# THE SWORDSWOMAN

JESSICA
AMANDA
SALMONSON

Illustrated by
Wendy Adrian Shultz

**TOR**

**A TOM DOHERTY ASSOCIATES BOOK**

Distributed by Pinnacle Books, New York

Copyright © 1982 by Jessica Amanda Salmonson

A TOR Book

First printing, March 1982

ISBN: 48-526-3

Cover art by: Carl Lundgren

Interior Illustrations by: Wendy Adrian Shultz

DEDICATION:
> to
> Eileen Gunn
> a latter-day Clorinda

Printed in the United States of America

Pinnacle Books, Inc.
1430 Broadway
New York, New York 10018

# TABLE OF CONTENTS

I · MAD-
WOMAN

Wendy Adrian Shultz

# I. MADWOMAN

"She may not seem dangerous," the nurse said. Her shoes resounded heavily through the lit hallway. The other's step was light. "But you've reviewed her history. Do be careful, Doctor."

He didn't bother to tell her he wasn't a doctor. He hadn't claimed he was. He was a paramedic; but that title wouldn't have gained him access to the woman's files or her room. It was never his way to exactly *lie* about such things, however. He merely misled.

"I'm sure it'll be all right," he said. His accent was heavy. He was Czechoslovakian. "I'll call out if there's any trouble."

The nurse unlocked the door. The lank Czech stood ready to enter the room, but held back, measuring himself. What if she *did* get violent? From her records, he knew her behavior had been calm to excess since commitment to the sanitarium; but no one had ever come with quite the same things to say. Could he handle the consequences? He was no fighter. She was. He didn't relish a genuine confrontation. He reminded himself that she was a third degree black belt in karate, a fourth dan in kendo and iaido sword styles, with at least a working knowledge of jujutsu and a motley assortment of additional martial styles to which her fickle interest had introduced her in the past several years. He wouldn't have a chance if she were riled. Yet he had a certain swiftness to his rawboned stature. Despite the greying temples which lent him an almost elderly, authoritative appearance, in actuality he was barely past thirty. He ran daily. He was fit. He could keep out of her reach, if worse came to worst.

He walked into the room. The door clicked shut behind. It could be opened only from the outside and by a key.

It was rather more than he'd expected, that room. The window was not barred, though it would open only a little ways. There were furnishings, even pointless knickknacks. It reminded him of the dorm room he'd stayed in when he first came to America, ostensibly to study medicine; though he'd become too depressive and emotional at the time and never became a physician.

There was nothing fancy about the woman's room, but it wasn't what he'd expected from a mental institution. What *had* he expected? A padded cell housing a raving maniac? She had rich parents. They made certain she had the best care in the finest facility. Then they forgot her. An accountant paid the bills, but otherwise her parents lived their lives as though the murderess neither existed nor required love.

The woman sat on the floor, in the corner beneath the window, beyond the foot of the bed. Brown eyes glared at nothing. Tousled hair was shoulder length and black. Her arms were locked around her knees. This, at least, met his expectations. Standing above her, he suddenly realized how imposing he must seem, like any number of medical personnel with authority over her movements, practically over her thoughts. Not wishing to seem a hovering presence, he crouched closer to her level. His face nearly even with hers, he looked at her a long time without speaking.

There was no hint that she intended to acknowledge his presence. After these few moments, he quoted to her:

"'Here I sit, mad as a hatter, with nothing to do but get madder and madder . . .'"

Something stirred behind that shadowed expression. The woman turned her head, looked him in the face. The corner of her mouth twitched. He thought she was about to smile, but she didn't. In a voice huskier than his, she completed the quotation:

"'. . . or else recover enough of my sanity to return to the world which drove me mad.'"

A longer silence then. The man's breath quickened; so did his heart. The madwoman, by contrast, was perfectly tranquil. He'd never seen anyone so beautiful, man or woman; for she might have been either with her amazing, androgynous strength. Swallowing, he calmed himself and said, "You're not really crazy, are you."

"I'm certified," she said. Evasive. "I killed a man."

"Do you remember me?" he asked.

She nodded. "You drove the ambulance. No. Someone else was driving. You sat in the back with me. I was, uhm, sort of hysterical I suppose."

Hysterical was the wrong word. Disoriented. Panicked. *Delighted.*

Why did he think that?

There was a powerful memory of her appearance that day. The gash in her forehead couldn't possibly have been made with the bamboo, surrogate sword (what was it called? *Shinai*) of the sort used in the kendo competition. That wound had been made by the close lick of steel. He'd have sworn it. But people saw it happen; no steel was involved. A safe, formalized exercise had turned into a nightmare. At least one hundred spectators and participants had watched the young woman break from the conventions of form to become a murderous whirlwind set on killing her suddenly frightened opponent. It happened too swiftly for anyone to intervene. She'd knocked the protective mask off his face with one incredible blow, breaking his nose in the process. It swelled instantly, bloody. She ripped her own mask off and glared at her opponent with "the face of a monster" according to one newspaper's quote. The poor guy managed one defensive strike to her head, then turned to run from the gymnasium's floor. As he turned, the madwoman cut him through the spine. *Cut him through the spine.* With a bamboo sword? More than a hundred witnesses.

The papers described it graphically. It had been big news—for three days. No one present had dared to approach her before the paramedic unit came. He saw the rest himself: the young man's corpse in a crimson pool; the woman with a terrific head wound, walking around and around the gymnasium like a gladiator in an arena, blood trailing in her wake. She was still muttering crazily about an "end to the evil; some people deserved to die; end to evil; deserve to die. Evil. Die . . ." Yet she responded with docility to the paramedic's gentle urging.

It never came to trial, which was why the papers forgot it. The woman was obviously mad; indeed, she had had a history of emotional problems. Minor problems, admittedly, but . . . There was a closed hearing. She had influential parents. It was an open and shut case. Decision: lock her up in a looney bin, save everyone a lot of embarrassment in the end.

So here she sat.

"I said some pretty strange things, eh?" She laughed. It was stout laughter. She had laughed in the gymnasium, too, dragging her bamboo sword as she circled around and around . . . "They put me to the polygraph, you know that? I said basically the same damn things. Polygraph said I wasn't lying. Therefore I'm crazy, right? You gotta be crazy not to lie. Or not to know you're lying. I'm not sure which."

"My name is Válkyová Idaska," said the paramedic as he held out his hand. He added with a naïve note of pride, "A naturalized citizen."

"Erin Wyler," she said foolishly, thinking for a moment that he didn't already know. She shook his hand. "A naturalized nut case."

"So I keep hearing. But I was with you immediately after . . . well, after the boy was killed. I didn't see what happened, of course, but I dressed the wound . . ." His hand reached out toward the scar on her forehead, mostly hidden by her hairline. He drew his hand away, thinking himself too bold. "Mine was also the first trained eye to look at the injury which ended that young man's life. Both of you had been cut with an edge sharp as glass or steel. The coroner who later looked at the corpse disagreed, and ignored my report, as did the doctor who eventually stitched you up. But I'm the only one who looked closely at *both* of you. I haven't been able to make myself believe it was done with a proxy weapon made of bamboo."

Erin laughed again, let go of her knees so that her legs slid flat to the floor. "Too many witnesses, Val. Surely you don't believe my ravings over the accounts of a hundred-plus pairs of eyes?"

"You seem reasonable to me. I don't see any raving."

"It's the nature of true pathos, my friend. Only a nut would believe what I was saying."

"Tell it to me again."

"Why? Pretty simple really. Suddenly, I was no longer in a university gymnasium in a simple kendo match. I was on a field of battle and the stakes were our lives. My opponent wasn't some kid from another kendo school either. He was the most monstrously evil tyrant *that* world had ever known, with a somewhat feebler moral structure than Genghis Khan or Nixon. I fought him, and I won. I thought I killed him. It was a trick, I knew too late. I'd killed that kid instead. Haven't quite figured it out myself, yet. But I know what I experienced. And I don't do drugs, either. It wasn't a hallucination." She shrugged her shoulders, then added as an afterthought, "If you believe any of this, Val-whatzit Ida-know, you need to be locked up too."

"There was no official investigation," said Válkyová. "Your attorney pleaded insanity in your behalf, during a preliminary hearing, and you ended up here without going to trial. I looked into it myself, though. Couldn't help it. I'd ridden with you to the hospital. Your madness gripped me, too, shall I say? Somehow, nothing fit together well enough. Everyone I talked to who had anything to do with it, they all sort of closed their eyes, as though they were afraid to look too closely at the strange parts. Kind of a conspiracy against . . . I'm not sure . . . against the unknown. You know anything about the man you killed?"

"His name. Jerry Mason. I'd seen him before; we never talked."

"That's what I thought. I looked into his case too, trying to sort it all out. He didn't have many friends. Kendo was his only outlet for the most part; otherwise, a fairly reclusive man. A bookworm with abominable taste in reading material. The few times he tried to get close to anyone, he ended up scaring them away. At least, that's how it seems to me, judging from the few people I could get to talk about him. Harmless kind of fellow whose life was pretty dull except for this swordfighting business—which I don't understand, by the way, if you don't mind me saying. Apparently

Jerry fought off feelings of helplessness and use-lessness with a very elaborate, almost pitiful private fantasy of being the heir of a recently slain lord on some far-fetched planet. As the fantasy went, Jerry was even more evil than his ferocious father had been. He had only one important enemy: the same woman warrior who had killed his father. This woman, said the prophets, would bring doom to a cruel dynasty."

Val paused. Erin was looking at the floor be-tween her legs. Val wasn't sure that she was listen-ing, but went on.

"It all sounded like what you'd related that day in the ambulance. Rather too unusual to be a coincidental pair of imaginings, I thought. Try as I might, I could find no connection between him and you before the night of the championship meet. No mutual friends. Kendo schools in differ-ent cities. No one ever saw you speak together. I couldn't figure how you knew a scenario from the boy's most personal fantasies."

"Coincidence," said Erin, proving she had been listening after all. "Maybe we all have private fantasies like those, at one time or another. And we're none of us too imaginative. The fantasies all come out sounding pretty much the same."

"I thought I had a better theory," said Val. "My hypothesis was that Jerry somehow projected his fantasy to you. You know, ESP, something like that; and you were as caught up in it as he. Only you didn't know it was a fantasy, and played for keeps. You killed him."

"Nice theory," said Erin. "I like it. But it won't get me out of here."

"The thing wrong with the theory was, well, it didn't explain the nature of your and his wounds. I looked at the tournament shinai. Made of strips of bamboo bound together. Makes a terrific cracking noise when it strikes, but relatively harmless. I

can't believe it made the clean gash on your forehead, or cut through a man's back the way yours
seemed to have done. I'd been mulling the problems
with my theory through my mind again and again,
when I achieved a breakthrough in my amateur
investigating. I made my most telling discovery
when I finally got through one of your parents'
defenses. Your mother agreed to talk to me. It
hadn't been easy to convince her."

"You really *do* stick your nose in things . . . "

"I was trying to help, believe me. I caused nobody trouble, and only a little pain. What your
mother told me was that you once kept a diary, but
that you never wrote anything in it that was real.
She showed it to me."

Erin's look was baleful.

"I hope you'll forgive me, Erin, but I did read it.
And the world you created in your diary was the
same world of Jerry Mason. The last entry was a
few years old, but it was virtually the same story
Jerry once told a friend about his father's death at
the hands of a swordfighting maid."

"You'd believe your own perfectly impossible
theories before the account of more than a
hundred eye-witnesses?"

"I'm not sure of anything, Erin. I just don't
know. My mind has fought with this for six
months, ever since that day I was sent to the university with the ambulance. In my birth country—
you'll pardon me if I stipulate 'birth' country, for
America is my country now—there are many old
legends about, oh, small deeds in paradise which
have major ramifications on Earth, and vice versa.
Break a mirror in your bedroom, and in some
other world, a nation crumbles. Mere 'stories,' I
know. Children's stories my grandmother told me
at her knee. But not so long ago, such tales were
held true. They explained the nature of the universe for a superstitious people. They were the

science of the day—and I've had enough experience and training to have learned how close to superstition modern science really is, and how often folklore comes closer to the truth. I don't scoff what sounds merely improbable."

Erin Wyler looked at the thin Czech crouched before her. She looked at him intensely. "I'm glad you came," she said. "I'm glad my madness was shared by at least two people. You, and the man I killed. But as I said before, it won't get me out of here. It's better'n prison, I'll grant, so I'm not complaining that much. If I'm a model looney, they'll probably let me out pretty soon anyway. So I don't really care. But I'd like to know why you came. What does it do, but reinforce my own mad fantasy? It might actually keep me here longer. Especially if I'm dumb enough to tell it to the shrink who comes in here once every two or three weeks pretending he cares, smiling and asking stupid questions and making me run off at the mouth. You're actually a troublemaker, Val, you know that?"

"My grandmother used to say so. But there really was a reason. You see, last night, I met a man. He found me actually, I don't know how. Must've heard from someone that I'd been asking after you or Jerry Mason. He came to my apartment last night, and asked if I had some reason to help you. He asked if I . . . if I . . ." Válkyova turned brilliant red.

"Asked what?" Erin's brows drew together.

"He asked if I was in love with you." Val's mouth was suddenly dry. Erin laughed that almost terrible laughter. The seriousness on Val's face quietened her. Then she asked,

"You told him you didn't actually know me, right? That you'd only seen me crazy in the back of an ambulance?"

"I couldn't resist him, Erin. He looked at me so

hard, I had to tell him the truth. I told him I'd been having private fantasies of my own, and they were about you. Your strength, your unique beauty, even your madness and the incredible skill of a woman who could cut a man in two, whether with steel or bamboo sword. It fascinated me. You see, I'm crazy too, as you suggested. I had never had such fantasies before, I assure you. But you were so beautiful. You *are* so beautiful, Erin!"

The slender Czech was close to tears, though he fought crying.

"Poor schmuck," said Erin. "Pardon me if I'm not flattered. I've read enough romantic drivel in my day, about men falling in love at first sight preferably with a crazy or even unconscious damsel in distress. I can't say it shows much maturity on your part. I stopped writing my diary when I was seventeen, and concentrated on martial arts instead. Sounds like you've just started yours."

Val bit back a bitter response. "I agree with you," he admitted. "I knew nothing about you. But I played detective, and I found out a little, and I loved you more. Or, if it isn't love, I became more obsessed. Then this man came, as I said, last night. He was perhaps fifty, looked like a typical businessman, except his eyes. There was more behind his eyes than you usually see staring at you from behind a desk. When he looked at me, I couldn't look away. He came into my apartment and took the best chair, like he was an old European lord or something, like he owned everything that was mine in the place. He asked for wine, and I gave him something I'd been saving. I obeyed him like he *was* a lord; I couldn't help myself. And he asked me if I loved you enough to help you, no matter what. He asked if I would risk my life for you."

Erin was not caught up in the melodrama. She was increasingly agitated. "There are bigger nuts loose than stored in this place," she said hotly. "What's this bastard's name? I don't think I know him anyway."

"He never said who he was. He just said I was to help you."

"Who needs help? These crazy stories aren't going to get me set free. Not that there's anything outside these walls any different than on the inside. *Everyone* is nuts; the whole stinking world is an asylum. I don't need any help from you or some businessman who thinks he owns the gawdamn world!"

Erin Wyler began to stand. As she rose, Val felt dwarfed in her presence, though actually he was a bit taller than her. He felt defenseless in her shadow, whether rationally or not he didn't know. He tried to step backward in his squat, but fell on his bottom, looking up.

"Listen, Val Ida-whatever-it-is. I *killed* a boy for no reason at all. I think I'm a really dangerous cooky, all right? I may be crazy enough to kick your teeth in!"

Their eyes locked, his staring up with something of agony, hers looking down with confused contempt. Val said,

"The man who came . . . he . . . he said you were in severe danger, that you couldn't last much longer in this world, that you belonged somewhere else . . . "

"Stop it!" She turned to face the window. It was starting to grow dark out. She looked at evening-shrouded lawns of a place ridiculously but in frank seriousness referred to as The Home. There was nowhere on Earth Erin would call home. She bit her lip, and it would be swollen later. She said again, "Stop it. I was born here. There is no place else. This is all there is!"

"No," Val said, almost too softly to hear. "There is much more than this. I don't know what it is you

see, or how, or where. I've never been blessed with
such sight, with such imagination, with whatever
it takes to see beyond this. But I've always known
it was there. It *had* to be there. The universe is too
awfully huge for this to be the only part to which
we are allowed access. The man said so, too, and I
believed him. He said you'd die here, or live a life
no better than death. He said to bring you this . . ."
Válkyová Idaska reached into his shirt as he stood.
Erin turned around slowly, tears streaking her
face. She looked at Val's outstretched fist. The fist
slowly opened.

In the hand was a transparent object: a sliver of
a knife; or a rhinestone-bright trinket carved in
the shape of a sword; or simply a glass needle, for
on closer look, it had an eye that might take a
thread. A harmless enough artifact for all appearances, but Erin Wyler recoiled in revulsion. Then
she looked again, fascinated.

"I don't want it," she said. Her breath came
heavily.

"It will take you there," he said. "The man said
it would take you there."

"No," she said. "I won't go. It's too cruel a place.
It's only good to think about. Not if it is real."

"You must take it, Erin! You must go. You're
needed. You must use the diamond blade to carve
a portal into the world you've always seen!"

The miniscule knife began to glow, for it was in
the presence of the one for whom it was meant.
Rainbows shone on all the walls, on Erin's and
Val's faces. Erin looked at Válkyova in helpless
rage. He saw this rage and wished he could elicit
love instead; but this was something he'd been
forced to do, forced by the man with strange eyes.
Val pressed the tiny blade to Erin's palm, pricking
her slightly. Immediately the crystal began to
grow.

Erin screamed hatefully. Válkyová could under-

stand only the sentiment, not the words. The
crystal sword shone two beams of light into the
madwoman's eyes, and she stared back with some
knowledge invested by the sword. Her gaze went
from shining sword to the man before her, and she
mouthed the gutteral maledictions of another
world . . .

*     *     *

Three insectoid creatures walked upright as do
men. They walked side by side, and their motions
were synchronized precisely. By their movements,
they might have been mirror reflections of one
another; but physically they were each different
from the other in coloration, number of joints, and
configuration of head. Each had two long arms
and two short arms, and held serrated sickles in
the multiply jointed pincers of their longer ap-
pendages. Blunt knives were held in the simpler
pincers of their shorter arms. They had mandibled
mouths. Their eyes were hard, perfectly round,
and luminescent gold like the eyes of moths in the
night. With such faces, it was not possible to dis-
cern expressions. They revealed neither cruelty
nor compassion.

The insect men—or women, she could not tell—
came to a cliff and stopped all at once, looking
down at a shining sea. Together they pointed with
their blunt knives toward the cove below, and long
tongues uncoiled from between their mandibles.
There was no sound with the vision, but Erin
suspected some kind of communication, either
among themselves or with others far away.

After a while, the three insectoids turned away
from the cliff and the view of the cove. They
turned as one, as though their thoughts were
joined and they did not merely anticipate the steps
made by the others, but made those steps as a

single entity.

All this Erin saw through a single facet of the diamond sword. Then the vision was gone and she felt herself bodiless in limbo. There was another presence with her: the lank man named Válkyová Idaska. She could not see him. After a while, she lost him, and felt only the faintest sorrow for having done so. An interminable length of time passed—moments or aeons, she did not know. During this time she heard angry shouting in the distance. She thought it was her own voice screaming. Then, with scarce warning, Erin lost all sense of being. Perhaps she slept. Perhaps she slipped into coma. She became the universe, and the universe was empty. Her last thought was: *I've died, but I don't mind.* Then there was nothing.

\*          \*          \*

The nurse heard the screaming. The light above the door to the madwoman's private room was blinking. The screaming was almost like a siren, not a human voice. She ran from the nurse's station, passing quickly down the hall, fumbling with her keys. She couldn't see into the room, because there was an awful, swirling light obscuring the view through the door's small, reinforced window.

Wrong key. Damn! She never had trouble with the keys! She got the right one in the lock. When she turned the latch of the door, there was a pushing force on the other side, powerful enough to throw her against the hall's other wall. She lay on the floor, dazed, looking into the brilliantly twisting glow of the madwoman's room. The nurse shouted,

"Code five!"

It meant escapee; or it meant someone needed restraint. In her daze, the nurse saw the madwoman gripping a long, glimmering sword. The man she thought was a doctor had fallen on the floor on his knees, covering his face from the sword's weird glow. Two beams of light held the madwoman's eyes, fascinating her. The madwoman was poised as if to decapitate the man. and she was shouting with a Pentacostal intensity of meaningless, emotion-charged verbiage.

"Code five!" the nurse screamed frantically. "Code five!" She couldn't think clearly, or understand what she was seeing. What the sword was or where it came from, she could not imagine; she could only wait for the doctor's head to fall. But the patient only carved designs in the air, like the ends of sparklers on the Fourth of July or New Year's in Chinatown. The after-image of that strange symbol etched into the nurse's memory indelibly, to haunt her dreams throughout her remaining thirty-seven years. She watched in mesmerized, almost mindless fascination as the patient helped the doctor regain his feet. Then the doctor was led by the madwoman through the center of the glowing design which drifted in the middle of the room.

"Code five!"

Orderlies appeared from down the hall. Six of them. The nurse pointed into the dark interior of a certain room. Two of the orderlies helped her stand. She was too shocked to speak intelligibly. She kept pointing. There was no one in the room, and no route out save down a hall filled with orderlies. The mystery of the two's disappearance would never be resolved, unless within the nurse's most private, fearful fantasy or dream.

II · FISHER'S
APPRENTICE

# II. FISHER'S APPRENTICE

Erin awoke as from a dream, disoriented about reality. She opened her eyes and found herself on warm sand. She lay naked on a beach which was otherwise devoid of inhabitants, sparsely strewn with flotsam and dry sea-grass. There were no footprints anywhere, not even her own, and this was strange.

A breeze off the water chilled her slightly. Raising herself to elbows, she gazed toward the horizon, over waters which shimmered in shades of jade and turquoise. The sun was going down. Plankton luminesced, giving the water its incredible brilliance. The sea was like a living, fluid gem with waves instead of facets.

Against the lowering sun's last rays, an unusual boat was silhouetted. It crossed the face of the huge, bright orb at an unbelievable pace. Despite the slightness of the wind, the ship's sails were swollen like the bellies of pregnant women. Erin pulled her legs up under herself, rose to her knees, and watched this dreamy apparition. She wondered: *Is this the dream, or that other?*

In her hand she held a clear, sparkling jewel carved to the shape of a sword, its miniscule hilt pierced as the eye of a needle. She had the eerie half-recollection of having somehow passed through that eye. *I have not awakened after all*, she thought. *Does no one ever wake?*

23

To Erin, there had always been only the present. The work-a-day craziness and routine of school and eventually a job had always blunted her senses. She strode through life an automaton. Little tempted her to greater response. All of her past, then, was easily questioned. She had never felt life's events strongly enough to count them real. Her parents, with a curious mixture of concern and annoyance, provided her youth with an endless parade of specialists and child psychologists, all eager to break through her generally disconnected attitude. Even as a tiny babe, she had never cried. Her elders presumed a repression of some secret, horrible event or emotional trouble, for no child should be so consistently calm. But Erin had searched her own soul for sources of her difference, and knew better than anyone that she kept nothing hidden there.

The feeling of actually being alive had visited her upon occasion, especially in the heat of sporting combat, when she sparred with a partner in the park or gymnasium. Even that had been artificial, never quite vital enough. Still, martial arts had sometimes lent the "here and now" a degree of sparkle and intensity forever lacking in memories of things past, or thoughts of years ahead. Yet no sooner would a sparring session end than it became part of the unreal past, or a plan of renewal in the unreal future. Thus reality was at best a fleeting sensation for Erin; she had never been sure of it on an intellectual level.

Her lower lip barely hurt, for she had bitten it in that former world. The swelling had already gone. She rubbed the scar high on her forehead. Though she retained clear enough knowledge of her life before this beach, she felt nonetheless like an amnesiac. A vague fear tugged at her, the fear that she was at this very moment strapped to a hospital bed in a totally catatonic trance. She might be staring at some ceiling, seeing this world instead.

The ship was growing out of the distance, its destination certain. It was heading for the very cove upon which Erin's dream—or her escape from former dreams—had deposited her. Quickly, she stood, and stepped backward, away from the margin. She left footprints facing the shimmering waters, so that it would look as though someone had walked into the sea to die. As there were no other footprints leading to or from the shore, the illusion might not be doubted.

She did not wait to see who piloted the ship. Instinctively she knew it as foe, and she knew herself not yet ready to face it. For the time being, she had another quest: to establish the actuality of her new environment—to learn, if it were possible, whether she had truly passed through the eye of a needle, or had merely withdrawn into her own interior. It would be pleasant enough to fall into such a trap, one of her own making, and live in the present as she had always done, never questioning, never knowing—even if she died of it, in a hospital elsewhere. Yet for the first time, reality had sharpness and clarity; and that was, perhaps, the true reason she had to question it as she had never done before. If all this was real, then it served a purpose; she had been brought here for a reason. There had never been a time in her entire life that she felt her existence had any reason or served any purpose whatsoever. Everything simply *was*, in all its brief pointlessness and tedium, broken rarely by dull anger, love, or pain. Now, suddenly, existence held a sense of dimension for her, and she wondered at the cause of this feeling.

It was possible she needed not so much to prove her current reality to be as valid as the one previous, but that she needed mostly to establish this new feeling of *purpose* as more than ego or illusion. If all else were fraud, she wouldn't mind.

Only, purpose must be real.

A winding upward grade took her through woodlands away from the sea. Darkness fell all around her, and no moon had yet risen. But the stars were bright, far brighter than she had ever seen them in the polluted world she'd known before. She stopped and looked at the sky, awestruck, seeing not one familiar constellation in that myriad of stars. Even the Milky Way was altered beyond recognition: a crescent highway arching from land to sea rather than dissecting the heavens.

A silver slipper of a moon rose in majesty, a slender sickle facing away from the crescent highway of stars.

Below, she beheld the sinister ship anchored in the cove, rendered visible by the bright sky and the gaudy glow of a trillion plankton. The sails were deflated; but furious, nearly invisible creatures hovered nearby the vessel, anxious to take up their chore, squalling like angry maids.

Men had come ashore in longboats. Erin kept herself hidden, lest her naked flesh be seen by those who searched the beach fruitlessly.

Cliffs soared to her left. The path grew steeper. Erin felt as though she were a pale specter of the night, a supernatural being from another world, winding its way to higher land and, perhaps, to higher knowledge. With this feeling, she strove upward.

\*      \*      \*

Anxiety held weariness at bay. Erin walked the night through, along a narrow path, as the young moon scythed across the sky. Upon occasion she glimpsed the shape of a far, many-peaked mountain, black against the starry night. Morning outlined the mountain more clearly, black against fiery bronze. The day grew progressively warmer and, as noon approached, Erin felt her skin redden and smart. The night had chilled her and the day burned her, but until now she had given little thought to clothing herself.

The path widened and looked more commonly used, though not once had she passed or seen another soul. At a bend, however, she saw a shrine. It looked ancient and unattended, no larger than the smallest cotter's dwelling, its stone masonry crumbling.

As she neared the structure, she could see into an oval entry. A ferocious female deity, carved in jet, sat crosslegged on a grey block of stone. Before this idol an old man rested on his knees, head bowed in prayer. He was clad in rags, but on the floor behind him there lay neatly folded raiment of freshly woven cloth. Beside the clothing were weapons: three swords of graduated length. It seemed unlikely that any of these rich accoutrements could belong to an elderly beggar.

At Erin's approach, the old man raised his head, and Erin saw that he was blind. He did not rise from his knees, but smiled toothlessly.

"Alms?" he said, and stuck out a hand with six blunt fingers.

"I've nothing, old man, but a needle and no thread. I lack even clothing, but am spared embarrassment because you're blind."

"I'm a beggar priest, sworn against lust, so you could spare yourself embarrassment even were I sighted. As for your need of dress, it seems I've lately come into possession of garments unsuited to my austerity. These are of soft cotton whereas I prefer rough hemp as you can see. If you would be so kind as to use your needle to patch my torn hemp robe, the cottons will be yours in exchange."

"A fair bargain. But I've no thread. Otherwise I would be glad to repair your robe for you."

He crawled on his knees to the threshold of the shrine's entry, where Erin stood. There, he bit at the sleeve of his robe until he caught a thread, unraveling a bit. "This will do," he said, handing her the dirty string.

Thus Erin fell upon a domestic chore. She threaded the needle-sized diamond sword and, bending to the level of the kneeling priest, sewed the rips of his wear. He was grateful, and happily gave her the folded cottons. Erin was unfamiliar with their design, and asked the blind man how the garments were worn.

"You must be from elsewhere than Endsworld not to know so simple a thing," said the old priest. "I pray I have not fallen in with a demon of another place."

"I pray the same thing, old man, for you are too handy an acquaintance for me to have made by chance. It is true, however; I am not of this place you've named for me. I am late of Earth, but feel Endsworld will be my first true home."

These words pleased the old man. "In my order, we believe there are twenty heavens and twenty hells, and if all of these are escaped or evaded, Endsworld is our blessing. The world you call Earth, is it one among the heavens or the hells?"

"I do not know," said Erin. "I'm not sure it is either, or that I would know the difference. The matter of this clothing confounds me the most just now."

He bowed apologetically, then directed her in the elementary matters of dress. The main garment was long, wrapping tight from shoulder to waist, but hanging loose from the thighs down. Over it was worn a narrow girdle or belt of contrasting coloration and criss-crossing print. "On Endsworld," said the priest, "we recognize status by our girdles. This pattern on yours represents crossed sticks; it means you are a student. The pattern on my own—if it is still visible beneath grime and age—represents the Hammer, and signifies the order to which I'm sworn." The girdle encircled the body three times and was then tied in a manner the blind priest was not able to describe in words, but which he easily demonstrated. His hands carefully did not linger anywhere they did not belong, vowed as he was; and Erin was quick to memorize the knot.

"When you need to wade through mud or water, or to free your legs to run with the longest strides," the blind man directed, "gather up the hem of your robe between your legs and tuck it all up in the back of your girdle."

"I feel like a monk," Erin commented, finally dressed.

"The monks of Endsworld are warriors," said the priest.

"And the priests?"

"Warriors also," he replied.

"Then those weapons are yours," she said, meaning the three swords on the floor of the shrine. The priest shook his grizzled head and stated,

"My sect is a rare one. We do not carry swords or spill blood. I carry only a hammerheaded staff." He reached behind himself, where a walking staff had lain. Erin had not previously noticed the wicked double-headed hammer at its top. "With this, I crush bones and end lives. I keep tufts of raw cotton in a girdle pocket, to plug the nose, mouth and anus of foe I've killed, so that nary a drop of crimson need be shed."

"A weapon that draws no blood, but kills," reflected Erin. "A hypocritical faith, I would suppose."

The priest's white, unseeing eyes became shadowed with anger. He stood abruptly, speed belying age. "Endsworld is cruel, woman! You travel in it without clothes or swords. You are like a child, yet risk much to insult me. But I am austere after all, bearing neither sword nor pride. Though your lack of knowledge appalls me, I will pardon you for a while. I was sent, as you might have guessed, to present these very gifts to whoever bore the diamond needle. I did not expect a woman, nor an insult."

Erin was stung. "I bow my head in shame," she said, trying to make amends. "I am a child, as you say. I know little. I would like to know who sent you to meet me."

"It was the Teacher of the Black Mountain, man of the four-legged race. Because I owe him my life, I came to this road in service to him. I am directed to give you at least the shortsword. Take it!"

Erin hesitated.

"I am ordered to kill you!" said the priest as he lifted the walking staff menacingly. Erin snatched the shortest of the three scabbarded swords and leapt through the oval doorway before the staff's hammerhead made contact with her skull. She drew the smallsword and cast the sheath aside, turning to see if she was followed.

The priest took up the two longer swords from the floor of the shrine, then stepped out into the sun. He was disinclined to use them, so thrust the shorter of the two into his girdle, and then slung the longest across his back by means of the sheath's cord. Then he approached Erin with as much surety of step as would an enemy with sight. The iron hammer faced her as though it were the old priest's eye.

"I will not fight a blind man!" she protested, squatting and backing away, prepared to guard herself if he continued the attack.

"Then a blind man will kill you!"

A flurry of strokes were around her, and she was taxed to the limit of her ability to keep the long-handled hammer away. Once, she was struck soundly with the butt of the weapon, so intent had she been on watching the iron head. It sent her sprawling, but she rolled, and came back to her feet gracefully. The blind man was definitely not handicapped by his lack of sight. His sense of hearing obviously more than balanced any potential handicap.

Erin could not step quietly enough that he would fail to hear and follow. She doubted that *anyone* could step so lightly as to evade his notice. Soon she realized he could hear even the sound of her arms moving through the air, manipulating the shortsword. So keen was the priest's sense of hearing that he could match her every stance and posture.

She quickly began to tire, having had no sleep in a day and a night, and having lacked the calm necessary to reserve energy for an extended encounter. The seriousness of her plight overwhelmed her. She said at last,

"Much as I hate to do so, I must kill you lest I die."

Drawing on everything she had learned of fighting, Erin Wyler brought her utmost skill to bare upon the oldster. She was still not certain she could win. Then, to her surprise and relief, the priest turned and ran away from her. At a safe distance, he turned around and took the middle-sized sword from his girdle and set it on the ground.

"You have won this one, too," he said. "You are very good, as I was told you would be. If you are not yet the match of Father Kes, it is because he has never been defeated in all his long years, though blind from birth." He chuckled. "But restrain your pride, woman, for there is a third blade which only true swordsmasters carry, and I will not give it to you yet! The first sword I gave you is called *i*, and every student of warrior caste is granted one. The second is called *mai*, and is won in combat, as you have just won yours. The third is called *oude*, and you are not worthy of so great a length of steel; few such fighters are. My advice: pray to the Goddess Durga, whose shrine this is. Pray that in a year's time you are worthy of the third blade, a long one for your back. I will come to you again, in obedience to the Teacher of Black Mountain, who taught me the ways of battle in my long ago youth and who owns my life. When I come again, you must win the final blade, or die as I have promised."

This said, the blind priest whirled about and dashed into the wood, spry as a youth, and by no means clumsy in the underbrush.

\*          \*          \*

Shaken to the core by her ordeal, Erin's heart still pounded in her chest. She regained the short-sword's sheath and claimed the longer *mai* as well. These she placed in her girdle. Then, because Kes the Hammer had bid her do so, she entered the shrine and fell upon her knees.

The statue of Durga was a fine work of art, but grim for all that. She was carved in a single ebon rock, her face grotesque, her breasts mere dugs. She bore three swords of varied length arranged in a particular way: two at the waist and a third over one shoulder. The idol was not large, and Erin wondered that it had never been stolen. Two could carry it easily. At this stage of her discoveries, she could only guess the intensity of fear, respect and awe afforded the warrior goddess, extreme enough to preclude the possibility of theft even by Endsworld's vilest.

"Durga," Erin began, feeling slightly foolish and yet, somehow, also slightly profound, "I am new to this world, and ignorant. I do not even know that I believe in gods. I feel I've come to learn, however, and my first instruction was to pray. Therefore I am praying. Protect me if that is your way. Give me strength if that is your way. Hinder me in no event, I beg you, for I am to the Black Mountain to confront a Teacher who issued warrant for my death."

Upon the floor lay the diamond needle, still threaded. Erin took up the ends of the hemp thread and tied them around her neck, so that the needle-sword became her pendant. By it, she might be recognized by a special friend or foe; the priest had as much as said so. It might be safer to travel incognito, the miniscule blade hidden in a fold of her girdle. But she had not come to Ends-world to sightsee in safety. As yet, she did not know what she had come for. She hoped it was not only for the will of others.

                    *       *       *


An unevenly cobbled road wound along a river. The source of that river was the Black Mountain, a multi-peaked hulk standing lonesome in the distance. Erin had been afoot for three days, but the mountain did not look much nearer.

On the banks were fishing villages, each with rickety piers and poor, grey boats and houses. Men and women with long, thin pipes smoked a foul tobacco. They busied themselves either repairing nets or throwing them into the river and drawing them back again. The industry was less than colorful and by no means merry; for the people were too sad and grim to appear so much as quaint. They were reticent as well, though Erin wheedled a little knowledge of the country by carefully phrasing queries and through constant observation.

The rough fishers measured Erin's weapons,

and noted the pattern of her belt. By their expressions she knew that it was rare, though not altogether unlikely, that a mere student had already gained her second sword. They afforded her as much respect and assistance as was due a two-bladed fighter, and no more. They offered her fishcakes and pickles, but only the scarcest conversation. They were always pleased to have her leaving their villages. A three-sword, she gathered, might command more aid, as much as a boat to hasten a trip along a river. Erin could expect only to be fed.

Although she often misunderstood their customs, the peasants were careful of her feelings. Undoubtedly her degree of ignorance about Endsworld made her seem foolish-minded to some. But they were peasants, and she well armed. Therefore they guarded her esteem.

She played the chameleon as best she dared to garner what information she could about day-to-day life on Endsworld and whatever else she might need to know merely for the sake of survival. She felt vaguely that it was a dangerous game, for the tension between peasant and warrior was great. She was not yet certain how patient these people could be in excusing her lack of manners.

"I am from a far province," said Erin. The fisher smelled oily and looked old, though he was probably younger than his weathered features indicated. "What place is this?" she asked.

"Thar of Delmo Prefecture," he replied, his face registering neither pleasure nor disdain at her presence. He did not look up from net-mending, but was careful of his tone when speaking to her.

"And the country?"

Surprise etched his brow the barest moment, then passed. "There are many names for the country. Peasants call it Durga's Lathe, and have

called it so for many generations. You would call
it Wevan."

"Durga's Lathe is a famous country," she said,
not knowing whether or not this were true, but
thinking even peasants might be patriots. She
hoped he would appreciate her using the peasants'
older name for the country. "I would have known
it already, but that I came to your land from the
sea, and was lost before then." Which was not
altogether a lie, she recollected.

He nodded the slightest amount, accepting her
excuse. He sat on the stoop of his porch as he
worked to repair the fishing net. Behind him, a
door opened, and a woman stepped out. She
looked older than the fisherman. No; on second
guess, she was younger. She was carrying fishcakes, having heard the conversation between a
warrior and her husband.

"Times are poor," she said. "My husband has a
bad knee." These excuses were given as a kind of
apology for the meagerness of the offering.

"I've been fed already, so will decline," said
Erin. "I have been afoot for three days, and am
going to the Black Mountain. The road has been
lonesome, and I am ignorant of the local ways. I
am offered food at every town, but no one is
pleased to converse with me."

The fishwife drew back. At last the fisher registered strong emotion, and it was anger. "Fishers
are lowborn, two-sword! We serve warriors as
custom, and our own safety, demands. But we converse among ourselves."

Erin mimicked the man's earlier bow, as slight
as she could make it. When she spoke, she con-
veyed genuine sorrow: "What you say is that it is
not possible for us to meet."

"No more than we have done," said the fisher.
"You must be of a far land indeed to know so little.
There is a city in the foothills—" He pointed its

direction—"with warriors of many nations. It is called Terwold. There you will find company in the drinking establishments, temples, and whorehouses. Each caters widely to warriors."

The woman behind the fisher was afraid for her husband, who spoke so boldly. She ran to the edge of the stoop and held forth the fishcake, insisting with her eyes that it be accepted. Erin took it and turned away, not thanking them.

She did not relish lodging of the sort promised from Terwold; and more, she doubted her ability as chameleon would see her as safely through a city's pitfalls as through the villages of uneducated, untravelled fishers. Turning once more to face the fisher and his wife, Erin removed both her swords from her girdle and set them on the step between the man and woman. She did not realize that her act was one of supreme trust, even obeisance. The fishwife could not contain her shock.

"Why this?" the fisher asked, his ill mood nearly subdued.

"Without swords," she said, "I am no longer a warrior. Therefore we can meet after all. You can see by the pattern on my empty girdle that I am merely a student. The criss-cross does not represent practice-swords, but netting. I seek an apprenticeship as fisher."

The fisher looked away from her. "You mock us!"

"I do not," said Erin. "I would linger in this village, to learn a smidgen of your honorable trade. Do not hold back! Work me until I ache in every bone. Pay me nothing but a portion of your own knowledge." She got down on her knees as she had done before the Goddess Durga many days before. She said, "I am alone in this world, without a friend or family. I beg your tutelage, even though I might not stay long."

The two peasants gaped at her in awe. The man said, "You are a strange warrior . . . no, a strange apprentice fisher. Very well, I will teach you to repair and throw small twin-nets, and to draw fish to the shore. From this moment, for the duration of your stay, my station is higher than yours."

Erin looked up from where she knelt before their grey house. She saw the gaping surprise on the fishwife's face. The fisherman, however, had resumed his mask of no emotion. "Senior," said Erin, "my gratitude will be revealed in my labor."

*      *      *

Nowhere in her past life could Erin recall a moment when toil was so rewarding. She had never worked so hard on Earth, but it had seemed more wearisome because she had never honestly seen or believed in the fruits of that labor. Here, she could sit by firelight far into the night, knitting the twin-nets in the company of a fishwife and her husband. On the dawn, and on the night of her first full moon, she would go with the fisher to the shallows, or the pier, or upon the narrow boat, and stand throwing the nets, drawing them back; throwing them, drawing them . . . It took considerable skill. Erin strove to master the art. She learned to recognize signs of fish beneath the waters, to judge whether it was good fish or poor, and to aim her double-net precisely. The fisher, whose name was Rud, was hard pressed to conceal his pleasure. His apprentice learned fast and well. Erin's nets helped the small family prosper a little bit and allowed Rud an occasional opportunity to rest his lame leg; so she felt no burden for staying.

She kept no calendar, but doubted three entire weeks had passed. The days were somewhat shorter and the months apparently longer than those of Earth; she had thus far seen but one full moon, and remembered the night more for the good fishing than the beauty of the sky. Knowing the specific time of day or month was less of an obsessive concern than it had been before.

Sometimes she would sit on the porch of the house and see, over the roofs of the village, the black and brooding mountain beckoning her. She wasn't sure why she refused to move on. Perhaps it was only fear—the same fear that made her leave that beach when a foreboding ship came too near. Perhaps it was only wisdom. She had foe on Endsworld, though how or why she did not yet know; and though she might be willing to fight them, she had to understand them first.

Yet she recognized her own rationalizations. She was good at making excuses and asking pardons when dealing with others, but she oughtn't fool herself. Even a blind man was a better swordsmaster than she! It was consolation to know he was famous for his skill. All the same, it had been unsettling. She had been good with swords on Earth; but skill in a formalized artform was a far cry from actually cutting someone in half. Or risking the same fate! The glamor was somehow lost in the realization of the dream. Here, she knew, on Endsworld, death could come quickly . . . death, or reward.

Was she a coward?

She wasn't certain.

There was something else holding her to the village of Thar in Delmo Prefecture: Rud, and his wife Orline. When first she saw them, they seemed little different from other fisher families: dirty, ignorant, narrow minded. She thought them all wretched; and without exception, the families she had seen were indeed unhappy. But she had gotten to know this one couple too well. They were beyond their prime and childless, and they considered their own lives to be somehow bettered

simply because Erin had set her swords aside to
live with them like a daughter and an apprentice.
That they loved her was certain; and Erin had
never experienced that same degree of certainty
with her blood parents.

Their dirtiness, ignorance, and prejudices were
still intact. But when Erin was covered with stinking fish oil, with nothing to dwell upon but the
flight of her double-net, the narrowness of the
peasants was her narrowness as well; and it was
no less profound than the gravest or wisest intro-
spection.

For all this, the unhappiness of Rud and Orline,
and of their fellow fishers, was no less real than
before. She wondered at its cause. It no longer
seemed sufficient to believe their simple life was
in itself a source of misery. Constantly she was on
guard for an explanation regarding the atmos-
phere of melancholy. She said to them one night,

"You have taught me the meaning of work in its
proper perspective. You have made my muscles
happy to ache. Yet the people of this village are
not happy with their lives, I can see it. You, my
friends and teachers, my family if I dare say it, you
are not happy either."

They sat crosslegged on the floor, the nets
spread out between them. Firelight danced over
the faces of Rud, Orline, and Erin.

"The work would make us happier," said Orline,
"but there are the . . ."

"It is easier for you, Erin," said Rud, interrupting his wife. "You can play fisher to your heart's
content; and we have come to love you as a
daughter, so do not be angry if I am critical. It is
always there, the fact that you may leave at any
time. This is not your life forever. For us, it is our
beginning and our end."

Erin lowered her eyes, concentrated on the
knots which would hold the net together, against

the wickedness of pikes and carp. She said at last,

"I am not certain that a warrior's life is better than the one you have shown me. If I am so foolish that I do not stay, it will not make my life better to have gone. That is why I think there is some danger hovering over the people of this river, or you would be happier with your lot."

"There is always fear!" said Orline, her eyes gone wild, but again Rud cut her off.

"The warriors have the right to slay us," he said, "and we've no recourse. We are non-people in the eyes of the Wevan government. Even those warriors not aligned with this or another government share certain privileges in common, including the authority to slay anyone beneath their station. The most starving peasant must feed a warrior who knocks at the door. We must respect the foulest of their class! If we fail our duty, and sometimes if we perform it well, our reward is to be gutted! My own father was . . . he was . . ."

Rud's lips quavered. His sharp, dark eyes grew moist. It was the most emotion Erin had ever seen from him; and he could not speak. She knew the fisher was torn between his dislike of the warrior elite, and his grudging love for Erin. His fists wound up part of the netting and he tried to tear it, but the knots of the hemp were too strong to break.

"Your father was slain without cause," said Erin, guessing.

Orline whispered in Erin's direction, "A warrior named Shom Bru slew my father-in-law many years ago, only to test a sword."

Erin felt ashamed, as though the misdeeds of other warriors should reflect on her. She said to Rud, "I see by your face that you hate loving me, father, because you think I am born of the warrior aristocracy. I cannot tell you of my birth, but . . ." Her voice trailed off and two words came unbidden from her lips: "Forgive me."

Rud covered his face with fists caught in re-paired netting, and he wept. Orline stroked her husband's hair. For a while there was only the sound of a man's weeping.

Silence might be best, but Erin felt compelled to pursue certain matters, because her weeks in Thar had given rise to as many questions as answers. This evening was by far the highest emotional peak they had achieved together. Even though it had been born of sorrow, it was yet a moment that required painful inspection. She said softly,

"Although warriors are authorized to slay any peasant who neglects certain amenities, it is also clear to me that peasants would rise in numbers to defend themselves if warriors demanded more than their due, or if warriors in no way benefited peasants. I do not say the caste system predomi-nant on Endsworld is good for the peasantry; but it does provide a stability which few question or abhor. The reason you hate warriors, Rud, is be-cause one of them killed your father, not because you must honor them. I am given to believe, then, that there are other dangers than you have told me. Something *else* keeps the spirits of the fishers dour. You must tell me what it is so that I can help."

"No!" cried Rud, looking up. His face was wet with tears but his expression was angry. "What right have you to demand our secrets? You have told us none of yours! Are you an orphan? What land do you come from? Why have you no family? Why did you give your swords into our keeping? *Why did you make us love you like a daughter?* Warriors are cruel! You are more cruel than any!"

The fisher stood, untangled himself from the netting and limped toward the door. He marched with a broken gait into the misty night, and neither Erin nor Orline moved to stop him. Erin's heart went after him, and she was cut by his accusations; but she let him go. When he was away from the house, she said,

"Mother, you must tell me. You have tried before." She was not certain it was moral to exploit the situation; but she felt there was a way to help these people if they would invest but an iota of confidence in her. Orline said,

"We feared to tell you, because either you would leave us, or you would take up your swords again, which would also be a kind of leaving. But soon enough you will know. On each dark moon it happens, and the dark moon is scant days from now. You will see it then! You will see it happen! Our terrible secret cannot be kept beyond that night!"

\* \* \*

Erin brooded for days, striving to be as melancholy as the other inhabitants of Thar. She walked the muddy street at dusk, exchanging weighted looks with dour citizens. The moon grew thin as a thumbnail while each day Erin searched faces for a clue.

Because she did not as yet know the moon's full cycle, she was uncertain as to which night it would not be visible. She suspected, however, that the night of the lightless moon would come upon this very eve. She woke early in the morning and discovered that both Rud and Orline were gone from the rickety house.

In panicked haste, she donned robe and girdle and scurried out onto the porch. When she saw Rud standing on the crooked pier casting a twin-net, her fears were allayed. All appeared as usual.

"You let me oversleep, father!"

He looked at her askance and said, "Not I!

Orline is the one to wake you, but she's gone upon an errand."

The fisher's apprentice took her own nets down from the hanging place on the porch. "My nets are strong," she said; the phrase was a common one, meant to bring luck. "It will hold big fish today."

Rud had drawn his own nets back and they were empty. Erin bounced along the planks of the pier, keeping her balance. When she was by Rud's side, she cast off her seeming good mood and asked him pointedly,

"What is mother's errand?"

Fisher and apprentice looked one another eye to eye. The fisher said, "Suspicious daughter! Why not ask her yourself?" He pointed across the river and up a hillside. Orline was hurrying down a trail, red-cheeked and breathless. She was smiling and waving and carried a package under one arm. Erin and Rud waved in return.

The small fishing boat was tied to a branch near the far bank. Orline climbed into the boat, tossed her package on the seat, and took up the oars. When she came to the end of the pier, puffing and straining, Erin grabbed the prow and Rud tied the vessel down.

The pier creaked and bent under their combined weight. Lest all be dumped into the drink, they took to shore.

"Why this gaiety?" said Erin sharply. "I thought this the night of the dark moon."

"Don't speak of it yet!" said Orline, refusing to have her rare fine mood destroyed. "The dark moon is tomorrow, so we must share today by being close together." She held the package out to Erin.

"We are too poor!" Erin complained. "You cannot buy things for me!"

"Be courteous," Rud reprimanded. "You have

made our burdens lighter. Please accept a small reward, and do so graciously."

She took the package from the fishwife and unwrapped it carefully, saving the handsome paper for Orline. Inside was freshly woven cloth: a girdle, dark green, with interlocking diamond patterns which Erin knew represented a school of fish. "It's a fisher's girdle!" she said excitedly.

"It was made by a famous weaver in a nearby village," said Orline. "But she's a peasant nonetheless, so do not think it costly; it was not. I slipped out before the dawn to fetch it for my daughter."

"You are no longer mere apprentice," Rud said. "I can teach you nothing more."

"Does it please you?" asked Orline.

The young fisher nearly wept. She said, "It pleases me, mother. Help me put it on."

She removed the girdle of a student. Orline helped tie the new girdle around her daughter's waist. Erin felt an overwhelming pride and spoke loudly, "It is a good day for fishing!" She snatched up her nets again.

"It is indeed," agreed Rud. "I will show you a secret place that I have shown no other: a fishing hole known to no one else in the village."

"Be home early!" Orline called after them. "There'll be a meal to delight!"

The two fishers wound their way through brush and woods, along animal trails and no trails at all, until they came to a tiny tributary and, ultimately, a wide, serene, shallow pool. It was so hemmed in by drooping trees that few could hope to find the place. Trout leapt in the shallows. Their pond was so lovely that Erin felt almost a sinner to spoil the fishes' safe seclusion.

"It's beautiful," said Erin. "I've seen nothing so wonderful in Delmo Prefecture!" She looked at Rud lovingly, and saw that his eyes held tears. He gazed at her intensely. Erin had suspected all along that this day was planned to be ideal; for Orline had suggested this would be the last day of Erin's ignorance regarding the villagers' grim secret. "Father, is there something wrong?"

"No, Erin. It is only that this place is beautiful to me as well. Come! I must show you something before we fish."

She followed him to a tree more gorgeous and leafy than all the others. Rud hugged the tree tightly, as though it were a friend. He said,

"This is my hugging tree, planted by my father when he was a little boy. The tree has a strong spirit and means only goodwill. I pray to it as warriors pray to dark Durga. I hope, daughter, that you will pray to the hugging tree."

"I will not hesitate!" she said. "I'm a fisher, not a fencer!"

Erin embraced the tree. Rud had stepped aside. Then he wound his net around Erin's wrists so quickly that it hardly registered what he was doing. She was bound to the tree.

"Father!" Erin cried. "What game is this?"

"No game, Erin. There is a gathering in the village this afternoon. Important matters will be decided, and you must not intervene. I think that I will see you never again, for tonight is after all the dark moon. I have asked this tree to keep you safe."

"You lied to me!" she said angrily. "You tricked me with love!"

"The love was no trick," he said. "There is a sacrifice to be made on each new moon. Commonly the choice is someone old, or sick, or crippled. Because of my knee, I think this time it will be me. I do not hesitate to go, now that Orline has a daughter who is a good provider."

"What do you say to me! A man who prays to trees does not sacrifice to cruel gods!"

"Not to gods, Erin! Not to gods!"

Before she could challenge him further, Rud hurried away, hobbling on his lame leg and vanishing into the trees. Erin struggled at the netting which held her hands around the trunk of a tree. She knew that fishers' knots were strong and that she might not escape. A sound rose in her throat which was like the sound of a baying wolf, a horrible lament that could shrink the soul; the cry of an injured heart.

*     *     *

A burl on the tree met the knot of her bindings so that Erin could not sit down. She stood beneath the hugging-tree until her legs cramped and her arms felt drawn upon a rack.

Dappled sunlight wandered in the shade. It was a sweltering day, but the tree kept her relatively cool, as did the breeze off the tiny lake. She grew thirsty. Thirst, atop the aches and sorrow, was enough to make her dizzy.

Periodically she'd take up the struggle anew, thinking that the net holding her hands might be worn apart if not actually broken. She rubbed the net against the bark of the tree, but caused more damage to herself than the binding.

Birds fluttered from shade to shade, not singing. Fish leapt above the minute waves.

"I'm thirsty!" Erin complained. A whole pool of water was beyond her reach. It made her angry. "I'll write a letter to Congress!" she shouted. "You can't keep me tied up here like this! I'll go to the union!" She began to kick the tree, for her feet at least were free.

Then she stopped cold. References to things from the planet Earth struck her as potentially dangerous. If she withdrew her mind from Endsworld, she might find herself thrown back through the eye of the needle. She was not yet so distressed with her adopted country that televisions, automobiles, and appliances had greater appeal.

"But I *am* thirsty," she said in a subdued voice.

Water dripped on her head and she looked up. Another drop struck between the eyes. Cupped leaves held moisture from the previous night's rainfall. A bird was hopping from limb to limb, spilling water from the leaves. Erin opened her mouth and, with head thrust back, captured what she could. It sufficed.

The drink helped clear her mind. She steered her thoughts away from the likes of Congress and workers' unions, refusing to dwell on things of Earth even in facetious ways. Instead, she concentrated on the fragrance of the woods around the pool, the breeze on her neck, even the pain in her wrists and calves. "Thank you, Tree," she said. "Thank you for the water. If your bark weren't so bitter, you might have fed me too."

She craned her neck as far around as she could to see along the rarely trodden path. No one was coming. At the edge of her vision, however, amidst the leaves of the hugging-tree, she saw a round object hanging above and slightly to the back of her head. Of all the branches she could see, only the one bore fruit.

By shimmying up the trunk and hanging backward from her bonds, she was able to grab the fruit in her teeth. She slid back down with the prize and stuck it on the spur of a small, broken limb. "Apple on a stick!" she said, biting into the pulp. Sweet, sticky sap had dripped onto the fruit's skin, doubling Erin's delight. "Thanks again, Tree!"

Although she had gained food and water from the tree by perfectly comprehensible means, to Erin it seemed supernatural. She was by then confused enough and alone enough that she was glad to personify her captor. She began to believe in Rud's statement that the tree had a spirit which meant only goodwill. Perhaps fear of the unknown fate awaitng Rud had driven her a little mad, or at least a mite delirious. For whatever cause, the hugging-tree began to take on momentous importance to Erin. She started talking to it at an uninterrupted pace, as though certain it could hear. In this way she kept herself distracted and she did not feel abandoned or alone. All the while, she rubbed her bonds up and down, polishing the bark, weakening her bonds, though no longer consciously thinking of escape.

Hours passed and twilight approached. Erin began to doubt anyone would ever come to untie her. "You know, Tree, if Rud is sacrificed in some terrible manner, there'll be nobody alive who knows about this place. I could be left out here forever! Oh, you're probably right; Orline knows where to find me. She and Rud planned this out after all. But she's kind of forgetful, and what with cutting firewood and cooking and her other chores, she doesn't have time to come out fishing very often; so she might not be able to find the way. In that case, it's just you and me, Tree. Yep."

Erin sang songs. At dusk, the birds joined in, twittering in branches above her head, flying lower to inspect her now and then. She sang all the songs she'd learned since finding herself on Endsworld, most of them fishers' songs. She sang fragments of others she'd not learned in their entirety; and she invented some new ones. "Wee toddler Tin's been sitting in the bin, playing with the coal while no one's home. Wee toddler Tin's been sitting in a tree, throwing all the acorns down to me." Oddly, she couldn't recall a single song she'd ever heard on Earth. She could think of the names of singers, but the songs were blocked from her mind. She wondered if it were a good or bad sign that Earth receded further from the grasp of her memory.

"It's getting late, Tree," she said, ending a tune she'd half made up. A few birds sang on; others were already sleeping. Insects chirruped. "Orline won't be able to find her way at night," said Erin. "I can't expect to be untied before tomorrow, and maybe not then either. If I die here—I hope you realize this, Tree, because you're an accomplice— there'll be nobody to take care of Orline. She's only got a few strong years left you know. If we take Rud's word for it, those who are a burden to any village end up official sacrifices. We wouldn't want that to happen to Orline now, would we?" She looked at the tree, waiting for an answer. Receiving none, she said, "No indeed, we wouldn't."

Insects and birds shushed when night was total. All was very still, but for Erin's voice, which sang ever so softly: "wee toddler Tin . . . wee toddler Tin . . ."

She began to laugh. It was helplessness that made her daft. It had made her daft on Earth, and it made her daft on Endsworld. She had cast down swords in favor of a simple fisher's life, afraid to take the risk of greater courage and adventure. What had her reluctance *and her cowardice* gotten her? Tied to a tree!

In her dreams of Endsworld, long before the reality of it, she had never been like this. She had been strong . . . a fighter . . . the champion of the meek . . .

The idiocy of frail, human dreams made Erin stop her laughter.

"I'm supposed to be a hero!" she shouted to the night, yanking at her bindings until her wrists were bloody. The roosting birds scattered in search of quieter perches.

The sky was clear, the stars bright. There would

be no moonrise.

"Tree!" she said. "Tree! You've got to let me go! I've got to save Rud! I've got to find out what it is that terrorizes the villages along the river! I've got to be a hero! Let me go, Tree, let me go!"

Her struggle was crazy and valiant. She'd have worn her flesh to the bone to escape, as a wolf might pay a leg; but such damage was unnecessary. She fell backward, away from the trunk. Adrenaline madness had burst every string of the net.

Breaths came quick and deep; she was nearly hyperventilating. This added immeasurably to her slightly crazed state. To the end of her life, she'd remain convinced that a tree had of its will given her water, fed her, kept her company, and finally let her go.

She picked herself up from the ground, exercising aching legs. Rud's net had been completely ruined. She unwrapped the last of it from her sore wrists and threw it aside. Her own twin-net was intact. This she took up as she scurried through the dark woods toward the village. She looked back once and said, "Goodbye, Tree," and kept on running.

Though her mission was serious and she knew that wicked answers lay ahead, Erin yet felt giddy. It seemed as though she'd survived a mere children's book adventure, and that more of the same should be expected. She felt that the only things ahead of her were further successes: greater heroism, charmed escapes, and merry deeds. Sprinting through woodland darkness, she fancied herself a combination of Zorro and Sheena of the Jungle, unchallengeably powerful, destined to live happily ever after—after the script had run its course and the lights in the theater went up. This was still, in all, a game to Erin . . . a dream . . . and she was therefore less a part of Endsworld than she would like to believe.

Because of all this, she was not prepared for the horrors to be confronted.

\*     \*     \*

An obscene, moist clicking warned her that something used the path ahead. When she caught the first faint outline of them, they looked like marching men, going three abreast. As she came nearer, they looked more like robots; but that wasn't right either. Erin crawled through an out-cropping to get close enough for a good view. When she saw them clearly, it was difficult not to cry out in alarm.

They were insects, walking upright, large as men. They walked in rows of three, keeping a precise rhythm to their pace. Their long, fierce mandibles clacked and clicked. Their eyes shone gold and red. They were armed with knives and sickles, all comfortably and thankfully (thought Erin) sheathed. Their long hind legs gave them an odd, broken gait. Midway between the long upper arms and their legs, there was a secondary, much smaller pair of arms.

These rudimentary arms held bundles of flesh, newly sliced; and the creatures' mandibles shone in the starlight, dark with blood. At first Erin thought the meat was from wild game. Then she saw the frightful, severed head of an old woman packed along by one of the fiends. Another carried the splotchy torso of a child who had suffered pox.

Erin might yet have contained her bile, were she able to think them merely vultures and ghouls. But they were not grave robbers. The severed parts of human bodies were so fresh that some of the muscles yet flexed. One trio of marching insects was carrying arms and legs on which the fingers and toes still wiggled.

The lines of marchers stretched out of sight, along the winding backwoods path. They were headed in the direction of the village Thar.

Erin withdrew from the awful sight. She crouched in thicker brush and emptied her stomach of foul tasting fluids. As quickly and quietly as possible she composed herself by drawing long, slow, even breaths. Soon, she found herself hurrying across a narrow bridge to the paved main road. She sped toward her adopted village, amazingly calm the whole while. She returned to the village's side of the river on a hand-operated rope-and-bucket ferry.

The uninterrupted line of insect soldiers cut her off from the house she'd been living in. She could not fetch her swords. The center of the village, however, was accessible. Erin ran along the single street, startled by the silence. All that she could hear was the repulsive clacking of gigantic mandibles over a brief rise. In the village proper, there was no sign of life: no fires in the pots, no candles at the windows. She kicked a few doors wide and quickly realized there were no people anywhere.

"Orline!" she cried out, then looked the other way to shout, "Rud!"

No answer.

"Anyone!"

The sound of the insect army seemed louder or more excited. Erin's blood rushed through her temples so violently that she could hear it like the river. It was not only her blood she was hearing, though; it was also a dirge of human origin.

Erin's sharp eyes scanned all directions, madness barely sealed behind the glaze. She recollected a small, comfortable room in a sanitarium, where she would sit for hours on the floor beneath a window thinking of nothing. She presently felt as though she needed to think about nothing.

*It's a nightmare*, she thought, looking all around. Darkness was everywhere. A mist was rising out of the east, threatening to block the starlight. The grey shacks of the village seemed to be hunched monsters, the porches like tongues and the doors like mouths. The sounds of the river, the blood in her head, the terrible droning of human voices, and the clacking of mandibles . . . she thought, *I've lost control of the dream*.

She covered her ears and shut her eyes, but couldn't tear the vision from her mind. There was a scream and it wasn't her own. Suddenly alert, Erin sprinted up the rise, for the shouting had been Rud's.

He screamed again.

*I'm not dreaming.*

Erin topped the rise. From her vantage point she could see all the villagers kneeling with their faces to the ground. None looked up as they hummed their deathly dirge.

One person was standing. It was Rud. A trio of insects had him. One held his neck from behind, another clutched his waist. The third leaned toward him with vicious mandibles snapping.

It bit through Rud's left arm.

Rud's response was immediate, extreme, and hideous to hear; yet he offered no struggle. He held his eyes clamped shut and raised his right arm to be treated like the left.

"Father!"

Erin charged through the group of prone bodies, not caring who she stepped on. The endless line of insects passed in the background, taking no heed of the ritual in Thar village. Only three were involved in the village sacrifice. Only three need be battled.

Rud's right arm was nipped cleanly from the shoulder. He almost fell, but was held by neck and waist. Erin didn't stop her headlong rush. The horror barely registered. She had one thought: save Rud. She took her twin-net from across her back and tossed it in the direction of the insects holding Rud. The webwork of the net's two halves fell over the two captors.

Her foster father fell to his knees, eyes still clenched tight. He continued to wail in agony.

Erin drew upon her advanced karate training as well as her glancing knowledge of other "empty hand" fighting styles. A flying forward kick took one of the netted insects full in the stomach. She felt as though she had kicked an iron firepot; but at least the fiend toppled, dragging the other with it.

The fighting woman turned, expecting the un-netted insect to come at her with its sickles and knives. Instead, it grabbed Rud. Its mandibles held him by the neck and dragged him backward, toward the line of marching, humanoid insects. Erin charged, cursing wildly; but before she could land a blow, the mandibles squeezed and Rud's screaming came to an abrupt end. His head rolled down the far side of the slope.

"Noooo!" Erin's fist contacted one of the fiend's huge, golden eyes. The eye collapsed like a brittle, paper balloon, then oozed yellow fluids. The insect staggered back, half blind, and drew its two sickles. The blades were not quick enough from the sheath, for Erin struck at the remaining eye with as much force as any third-degree black belt ever achieved. The fiend tossed its arms in the air and the sickles flew straight up, twirling. Erin caught one of the sickles before it reached the ground. It was designed for pincered hands and fit strangely in a palm. The other sickle struck the spine of one of the villagers. All of them were still face down upon the ground. Erin shouted at them,

"Get up! Fight or run! Get up you fools!"

They continued their dirge. They were under the

glamor of a self-induced hypnotism. It was probably the only way they could endure the horror of each dark moon. This ritual might be so deeply rooted in their traditions and themselves that it was a virtual religious rapture holding them motionless.

The blinded insect staggered to and fro, beating itself in the face with its pincered hands. The two which Erin had netted had cut themselves out of the snare, using mandibles and knives. They came at her together, multiply armed.

Somehow the blinded one regained its bearings, too. It had lost its sickles, but still held two knives. It came at her from behind. Erin ran sideways, out from the midst of the three. It did not escape her notice that they all stepped in precise unison. Unbelievably, she realized, the fiends were linked in sets of three. Even the blind one could find its way, led by the other two's senses. Erin wondered what would happen if she killed but one of them. It might break the whole link between the three.

She maneuvered around them so that only one could reach her at a time. It swung the sickles wide, not a particularly good fighter. She kept herself far enough back that the shorter hands' knives could be no threat; but she was kept no less busy blocking the long arms' sickles. Though it was the inferior fighter, it was doubly armed. Yet Erin felt confident. Unfortunately, the other two were approaching. She withdrew again, swiftly circled the three, then made a surprise charge at the one whose eyes she'd ruined. It "saw" her through the eyes of its partners, and faced her head on. But all it had were the daggers with which to fight. Erin's stolen sickle outreached the short weapons in short arms. She wrapped her sickle around the fiend's neck.

"Your head for Rud's!" she hollered, and yanked the sickle towards herself. The insect's head tumbled off.

The fiend did not fall. Its long arms caught her. The head lay on the ground, mandibles opening and closing; it was still alive, still part of the three-way connection.

Its middle arms jabbed out with the knives. Erin caught one of the short arms in her left hand, and cut the other off completely with the sickle in her right. Then she carved upward in a sweeping gesture, striking through the joints of the elbows, severing both its upper arms. She darted backward in time to avoid the other two insects.

The armless, headless one was helpless, though still living, still directed by the decapitated head and its shocking connection with its fellows. "Is there no killing you!" Erin shouted at them, and tossed the sickle toward one of the two approaching. It crossed its own sickles in front of itself, stopping her sickle's flight.

Erin withdrew further, but saw that she was heading for the line of marching insects who had thus far taken no notice of the events in Thar. She circled back, wanting to avoid the horde.

Ordinarily the sacrifice would be done by now. The villagers began to awaken from their self-induced trances. The dirge began to die. They expected to see no sign of the insects by now, so when they raised their heads from the ground they were horrified by the vision. Orline was among them. She called out,

"Erin! Stop! You don't understand!"

Erin had taken up a large stone as she circled toward the severed insect head. She smashed the rock upon the exo-skull and it cracked. She struck again and the head broke open. Inside was a brain no larger than a walnut. It was no wonder it took three of them to add up to any sort of intellect!

When the skull was broken, the other two

insects dropped their weapons and stood like dumb statues.

"I beat you bastards!" she shouted; but she was wrong. By breaking the bond between any three, she alerted the marching horde. The previously unconcerned hundreds stopped in their tracks. They turned their heads toward Thar.

They swarmed toward the sacrificial site.

The villagers were on their feet and running. Erin ran amongst them and grabbed Orline by the arm.

"What have I done, mother?" she begged. "Tell me what I've done!"

Orline's voice was harsh. "You've doomed us all," she said hoarsely. "You cannot fight so many." She pulled away from Erin and ran with the others. Erin did not go. A terrific guilt welled up inside her. She knew she could not defeat the whole army of insects; but she was willing to try. It was, after all, an excellent method of suicide. She felt that she deserved death, considering what evil her ignorance had wrought.

She approached one of the insects which stood statue-still, severed as it was from the three-way bond necessary to give it and its two mates a semblance of intelligence. She stole for herself a sickle in the right hand and a knife in the left.

She stood before the onrushing horde.

About a dozen of them surrounded her in an instant. The rest flooded into the village. The people had taken refuge in their poor hovels, which the insects could hew through with ease. Erin could not see it; but heard the dreadful cries of agony and torture. It appeared that the insects felt no pain even when their various limbs became dismembered; so it might not be that they truly meant to torture. They had no understanding of human terror. But the effect was the same. They cut and bit the villagers into pieces without killing them swiftly, then carted each piece off into the night.

The foolish, would-be hero fought excellently, intending to slay at least a few before her own end was sealed. It would help her atone for inadvertently causing the slaughter of her adopted family and friends.

The clouds had come in from the east, shrouding the stars. Erin aimed her weapons at the insects' shining eyes, for there was little else that she could see after the bright starlight was snuffed out. She might have beaten them off for an entire minute. There were too many for her to last longer than that, armed with weapons designed for claws and balanced differently than would be preferred. A dagger dragged across the front of her robe, scratching her. She could not leap back because she was surrounded. The next slash either from dagger or sickle would end her life.

The diamond needle slipped out from the folds of her robe, dangling on its hemp cord. It shone in the darkness—and the insects stopped fighting.

They backed away from her, though keeping her penned. More of them came to see the shining object. They pointed with pincers. Directly, they began to squat down on their big grasshopper legs, watching her with those glowing eyes.

When she tried to break out of the circle, they bunched together with weapons pointed at her. But they did not attack. The clicking of their mandibles sounded like heavy rain, for they were very excited among themselves.

"You fear this?" she said, removing the miniature sword pendant from her neck. "Or do you worship it?"

She held it before herself like a small lantern; and they would have allowed her to pass then. But there was a fluttering of wings above her head and

Erin looked up. An insect—larger than all the others, gorgeously winged, and quite singular rather than part of a trio—hovered in the sky above the site.

Erin held the little sword upward, casting faint light upon the winged creature against dark clouds. The thing was vaguely feminine though it lacked breasts. It was inimically beautiful and wonderfully curved. Erin guessed it was the Queen.

"Err! Err!" the Queen rasped.

"Go away!" Erin shouted, swinging the little sword as though it were a big weapon.

"Err-ta! Err-ta woh-mon! Erta wohmon!"

It was talking. Erin was taken aback to understand the words: Earth Woman.

"How do you know!"

"Err-ta Woh-mon!"

The queen fluttered in a semi-circle to inspect Erin more closely.

"Bah-tree!" said the queen, pointing with long, slender fingers which were nothing like the soldiers' pincers. She repeated: "Bah-tree!"

"Bottry?" Erin said, captivated by this attempted communication despite the horrors. The queen had indicated the needle-sword. Erin asked, "This is a bottry?"

"No. No. No. No." The queen dropped down a bit, though keeping out of Erin's reach. It tried to enunciate better: "Bah-tra-tree! Bah-terr-ree!"

"Battery? Battery?"

"Ssss! Yo-ssss! Bah-tree."

The queen flew higher, then headed west without looking back. Directly, the group surrounding Erin picked itself up in threes and sixes and followed their queen on foot. Those in the village went carrying pieces of meat. The three insects Erin had killed or decommissioned were also sliced to pieces and hauled away.

Before long Erin was left standing alone. The first rays of dawn touched the undersides of distant clouds.

She held the crystal blade near her own face and looked at it with a puzzled expression. The queen's knowledge confounded Erin. How could so terrible a creature have known she was of Earth? The queen had also known something of the miniature blade.

"Battery," said Erin. "A battery to what?"

III·SUR-
VIVOR

# III. SURVIVOR

Teebi Dan Wellsmith piloted his boat twixt the banks of the river Yole. A warm, light drizzle dampened the morning from sky to ground. Teebi had pulled his arms out of his robe's sleeves so that the top hung behind, held to him by the cloth belt. Sweat and rain beaded in the thick hair of his bared chest.

He sang a tune about a handsome man, whom Teebi fancied was himself. The chorus, which went in part, "and a good fine man was he," became, after Teebi's illiterate fashion, "a good fine man was me." But if Teebi had ever been handsome, it had worn off with time, although he wasn't far into his middle years. He had a crooked eye and a cleft in his chin that might have been natural or might have been put there by a sword; Teebi never said which.

"O! Me went out hunting on a good fine day, and me poached a hen in me neighbor's hay. I was caught red-handed but they set me free, for me neighbor's daughter had a crush on me . . . huh?" Teebi left off singing. The village Thar had always been one of his regular stops along the way. He knew instantly that something was amiss.

The place looked deserted in the drizzle's mist. There was only one vagrant soul in sight, sitting on the end of a pier, thoroughly drenched but not moving to cover. The poor lad was looking off into nowhere and didn't seem to notice Teebi's boat approaching.

"Ho!" cried Teebi Dan Wellsmith. "Ho!" The lad on the pier wouldn't take heed. No, on second look, it weren't a lad at all! It was a wet, bedraggled woman. She bore weapons through her girdle, short *i* and long *mai*.

"Ho!" he shouted again, poling his boat toward the pier and acting merry enough to ward off danger. "Name's Teebi Dan Wellsmith, a fishmonger on a buying spree from Ucho-by-the-Sea to Terwold-by-the-Mountain! Any fish to sell today? Good prices will be paid, Oh! Good fish is loved in Terwold, salted down and dry, My!, it does go good with whiskey-rye and city folk loathe being dry!" He carried on in a roughly poetic way, far more impressive than the average hawker shouting about his wares to buy or to sell.

The boat came to a halt near the rickety pier and Teebi ceased shouting. He looked the woman up and down, but she still did not notice him. "Can't hear me, hey? Mute as well, hey?"

He looked beyond her to the village. A muddy street was tinted with blood. Pink runnels washed into the river Yole. There were no corpses to be seen, however, and Teebi recognized the signs. "Ain't seen it in a dozen years!" he exclaimed. "So that's what got your tongue, hey? Vengeful critters, them bugs. You the meddler what set it off?" He measured her swords and tried to collate these with a fisher's girdle. "A fencing fisher!" he declared, laughing. "I've seen it all today!"

Teebi snatched up a sack made of loosely woven hemp and jumped off his boat. He hurried along the pier, leaving the mute woman behind. "Guard the boat, me silent gal!" he called back. She turned her head slowly, apparently noticing him for the first time. Her expression was sad and far away.

The fishmongering boatman checked all the

houses, sheds, and boats. He loaded fish into his hemp bag. When he came out of a certain old shed, the sword-wielding fisherwoman was standing there. Teebi grinned sheepishly.

"No sense letting all this good fine salted fish go to waste, now, hey? Pretty penny for it in Terwold. And I's be giving you your share, you understand, as how you're the only survivor of the massacre and all."

The woman didn't speak. She seemed barely to look at him. Slowly, Teebi grew afraid.

She drew a sword from her girdle. It was the *i* or smallsword; but "small" was a comparative value. It was a sight longer than Teebi needed held before his face. He dropped the sack of fish. His crooked eyes went two ways at once looking for a good route of escape.

"Meant no harm!" he said, edging along the porch. "A shame to waste the fish is all!"

She came on.

"Hey, wait," he said, waving her away. "You've been through a bit; I understand all that. But let's not go killing innocent fishmongers about it, hey? You're feeling under; I can tell. I've a spot of medicine on the boat; if you don't mind, I'll go and get it for you now." He tried to run off the shed's porch, but the woman reached her sword sideways to block his path.

"Stand there," she said, her voice harsh and guttural. Water dripped from her soaking hair, trailing around her face. Her eyes were wild like someone fevered.

"Why, yes, I think I'll do that," he said, grinning and trying to look helpful. "If it pleases you, I mean."

"Those are my mother's fish," she said. "And my father's."

"Oh! Right! I see your meaning. I'm a thief caught red-handed; I admit it! But I'm willing to make amends. I'll pay you twice the going rate. To atone, you understand."

"Do you know what happened to this village?" she asked. "Well, I'm the one who caused it! I'm an evil girl! I could kill you like *that!*" She swung her sword meaningfully.

"I'd rather you didn't!" he said, more indignant than afraid. "Why are warriors bullies? Go ahead, then, kill me! Kill me if you can, hey!" He reached behind his back and came out with a short, barbed pole. It was for grabbing sacks and bales, but it made a dandy weapon.

The woman stood poised and calm. She didn't seem to care if she were hurt or killed. Her lack of fear unnerved him once again.

"I'm a good fighter!" he warned, crouching to attack; but he was shaking.

She took another step forward, sword raised.

Teebi dropped his barbed pole on the step, then went down on his knees. "Reconsider!" he shouted, clutching both his hands. The woman held off. "You've a good nature," he said, hoping to flatter, "I can see that. It isn't you what wants to kill. The blood upon the street was spilled by bugs, not you. You mustn't blame yourself for them! But if you kill a hard working fishmonger, now hey, what excuse for things then? Y'are too sensitive to live with that, I know, or you wouldn't be so sad today!"

She backed away and sheathed the sword with a deft motion. "You're right," she said. "I could not live with it. I cannot live with it now."

Teebi wiped sweat from his brow and stood up very slowly, still afraid to make a sudden motion lest her sword lick out anew. He slipped his arms into the sleeves of his robe, pulling it up from his waist to cover shoulders and chest. After he arranged his girdle into a neat position, he fancied himself so tidy and attractive that no woman would kill him now. He picked up his hook from the step of the porch and hung it from the backside of his girdle.

"Your mind's upset," he ventured. "I've seen it before. People die of melancholy. We die of shame and broken hearts. It's a difficult sickness to endure. But there's a healer traveling from a foreign land. I saw him in Ucho-by-the-Sea and heard that he would go by route of Terwold, same as me. He can cure melancholy with the touch of his hand, I'd wager! He cured me of a crick in my knee, and asked no payment for the deed. That knee had bothered me seven years! His name is Valk the Ear, so called because he listens to the weak and the poor."

"Valk?" she said, trying it out. The name seemed to annoy her. "What does this Valk the Ear look like?"

"He is fair," said Teebi, "of complexion and of spirit. Dresses all in white as befits a healer. Even his girdle is white, with no designs whatsoever; he calls himself Man Of No Trade. He is a minister, though: minister of the sick of body; minister of the sick at heart. His sermons are fine to hear! He preaches pacifism, which annoys certain folk, such as those who carry swords. He impressed me, talking bold without a knife or barb. That is why I threw down my hook, hey! You might have thought me afraid? I thought we might hurt each other fighting, and Valk the Ear would be ill-paid for tending to my knee."

"What's your name?" the woman asked. "Teebi something? You yelled it on the river."

"Teebi Dan Wellsmith!" he said proudly. "From a fine good line of well diggers. My old brother got the business, hey, so I took out to sea. You can tell by the triangle designs on my belt that I'm a sailor by profession, or a pirate some would say. The seas are dangerous with action of late, so I wend along this river instead. Seems hoary river Yole has got a bit of action too!"

"My name is Erin," she said, once he had finally paused. "Erin of Thar, in this country called Durga's Lathe."

"You call it that! Y'are a fisher after all?"

"A fisher," she halfheartedly agreed.

"And a swordswoman too! That's fine. I always said if more fishers carried swords, fewer warriors would kill them! I was reared in Sandor Prefecture, so we're neighbors of a sort. Sandor holds the capital seat of Durga's Lathe. Therefore, those of us who live so near Terwold learn swiftly to call our country 'Wevan.' Warriors believe the name of the war goddess cannot be said by peasants' lips, and they slay us for using the country's older name. But always in our hearts, hey!, and in the reality around us, this country *is* the lathe of black Durga!"

He laughed. Then he grew more serious, and warned her, "All the same, me good fine friend: if you venture near to Terwold, pretend the nation's name is and always was Wevan."

"I will reflect on that advice," said Erin, "but might prefer the trouble."

"A fencing fisher is no match for proven warriors!" he insisted. "Start no fights with them! It would be the same as leaping from a cliff!" He looked at her sideways, seeing that his lecture didn't penetrate. "Ah! Then death is your quest? Because of this slaughter? Y'are mad to think as that!"

"Maybe I am," she whispered, her gaze once more far away. "I cannot help my thoughts."

Teebi grew quiet for a moment. He looked all around him at the empty village. When he burst into renewed chatter, his voice was lower: "Them bugs left nothing to bury, hey? Of your mother and daddy not a bone? I'm sorry to hear. I give you my word on this, O Erin of Thar: full half of all receipts gained from salted fish gathered in this village will be spent on funeral prayers in Terwold's finest temple!"

"You still think of business," said Erin, turning her back to him. She said so quietly he barely caught the words, "All the same, that would be welcome."

Teebi laughed again. "Good and fine!" He grabbed his sack and went scavenging through the rest of the houses. Eventually, loaded down, he led Erin to his boat.

The light rain had stopped and the sky was less overcast. Erin dried herself near a little firepot on Teebi's boat. He fetched together a small, cold meal.

"For you," he said, holding forth a hand. "Dried shrimp from the briny sea near Ucho—a treat for a river woman, hey?"

"Thank you no," she said, spurning his offering.

"No, hey?" He was injured. "You'll make yourself grow thin." He held the shrimp closer to her face.

"I'm not hungry!" she scolded, and slapped his hand away.

Teebi looked upset. "A bad sign," he said. "Valk the Ear would help you."

All that day, she helped steer as he poled the boat up the turgid river. They'd stopped at two villages before dark. Teebi dickered for quality catches and gave the people free news. Of Thar he said nothing. As he explained to Erin later, "They never speak of the bugs! Soon enough they'll know that Thar is uninhabited."

As night approached, they searched for and discovered a quiet place to tie up the boat. They made beds at opposite ends, a pile of packed fish between them. Erin couldn't sleep. Neither could

Teebi, who directly went peeking over the pile of fish to ask,

"How did you survive it? Why didn't they take you too?"

"I don't know." She shrugged and didn't look at him. She reached into the fold of her robe and withdrew the end of her diamond pendant. The miniscule sword no longer shone. "They wouldn't come near this," she said. "A charm against them, perhaps."

Teebi squinted at it, one eye at a time. "It's an artifact," he said.

"Artifact?"

"Very old. Maybe it saved you once, but do yourself a favor: sell it to a magician. A rich magician. Get rid of it fast."

She dropped it inside her robe, near her throat. "I think I'll keep it," she said.

"As you please," he said, crawling back to his side of the boat. He added testily, "Teebi Dan Wellsmith don't know a good fine thing about it, hey."

\*   \*   \*

Most of the morning went without hazard or complaint, although Erin had not eaten and this made Teebi fret. He poled the boat along the river, trying not to worry too much about his sullen passenger. Since her conversations were not the most delightful, he fell singing, as was his usual pattern. It delighted him to think that his rider probably enjoyed overhearing the tunes. An audience was a grand thing to have; and a lack of applause did not necessarily mean a lack of appreciation. He went so far as to fancy his music might well soothe her dreadful sorrow.

Generally it was his practice to sing the same

song for many hours; but in the spirit of greater adventure, and so as not to bore the fencing fisher on his boat, he tried every song he knew and repeated not a one. When he got around to a lullaby his mother had sung him as a baby, which went, "Wee toddler Tin's been sitting in the bin, playing with the coal while no one's home," the woman gave her first response. She drew her sword.

Teebi reeled about when he heard the bothersome "shhhk" of a drawn sword. The woman was glowering at him from a crouch as she commanded,

"Sing any song but that."

He sang none instead. The rest of his morning was spent being as sullen as she.

By afternoon they had passed into Sandor Prefecture, stopping at every riverside village along the passage. Teebi bargained poorly, partly because the people had known him as a child and they knew his dickering tricks too well. It was also partly that his heart had grown heavy about his sad and temperamental ward. His boat was already close to full, though, so his livelihood was not at stake.

The highway was a more direct route to Terwold than the winding river Yole. The way was made longer still by Teebi's stopping and bartering and sometimes lingering among old friends. "We'll make it to the city before night falls," he promised, seeing that Erin grew edgy on the trip.

Yole wound furthest east at a certain point in Sandor. The area was far from the highway and there were no villages on the banks. Teebi poled faster through this quiet stretch.

Erin pointed to the eastern horizon. "What's that?" she asked.

"Nothing that means a good fine thing to you and Teebi Daŋ Wellsmith," he said. Erin untied the rudder so that it flopped sideways. The boat was sent toward a muddy bank. Teebi looked at the back of the boat, annoyed. "Now what's the point of that, hey? Y'are trouble all the time."

"Tell me what it is," she demanded, sitting by the loose rudder's handle. There were spiral-shaped metallic structures poking up on the skyline, bent and corroded. "Is it part of Terwold?"

"Gods no, gal!" He pointed straight down the river. "Look for Terwold that way, in the evening shadow of many-spired Black Mountain." When he clambered to the back of the boat to tie the rudder straight once more, Erin stood up from her seat and blocked Teebi's path. He said, "There you go being threatening again, as though we weren't good fine friends and all. Are you sure you're from this country, hey? You'd not be asking about that land out east if you'd lived around here long."

"It's my adopted land after all," she said. "There's a lot that I don't know."

"Well that place out there is full of artifacts. Ain't no one visits there but sorcerers, and some of them's too scared."

"The ruins of an ancient race?" she hazarded. "I want to see it."

"Nah, you don't want any such thing, me gal! Teebi Dan Wellsmith's never been closer than this and never intends."

"Does a tributary go near the ruins?" she asked, ignoring his complaint.

"What if there was, hey? You going to be swimming up that way alone?"

"You'll take me," she said. "You've always been curious about the place, hey?" She mimicked his tone.

"I'm too old for adventures anymore! Only a fool would go to a dangerous place with a woman who wants to die. I'd sooner see familiar Terwold, which is dangerous enough. I've salted fish to sell."

"It'll keep," she said, grabbing up the pole from where he'd set it down to fix the rudder. She said, "You steer."

He obeyed, but looked cranky about it. "To tell the truth," he confessed, "I went there when I was young and bold. There wasn't much worth seeing; that's the fact of it. We might as well not go."

Erin kept poling. She found a tributary and turned the boat that way.

"If you're confirmed about it," Teebi said, "you'll need something for your feet. Barefoot might serve on a smoothly cobbled highway, muddy roads, and wading in the river . . . but there's splinters of steel and shards of glass all about the ruins. The very soil of that unwelcoming place would gnaw through your callouses and cut you to the heel bone. Perhaps we should come some other time, when you're better shod."

"You've spare sandals," she said, knowing where everything in the boat was kept. "You can deduct the value from the funeral fund."

"Mine or your folks', hey?" He shook his head. "Won't see Terwold tonight, I say. Got a new captain on this ship, I say. It's mutiny is all, and quite a common thing."

\*     \*     \*

The tributary grew shallow, then thick as sludge. Tall shrubbery with succulent, fingery leaves obscured the view in all directions. They couldn't tell how much further it was to the ruins.

"Don't eat the berries, hey," said Teebi. Erin eyed the small, pale, blotchy fruits and stoutly replied,

"I wouldn't."

The pole bent with her efforts to move the boat forward.

"Keel's rubbing bottom," she said. "I don't

think we'll get much closer by boat."

Teebi didn't look happy. "That wall of brush looks impassable," he said, "and the ground's all quagmire and quicksand. We wouldn't dare it afoot. I seem to remember this stream being higher in the springtime. Maybe we could come back when . . ."

"My sword can cut us a path," Erin promised, "and we can grab hold of the overhanging shrubbery if it seems we're sinking too deep." She pulled up the hem of her robe and tucked it in her girdle. Teebi did likewise, without much enthusiasm. They tied the boat to shrubs along the bank, spied the vicinity for landmarks, then slid off into the foul water. Erin tied a pair of sandals together and slung them over her shoulders, keeping both hands free. The sharp edge of her *mai* carved a path through the overhanging bushes. On obtaining the bank, their legs went to the knees in viscous mud. After a while, Teebi said,

"Something stinks."

"Mud," said Erin.

Teebi had it all over his face from falling twice. He wrinkled up his nose and said, "No, hey, it ain't the mud. Musky smell. It's an animal, I say." He reached behind himself and fetched his wicked hook forward. "Never cared much for a good swamp or bad," he said. "Plenty stories about this place."

Erin sniffed the air. "Phew! You're right about the smell. It's getting worse."

"Don't know what it is," said Teebi. "I'm hoping we don't find out."

"Might be a mudfish or the like," said Erin, then added teasingly, "If we catch it, you can salt it down and sell it."

"It might be a-thinkin' the same about us, gal. Cut faster up there! Your little tag-along is getting anxious to see some ruins after all, he is."

The sun was filtered thin by the pudgy leaves of the swamp's tall brush. The air was stifling. "Sort of gloomy," Erin understated. "How about singing us a song to make us happy."

Teebi grumped. Erin started singing one instead, one she'd learned that very day:

"We went out hunting on a good fine day . . ."

"Something bit me! Yai! I'm bit!"

Teebi was chopping the mud with his barb when suddenly he was sucked under entirely. Erin rushed to the site, where the turbulence had already fallen still. She was afraid to stab anywhere for fear of knifing Teebi. Sheathing the *mai*, she felt all around with arms and feet, risking whatever might be risked to get hold of some part of Teebi and pull him up before he was eaten or suffocated. All she felt was mushiness and slime.

"I've lost him," she whispered in disbelief. She could find no sign of the man nor whatever it was that bit him. Erin felt instantly to blame, as the fishmongering boatman would never have come this route of his own accord. "Just like that I've lost him." Although she said it, it didn't yet settle in all the way. She plowed left and right, searching the area frantically. When she stood from her bent posture, arms muddied to the shoulders, it began to hit her more fully. She said to herself again, her voice husky, "Durga be damned! I've lost Teebi."

There was too little drama in a quick, unexpected death. It was somehow wrong. She wasn't prepared for it. Angered and sorrowed and defeated before she'd tried, Erin felt the depression well up anew. She shouted the phrase a final time:

*"I've lost Teebi!"*

The mud erupted before her. An ugly muddy shape burst upward.

"Gods help, hey!"

It was Teebi. His darkly stained hook reached straight up in the air. He grabbed a limb with it and pulled himself upward, then clung like a sloth in a tree, panting.

"Teebi! Teebi!" Erin strained against the pull of the mud, wanting to hug that stout mudball of a man. He spat gobbets of filth, choking out a warning:

"Out of the mud, gal!" He coughed twice more. "Get out of it, I say!"

Delirious with relief, she paid him too little heed. All she wanted to do was touch him. "I thought I'd got you killed for sure!" she called. Manic after the depression she'd felt ever since the massacre at Thar, Erin could scarcely think of anything but the fact that one friend had been sent back to her from certain doom.

"Damn fool woman!" Teebi shouted.

The quagmire erupted a second time. An uglier shape than Teebi's arose. It was an incredibly toothed, wormlike salamander rearing its arrow-shaped head up from its dirty habitat.

"It's an elt!" cried Teebi, climbing higher into the huge, closely entwined network of branches. "Never seen one before, but heard about 'em plenty! It'll suck your blood if it gets a hold of you, gal!"

Erin drew both the shortsword and the lengthier *mai*. The arrowheaded elt rose higher and higher, until its tiny black eyes looked at her from above. Its round, slimy maw undulated menacingly. Sharp teeth moved in some hinged fashion, opening and shutting like a circle of scissors.

To her left, a second arrow shaped head began to rise; and behind her, a third.

They had little, useless hands below their heads. Slime oozed from their greenish grey skin. Their skeletons must have been gristly and elastic, for the elts could not keep their narrow bodies from wavering in their stance.

The first one to rise began to topple forward, its

scissory maw stretched wide enough to enclose Erin's entire head. Her *mai* swept outward at an angle, cutting halfway through the thick trunk. Its tiny hands grabbed at the sword to no avail. As the creature fell, she caught its throat on the point of the shorter *i*. The elt gurgled and spat cold, acidic fluids on her.

To the side, the second elt was falling toward her in that peculiar mode of striking, collapsing like a sawed tree. The first elt was still thrashing at Erin's *i*'s point. It threw her off balance before she could push it aside to die. Only Teebi Dan Wellsmith's quick action saved her from the plunging elt.

Teebi dropped to a lower branch, hanging by his knees upside down in the thick shrubbery. His hook smashed into the back of the elt's pointed head, grabbing it by the brain and holding it before it could fall on Erin with sharp, round maw. Erin regained her balance while letting thick mud wash away the acidic bile that had previously soaked her shoulders. She left Teebi to wrestle with the one he'd hooked and turned her attention to the third.

It wavered in its rigid, upright posture. It began to sink back into the mire, not repeating the tactic of the two defeated. Erin fought the clinging mud, urging herself forward to get in range of the monster before it pulled itself completely beneath the mud. If it vanished under the surface, it would almost certainly attack in another way. She lunged forward, slashing with her sword, and fell full on her face in the muck. The last elt's severed head lay beside her.

Three elt corpses sank out of sight, thrashing below the surface of the mud.

As Erin picked herself up, she spied droplets of red blood spotting the ground around her. She looked up to where Teebi still hung upside down.

A white grin shone out of a muddy mask. "We got 'em, hey gal?"

"Are you all right?"

"I'm bit, I reckon. Hurts in the back of the leg. You strong enough to carry a brute like me?"

"If you can hang by it, you can walk on it. Come down from there and we'll get you out of this place and clean the wound."

*    *    *

Guilt plagued Erin afresh, for only good fortune had kept her from getting Teebi killed. Her own life she had a right to risk, but not the lives of others. It seemed as though the people of Endsworld could carry on in greater safety if she were dead; but before she did anything foolhardy, she'd have to see Teebi Dan Wellsmith safely to his boat.

They found a dry, packed path obviously used by the insect people on their moonless nights' treks. There was a clear pond nearby, in which the man and woman cleansed their bodies and their clothing. Erin ripped off part of the hem of Teebi's robe, saying,

"It's your wound, so we'll wreck your clothes to bind it."

"Y'are a mean gal, Erin of Thar." He gritted his teeth as she scrubbed his leg's wound and bound it with the clean, wet strip of cloth.

"How's it feel?" she asked.

"Stings a speck. Teebi Dan Wellsmith heals fast."

"It's a minor nip. You're luckier than I thought."

"Gonna limp a while, I reckon; but I'm used to that, from before when Valk the Ear healed my gimp." He slapped his wrapped leg with an open hand. Erin watched him hobble about in a practicing manner, and she thought of Rud with his rheumatic knees. It made her the more certain that Teebi be kept from danger. She scanned the vicinity for a quick way out of the predicament she'd led them into.

"It doesn't seem wise to go back to the boat through the swamp," said Erin. "We should be able to build a temporary raft from vines and reeds so as to float along the shallows to where we left the boat. You said you came this way as a young man. Do you recall if there's easier access back to the tributary somewhere?"

"It winds through that trash heap of a ruin," he said, pointing to the nearby spires poking above everything else. "I guess there's no getting around visiting the place, hey? Help me stand."

\*      \*      \*

"There," said Teebi, pointing. He hobbled out of the woods ahead of Erin, curious for all his reluctance in coming.

"Sun'll be down soon," said Erin, coming up behind Teebi.

"I reckon we're safe from them bugs all right, seeing's how they stay underground excepts on moonless nights. But that heap of rubble, hey! It looks ready to fall on someone's head." Teebi covered his scruffy head of hair with both arms. He looked back at Erin and said, "Better get them sandals on, gal. The road looks mighty cluttery from here on in."

She sat down on the path and took Teebi's spare sandals from her back, over which she'd slung them earlier by their straps. The footwear was woven from a tough, fibrous root and consisted of little more than a pair of soles with thongs. Erin tied the shorter thongs around each big toe, and the longer ones around her ankles, scarcely indi-

cating that she'd never worn Endsworld sandals
until today.

"Lead on," said Erin, standing.

"Nah," said Teebi. "You." Erin led her friend
toward a place eerie with early evening's shadows.
The ruin looked more akin to a massive garbage
dump than a once-inhabited city. Only a few buildings' spires poked up from the heaps and rubble
and machinery.

"What *is* this stuff?" asked Erin, looking all
around. On every side loomed monstrous, twisted
derelicts.

"Ain't nobody knows," said Teebi. "I've heard it
said that this place was here at the beginning of
history's records."

It was Erin's first sign of an advanced technology ever having been pursued on Endsworld.
Of course, she'd seen little of the one country as
yet, and the entire planet would of course be more
than she'd ever know about; still, she'd fancied it a
pre-technological world for all evidence—until
now.

Gargantuan, wrecked tractors, bent cranes,
wheeled iron tubes, globes held high on spidery
legs, and a vast assortment of additional vehicles
and machines were heaped one upon the other.
They formed an absurdly familiar pattern of dis-
array: to Erin, it was a nightmare version of an
automobile graveyard on Earth. The busted
machines weren't cars, however, but wild engines
of unguessable purpose. They might have been
used for construction or for war—or neither, or
both. One thing seemed likely. There was something *willful* about the massed stacks of destroyed
machinery, as though some ancient battle had
been waged against hard technology.

Although it would be curious if Endsworld's his-
toric records yielded no knowledge of a techno-

logical era as evidenced by these ruins, Erin suspected even historians might have limited information of the origin of all this. Where peasants lacked legends on a given subject, scholars generally lacked data. Erin's best guess was that chronicles were destroyed, scientists slaughtered, and the mere mention of technology severely punished by fanatically anti-technocratic tyrants of the distant past. After a diligent thousand years of that, the vaguest memory of ancient sciences might well be eradicated; on Earth, at least, whole civilizations had been known to rise and fall, leaving scarcely a trace to archeologists *or* the folk memory. Yet, in this case, the artifacts did remain, and were a mystery.

Sharp pieces of metal and glass were strewn about the bases of the mountainous heaps, creating dangerous obstacle courses for anyone who desired to inspect the structures more closely. Erin said,

"I'm going to climb inside one of those things."

Teebi looked upset. "There's no cause!" he exclaimed.

"I doubt there's need to fret," she said, stepping carefully between sharp objects. "These things haven't moved in a thousand years, I'd wager; my fiddling isn't likely to move them now. If anything among this junk still operated, some foolish stoutheart like Teebi Dan Wellsmith would've found out a long time ago."

"Not me, hey!" Teebi said. "No one like me!"

"Not even when you were a young adventurer?" she teased.

"Not then and not now!" He was adamant, defensively so. "Well," he added sheepishly, "maybe once. Not more than once."

Erin obtained the base of one of the piles and leaned against a particularly fantastic structure. She looked upward, into the skeletal bowels of the giant. The interior was shadowy and criss-crossed with narrow girders. "I see a kind of chair way up inside," she said. "I think a single person must have driven the entire juggernaut from there." She climbed along a twisted, unsteady ladder which ages before had provided safer access. She looked down where Teebi stood and called, "You coming?"

"Nah. Thanks, hey."

Her weight caused the structure to creak, but she felt no swaying and proceeded carefully. On gaining the high seat, she settled in as comfortably as possible. The seat wasn't designed for her particular bottom. Before her was a triangular control console. She began punching buttons and turning knobs at random. As she expected, nothing happened.

A certain lever wouldn't budge until she braced both feet against it. It moved the barest amount. Unexpectedly, a two-pronged fork popped forward from the console. The two sharp points stopped a mere finger's width from her eyes. Erin froze. Nothing else occurred. When she pushed on the prongs, they closed together as would a pair of tweezers. She was able to force the pronged extension back into its original position without much effort. "Spring operated," she guessed; it didn't indicate that anything still worked.

"How's it go, hey?" called Teebi from below. Erin stuck her head out an oval window and shouted,

"It reminds me of an amusement park ride!"

"A what?"

"Never mind," she said. "You wouldn't know."

"Well, have a good time at it," he said, encouraging her to play. "You've been a gloomy enough companion until now!"

He shouldn't have reminded her. Erin instantly ceased playing with the useless gizmos and started the descent. The sky was a deep hue of blue. The first bright stars were shining. The gargantuan derelicts stood silhouetted against the young night, looking like elephants and dinosaurs with heads bowed at a funeral. Erin's heart sank into emptiness.

When she stood by Teebi again, looking like a whipped pup, he shook his scruffy head and put hairy knuckles on his hips. "Y'are an unstable gal, Erin of Thar!" he said. "What you needs is a hug to cheer you."

He moved nearer with his strong, thick arms ready to hold her. Erin's fingers caressed the hilt of her *mai*, warding him off. Teebi backed away, looking embarrassed to have offered comfort, and sad to be mistrusted.

"Meant nothing by it, gal," he said. "If you didn't look like such an orphan . . ." He limped around exaggeratedly, as though to win some sympathy in turn. "My leg's aching," he said, slapping at his thigh. "Might should get back, hey? The tributary flows through these ruins, right over in that area." His finger pointed over Erin's shoulder. "We'll make a hasty raft from the big reeds like you suggested and be back to the boat in no time at all."

"I hear something," said Erin, turning her head to one side.

"You hear me yammering to go," said Teebi, somewhat frustrated by everything.

Erin started off in a direction away from the stream Teebi had indicated. He threw up his hands in exasperation and followed after her, forgetting to limp.

They followed the repulsive sound to its source: a gaping passage between and under a pile of wreckage.

"Bugs," said Teebi, standing beside Erin and looking into pitch blackness. "Sounds like an oyster farm down there. We'd best go, hey?"

Erin glowered into the entrance, hatred in her eyes. Her lips were held in a firm line. The moist clicking of joints and mandibles was the only thing she could hear.

"We're safer away from here, gal. Come this way."

Her breathing grew heavy, and she spoke with a voice harsh and cruel as the first hour of her and Teebi's meeting. "What are you shaking for, fishmonger? There's a slender moon rising. They won't come out."

"There's stories says they used to," said Teebi. "I ain't never heard about it happening in my life, but people oughtn't take chances with them critters. Here we stand thinking they don't like moonlight, but they just might come running out and tear us to pieces. The best place for us is far from here."

A sword slid from its sheath.

Teebi jumped with fright and said, "What you got in mind, gal? Tell me, hey?"

She took a step forward onto the dark ramp leading down. Teebi rushed forward and grabbed her sword arm. Erin wouldn't look him in the face; she kept glowering into the insects' hole. Her breathing was short and ragged. Her eyes were strange. She took another step, dragging Teebi. He put a little weight into drawing her back, trying not to seem too forceful.

"Another step, gal, and I'll punch your head," said Teebi.

Heedless of his threat, she stepped again. Teebi reared back with his knuckles and swung with every intention of knocking her silly. She blocked his swing without a thought about it; and before her mind caught up with her actions, she'd struck with the hilt of her sword and laid a man twice her weight flat on his back.

Teebi's head lay between two pieces of shattered steel. If he'd landed further left or right, spikes of metal would have taken him through the brain. He couldn't cuss or complain, and could barely breathe, for Erin's blow had been full in the throat.

The woman was at his side immediately. She knew she hadn't done any real damage; but once again, it was more due to Teebi's luck than Erin's fine grace. "Forgive me, Teebi," she said softly, the madness passed from her for the moment. Teebi looked at her with as much severity and indignation as he could muster. He took her hand and stood up, but couldn't talk yet. Erin looked at the blunt end of her sword's hilt, counting the single fortune that her rash reflexes had not responded with the blade. She said again, "Sorry, Teebi."

Teebi Dan Wellsmith reached up behind his back.

He brought forth his hook.

Erin backed away.

"Teebi?"

He was pointing with his weapon. He pointed over Erin's shoulder, into the darkness of the entryway.

Something was coming out.

\*     \*     \*

Three faces appeared in the tunnel, and then the shoulders. There was small chance of running for cover. Erin's *mai* was in one hand; the *i* was in the other. She crouched and, with Teebi, backed away.

They weren't a trio of insects coming into the light of star and moon. They were human warriors. Teebi whispered,

"By their dress, they're from Terwold. Why humans have commerce with bugs, I can't say. But I'm relieved to see it's men coming out of that hole, hey, or we'd be killed already."

"They're two-bladed warriors like me," said Erin. "If we work hard, we can kill them."

"No sense in that, gal," said Teebi, lowering his wicked barb. He started toward the three warriors with a friendly wave and a grin. "Ho, men of Terwold! A coincidence to meet other sight-seers in this forsaken heap of junk!"

"Spies!" spat one of the three.

"Kill them," growled another.

Two of them set upon Teebi at once, for he was nearer. The third rushed Erin, side-stepping the litter on the ground. Erin blocked the fellow's *mai* with her own, stopping his onslaught, then carved upward with her *i*, gutting him. Warm blood gushed over her fingers and hand. Erin felt, instead of revulsion, a curious thrill. She pushed the dying man away and ran to aid Teebi. He held one of his attacker's swords at the end of the barb, but was left with no way to guard against the second swordsman. Erin was upon the scene with her own two swords, jamming both into the surprised warrior's sides from behind. She stepped back and the man fell.

Teebi managed to push his remaining attacker away. The man stumbled over the rubble in the dark, fell, impaled himself on one of the very spikes Teebi had previously fallen between. The man writhed on the ground, but spartan fellow that he was, did not cry out as he died.

It was quickly done. Erin's *i* and left hand were drenched in blood. Her *mai* was slightly less reddened. She stared at the blood, almost black in the dim light of moon and star.

"I swore to Valk the Ear I'd be a man of peace," said Teebi, obviously disappointed in himself as he looked at the three corpses. "At least this impaled blighter died from his own clumsiness and not by barb . . . but that's poor rationalization in my behalf." He said nothing about the two Erin killed. She knelt beside one of the corpses, cleaning her hand and her weapons on his garments. The exhilaration was still upon her, though beginning to fade back into depression. She felt no remorse and no delayed fright. Killing was an easy thing.

"You had no choice," said Erin, trying to soothe Teebi of his sense of guilt. She sheathed her weapons. "They attacked us."

"A waste," said Teebi, unplaced. "A stronger man than me would have avoided the bloodshed—somehow."

"Or a stronger woman?" said Erin.

"Aye, or that. You kill without much effort, Erin my friend. Without much care. It cures you of gloom, too, I see; but how long will that last you? If you ever desire an undertaking somewhat more difficult than cutting up a foe, try another way. That's what the Prophet said on the day he healed my gimp. I've let him down."

"Don't tell him about it," Erin said sarcastically. "These men deserved to die. The only conceivable reason for not killing them would have been to find out why they go underground to visit the insect people."

"That's a curiosity for certain," said Teebi Dan Wellsmith.

"I'm an outsider, Teebi; maybe I've a more objective eye. And maybe not. But it seems to me that the peasants along the river—and elsewhere, I presume—are less a threat to the dominating warrior caste, so long as the insect race is the more immediate concern of farmers, fishers, and the like. What's the chance of a peasant rebellion under the present state of things?"

"Not much, I reckon," Teebi admitted, his slow

brain going as fast as it could with Erin's idea. "You suggest the warriors have something to do with the insects taking sacrifices from peasants each month? The thing wrong with your theory is that, in Terwold, even the warriors have to make their new-moon sacrifices, or risk annihilation of the capital city."

"Do they sacrifice warriors?" Erin asked pointedly. Teebi didn't need to respond. The sacrifices would be so-called "criminals." Activists, no doubt—or anyone who threatened the status quo.

"It's a fantastic notion, gal, and Teebi Dan Wellsmith don't like courtin' it. I ain't never heard tell of no human being talking to an insect, and don't care to hear about it happening. Them bugs got no way of thinking! They just kill and eat. It's all they understand."

"That may be the common belief," said Erin, looking toward the hole leading underneath the ruins. "But even assuming the drones are practically mindless, their queen is not. She already communicated with me once, however minimally. I think it's obvious from these three warriors we were forced to kill that the tyrant Shom Bru in Terwold has commerce with the insect race, if only through emissaries. The exact nature of this commerce, I can't guess."

Teebi seemed to digest these ideas reluctantly but completely. He sighed heavily and said, "If there's an answer—it's to be found in Terwold, hey?"

*     *     *

The river Yole passed beneath a high arched bridge into the heart of stone-walled Terwold. Archers stood atop the bridge, but Teebi's boat was given easy passage, for the fishmonger was a familiar face. His ward looked like nothing more than a peasant in his employment. Erin had hidden her *mai* among Teebi's baggage; her *i* was secreted in the folds of her long raiment. Since her girdle was that of a fisher, she was scarcely worth noticing in the eyes of city guards and warriors.

Teebi moored his boat along a canal near the market square. Along the canal's moorage were groups of children which Erin at first took to be street urchins, but they were too neatly dressed. Their thin girdles were all the same, implying some shared industry. The green cloth's design resembled small, docked boats, one lined up after the next. Erin said to her companion, "They're clad well for children on the street."

"They earn their wages here," Teebi explained. "A few jobs in Terwold are dominated by children, including that of guarding boats. It ain't safe to leave one's goods unattended, so for a small coin we can hire some brat to sit on the prow. They're honest brats, too; their profession depends on it. Their own Guild would punish them by severing an arm or two if they broke the regulations. Those with parents send a bit of their earnings home; some of them were sent to Terwold from the countryside to help their families. The ones who are orphaned have only the Guild to call their family. It ain't a bad life either, hey; I'll vouch for that."

Erin mused, "A children's Guild . . ."

"Aye. Belonged to it myself, long ago. Many a sailor started out along this moorage; and many a buccaneer has but one hand because he went against the Guild and was caught. Get a certain age, though, and the Guild forces a change of occupation, one way or another. The sea is the obvious choice for most."

"Doesn't seem like a child would be much protection for, say, a boatload of salted fish."

Teebi eyed his stock and did not look worried.

He said, "Ain't often one of them spunks gets robbed or killed, hey. The whole Guild membership can turn assassin at a moment's notice, if one of their own is so much as scratched."

"I see," Erin said, although she didn't. It was hard to imagine the tough, polite, and surprisingly clean young boys and girls doing anything in the way of murder. It was hard enough to imagine them doing the job she saw with her own eyes; and she suspected there was more to them, and their Guild, than showed. She recollected with a dream-like unclarity what childhood had meant on Earth: a culturally imposed and enforced kind of immaturity, separated from adulthood by awkward adolescence. Perhaps she should be less amazed that, given a different kind of society, children would gain another sort of socialization, possibly with business or survival sense, and unity.

Teebi Dan Wellsmith hired one of the passing spunks to guard his boat before leading Erin away from the moorage. "I've connections to make for the sale of fish," he said. "And, as promised, I'll be buying temple services for your ma and pa and the folk massacred at Thar. There's an inn down Cray Street here, if you want to rest and wait. Or you can tag along if you want, but it'll be dull stuff you'd overhear."

"The inn," Erin said, sensing that Teebi didn't want to babysit her during business, and as certain that she herself wanted to be alone.

"Fine. I'll meet you there later." He pressed a few coins into her hand, then took another street toward the market square. Erin watched Teebi's broad back as he walked away. Fingering the few coins, she whispered to herself, "Sorry, Teebi; but you won't find me waiting like an obedient daughter. Your mood's too cheerful and mine's too glum. I don't think we're good company for each other." She turned a direction away from both

Teebi and the inn he'd suggested. She could pretend neither amenities nor friendship. She needed to lose herself, alone, in this strange, big city. To lose her fear, her shame, her confusion. The option of being dependent on Teebi struck her as repulsive. She would have to make it on her own on Endsworld, even if it meant failure.

At first she circled back toward Teebi's boat, saw the young spunk standing near the prow like a proud imp. The boy would of course let her get her longer sword; but what would she do with it then? Weapons would draw attention to herself. Better to rely on the shortsword hidden in her clothing. Teebi could be trusted with the other blade for a while. She knew enough about his fishmongering circuit to make good guesses as to when he would be through Terwold next, and when she might reclaim the weapon.

A strange sort of plan for survival unfolded in Erin's mind. The streets she walked were littered with the outcasts of society: cripples with grimy hands cast forth, or cups; old women and old men with no place to live but the damp alleys and stairwells; drunkards; drug users clinging year upon year to the very brink of death; purveyors of the weird plants and chemicals that left those people clinging; procurers of odd, personal events . . . She saw these various loose cogs of society, and was drawn to them like a chameleon into foliage. Perhaps she had thought herself capable of being a hero in this world, but really, what could an outsider be but a misfit? Here she would be safer than in places such as hostels or honest employment, where her alienness would be constantly scrutinized. Here, her ignorance of things might go ignored as the simple, harmless behavior of a lunatic. She'd had practice on Earth playing crazy —presuming it *had* been mere play—and there

seemed only one safe disguise for her now: a wit-
less beggar.

If a crazy street-woman seemed easy prey to
men of certain persuasions, her secreted shortsword and her skillful foot and fist could correct
their first impressions. Indeed, sick as it seemed,
sick as it may have been, there was a kind of half-
eagerness to find herself in peril, to exercise her
ability to slay. The figurative taste of blood had
been intriguing. She knew that she had only
glanced the surface of her murderous capacity.

*I shouldn't think like this*, she knew; but the village Thar in Delmo Prefecture loomed in her consciousness—and her consciousness, like Thar,
crawled with gigantic insects she alone unleashed.
She fancied herself the greatest of villains. The
tragedy which she had accidentally instigated
was, in her mind, dreamlike; so much of Endsworld was dreamlike; and Earth was dreamlike,
too. As always, she was not certain of her own
existence. Endsworld, she had hoped, would cure
that old feeling, but it did not. She could not even
remember her foster mother and father with any
depth of reality; she had never really gotten close
to them, or, if she had, the memory had faded,
being after all a dream. Yet some *feeling* of them,
of Thar, remained. It was a feeling of evil that was
internal, not outside. She could not recall the individual folk of Thar because of her introspectively
selfish perspective. Nothing was quite as important as herself, not that she was important either.

She felt the need and inclination to lash out and
slay the ghosts around her, if they threatened her
the least. Soon, she hoped, even the endearing
visage of Teebi Dan Wellsmith would fade from
her memory, and there would be nothing tangibly
*good* about Endsworld to recall. Teebi had been
more vibrant, more alive, more real than anyone

else she had met . . . she did not know why. Perhaps it was because he had reached out to her in no way frightening. Perhaps—and she could barely stand to consider this—perhaps with each week and month in this new world, the people and events became more real, and there would be more people as sharply seen as Teebi, if she were not careful, not insulated. As Earth receded into her subconscious, Endsworld might well surface more completely. This she must repress. Endsworld must remain a shadow, too. Nothing must touch her. Nothing must hurt.

Erin thought: *I am afraid to know that I exist.*

She withdrew into the shadow of a niche along the walls of the city streets. Her hand went to a fold in her garment, where steel was warmed against her flesh. In all those years she had kept the diary, in all the writings about a place she'd thought a mere illusion, she had never suspected, or recorded, that among the many monsters of this world, Erin of Thar could be found.

IV · BEGGAR

# IV. BEGGAR

The filthy beggar climbed the crooked stairway, up the side of a tenement building. She stopped a moment, looked out across City Terwold, unused to it from any height. Even these foul, leaning apartments were beyond her means; she usually slept in the streets. From her view at the third flight, it seemed the city was nothing but homely tenements throughout; but she knew there were other kinds of views elsewhere within great, walled Terwold. She turned her face from the vision of decrepitude and climbed the next flight of stairs, and the next.

Near the top, she slapped a door with an open hand. A peep-door slid sideways and two red eyes in a black face looked out. "You want?"

"Yes," said the filthy beggar.

"What you want?"

"A place! A place!" She was agitated.

"Full up. All day all night full up. You wait somewhere other."

"All the places say that; but you'll make room for me, you black devil."

"Not black as you. You black with dirty."

A smallish hand darted through the open peep-door and snatched the man by the throat. The fingers were strong and clenched deep. The man gagged. The beggar said, "I'll let go when the lock comes undone. I won't be left out here for those damned Bugs to eat!"

It was the third new moon since Erin came to Endsworld; she knew well enough what the darkest nights would bring. It was the second new moon since coming to Terwold and the beginning of her street-life, surviving from trash-heap to trash-heap. She was already somewhat street-wise, but there were things yet to learn.

She knew the places beggars went on the nights the Bugs marched. On these nights, "criminals" were staked outside the city walls as sacrifices to the insect people . . . usually there weren't quite enough bodies to fill the stakes, and so any vagrant was fair game for warriors to capture as night approached.

There were various groups of beggars, cliques within outcasts. Each group provided itself with a measure of protection against the sacrificial nights. And there were low businessmen who managed to profit from the plight of these groups, renting even narrow hallways or rat-infested lofts and cellars to the street-people who would cram themselves into small spaces by the dozen-score to wait out the monthly night of horror. On these periodic, gruesome nights, the population of vagrants vanished from the streets . . . all but the ones who were too sick to find their places, or who had failed to raise their portion of the cooperatively shared one-night's rental. These would be left in the streets and to their own devices, which might be few and useless when the Warriors marched in prelude to the Insects' march.

There were others who failed to find their places, too. There were those overcome with ennui, who had given up hope, and these might buy some drug or wine and sit glaze-eyed in the alleys awaiting some warrior's vice-grip on the shoulder, dragging the uncomplaining beggar to

the stakes outside the walls of Terwold. Others
were not as willfully suicidal, but were emotionally crippled, or addicted to the same drugs and
wines; their minds had lost the ability to track the
time, to know when they should find a place away
from doom. These would go screaming. Still
others were elderly and forgetful and lost their
way to those waiting-places; or they walked so
slowly through the streets that night fell before
they reached their destinations.

There was a final group of individuals who were
often left in the streets, fair game for the stalking
warriors to feed the Bugs. This latter group were
the rogues, the loners—anyone who belonged to
none of the sub-groups of beggars: did not fit with
winos, did not fit with the collectors of broken
things, did not fit with the blind, did not fit with
the drooling mad, did not fit with any of those who
banned together in grotesque, unnamed societies
like huddled mice against some monstrous cat.
Erin was one of these, an outcast among outcasts;
and here upon her second new moon in Terwold, it
was hard to find a waiting-place, for all the places
were taken by established groups.

The man at the door tried to pry the woman's
fingers from his neck. When this seemed difficult,
he frantically unworked a multitude of locks
while his face went from its natural black to the
purplish color of ripe plums. In a moment more,
he had pulled the door inward.

Inside, Erin was witness to wall-to-wall flesh,
stinking flesh but no worse than her own, sitting
or leaning on one another, bleary-eyed, waiting
without thought, waiting for the night to be done
so that they could return to their territories in the
city streets. There was hardly room to squeeze one
more body in. The man at the door rubbed his
throat, let Erin take two steps inside. He was surprisingly unperturbed, but put a light hand on her

shoulder and asked, "You got penny? Got pay penny."

"Up yours," she growled and tried to push further into the crowded room. The dark man raised his voice and said,

"She got no penny."

In response, a big, fat warrior detached from the shadows and picked across the body-littered floor. People moved their toes and fingers out of this one's way.

It was a common enough sight: a two-sword fallen from station, taking odd jobs like this one, earning money enough for the next flask of burning liquid, or enough for some drug to last until the next new moon and the next appalling duty. Such as this were called renegade. They had lost their privileges and rank, were considered by others of their class to be no better than any other element of street-trash. To the street-people themselves, however, even a renegade commanded some degree of respect, so that a warrior far from grace might still be granted a sort of dignity among the lowliest and least dignified.

Though such renegades were no uncommon sight, Erin was yet surprised by this one, for it was a woman. In addition to her *i* and *mai*, she kept a looped rope at her thigh, and the rope's end sported a pointed steel barb.

Despite her obesity, the woman held her sword exact, drawn forth to threaten Erin.

Erin smiled.

The fat renegade paused, seeing that smile. She took it, perhaps, as evidence of another warrior ruined in some way.

Erin's *i* was close to her flesh, hidden in folds of her robe; but she did not reach for it. Instead, she said, "I will find quarters elsewhere for this bloody night," and she turned to leave. Before the black man could close the door on her, she turned and looked at the fat warrior once more and said, "Tell me your name."

The warrior barked, "Dee the Rope. You?"

"Erin of Thar."

The name of Thar drew a gasp from the crowd, quickly stifled, but no surprise registered in the eyes of Dee the Rope. Although few spoke of Thar or any of the other towns to vanish over the decades, it was intrinsically known what happened to places like Thar. And it was known that survivors never existed. The black man pushed the door closed, and Erin descended the long stairway to the street.

*     *     *

The chameleon may take on the color of the tree, but is not the tree; however, the Earthling played the role so well that, in a little time, she had become one with Endsworld and was not a chameleon after all, but a tree. Would that she had melded into a higher level of that world's society! She haunted the streets like any of the other cast-offs of Terwold. She knew the routes: where garbage was thrown, where it was safe to sleep most nights, where hand-outs were likely, and where beggars were not welcome. She was dirty. She was the color of the walls of Terwold, the grey walls of the slum districts. Among the many communities of beggars, each presumed that the strange one belonged to some other group than theirs, or else they understood that she was a rogue among them, more clever than they and more alone. They did not sense that she was in some way unlike them, for they were unlike each other; and by some queer measure, she had become more like them than they were like themselves.

It was already twilight when Erin was turned

away from that beggars' waiting-place. She had lied about finding somewhere else; the flea-bin atop the stairs had been her last bet. She was gripped with a perversity of carelessness, however, and made no effort to hide among the shadows of the descending night. She heard the tramping soldiers, but could not tell from what direction, for the sound of their feet echoed off every wall. Erin of Thar strode around one corner and around a next, expecting any moment to come face-to-face with twenty soldiers.

They'd be gleaning the streets for the city's excess baggage. Some of the sacrifices would go silently, drugged or drunken; some would go screaming, some with only a moan. A few might even have earned their fate, but that would be the rarity. They would all be taken alive, for the Bugs took only fresh meat.

The situation was surprisingly unhorrific to Erin, for she had come to take all such things for granted. When first she was deposited on the beach of a luminescent sea, the strangeness had made everything seem sharper and more real than anything she had experienced on Earth. But somehow Earth had receded from her consciousness; there was nothing for contrast, Endsworld was all that had ever been. She had grown so used to the new world that it was no more phenomenal to her than had been Earth, when Earth was all she knew. Even the massacre at Thar was a dim nightmare from which her memory cringed. In these ways she was like someone prematurely senile; she was a forgetful woman. And the old question of reality plagued her as it had done before coming to this world and becoming part of it. Once, to answer that question, she got down on her knees before the sludgy stream which ran through the slum district, but the waters had been so polluted they cast back no reflection at all. She had never searched for herself like that again.

As she walked the slum districts beneath impending night, her mind walked darker alleys, finding nothing of her past. She scarcely recalled a time when she had been anything but a vagrant in the streets of Terwold. This had been her only life. If a man attacked her in the streets with murderous intent, she had been known to fight, to use skills she did not remember learning; afterward, she would forget the encounter, and not wonder about her past.

What began as a game of survival, then, quickly swallowed her whole. She was the madwoman after all, but she was also the survivor. Nothing could kill her. Nothing could harm her body. More than that, nothing could harm her intellect or her emotion, for these things were hidden away, secure, inaccessible to attack.

Few of these notions impinged upon Erin's consciousness; it was, of late, unlike her to reflect. She would regain her memories and her ability to meditate when she was ready, and not before. Yet there was a manifestation of these notions in Erin's behavior: she sensed her invulnerability, especially tonight, and it made her reckless.

She wandered to a place near the gate of the city. There, she saw about eight soldiers standing guard. She withdrew into a shadow and watched them momentarily, but the soldiers did not really interest her. She moved along dark alleys and found a wrought-iron ladder set into the wall of a building, bottom rung above her head. It was supposed to be out of reach, for it was intended only as a fire-escape; but Erin leapt upward and grabbed it. She climbed high enough to peer over the walls of the city.

Men and women were staked against the bloody sunset in an even row, one after the next, upon the path used by the insect folk—for like common ants are wont to do, the Bugs followed set routes.

They were staked far enough from the wall that Erin could not make out many faces really, but she could distinguish between recently acquired beggars (who were either limp, or struggling feebly) and the so-called criminals who stood stoutly with useless pride. Some of these latter were mere youths, militants no doubt, caught in some infraction against Shom Bru's regime, arrested on any pretense and dungeoned until this night of sacrifice. Unlike the beggars, not a single one of them cried for mercy, for they knew the regime too well.

"Come down from there!" an unexpected voice demanded. Erin looked below and saw where a small group of warriors were standing. She started to climb the rest of the way upward instead, then saw some other warrior looking down at her from the top of the building. *Trapped.* There was no avoiding it, so she descended to the bottom rung, then dropped to the pave amidst the men. Her teeth were white in that dirty face, as she smiled.

They surrounded her. "With us!" one of them growled. None of them had drawn their swords. The one on the roof had just come down. They were all two-swords, for three-swords considered this sort of nightwork beneath their dignity.

The crazy beggar kept smiling. She squatted down as though to rest, and the same growling voice commanded,

"Stand up!"

She did not stand up. She held out her hand, showing them a dirty palm, and said, "Alms?" One of the group of warriors was young and handsome. Judging by the gentleness of his voice, he did not much care for his task. He said,

"She's mad. She'll be no trouble."

They took her by the shoulders and arms and

half-dragged her away. Erin had by now ceased to
smile and was calculating. The city gate was only a
short ways ahead. The eight guards she had seen
earlier were out of sight but in ears' range. She
could fight now, but the eight additional warriors
would come running to the sound. She could fight
when they were outside the walls, but the gate-
guards would still hear, and come out.

Another group of soldiers appeared from some
other alley, lugging victims along. The group
which captured Erin held back to let the larger
group pass. One of the wretches was being dragged face-down by his feet, dazed possibly by some
drug or fiery blend. He stirred and must have
realized his plight, for he began to kick and complain. One of the warriors' swords licked out, reflected in the torchlight, slipped back into its scabbard. The kicking fellow ceased his struggle, but
was not dead. The muscles at the back of each leg
were sliced. He went howling the rest of the way
to the stake, upon which he'd be tied with legs
dangling limp.

Before reaching the gate, Erin twisted slightly
in the grip of the two men pulling her on. Her
elbows went left and right; the men went "oof"
and she was free of them. They buckled over and
her elbows went again, cracking them on the tops
of their heads.

The rest of the men were around her. She heard
at least six distinct *sshhk* sounds as swords came
from scabbards. They had all drawn shortswords,
the *i*. Nothing longer would be needed, they undoubtedly believed.

They were surprised to see the beggar had an *i*
also. She had kept it hidden in her robe, and they'd
never thought to check for such a weapon. She
held the scabbard in her left hand, the blade in her
right. She crouched.

Two of the six warriors drew their *mai*, perceiving, perhaps, the sureness of Erin's handling of her weapon. The other four still did not believe they were in danger. The gate-guards—eight sturdy men—were in eyes' sight, but did not move to help, for it looked unnecessary, there already being six warriors against one beggar-woman.

Not more than three warriors could really close an attack at any given moment without risking a cut to a comrade, so three held back and three came forward. One of the two she had knocked in the belly and head was still conscious, but clutched belly and head, unable to see or join the battle.

None of them seemed particularly worried. They were methodical in their approach, certain they could disarm her at minimal expense of energy. They would not kill her if it could be helped, for they were to stake out live meat for the insects. But they would have no qualms about seriously crippling her, and they might even kill her if need be, for the insects would still dismember and haul her parts away if she were so freshly slain that there was no smell of rot about her and her death-throes mimicked life.

If they thought in this manner, it was soon altered thinking. Fresh meat fell, but it was not the woman. The stricken warrior clutched his slit side, groaned once, and no more. Two more attacked at once—two men and three swords, for one of them used *mai* and *i* simultaneously. The beggar woman jumped away from them, practically into the embrace of a startled fourth. He began to slash at her with his *i*, but suddenly his fingers were removed. The woman's *i* had clipped the fingers off, leaving only the thumb, and he dropped his weapon as a result. She turned to block with the scabbard and slash with the *i*, killing the attacker she'd evaded a moment before. By now the warriors were backing away to regroup and rethink the situation.

"A monster!" one of them cried, for no begger should fight like this.

"No," another man's voice corrected. "She is warrior-blood: a renegade."

They had backed away from her but kept her penned in. The young warrior who had spoken earlier with a gentle voice stepped closer. He had both swords in his hands, but did not attack. He said,

"You are of warrior caste; it cannot be explained any other way. What country is yours? Maybe we will let you go."

"Country?" The smile returned to Erin's face, shining in the dark. She replied, "Durga's Lathe."

The men around her groaned, insulted, for Wevan was the proper name and Durga's Lathe was the name used by rebels, peasants, heretics, and suicidal fools.

"By your girdle, you're a fisher," said the young warrior, less perturbed than the rest. "You're from Delmo Prefecture, I will hazard. How did you learn to fight?"

She didn't seem to know the answer herself. The question made her look confused.

"What's your name?" asked the young warrior, circling to one side of her.

"What's yours?" she countered. A peasant, let alone a beggar, never asked for a warrior's name. The men grumbled again, but the youthful warrior was still not ruffled.

"I will tell you," he said. The other warriors looked at him, startled; not only did peasants not ask warriors' names, but warriors did not offer them. "My name is Cassilow the Boar's Son. Now you tell me yours."

"Erin." She watched the young warrior's footwork. He was in a good position to attack if he chose to. "Erin of Thar."

"Don't lie!" the warrior shouted, and looked

angry now. "You are someone I have seen before! Tell these other men your real name!"

She looked at the others. They all held swords ready, but were a safe distance away. The young warrior's insistence that she tell the others her name confused Erin all the more. Still, she obeyed, shouting to the ones on her right, "Erin of Thar!" She looked to the ones on her left and said it again, "Erin of Thar!"

"Liar!"

Cassilow was insistent on this. Erin's name was not Erin, he seemed convinced of that. Erin was quite as convinced it *was* her name, although, she would have to admit, she could not recall all of her life very clearly. She could not remember where she was born.

Warriors surrounded Cassilow, too, as though he were as crazy as the woman. They did not understand what he was doing anymore than Erin understood it, and they clearly did not trust his judgement or his actions. Already they could hear the clicking sound of the marching insects, and the rest of the sacrifices had to be staked out at once, and the city gate sealed.

"We dare not dawdle, Cassilow," a rough voice said. "Kill her at once and have done."

"Stay back from me!" Cassilow threatened, sweeping through the air around him with his *mai* but not taking his eyes from Erin. He said, "Shom Bru must know of this woman! Look at that scar on her forehead! I swear by Durga Herself that it was Shom Bru and none other put that mark on her! I saw him strike this very woman dead, but she lives, somehow, though crazed by the blow as you see her."

Now Erin was confused more greatly than ever. She did remember something of the sort Cassilow described, but could not draw it completely into the context he would have for it. The other warriors were now gazing at her intently, trying to see the face beneath the grime. Their response to what they saw, or thought they saw, was evident on their faces: superstitious terror.

"Tell them your name!" said the young warrior, and if he had looked handsome and concerned before, he looked like that no more. He was angry. He was loud.

Erin's eyes narrowed and she set her teeth together tightly. Now she answered testily. "Erin of Thar."

The young warrior attacked her, and he screamed once more, "Liar! You are Merilia of the Black Mountain, slayer of Cal Bru!" When the distance was closed between him and Erin, she dropped to one knee, evaded his *mai*, smote his other arm with her empty sheath thereby stopping his *i* from cutting. With her own *i*, she carved into his stomach. He dropped the shortsword, stepped back, held his intestines and looked at the other men, "You see? It's true! Merilia lives! The cause of the people lives, too!" Then Cassilow the Boar's Son looked at Erin again, his eyes full of tears, and she realized his sentiments were not with his own caste; he was a secret rebel, perhaps a spy. He exulted, *"Praise Durga's Tits!"* Then he began to cut a large swath through the ranks of the men he was with, throwing them into panic. The gate-guards, having seen all of this and heard most of it besides, were coming to fight the traitor.

"Run!" Cassilow shouted to Erin. He held his guts in with one hand, and fought with the *mai* in the other. "Run! You've killed me already; now I will kill some of these for you!"

*     *     *

The bold Cassilow died slowly, and even when his entrails slipped through his grasp, he was still fighting, keeping the warriors from going after the woman he had mistaken for someone else. Erin fled swiftly. She had almost forgotten who she was in the last weeks, but she did not believe she was this Merilia. She was Erin, the Fisher's Daughter.

But all this confused her to greater madness. There'd been a dream, only a dream, of killing a tyrant, no, of killing an innocent boy in a game, no, of killing a tyrant, no . . . it had been a dream she'd had many times, and no two times the same. It hadn't really happened.

She found a dark staircase leading up the outside of a building. It led to the roof and a leaning, deserted tower. Her back against the tower, she could see over the walls of Terwold. She could see beyond the city to the place where insects grotesquely dismembered living and half-living victims and carried off the parts to their storehouse of flesh. The sight of it reminded Erin of before, of the time in Thar, but it only made her more determined to not remember it again.

The warriors had sealed the gate. Those among them slain by Cassilow, or dying, were preserved against the insect folk, saved for rites and burial. But Cassilow's body was carried up to the top of the wall and thrown off. A trio of insects detached from the main line, came in unison to dismember Cassilow in his death-throes.

Erin could not bear to watch. She hurried along the roof, away from the horrible vision at the wall and beyond. She leapt across a narrow alley to another roof. She climbed a tiled slant, slid down the other side, dug heels into a gutter and leapt again. She went over the top of the city until she was too tired to go further, until she realized she had come to a rich area where beggars never came. On this night, however, even this place was shuttered against the horror; and people amused

themselves quietly, pretending they had no reason
for staying indoors this night, pretending there
was nothing terrifying outside Terwold's walls.
But they did not go out.

The dirty beggar sat on the edge of a rich
family's house, swinging her feet and kicking the
shingles. No one came out to see who was doing it,
to find out what it was. She imagined it frightened
them, though. She hadn't yet captured her breath.
She was trying to remember why she had run so
far. Her *i* was in her right hand still, the sheath in
her left. She cleaned the blood from the blade,
wondering where it came from. When the weapon
was sheathed, she hid it in the folds of her
garment again, hid it from her own memory, forgetting she had drawn it out. Childlike, she looked
into the sky, and whispered, "Where's the moon?
Where's the moon, Orline? Where's the moon,
Rud? Where's the moon?"

\*       \*       \*

The moon was invisible, unless one looked for
certain stars and found them missing, gone behind
a black pit in the sky. Shom Bru glared from his
tower window, a window from which an iron grate
had been removed and set aside. The room behind
the man was dark—no torch, lamp, or fireplace
giving light. It was cold in the room. Only the
bright stars lit his visage, silvering his front,
making    him    almost    handsome . . . which
ordinarily he was not. He was, however, imposing.
Heavyset from childhood, whenever he grew sloth
—which was rarely—his muscular girth quickly
went to fat. He was only a little taller than the
average man, but those meaty, thick bones made
him seem bigger.

He wore a slender girdle around his waist, holding the long robe loosely closed. The robe's sleeves

billowed. The standard wear of Wevan was the same for both sexes and for all classes, but only warriors of the highest echelons wore the glistening, silken red such as Shom Bru presently sported. There was a single, small mark on the girdle: a crown printed on the back. It was the one concession to the old reign, now three generations overthrown: the symbol of kingship. A warrior, unlike the slaughtered and extinct aristocratic rulers, would not wear a literal crown, only the subtle likeness of it printed black upon the sash.

He raised a foot to the sill of the window, revealing the thick, muscled thigh.

There was movement across the roofs outside; something leapt, slid, leapt again. Shom Bru gasped, imagining there was something familiar in the way the ghost had moved. It vanished as quickly as it appeared, and Shom Bru chided himself for his momentary sense of danger. It had probably been nothing more than a cat-burglar taking advantage of this moonless night, a night when sounds were rarely inspected by the inhabitants of the houses. Still, that burglar's gait and grace had reminded him of a certain war-woman he had killed for killing his father . . . although truth be told, his had not been purely a mission of vengeance. Merilia had been a key leader of rebels —but it had been politically advantageous to present the duel as a matter of revenge.

As heir, and as an abused child grown to bitter manhood, Shom Bru was glad enough to see his cruel father slain, might eventually have arranged it himself. There could be no hint of glee in his response to his father's defeat, however, for the change of command in Wevan was a touchy enough affair at best; it was a weak moment for the government, and the small groups of rebels ceased bickering among themselves long enough to stage a desperate lunge against the Bru

Dynasty. Merilia was at the forefront of that attempt; and it was omened by the astrologers and prophets that she would rule the day. Shom Bru's own soothsayer had said that she must be slain with steel and burned to ash, or she would rise a corpse to annul the relatively young dynasty.

It was during that last rebellion that the encounter came to pass, outside the walls of Terwold. The combined strength of the generally splintered groups of militants was not enough to take so old and fortified a capital. The rebels had expected the peasants to rise in arms, but they had not come, and so the professional warriors swarmed out of the city onto the battlefield, clearing the land of unrest as a scythe clears a field of grain. Only one had not died easily—that remarkable woman, fighting earnestly for the gate, killing all who stood between her and Shom Bru, the hated general. No one could stop her, and so he had had to face her himself. Even knowing she had proven strong enough to slay Cal; even knowing the numerous prophecies against himself and in Merilia's favor; even seeing her cut a path through his best soldiers, coming for the hill on which he had directed the battle . . . even wtih all this, Shom Bru had shown no fear. He was prepared.

He knew himself every bit the three-sword his father had been. More than this, his sword-style incorporated as much of the occult as it did of skill. Cal Bru had fancied himself above magic; but Shom had no qualms about the added aid of supernatural craft.

Merilia's defeat had not come without cost, for Shom Bru would carry a scar on his side the rest of his life—a stroke that had nearly reached the spine and rendered him incapable of seeing to the burning of Merilia's corpse. In the confusion, her body had been lost. The soothsayer's advice had gone unused. Shom Bru later had the soothsayer burned instead, but those ashes did not cover the tyrant's unease. Despite his occasional fretting, as on nights like this one, it was unlike him to fancy ghosts out open windows!

It was perhaps understandable that on *this* of all nights, Shom Bru would look haunted, and imagine specters in the night. He stood in the dark tower room, like a ghost himself, brooding and waiting for his special tryst. It was these trysts that haunted him, not Merilia; so it was easier to dwell on old problems and ignore what was current and on-going.

The tower's window was high enough to see beyond the city walls, but faced the opposite direction from the new moon's sacrifices. Multipeaked Black Mountain was itself a glum sight, upon the horizon, outlined underneath the stars. It was there that great heroes had always been trained by Endsworld's one immortal. Merilia had been trained there, as had been the founder of the Bru Dynasty, Saint Jorr. There was rumored to be only one warrior alive trained by the Immortal four-legged man . . . and that one was now old and obsessed with his religion, and blind as well. Effectively, Shom Bru had slain the last true hero of the land; for the legends were honored religiously by the people of Wevan, and tradition said that *only* disciples of the Teacher of Black Mountain could be true heros, though false ones might abound.

It had been a thorn in the side of Cal Bru that he had not been accepted for training on Black Mountain. Shom Bru was less concerned about the cultural prestige of the Immortal's instruction. Yet the presence of such unharnessed power as that was always cause for worry. The Immortal maintained an aloofness from societies and governments—a long dynasty, to a being who had lived millenia, was not much time at all; no atrocity was great enough to make the four-legged hermit come

down from his seclusion and trouble tyrants. Yet
. . . Shom Bru could not help but wonder, from
time to time, what hero would be trained next, and
stride down from that mountain to wreak havoc on
the world. If it ever became conceivable, Shom
Bru intended to snare the power on that mountain, to be sure those aeons of military knowledge
and fighting expertise were handed down to no
one but heirs of the Bru Dynasty. It would take
magic, perhaps; but Shom Bru had shown before
that he was not above such devices.

Again, he had allowed his mind to dwell on problems somewhat remote, in lieu of preparing his
mind for the immediate encounter. He forced his
mind away from thoughts of Merilia's ghost,
hatred for his slain father, controlling the Teacher
of Black Mountain . . . . he forced himself to prepare, instead, for the night which was around him.
He turned from star-gazing and reached for a
cord, pulled it. Directly a servant appeared, the
scrawny man's eyes darting back and forth from
an abruptly opened doorway, trying to adjust to
the dark and see where his Lord stood. A voice in
the darkness said,

"Bring light. Warm the room."

The voice was not deep, but almost musical, although utterly commanding. The servant snatched
a brand from the hallway and entered the room,
lighting oil lamps, then tending the fireplace,
striving for a healthy blaze. Soon the room was
less gloomy. It was a bedroom, and the bed was
huge, soft, unlike the pallets of warriors. It did not
look often used. Even Shom Bru adhered to the
austere habits of his class, regardless of his
wealth and veritable godhood to his nation. The
bed was for rare occasions, obviously; it was
canopied and designed more for lovers' sports
than for sleep.

"The sacrifices have begun?" asked Shom. He

knew the answer, and his tone did not really command a reply. The servant still dashed about tidying the room. Shom Bru said, "There were no troubles."

"One," said the servant quickly. The hairs of Shom Bru's nape prickled.

"One," Shom Bru echoed, not looking at the busy servant.

"You'll have your report from your generals later," said the small fellow. "But I was told to inform you, if I had the chance, that Cassilow the Boar's Son is dead."

Shom Bru sucked in a long breath. Cassilow had been sent on this night's duty as a test; ordinarily, so fine a warrior would not be handed such an occupation. It was for poorer two-swords than him.

"How?" said the warrior-in-red.

"He went berserk to save some woman from the stake. He took several warriors with him into the Shadowed Realm."

The warrior nodded. He had hoped eventually to trust Cassilow, a man destined to be a three-sword and a leader among warriors. But his heart had been tender, and that was a weakness . . . or a strength against Shom Bru's reign, which some perceived as tyrannical. Shom Bru felt some small loss because of this news, but nothing terrible; Cassilow would have been killed eventually anyway, if his loyalty could not be completely won.

"That's all?" asked Shom Bru.

"More . . . I think. Your generals are furtive and will tell you the rest personally, I suspect. It was not for this humble messenger to hear."

This was unsettling. By rights, Shom Bru should repair to the war rooms and see what this trouble was—or is. But there was yet a responsibility waiting for him in this tower room. He would have to wait for other news . . . or, his generals would have to wait for him to receive it.

The walls of the room became clear when the lamps were lit and the hearth fired. Those walls were hung with tapestries unlike those in other rooms of the warrior-dictator's mansion. There were no heroic deeds portrayed on these tapestries, no bloody battles woven from the threads. Rather, there were woodland scenes which on first glance seemed quiet and peaceful. On closer examination it was not so peaceful. Here, by a stream, there was the rape of a maiden; and there, in the shadows of gigantic evergreens, an unspeakable act between a goat and a man was attended by children who were obviously the get of previous encounters like that one. Hidden in various places were the sexual activities of demons and beasts. There were satyr-like beings lurking in other dark areas while, in the lighted areas, unwary children and maids and wives and even grannies were portrayed at innocent work or play, performing trivial deeds such as washing at a river's side, hoeing in a garden, each unaware that sexual danger hovered around them.

The theme of the tapestry was not so simple as this, either, for on yet closer inspection, there were revenges taking place: the skeleton of a satyr lay half-buried in a muddy place, a woman's gilt knife in his rib cage. A haggard, ghoulish woman stalked through the sinister shade behind where leering men and satyrs hid.

Shom Bru did not look at this tapestry, a work of art made by his grandmothers at Saint Jorr's request especially for this room. The servant had seen it often enough, too, yet could not resist uncomfortable sideways glances. When the room was warmed by the roaring blaze and lit from a half-dozen lamps, Shom Bru said simply,

"Go."

The servant went. Shom Bru locked the door behind the little man, then turned to look about the room carefully, as though expecting the ghost still, as if ghosts could appear once fires were lit.

No one or nothing appeared in the half-sinister, half-erotic room. Shom Bru strode to a standing partition and folded it to one side. He gazed at the objects of pleasant torture kept there, but his expression did not change.

There was a fluttering at the window. Shom Bru tensed. He calmed himself immediately, remembering his duty, remembering the pact inherited, with the rule, from his father and grandfather. He turned slowly, facing the monster perched in the window.

It was the sleek, black queen of the insect-folk, gorgeously feminine for all her lack of breasts. She said in her rough voice, "Play . . . play . . . play."

"Yes." Shom Bru reached behind himself, to the store of toys. He grabbed a whip. "Yes, we will play." He moved toward her, as she moved toward the bed. He swung the soft whip meaningfully.

*     *     *

Dee the Rope pushed through the crowd. Folk moved away from her path, for not only was she stalky and brutish and hard to stand in front of, but she stank as well. She must have stunk very much if even the noses of noxious plebians wrinkled at her passing. She carried a bottle in her left hand. It was round-bottomed and had a long neck. Periodically she held it to her lips. Her right hand rested on the hilt of her longsword, as though relaxed upon the arm of a chair. From her left hip there hung the spike-ended rope, coil upon coil.

There was a ballyhoo in the shopping district

which scarcely interested Dee. A new fanatic and miracle-worker was visiting Terwold and had come to this particular district to preach and heal. His voice was not a loud one, and therefore the audience became unusually quiet in order to hear him. Dee sniffed and snorted just to hear people go "shhh" as she went by. The fanatic was hardly the first she'd seen in the city and certainly would not be the last; but, if only transiently, the common folk would dote on him, as they had doted on the ones who preached before.

She was mildly surprised to see a fastidiously dressed warrior here and there, listening intently to some banal rhetoric about peaceful this and that; but she reckoned they were only pretending avid interest, and were sent to be certain the new fanatic's followers represented no danger to Wevan's capital city.

There was shockingly little business in the square that afternoon. Not only was the press of the crowd too great to allow movement from storefront to storefront, those shops were actually closed against patrons, so that the shopkeepers could themselves listen to the white-clad preacher. Now that was something to consider! Warriors might pause to hear a new idea, but greedy merchants sealing up their stalls?

Dee scratched the short hairs at the back of her neck, but refused to consider the puzzle at any length. She had other business in mind. She knew of a particular fellow enamored of that preacher out there in the square; and it was this fellow she was seeking. She held the bottle to her lips again, then scanned the area for that certain face. Although the obese swordswoman was tough and solid and heavier than any two people standing around her, she was by no means taller than average, and so could not scan the crowd easily. She was of a mind to slice a few heads from their

shoulders with the sharp edge of her *mai*, and
chortled when the grotesque notion came into her
mind. Someone went "shhh" when she laughed,
and she gave the tall fellow an evil eye which made
him blanch. She pressed on, people parting like
the grass of a meadow.

There was a familiar curb and she encouraged
others to vacate it so that she could get above the
heads of the crowd. From this vantage-point, the
fanatic was quite an eye-sore halfway across the
shopping square. In between lectures, he was laying on the hands, easing the pain of cripples, offering advice regarding health, prescribing herbs or
whatever. Of true miracles, she saw none, and was
all the more curious how he captivated his crowd.
Dee's old granny could put on a better miracle
show, but preferred the easier prestige of a village
doctor. The possibility that the gathering here in
the square was interested in the preacher's
message, not in a show, was difficult to swallow.

The healing-preacher stood slightly elevated, on
the front of a pedestal meant only for the statue
behind him. It was a gigantic bronze casting of a
warrior: Saint Jorr Bru, founder of the three-
generation old dynasty. Dee believed in neither
gods nor saints, yet she bowed to Durga at
appropriate ceremonies and praised the names of
Her favorite warriors. She thought the fanatic
unwise to stand disrespectfully upon the bronze's
dais, as though a religious man and not a warrior
belonged there.

The current ruler of Wevan was not popular,
but the earlier Bru represented in that mammoth
casting was a bit of a cultural hero. The merchants
respected his memory because he had chosen
Terwold as the new seat of capital, a boon econo-
mically. The peasants liked him because it was
easy to forget a man's crueler moments once he's
dead and once even more wicked men have filled

his shoes. Peasants old enough to remember—and too old to believe without a few grains of salt— told the tale of Jorr Bru battling the insect-folk in their holes beneath the ground. Before that time, the tale went, those insects stalked the face of Endsworld nightly, not merely once a month. Dee was atheist even in the matter of legends; she did not know if Jorr Bru had bound the insect-folk to limited sorties or not. But she did not doubt that Jorr Bru had been mighty in his day, having put an end to a previous dynasty older than legends could say.

The fanatic stood there with the bronze statue, berating the ethics and philosophy of the ruling warriors. It was amazing how the few warriors in the crowd remained relaxed. That preacher was so bold as to reach up with his crooked staff and smite the metal face of Jorr Bru! As well to copu-late in public as to strike the memorial of a venerated saint! It was no wonder people gathered to see it.

The preacher was clean shaven and pale, thin and sickly. His voice carried badly, which sug-gested he'd taken up the wrong vocation in preach-ing—although he *did* manage a crowd all right. Annoyed to realize even *she* was listening to the impuissant fellow, she turned her attention to the crowd instead, spotting the man she sought.

She leapt from the curb and shoved people out of the way, coming up behind the stout, hairy man whose shoulders were bared, his arms pulled out of his robe. He smelled of fish, which wasn't much more pleasant than Dee's odor of cheap liquor. She made a polite salutation to his back, but the man did not look at her; rather, he shushed her, so she punched him in the kidney hard enough to make him wince and look around. "Dee," he breathed. It was Teebi Dan Wellsmith. Dee the Rope said to him,

"Where you been, you cockeyed codpiece?"

A half-dozen faces looked at the two severely, wishing them to be silent. Teebi took Dee's elbow and led her gently toward a shadowed alley where no one else was standing, there being no view of the preacher there. Despite the obvious privacy, Teebi whispered in a furtive way. "You're drinking still? Your tongue gets loose when you drink!"

She handed Teebi the bottle and let him take a pull from it. Then she held it to her own lips once more, wiped her mouth dry with the back of her other hand, and smiled ingratiatingly. She said, "Been looking for you the whole week. You holed up with some gal I don't know about?"

"There's fish to sell on the River Yole, Dee. It's me honest wages now—no longer just a front for my old activities. I've gone straight, gal!"

"Ya, I know; and it's that damned preacher out there done it to you. So you'll let Shom Bru rule unmolested in this city, let him rule all Durga's Lathe, or Wevan if you prefer, now that you're an 'honest' man. You were useful to the conspiracy, Teebi, but now . . ."

"There's your tongue loose again! Walls got ears, hey. I help where I can, you know it well; but I'll not be helping in any killings."

"Well then that's no help at all, my cockeyed fellow; but I keep helping you all the same, don't I? That girl you said to keep my eye out for— girl with the scar here." She ran her thumb down from her hairline in an exaggerated portrait.

Teebi gasped. He pulled Dee further into the high-walled alley. "You found her?"

"Saw her." She shook off Teebi's grip. "She the one you been holed up with?"

"She's just a poor orphan, Dee. She'd break into little pieces the way I make love."

"I was thinking that. You need a solid hunk to screw. So, she's like a daughter, like you said.

Good. I'd feel inclined to beat her up otherwise."

"Where is she? I've been worried sick about the poor sad thing."

"Don't know where she is; but you've been looking in the wrong places, I can tell you that. You better start looking in garbage cans. She's a street wench now."

"I don't believe that, hey!"

"Nay, not a whore, you blamed hairy fool. *Look* at the street wenches sometime. I mean, look at the ones with*out* the paint. There's more ain't whores than is. And pretty damned wretched, I should know, being as how I'm practically a street wench now myself." She raised the bottle to her lips again and Teebi watched closely until she lowered the thing. He said,

"So she's a beggar. Nothing wrong with that." He put his arms into the sleeves of his robe and pulled it back over his shoulders, tucking and folding and straightening the garb without untying the cloth girdle to get it perfect. He asked, "When did you see her and in what part of town?"

"Lowest part you think about, that's the place to look. Seen her early this week, night of the New Moon. She was looking for a night-dive, and nobody'd give it to her free."

Teebi whistled and looked upset. "Not seen her since? You think . . ."

"Nah. She didn't get fed to the bugs. That's one tough gal; you should of told me about that part . . . she can fight."

"I left that part out on purpose. I didn't want you indoctrinating her to your bloody revolution."

"Ain't *my* revolution." She pointed out into the city square, where masses listened to a fanatic whose voice had raised a bit. "It's theirs. I'm just a rouser, a mercenary; just a cog. I've a rope, two swords, and big ears, you'll notice. I hear things. Ain't seen this orphan gal of yours again, but I've listened in on things. She gave some two-swords a good run. Killed a particular fellow who had a good future in Shom Bru's army—he was wavering toward our cause, so it's unfortunate she got him; but it's interesting she could cut him as easily as she did. The men who let her get away were in a stew of trouble when Shom Bru got the story. They had some weird excuse about her being Merilia sprung back to life. I'll tell you, Teebi, I saw Merilia a long time ago, at the Battle of Cadra where the late Cal Bru fell to her sword. She was young, but fierce, and a damned good swordswoman—youngest three-sword I ever seen, and a disciple of Kiron of the Black Mountain, some say. Frankly, I was surprised to learn she'd died in a later battle, Shom Bru avenging his father; I wished I'd been in these parts at the time to take part in that battle. In any case, I admit this Erin of Thar looks a lot like her, but it ain't Merilia, it just ain't. Warriors is superstitious, though, all but me. They're scouring the city for her . . . or, well, I don't think they intend to imprison her—yet—but surely she's being looked for. Shom Bru wants to see what she's up to, if she's up to anything, which you and me know she's not. He's too smart to believe it's Merilia who he killed with his own sword; he took a scar in his side in the doing, and it's not a victory to forget. He won't go for the idea that Erin's someone back from the dead, but he's bound to wonder what this look-alike is doing living in the gutters . . . a look-alike that can fight pretty good. Not as good as Merilia, I'll wager, but good."

There was a ruckus out in the square, but Dee and Teebi could not hear much of it, tucked as they were in the back of a dead-end alley talking private. Teebi said, "It *is* a bit of a coincidence, isn't it? I never knew anything about her looking like Merilia—I was a pirating in the Isles during

her short, fiery career and never saw her, only
heard the tales. Word is that she was defeated by
Shom Bru only by the aid of sorcery, for 'Bad
Shom' ain't no better fighter than his daddy, his
daddy who was defeated by . . . hell. It's the wrong
dead hero to go about looking like, I say, and a
good fine lot of trouble it's going to cause her."

"I say she's good for a certain cause, Teebi, and
that's where you come in."

"Not me, no, hey."

"Listen, man. This look-alike business can come
in handy. If we can get that gal on our side, we can
*use* her. I'm not sure how just yet, but it just
sounds handy."

"Don't ask me to help you use a friend of mine,
Dee the Rope. It'll be a good fine day when Teebi
Dan Wellsmith helps one friend abuse another!"

"You blasted cockeyed idiot!" Dee practically
shouted, but the crowd in the square was a bit
rowdier than it was before, so Teebi didn't feel
compelled to hush her. She continued, "You may
have lost the fighting spirit, listening to that
damnable fanatic, but the girl you're looking to
protect is a fighter-born; I saw it in her eyes, and
she's eager for it, I'm certain. You can't make her
decisions for her. You find her, all right; I've a sus-
picion you're the only one she'll trust right now.
She seems pretty far down. You go find her for her
sake, and you introduce her to me for the sake of
Durga's Lathe. If I don't get her, Shom Bru's spies
are bound to. They may already be marking her
every movement, awaiting an order from Shom
Bru before slitting her throat as she sleeps in
some pile of trash in some alley darker than this
one : . ."

"Listen!" Teebi interrupted. He looked toward
the light outside the shadowed alley. He said,
"That crowd's upset out there."

"Probably decided to lynch that fanatic for berating the Saint."

Worried, Teebi Dan Wellsmith hurried to the mouth of the alley and looked across the square, where Valk the Ear was being dragged from his makeshift podium by a half-dozen soldiers. "Damn," he whispered, and reached up behind himself to get the barbed hook from its place in his girdle. Dee the Rope grabbed him before he could do anything rash. The whole crowd of devotees seemed ready to spring upon the warriors for interfering with their latest guru's speech.

"I don't like this," said Dee.

"Nor I," growled Teebi, looking less like the man of peace he'd been trying to remain.

The fanatic twisted from the grip of the soldiers, but did not try to escape. They let him speak a moment, for his words calmed the crowd, and that was fine with the group who had come to arrest him. He raised his arms to silence the crowd and offered some idiotic sentiments about non-violence and this being their test. The crowd grumbled, but listened, and watched their stupid hero being hauled off to some dungeon or another. Teebi forced himself to stand still, to put the barbed hook behind himself again. He turned to look into the intense eyes of the woman who was shorter than him, but bulkier. He said, "They'll torture him, then feed him to the bugs come the new moon. Dee, will you help a good fine man of peace get a better one out of trouble?"

"I ain't up for aiding self-styled martyrs, Teebi; not you, not Valk the Ear. But I'll make you a trade. I'll get that fanatic out of his fix at any cost, if you'll get me that girl."

Teebi Dan Wellsmith grumbled deep in his throat, but agreed.

\*     \*     \*

That self-appointed Purveyor of Peace had been led from the business district by four burly guards, one of them a three-sword. In their wake went numerous other warriors, mere one-swords, who were to be certain that the crowd did not become a mob. Had Valk the Ear been urging them to overthrow the Wevan government, surely the masses would have risen at that moment, for they were greatly disturbed by the arrest of their latest messiah. But he had advocated non-violence. There would be no rising in his behalf, for it would only insult the philosophy he proposed.

Dee the Rope was not so impressionable or gullible. She was not afraid of the several guards who held back to make sure no mob would follow. She was not afraid of the two-swords that went with the prophet-healer himself. She was only respectfully leery of a direct encounter with the single three-sword in the company. She *certainly* did not care whether or not she insulted Valk the Ear's philosophy by saving him from the torture and imprisonment he was being led toward. Dee thought: *Masochistic cod.* She circled buildings through shadowed causeways and got ahead of the small troop. She knew exactly where they were going; she'd spent time in the prisons herself, not so long ago.

She was also secure in her motivations. There was no sense of duty in it; it was only a bargain. She wanted to get close to this Erin of Thar, who had thus far evaded arrest, and was therefore probably unapproachable except by someone she would trust. This look-alike business could come in handy; Erin of Thar was potentially a commodity. Dee was first and foremost a mercenary; she was for hire . . . she had for the past year been employed by rich merchants to undermine *both* the militant forces and the Wevan government. To Teebi Dan Wellsmith, to most of the people she

knew from the last year since her arranged release
from prison, Dee the Rope was merely a warrior
"out of favor," sympathetic to revolutionary
causes; they also presumed her out of favor because of a problem with a drink. In fact she
loathed liquor and, though often holding the bottle
to her lips, she rarely let the horrid, burning fluid
reach her throat. Her bottles were emptied only
because she was generous! She smiled at her own
cleverness in this; she was thought by all a
reasonably pleasant drunkard eternally willing to
share a nip. They also thought her loose-tongued,
when actually she was fast-talking and skilled at
loosening *their* tongues.

Dee made a leap surprising for her size and
caught the lower rung of a fire-escape ladder. She
pulled herself up quickly to the top, and ran along
a widow's walk. At a narrow alley she leapt across
to a building almost of identical height. Soon she
came to a place along the roofs overlooking a
street empty but for five pedestrians: the four
warriors with Valk the Ear between them. Dee the
Rope took from her thigh the coils of rope which
gave her her title. Below, the five men were passing, and the last in their small troop was her
target. The rope shot downward and looped
around the hind-most warrior's neck. It caught
tight. Dee pulled upward, the muscles of her arms
taut; the rope taut, too. The man could not cry out,
for he was choked silent. He was jerked so suddenly that his neck snapped. With a deft twist, Dee got
the rope loose, and the corpse fell back onto the
street, kicking with false life.

When the others heard the thrashing, they turned and retraced their steps. By then, the length of
rope had been withdrawn. There was only the
body of one of them laying in the street, apparently garroted. But there was no evidence of who
had done this, and no clue as to where the assassin

could have fled in scant seconds. Dee the Rope did not look over the ledge of the roof, for she trusted the three-sword among them to see her if she did. She could well imagine him looking left and right and up and down, striving to resolve the riddle Dee had left them. He might be clever enough to have earned his *oude*, but he could not suspect a felon on the rooftops capable of reaching down with long arms and garrote . . . unless the culprit showed herself.

Two of the men hefted their fallen friend and the troop continued toward the prisons, warier than before. Dee the Rope scurried along the roof and leapt across another narrow alley to the window-ledge of a higher building. She pried the shutters loose and found no glass on the other side; the building was a poor one without such luxury. When she dropped into the room, she found some man and woman sharing a bed in the middle of the day. Dee said, "Pardon," and hurried out into the hallway, leaving the two lovers forever to ponder how anyone could have leapt into a window three stories in the air.

At the end of the hallway was another shuttered opening. She unlatched it and peered out to see the three warriors, their corpse, and Valk the Ear. This time they would see her, but fat lot of good it would do them. Her rope shot out again, weighted by the hook at its throwing-end, and snatched away the warrior who carried the dead one by the legs. The rope held like a constricting snake. The warrior let go of his end of the corpse and made a momentary gagging sound. Then his neck snapped. The rope came loose, but before Dee could draw it back, the quick three-sword had snatched a hold of the steel-weighted end.

A tug-of-war ensued, the three-sword attempting to pull the woman through the window. She could let go of the rope, but there was a matter of pride,

and an element of simple fun involved. Deadly fun.
His eyes bored into hers, for he knew himself to be
the superior warrior, with the revered third sword
upon his back to prove it. To let go of her rope
would be an admission of inferiority; and Dee had
no desire to admit such a thing, unless it served
some plan.

There was an undeniable advantage on her side.
She probably weighed the same as the tall man in
the street; but he had no leverage to keep her from
pulling upward, whereas her knees were braced
against the window sill. She laughed, and pulled
him toward the wall. He, too, could let go of the
rope, but had already committed himself to the
game; by challenging her with his surly expression, he dared not give in, lest it prove *her* the
better of the two!

The other warrior was left to guard Valk the Ear
and so could not enter the building to trouble Dee
from behind. She began to pull the three-sword
upward. He braced his feet against the wall, but
could not keep Dee from dragging him up. His
eyes still bored into hers, and he seemed calm. Dee
laughed again, but was not certain what good such
sport would do her. The three-sword could no
doubt fall two stories and land on his feet un-
injured—he was in good shape. But if she could
drag him close to the third-floor window, and *then*
let him drop, he might break his ankle at least.
Even the best roll could prove insufficient upon a
flat, cobbled surface.

He was a wise one, though. When he got as far as
the second-story window, he planted both feet
against the top of the sill and hung upside down. *A
sorry fix for me*, thought Dee. He now had the
better leverage, though the more precarious position. If he pulled her out the third-floor window,
she'd probably fare nastily; she was strong, but
plump, and the fall might break both legs, if not

her head. The three-sword on the other hand
would probably do a simple back-flip and end up
on his feet in a crouch, ready to finish her where
she lay in the street. *Not to worry*, she reminded
herself; she could still let go. But that damned
three-sword's eyes were locked with hers, his expression haughty as a nobleman's daughter. Dee
could not bring herself to let go, despite the fact
that she was already being drawn through the
window-frame.

The full length of her rope was not used up.
Wedging part of it in the crack between the
shutter and frame, she saved herself from being
pulled further. Then, trusting the wooden frame
and shutter to hold, she slipped out the window
and went down the rope as might a fat, healthy
spider.

The three-sword began to climb upward. They
met halfway between the second- and third-floor
windows, and there clung with one hand each, and
brought swords to bare with their free hands. The
three-sword had drawn the *oude* from over his
shoulder, and so outreached Dee's *mai*. He was by
far the better swordsmaster on level ground, but
Dee was more familiar with ropes. She knew
better how to plant her feet upon a wall, cling to
the rope, and fight one-handed. Her sword was
lighter, too, increasing the excellence of her balance.

It was not such an unusual fighting method in
Terwold, whose high walls had in past wars been
defended by warriors trained in this manner; and
in years before that, battles had been waged on the
cliffs of the Black Mountain, with fighters like the
two presently engaged in a vertical fight.

"We're even here, three-sword!" said Dee,
laughing still; and the man below her looked no
longer calm, but concentrated mightily. Since he
was lower on the rope, she could cut him loose;

but it was a fifty-fifty chance that he'd be hurt enough by the fall to cause her no more trouble. So she let him hang, and fought him there.

He let himself slip down a ways, but the rope ended at the second floor, and he could not bait her to the ground; still, he decreased his chances of injury should he fall or should Dee cut the rope. He had also gained access to the window, but it was fortunately locked from within. His first kick against it failed to break the wood open. Dee started the rope swinging from side to side so that her opponent could not easily burst the wooden window through. If he gained the hallway and his footing, she could not hope to win the encounter.

Their swords rang together. He kept her from cutting him because his sword was longer. She evaded his cut with plump, spider quickness.

Heads appeared from windows on both sides of the street. Dee called out to the spectators, "Watch! Watch! See how a three-sword falls before a two!" They swung perilously; and now the three-sword was good and unsettled, looking close to panic. He finally spoke, but not to Dee. He called to his man in the street: "Let the prisoner go!" It was basically a command for the other warrior to get to the third floor and cut the woman's rope.

Valk the Ear had this while refused to watch the spectacle. But he was not fool enough to stand around waiting when the guard left him. He took off running, and Dee considered her part of the bargain with Teebi Dan Wellsmith completed at that moment. She continued to fight from the swinging rope until she reckoned the other man was more than halfway to the third floor. Then she left off the battle and climbed upward. When she reached the window, she saw the two-sword running down the hall, already out of breath from hurrying up several flights of stairs. Dee stepped into the hall from the window and her *mai* struck twice: once to deflect his blow, again to open his throat. When she turned, she saw the three-sword's fingers clutching the sill of the window. Her sword flashed again; fingers were severed; she was saved the encounter on a level surface, and the three-sword fell without screaming.

Dee went to the sill to reclaim her rope, and looked down to where her opponent lay in the street with leg and ankle broken. He writhed, but made no sound of pain. With the steel hook at the end of her rope, she pushed the three-sword's clipped fingers off the ledge. Windows on both sides of the street clapped shut and were bolted. Dee's laughter echoed between the walls.

*       *       *

In the days following his agreement with Dee, Teebi Dan Wellsmith felt increasingly uneasy about that meeting in the square, the bargain he'd made with the swordswoman, and their three meetings since. He was pleased to learn Valk the Ear had never reached the grim prison wherein were tortured the enemies of Shom Bru's regime. He was less pleased to learn the Healer had taken residence in a forest too near Terwold for anyone's genuine comfort, and where he might easily be recaptured if he and his devoted band were the least careless. Yet it was undeniable that Dee had lived up to her part of their bargain; she was eager for Teebi to live up to his. She was almost too eager, in fact, and it set Teebi wondering what he really knew about that woman. They'd been lovers for a spell, but she'd wheedled more from him than he'd ever learned about her past . . . not that he'd shown much interest at the time; he was only too eager to unburden his own pains and never query about hers. It might then be his own fault that Dee the Rope was such a mystery to him. That she was part of some conspiracy against the three-generations old regime was certain; Teebi had himself been party to conspiratorial deeds and meetings in days past. But Dee's real superiors were unknowns. Teebi disliked the idea of involving Erin of Thar in dangerous doings with people he knew nothing about.

"I've been looking for her," he reported on each of three quick meetings with Dee; and each time she said, "Shom Bru's spies are looking for her, too. So it's best for her that you don't dawdle in bringing her to me." And Teebi reckoned he hadn't been looking as hard as he should. Although . . . he did have fine excuses. He was no spy, after all; and if Shom Bru's professionals could not discover where the look-alike to Merilia hid, how could one cockeyed pirate-cum-fishmonger find her?

He'd have to think up some plan, but cleverness had never been his most famous trait. He walked the low districts of Terwold with no idea of how to draw the young woman out of hiding. Where he walked, he was appalled by the odor of the streets, the disrepair of the buildings. He'd been down in his life, but always near the ports of River Yole, protected when young as a member of a children's guild, later by his own toughness; he scarcely realized the dirtiness and poverty could be worse away from the piers.

There was but one narrow canal in this part of Terwold, really a sewer, on which no boats floated. There wasn't the feeblest of economic access here. The unemployed along the river were wealthy compared to these sad sights.

The buildings were crumbling; the streets pot-holed and coated with excrement. A single, ancient temple of note—built long before this part of the city fell into such disrepair—was still used and visited by pilgrims and patrons. The street leading to it was lined with beggars, dirty hands thrust out, some with hats or baskets, mouthing the phrase "alms, alms" without any genuine sound coming out. "Beggars are holy," said the priests, and so the visiting pilgrims sprinkled the lowest value coppers at random, hoping thereby to shorten their own stays in the Twenty Hells, through hand-outs to pariahs thereafter ignored and despised.

That Erin lived in this district was almost unthinkable, and unbearably sad. Yet it was indeed the one place someone might actually be able to hide indefinitely, whether from friends or authority. All these filthy faces . . . these tattered rags draping from bony bodies . . . it was hard to distinguish the sexes of many of them, and no face looked different from another, pleading white orbs staring up as he walked by. These beggars squatted on the left and on the right of the street and he ignored them, and yet didn't really ignore them, for each face he wondered about: behind these masks of caked soil, might the face of Erin of Thar be watching?

Teebi Dan Wellsmith crossed a bridge. The bridge straddled the filthy, narrow canal through which floated vile, small objects and shapes. The water itself was thick and oily on the top. Did the people here drink it? Where else might they get their water? It was no wonder the place was full of sickness.

He lingered on the bridge a scant moment, then fled the odor of the waters underneath. He told himself over and over, "I must find Erin and tell her to speak with Dee the Rope." But as it had been on previous days, his search through the slum districts had been half-hearted. He returned to a pier and to his boat, and pondered unhappily the fate of a swordfighting fisherwoman from Thar . . . a sad, orphaned waif who had no friends

at all, not even one, for even Teebi Dan Wellsmith
had bargained her for a Healer's freedom, as
though a cockeyed fishmonger had some right to
Erin's life . . .

When it was dark, Teebi fell asleep in his boat,
tears streaming from his eyes while he dreamed. A
colorfully dressed boy who worked on the piers
watched over the sleeper and the sleeper's boat,
and saw those tears, and wondered.

\*        \*        \*

Beneath the bridge was a secret place. There
was a mattress laying flat upon the ground, and
worms had half eaten it underneath. Bugs lived in
the creases and folds of the mattress's topside.
Seven stinking bodies were crowded upon this vile
bed, each making noises peculiar to themselves,
sleeping.

The odor of the narrow canal was profoundly
putrescent beneath the bridge, for there was
almost no ventilation. The narrow places where
bodies squeezed in and out were always plugged
and disguised when no one needed a door.

The mattress was on the eastern side of the
canal. On the western side there was nothing but
ha. d ground and refuse for the miniscule population to share. The western side of the canal, underneath the bridge, was the dwelling place of the
sadder of two sad groups. The mattress to the east
was a treasure; there were cracked pots and other
useful things on that side as well. The folk who
lived under the bridge were, then, of two factions,
the eastern faction considered wealthy, the
western faction envious and poor.

There was a fire on the western side, tended by
the only inhabitant not sleeping. She was black
with caked-on dirt, except for a place on her forehead which was a slick, white scar to which dirt

would not adhere. That place shone in the dim firelight.

Someone stirred on the eastern bank of the canal. A man crouched there, for the bottom of the bridge was too low to allow anyone to stand beneath it. The man waddled duck-like to the edge of the bank and showed his ass to Erin's firelight. Three long, hard bits of feces dropped into the canal—splosh, splosh, thup—and were slowly carried off by the turgid waters. The fellow waddled back to the mattress and fell onto a portion of it as might a jig-saw puzzle piece.

The small fire ate away some of the stink in the air, but ate the oxygen as well. People coughed in their sleep. One old woman was not coughing; usually she did. Erin suspected she was dead. It was common enough to find someone had died in the night. Their bodies would be rolled into the thick, vile water to be found by the *rint*, low officials whose task it was to dispose of dead animals and "untouchables." Animals and pariahs were burned in the same pyres; Erin did not know what the *rint* did with the ashes afterward.

When she was certain everyone slept, Erin reached into a fold of her cloak and withdrew the i. Miraculously, she had kept the blade clean, although her finger-marks soiled the scabbard. She withdrew the blade halfway and looked at the fire reflected in the glistening steel. She thought: *I once believed my destiny was to be a hero.* She could not fathom where she'd ever gotten such a notion. She sheathed the blade and tucked it back into the hiding place in her garment, accidentally revealing the tiny crystal dagger which she wore as a pendant. It gathered in the firelight and reflected rainbows across Erin's face. She hid the colors away, lest someone wake and wonder about her treasures.

When she lay upon her side and slept, she

dreamed of a world unlike Endsworld, where
roads were black ribbons knitting the whole world
together, and cities were great huge things made
of buildings twenty times the height of trees, and
carts were big iron monsters with humans trapped inside.

In the morning, it was discovered that the old
woman was dead. Her body was rolled into the
stinking sludge of the narrow stream. Erin watched, unconcerned. The only reason she'd been accepted under the bridge when she accidentally
found the place was because someone had died
similarly. Violence was muted in the low districts,
compared to the deeds of warriors; but death was
no less common, and far less noble.

On the farther side of the water, an unusual
amount of activity was taking place. Some unexpected stranger had found the entrance and was
trying to get underneath the bridge. Had he found
the western entry, he would have been lucky; he
would be allowed to take the place of the woman
whose body floated away through a culvert. But
he had found the eastern entry, where the population was already at its maximum of seven.
*There'll be a fight*, thought Erin. *They'll kill him.*
They let him enter so that no one outside would
see what was happening. Monstrously filthy vagrants surrounded him threateningly, all of them
crouching beneath the low underside of the
bridge, looking ape-like and all the more horrid.
The newcomer didn't look fretful. Indeed, for a
man who found himself in a place where he could
not stand upright, it seemed as though he carried
himself with a degree of distinction—a prince
among beggars.

He reached into a fold of his robe, a robe less
tattered than theirs. So certain was his gaze that
Erin thought surely he'd produce some weapon
and kill everyone on the eastern bank. He pro-

duced no weapon. Too little morning light filtered through the cracks of the bridge's boards above, so Erin could not see what the newcomer had— some offering, no doubt, to buy a spot under the bridge. He would be turned down; the number seven had various connections to superstitious beliefs, and the population could not exceed that number on either side of the canal. They might still accept his tribute, in exchange for a safe journey across the tiny canal, to the western bank which could accept a new tenant.

Whatever the newcomer had, it seemed to produce an almost unprecedented change of attitude across the way. Hostility had been transformed into welcome.

One of the seven dug up coals from the last night's fire and started the smallest conceivable flame inside a rusty pot. The group gathered around it as the newcomer tossed a small packet into the pot to burn. *Ah*, Erin realized. It was Terwold's opiate, *penm*, probably cut with ordinary incense, but still effective. Soon the ones breathing the weird fumes were lost in dreams.

On Erin's side of the canal, awareness grew among the small population as to what was happening so near. All but Erin lined up along the bank, packed close and side by side, striving to capture a waft of the fumes.

Their slavishness reminded Erin that she had not sunk so low after all. She was apart from them in many ways and, though usually she perceived this difference in herself as a weakness, betimes she saw it as dormant strength. Not that it lent her a sense of superiority. She felt herself to be as useless and lost as these *penm'd* pariahs.

The *penm* altered the odors beneath the bridge, not for the worse. Despite her desire to avoid the trails of drug-smoke, a little of it was inescapable. It made her a little nauseous, but the dreams it induced in others did not come to Erin of Thar. Perhaps she had breathed too small an amount, inasmuch as she was trying not to breathe any at all. Perhaps she was immune. She recalled echoes of dreams she'd had in the past nights, and doubted any drug could produce anything as strange or as strangely familiar.

Morning traffic used the bridge. Erin listened to the stomp of feet above, the creak of the boards, the rumble of hand-drawn carts. She would have to wait for a break in the procession before crawling out to go on her morning begging-rounds to the temple and the shrines. It was the rule of the bridge-community that no one be seen entering or leaving, so Erin tried to be patient, though she was more anxious than usual to go because of *penm*-smoke in the air.

Priests and priestesses of the holy places Erin visited daily considered begging a higher occupation, believing its humbleness and simplicity to be divine. The exact philosophy evaded Erin's understanding. She only understood that they were always willing to spare coins for beggars—coins which were almost worthless, having been minted in cheap metal before the Bru Dynasty. Still the coins were honored in various places, at tremendously deflated values. The holy caste refused such alms only to beggars whose eyes revealed the effects of *penm:* dilation, redness, a sleepy look. In this Erin had a distinct advantage, for she was never *penm'd*; but she fretted about the air she was breathing now. She covered her nose with her sleeve, feeling agitated.

If she received a few coins everyday and used them sparingly, she'd have enough to equal a penny by the new moon, and could spend it on one night's lodging during the Horror. It was not her intention to remain part of the tiny community beneath the bridge. On each new moon, they had given her to understand when they accepted her among them, they would all become killers in the defense of their secret place. A few desperate souls invariably tried to burrow beneath the bridge when the Horrors began; but for them, death was to be unavoidable.

Erin wasn't interested in collective action of any sort; she preferred her rogue status. The devalued coins from the holy caste and the pilgrims was her means of independence among pariahs.

Someone had sat down upon the bridge with a thump, covering one of the few small cracks with his buttocks. It was almost entirely dark beneath the bridge as a result, save for the pulsing glow from the pot, reflected on the sleepy faces of the crouching eastern faction. As long as there was someone sitting on the bridge, Erin was bound not to leave, for it would give away the secret place. Perhaps the upstairs sitter meant to beg from passers . . . if so, he'd leave soon, for the ones who used this old bridge were usually off on begging rounds themselves.

She heard a metallic cup placed upon a board above. Then the bridge-beggar began to sing: "Me went out hunting on a good fine day and me poached a hen in me neighbor's hay . . . " Erin recognized the song and the voice of the singer and knew she had to get out from under the bridge to see Teebi Dan Wellsmith, to find out why he would be begging in the streets like vile pariah, like Erin herself. A breach of rules meant the two factions would try in some way to kill her . . . and though she knew they couldn't succeed, there was no need riling them after they'd been good enough to let her inherit a corner of their shelter.

The western faction with whom she lived had captured enough whiffs of the incense to be quite unaware of anything but their own meaningless dreams. The eastern faction was even more deeply

entranced. The newcomer alone had not partici-
pated in the *penming*. He watched Erin with intense, narrow eyes the color of sand.

Erin scrabbled toward a hidden opening, moved
two rocks aside, doubting the drug-provider cared
about rules any better than she did. None of the
others would even realize she'd broken rules. She
crawled out into the startlingly bright morning,
went on hands and knees through some brush,
then stood abruptly and climbed the side of the
bank. She walked onto the bridge. Teebi had been
facing another direction; no one had seen her after
all. He was still singing his foolish song, but left
off immediately when he saw Erin standing by
him.

He got up, leaving his tin cup behind, and faced
Erin eye-to-eye. He said, "The plan, me good fine
and dirty friend, was to sing every song you and
me knew, right up to 'Wee Toddler Tin' which you
don't much like. I thought I'd be doing it all day
. . . but hardly a stanza from me lips and here you
are, hey, appearing out of thin air like a devil.
Well, me gal, it's me good strong suggestion that
you give up this life of begging, just as I'm about to
do (short career that it was), and follow me back to
a slightly if not greatly better part of Terwold."

Teebi walked away from the bridge. For a few
paces, Erin followed. She stopped and asked,
"Why am I following you?"

"Because you're bloody tired of being a vagrant,
hey. Teebi Dan Wellsmith don't make many commands in his good fine life, but he makes this one:
you come with me."

He led her some more. She thought about his
"command" to follow and the more she thought
about it, the more annoyed she felt. As they approached the boundaries of the low district, Erin
paused again.

"Don't think I'm ready to leave here, Teebi. I

don't think I can."

Teebi looked perturbed. "There's a sword of yours on me boat," he said. "I ain't been oiling it for you. It needs taking care."

"Nothing's any different from before, Teebi," she said. "I couldn't cope with things. Now I've found a place for myself where I can get by."

"At the very fringes of society, gal?"

"The very fringe; the very pit."

"Well then now what can I say to you? I'll tell you some things. There's a woman I know— friend, sort of—who thinks she's found a better place than this for you . . . in some fool revolution probably, though I'm never much certain of her plans, hey, she's a curious gal. For a certainty some sort of rising is brewing; the only thing hold-ing it back is fear of them damned bugs. But if timed perfectly—as far away from the new moon as possible—something could happen. Might be a year from now; might be next week. Me, I try not to know too much about it, good fine man of peace that I've become and all. But I'll be straight with you, Erin of Thar: you bear a startling resemblance to a war-woman named Merilia. This friend of mine, Dee the Rope, thinks she can use this resemblance in some way. You see, Shom Bru cleaved Merilia through the forehead, right in the place where you, coincidentally, carry a scar, and . . ."

Erin's eyes grew round and white in her dirty face. Such a look of surprise or terror was in her eyes that Teebi was given a tingle of superstition up his back; it made him shiver. He moved closer to Erin and whispered, "Now don't go telling me you *are* Merilia of the Black Mountain?"

Erin whispered, too. "I've never been there. I was told to go to the Teacher there, man of the four-legged race. I didn't go."

Teebi's mouth was hanging open. He said, "I

didn't think such a man existed! Do you mean to tell me he's more than legend?"

"I've never seen him. Kes the Hammer says he's real."

"In the tales, Erin, he's a trainer of good fine heroes only. If he beckons you, you should go."

"Or go hide."

Teebi stared at her long and hard. She couldn't tell what he was thinking, but it must have been quite a negative train of thought, because he said,

"You're not coming out from this place with me?"

"I don't think so, Teebi."

"Well then now. I'm sorry I came looking for you gal. You don't have to follow me anymore if you don't want, hey."

When he turned to walk away, his shoulders sagging, Erin called after, "Don't be judging me, Teebi Dan Wellsmith. You came to sell the visage of a dead warrior to someone who would use me for her own purpose! You were honest with me about that, but it's a shame all the same. You didn't look for me out of love or friendship."

Teebi wheeled on her, stung, guilty. "I've looked for you harder than you think, you damned monster-wench! I'll admit my weakness, but Dee the Rope offered to risk her life getting the Healer Valk away from torturers, if I would bring you to her. She lived up to her side of the bargain, and here I am refusing to finish my end—for 'love or friendship' I don't know. I won't take you to her, gal. Dee is interested in fighters, but it's a good fine fighter a coward like you'd make anyway, the stink of *penm* clinging to your dirty clothes . . . I wish I'd never thought up the good fine trick of singing on that bridge, and I hadn't seen you now."

When he turned to stomp away, she called his name, thinking to explain how she came to have a little odor of *penm* about her person; she didn't want him thinking she had fallen quite so low. But when Teebi looked back with his expression hopeful, Erin suddenly felt cruel and, having gained his attention, she thrust out a soiled hand and said, "Alms, my friend?"

He tossed her a better coin than the temple people ever spared, then snorted in disgust as he went away.

\*          \*          \*

The man with sandy eyes had watched all this from the shadows. When Erin turned around, she saw him; he had let her see him, she was certain, for he was too clever for it to have been by accident. She called to him, "Who are you, man? You're no beggar; you're Shom Bru's spy."

He reached into his robe and pulled out a small, oblong box, holding it up for Erin to see. She was quite a ways up the empty street, but the sun was bright on that cloudless morning, and she could see the box.

"If it's the drug you purvey," she said, thinking he might not be a spy after all, "then you waste your time on me."

The box snapped open, and Erin saw that it had an indentation inside, intended to hold a jewel. The jewel to fill that space would need to be shaped like a sword—the crystal needle-sword Erin kept secreted on a string around her neck.

For the first time, she heard the man's voice, and it was not accented with any dialect she had heard in the streets of the low district. Like Teebi Dan Wellsmith, he had only been disguised, and intended, it appeared, only to find whoever had the jewel which belonged in that box. Not Shom Bru's spy, perhaps, but a spy in any case. He said, "You have disappointed many, Erin Wyler."

She did not remember the name Wyler. She

said, "So now my name is Wyler. Someone else called me Merilia."

"Would that you were she," said the man with strangely colored eyes. The box snapped shut in his hand, and he put it away. "We are not prepared to forsake all faith in you as yet; you may keep the jewel a while longer. But someday I may reclaim it, for it is mine, and it was I sent it to you on Earth. Had you partaken of the *penm* which I brought to test you, then I'd not talk to you now, and you would never know where the crystal sword had vanished to."

Erin had taken several steps toward the man, trying to see more of him than his strange eyes. He was not young. He did not look particularly strong. He *did* look well-fed and was not of the streets, it was certain. Doubtless he was rich, and his mission must have had some ultra-personal importance to him, or else he would have sent hirelings with his message.

"So I have passed your test," said Erin indifferently. "Should I be impressed, or should you?"

"It is possible neither of us impress easily," he replied. "Stay where you are please!" Erin ceased edging nearer. She scrutinized him carefully, to be sure she would recognize him should she ever see him in another context—be it a different disguise, or in his usual habitat. He said, "Since we are speaking plainly, I would like to remind you of certain things before I take my leave. One-third of an Endsworld year has passed since you came; when a full year has gone by, Kes the Hammer will challenge you to a duel. It is well that you bear this in mind, for he will surely kill you if you have failed to practice the sword this whole time. Only the Teacher of Black Mountain can train you well enough."

"You are a friend of that Teacher? Does he send you?"

"As a rule he does not meddle in mortal affairs; probably he does not know that such as I exist. He has a few delights, though, and one of them is training heroes, for it makes him less lonely in his self-imposed exile. He would like to see you, for he has been informed that you are an otherworld counterpart to Merilia, once his disciple. You act as though you forget that world you came from! You may be reminded of it if someone with the power sends you back . . . someone like me, who arranged in the first place for you to fill the vacuum of Merilia's unforetold demise."

It was almost true that she had forgotten the world he'd called Earth; but it was not entirely true, for the threat of being sent back frightened her. She did not reveal her feeling that she was endangered. *That Hell I dream about*, she thought; *he means to send me there.* Her hand crept toward the *i* hidden in her robe. She spoke to him, partly so that he wouldn't notice her hand moving, partly because she was curious: "Are you some dark magician who conjured me, a demon, out of some darker Hades?"

The impassive face almost let escape a look of humor. His unusual, sandy eyes sparkled. For a moment he did not answer her. Perhaps he *could* not answer! Finally he said, simply, "Yes."

When her hand closed upon the hilt of her *i*, she drew it forth, leaving the scabbard in her robe, and leapt upon the man in a flash. Her shortsword slashed where he had stood threatening to send her to one of the twenty hells . . . but he was not standing there now, nor could she see where he had gone.

There was no place he might have run, yet she could not see him on the street. In the blink of an eye and the bright of day, he had vanished. *A magician after all*, Erin realized. She tried to cloak herself in that self-made syndrome which was

akin to senility. She tried to forget that she had
seen the man with sandy eyes, to forget what he
had said. Now that he was gone, it seemed he
might never have existed. It was the *penm* that
she'd accidentally inhaled, that very small
amount, which had caused her to dream him up, to
dream he'd brought *penm* to the people under the
bridge. As he had not been real, then he hadn't
brought *penm*; therefore she hadn't breathed a
small amount, and hadn't dreamed him at all. If
she hadn't dreamed him, then he had really
existed, had brought the *penm*, of which she'd
caught a whiff, and dreamed him . . .

Her mind raced toward oblivion, raced along a
labyrinth of conflict and dilemma. When she could
think again, think without remembering, she
found herself outside a certain shrine. To the
passers-by she was saying, "Alms?"

She did well on her begging rounds.

*       *       *

Days later, Valk the Ear's small encampment
was raided by three warriors. The warriors were
vastly outnumbered by devotees and by sick
peasants who had come for free treatment of ail-
ments of various sorts. Yet no one in the camp of
the Healer resisted. All but one were slain. Valk
the Ear's arms were tied painfully behind his
back, the rope drawn so tight that his elbows came
together. He was taken from his forest retreat,
back into City Terwold, along dark streets and
seldom-used alleys to a prison wherein he was tortured. The means of torture were two huge stone
weights suspended from the ceiling, lowered by
increments upon his shoulders, as he sat bound to
a "throne" (as the torturers termed it) made of the
same grey stone. Valk the Ear had strong lungs.
He screamed and begged for mercy, receiving

none. His torturers were careful, for this one was
to be preserved whole for the insect folk. They
broke nothing, bruised little; the white garments
the Healer wore were scarcely soiled. Yet the pain
was extreme and constant. When finally he lost
consciousness, the torturers rested, but in the
prisoner's dreams the torture continued.

He awoke in a cell with no light, no toilet, only a
stone door in a stone wall, once more the same
grey rock which had been upon his shoulders for
hours or days. There was a window in the door,
too small to need bars, too small for more than
one arm to escape. Light appeared at the window:
a torch. Then a face: a man with a crooked eye
who Valk the Ear vaguely recollected as the face
of someone he had once healed. The man with the
wandering eye said, "It's a pleased man I be, to
find you still alive, and a devoted peaceful man as
well, who has broken in this place to save your life
at any risk!" For a moment, Valk the Ear felt the
weights released from his shoulders. They had
been released long before, of course, after he had
passed out and before he was deposited in the
small room. But only in his moment of hope did it
seem the weights were gone. In the next moment
there was a quick, dull sound and the man with
the crooked eye collapsed from view. A torturer
peered in, leering, and the door was unlocked.
Valk the Ear was resigned. He had risked this
from the start. His lungs were rested. He was prepared to scream anew.

V·FIGHTER

## V. FIGHTER

Erin had not marked the time well. She seemed capable of going long periods without the least thought passing through her mind, and in this psychological state, days passed as minutes. Yet she did realize when the sacrificial night was pending, for there were overt signs among the street people, and particularly among her own group beneath the bridge. Procrastination, and her practically-mindless state of oblivion, found her still living among the bridge people when the Grim Day began, although she had earlier promised herself never to become a fixture of any given group.

There were fourteen members living there, including Erin: seven on the eastern bank, seven on the western bank. Only one was a more recent tenant than Erin. She and the newer arrival were being lectured by an extraordinarily ugly man about protocol and procedures for the night which was yet hours away.

"You must have weapon," said the ugly man in one of the odd street-dialects. The newest tenant reached into his robe and pulled out what looked like the tip of a broken, rusty sword, tied haphazardly to a length of wood. The newcomer grinned. Erin ignored the ugly man who lectured them, and he repeated to her specifically, "Must have weapon! It is regulation of new-moon-night!"

Erin turned her gaze on him slowly, no emotion in her features, and she said,

"No one knows of this place. There'll be no need of weapons."

The ugly man sputtered. Then he said, "Always on new-moon-night, one or two try to hide under here. This cannot be! Only seven live this side; only seven live that side." He half-pointed to the eastern bank. "We cannot turn others away, not so simple; they go get other people, come back. We cannot let them stay here either. Too many people learn about our bridge-home, run out of room quick. So we have to fight who finds us by accident, unless we need one more. No need one more tonight; have seven live here now. All must be done quick, without sound, or Warrior notice, then not safe on new-moon-night no more. You understand all this?"

His tone had seemed patronizing. Perhaps he was merely trying to talk across the barrier created by their varying dialects, but Erin felt insulted. She turned her face from him as though she had not heard a single word. This made the ugly man very angry, and he spoke hotly: "All of us fall upon anyone try to come in here! All of us go *poom! krtt!*" He made motions with his hands: punch! slice! "Then throw in canal, leave for carcass-collecting *rint* to find next day. You live with us; you obey regulation. Must have weapon!"

She folded her arms and snuggled further back into the tight corner under the bridge. Without looking at him, she said, "There are plenty of you to do it."

"No! No! Less than seven not lucky. More than seven not lucky. You live here, you fight this night. It better than having to find penny every month!"

"If I refuse?"

The ugly man motioned toward her and made the sounds, "*Poom. Krrt.*"

Erin suppressed a smile. They didn't know she could fight, or this one wouldn't threaten her. Still, she shouldn't go against their rules, for it would do her no good to sleep nightly among those committed to harming her. She usually slept light, but not always. Some bit of devilish mischief kept urging her to be disagreeable, though, so that she said to the ugly man,

"I will be your back-up."

"Back-up? What you mean back-up?"

The newest tenant had been the only one listening to these exchanges at first, but the other four had now gathered around. Erin explained loud enough for them all to hear, "If someone is too big for you to handle, or too tough, I'll take care of them for you. By myself. If no one big and tough comes, I'll keep sitting up here in my corner. Got that?"

"Stupid deal to make!" The ugly man was incensed. He sputtered so badly he couldn't say anything else. One of the other tenants-under-the-bridge echoed the sentiment, "Stupid deal!" It was a toothless hag who spoke, and she continued, "We all kill to preserve our home. Only when someone dies do we let new one come in and be safe. You be one of us now, so you fight. You kill. Once a month only; no other work we require to live here. Is easy."

"Is easy," said the ugly man, finding his speech and seconding the hag's opinion.

"I said I'll fight," said Erin, improvising an agreeable-seeming air. "But on my terms. Maybe a warrior will find this place. If so, all of you together could not hurt him. In that case, I'll fight."

"You not hurt him either!" said the hag, spitting through her gums with indignation. "You try make stupid deal with us! If no big-tough one try to break in here, you don't have fight at all, so not fair to us. If big-tough *do* come, then maybe you fight, but you die for sure, and he get us. That no help either."

"I wouldn't die," said Erin.

"Because no big-tough come!" exclaimed the ugly man.

"Stupid deal!" the hag reiterated, and the others, even the newest tenant, nodded in agreement. At that moment, heavy feet trod the boards above their heads and everyone became perfectly silent so as not to give themselves away. All eyes glared at Erin malevolently, but the argument was stilled. The heavy footsteps stopped near the top of the bridge, just to the west of the turgid canal. Everyone waited for the footsteps to pick up again, waited for the one dawdling above to go away.

The boards creaked, as though the dawdler shifted weight from foot to foot, but did not move on.

The vagrant pariahs looked suddenly terrified. Clearly someone was nosing around their place. The ugly man whispered to the others, "It not dark yet, but already we must kill someone." Low as his voice had been, the one above had heard him. A sword was forced powerfully through a narrow crack and stopped in front of the ugly man's face.

Everyone's breaths came to sudden halts.

Erin said sardonically, "No big toughs ever come?"

The sword point was not withdrawn. It remained poking down from between the boards. A vagrant's dirty hand reached out, touched the tip, withdrew the hand with a stifled yelp, sucking at the cut on the finger's tip. A voice from above called down:

"It is not my sword sticking in the bridge. It belongs to Erin of Thar."

Erin squinted in the darkness under the bridge, looked at the *mai*'s point. Could it be the one she'd left with Teebi Dan Wellsmith nearly three months before? The voice that spoke above was almost familiar. Erin concentrated to remember where she had heard the voice previously.

The vagrants gaped at Erin with slack jaws. They could scarcely believe the threatening *mai* belonged to someone in their own midst, although it gave sudden sense to the arguments she had given them.

"Come out and claim your sword!" the voice commanded. Hearing it again, Erin remembered who it was: a renegade she'd met a month earlier, who gave her name as Dee the Rope.

The ugly man said, "We accept stupid deal! We not understand you are renegade. You no have fight unless with big-tough. You fight now, okay? This your sword poking down? You go out and get it! You fight! You kill!" He bowed his head in front of Erin, and the other pariahs did likewise, their attitude toward her reversed as suddenly as that. On the other side of the canal—the richer side, where there was a mattress—the rival group had lined itself up to overhear. Someone over there whispered loudly, "We on this side never one time say stupid deal! Renegade warrior should live our side, sleep at top of mattress, honored space. Old Treepit die soon anyway; we kill him now and make you our Number Seven!" Another voice from across the way added, "We share cup with only one chip on it!"

"No, you stay this side!" said the ugly man. "This your home, yes? We give you many special honor. We make many apology for not realize you are warrior." He banged his head on the ground so hard that Erin heard the thump. The voice above said,

"You're a noisy bunch down there. I weary of waiting."

The beggars became more pitiful than Erin had

ever seen them, suddenly begging *her*. When they grew silent after Dee the Rope chided their hoarse whisperings, Erin said softly, "Maybe I won't live on either side of the canal anymore." The vagrants gave a collective worried look. "All the same, I'll fight my challenger." That relieved the two groups immeasurably. Erin reached into the folds of her garment and withdrew a sheathed *i*. The vagrants moved away from both her and the weapon, aghast that someone had been living amongst them who secretly bore such a thing. "Idiots," said Erin. "You just *told* me I had to have a weapon. This is it." She placed the sheathed weapon through her fisher's girdle, then crawled toward the rocks that led outward to the day. The toothless hag moved the debris from Erin's path, and she left them.

Outside, she brushed herself off, as though the ground-in soil might fly away with the swipe of a hand. Then she looked Dee the Rope in the eye. She said, "You have revealed me to my friends and upset my happy home." The sarcasm escaped those beneath the bridge, who swelled with pride to think a warrior might consider them her family, or their bridge her home.

Beside Dee the Rope, the hilt of Erin's *mai* stuck up from the bridge. Dee pulled the weapon out and put it in its sheath. She said, "I came to deliver this to you."

"As a challenge to a duel?" asked Erin.

"Perhaps."

"I might refuse to claim the sword. I might refuse to fight."

"I don't mind," said Dee. "It may not be an encounter with swords I require. In any case, I expect to win."

Erin climbed up the bank, away from the canal, stood on the verge of the bridge looking at the fat warrior standing on the bridge's high mid-point.

Dee the Rope set the sheathed *mai* flat on the planks, then backed to the opposite side of the bridge. She said, "Now you may pick up your sword without worrying about me."

"I was not worried about you," said Erin blandly. She walked to the top of the bridge but did not bend down to pick up the sword. She said, "Your hand is near the rope at your hip. Do you intend some trick?"

"Perhaps."

Erin bent slowly, her hand reaching down for the *mai*. At that moment, Dee's rope was to hand and the weighted end shot toward Erin. Erin grabbed the *mai* by the hilt, leaving only the scabbard laying on the bridge. The blade swung in an arc, and the hook-weight at the end of the rope was shorn off. When Erin reclaimed her *mai*'s scabbard, she simultaneously pushed the severed hook into the murky waters of the canal.

"That was unnecessary!" complained Dee. "That hook was good steel! It will cost plenty to replace!"

"Afford it," Erin suggested, placing the *mai* in her girdle next to the shorter *i*. "You don't seem to have come as a friend, so Teebi Dan Wellsmith did not send you with my sword. You stole it from him."

"Perhaps not!" said Dee. "I had to kill in order to get it, I admit . . . but only because Teebi's boat-guard refused me freedom to take anything off the boat without Teebi's express permission."

"You killed a boat guard rather than talk to Teebi?" said Erin.

"Nasty little scamp," said Dee. "Not that I like killing a child, but, well, Teebi was in no position to give any permissions. He's in prison. Tortured no doubt. A few days ago."

Erin's indifference was dented. "Imprisoned! And the new moon is tonight!"

"Indeed it is. That's why I thought you might want your sword at any cost. He is a friend of yours as well as mine." Dee strode to the center of the bridge again, stood next to Erin, said, "You've forgiven him by now, haven't you, for dickering your whereabouts to me? He refused his part of our bargain, and I had to practically drink him under a table to get him to tell me where you were lurking like some horrible bridge-troll. Even then, in a drunken stupor, he tricked me. Told me it was a different bridge altogether. I don't know the slum districts as well as I might; took a while to find which bridge was *really* the troll's hide-out. The same night I got Teebi drunk, news of Valk the Ear being captured was going around the piers. Teebi roared that he'd save the Healer single-handedly, but passed out cold, so I didn't worry about him doing anything extreme. Next day, though, hangover or none, Teebi was gone; we know where, don't we, Erin of Thar? He likes that blamed weird preacher enough to die for him. Can't say I understand it."

Erin knew the moment for action was upon her, but she had lived as street-scum long enough that she was uncertain there was anything more than that to her. Could she swing back as easily as a clock's pendulum? She said, "I'm not sure I can help."

"All we've got to face is a bunch of bloody two-swords like you and me, only not nearly so good," said Dee. "Three-swords never take on such work. No one will give us trouble! We'll save Teebi's hairy hide all right, and maybe save some other hides for the fun of it and to shake things up a bit. Might as well save that idiot preacher while we're at it; make Teebi feel good."

"Last time I interfered with a sacrifice," said Erin, "the whole village Thar disappeared."

"Them bugs can't breach the walls of Terwold,"

said Dee. "If they try, it might give Shom Bru's army something useful to do."

Behind Erin, stealthy as ghosts, six vagrants had gathered, having dared crawl out from under the bridge. The ugly man cried, "Stay with us! We honor Erin-renegade!"

The east-bank group had gathered on Dee's side of the bridge, six of them too, for the one called Treepit was probably already killed to make way for Erin of Thar. Their leader shouted, "Kill the warrior and join our side! We give tribute! Find *penm*-vendor to make you dream!"

Dee said, "Perhaps you should listen to them. It may be that your place in this world is underneath a bridge breathing *penm*-smoke and guarding pariahs. It could be your fate. It could be your choice."

Erin drew her *mai*, insulted. "Fat woman!" she said, trying to be equally insulting. "I challenge you to the death!"

"Good!" said Dee. "But I refuse. You must help me save Teebi first."

The two beggar groups had sealed off both ends of the bridge. They brought their pitiful weapons to bare: rusty knives, broken bottles, staves . . . The speaker for the eastern faction said, "It is our rule that no one lives who finds out about the bridge."

Dee the Rope looked at them with disgust. "Fight me with puny weapons and bits of glass?" She laughed at their impudence. "I've a better suggestion. Back away slowly, and I will think about letting you live!"

Erin turned to the ones who'd been her companions for nearly a month. She said, "Don't press your regulations this time. It would be folly."

The toothless hag said, "Let those on east bank fight if they're stupid enough!" She turned and slid down the bank, toward the brush-hidden entrance.

The ugly man urged the other four to follow after
the hag, and he went last, looking back once but
saying nothing. The eastern faction vanished more
sheepishly. Dee the Rope and Erin of Thar stood
side by side on the bridge, then walked away together.

\*       \*       \*

In the merchant's quarter on a slope above the
business district, the streets were lined with
flowering trees. The walls of three- and four-
storied mansions were greened with ivy. The air
was fresh with a verdancy almost foreign to Erin,
who had never guessed a part of Terwold was
famous for its gardens. The architecture itself was
difficult to see, hidden beyond hedges, behind
trees, and under vines; but here and there a twisting spire or windowed turret poked out of the
greenery, suggesting a style which was alienly
baroque.

"Why do you lead me through this rich place?"
asked Erin.

"It's hours still until sundown. We need rest.
Food. A bath."

"Here?"

"Here."

Dee the Rope led the way through shady
avenues, over wooden sidewalks, alongside
wrought-iron and stone fences. On one fence, a
brilliant purple lizard sat and watched the woman
pass. Erin returned its stare with equal intensity,
causing Dee to explain, "Those queer fellows are
kept as pets around here. They keep grubs off the
flowers and they add a literal 'dash' of color."

At a certain intersection, Dee pointed down a
narrow side-street to an iron gate between high
stone posts. "We go in there," she said.

"The lock," Erin began, seeing the size of the

sealed bolt; but she did not finish her sentence, for she saw that Dee had already produced a key. Inside, the perfumes of a myriad flowering plants was almost as overwhelming as *penm*-smoke. Indeed, Erin wondered if she were lost in some drug-induced dream, so unutterably *different* this place was from her haunts in the low districts.

"You're all right?" asked Dee. Erin ogled the raging colors as Dee resealed the gate. Dee said, "You're breathing kind of funny."

"It's a fairy-garden!" said Erin, sounding like a child. Dee barked a laugh and said, "It's nice, but there's better. This one's rather neglected, since the owner lets no one in but me, not even caretakers recently. You wouldn't find it so impressive if you hadn't been living under planks outside grey shanties. Well, follow me—stay close, the paths are designed to be tricky."

The place was as wild-seeming as the forests around massacred Thar; and yet it wasn't wild at all, for the paths were clear and artfully placed to create illusions of vastness and to maximize the beauty of each bush and flower. Another of the purple lizards rested on the path. As Dee and Erin approached, a yellow sack swelled beneath its neck. When the two weren't scared away, it lifted itself from its repose and shot away, tail whipping.

"You can't *live* here," said Erin, still overawed.

"Why not?" They turned another bend and there was a tiny stone cottage with glass windows and a high chimney. It had been a gardener's home, no doubt. In front of it was a pool in which were yellow fish and blue lilies. Dee sniffed her armpit and said, "I don't like to mess up the place. Let's fertilize the lilies first, all right?"

"What?"

"I'm stinking with sweat and some cheap liquor I poured on myself, and you're filthier than a wart hog in a dung wallow! Ain't a one of us steps foot in that cottage without first taking a bath!" So saying, Dee the Rope began to strip. "Off with the clothes, nit!" she commanded. "If you don't, it's off with your head! I'm king around here; this retreat is part of my *pay*."

"Pay?" Erin still stood dumbfounded by everything. Dee looked annoyed.

"Yes, pay. I'm a professional trouble-maker if you must know. But keep it under your girdle. My employer said to take you into my confidence, that you're good at silence. He didn't say I had to let you track dirt into the house."

Only when Dee the Rope had slid into the pond and moved her hard obese body among the lily pads did it dawn on Erin that, indeed, she was in dire need of a bath, had been for many weeks. She started to strip. Dee said, "Throw the clothes in, too. You can scrub 'em after they've soaked a while. I've something in the house that'll keep you comfortable for the time being."

Erin found the water deeper than she expected. The top four feet were placid and warmed by the sun. At her feet, the water was extraordinarily cold, suggesting an underground source. She tried to stay horizontal in the warm zone.

Yellow fish slithered near her thigh, their pearl-shaped scales like cold gooseflesh. Dee the Rope swam toward the further bank, where round pumice stones had been stacked, and where stubby reeds grew with pale, unimpressive blossoms on long stalks. There, Dee grabbed a rock and broke off a stalk. She swam toward Erin and said, "This plant's juices can be worked into a cleansing froth; that's why it's planted there." Erin took the bit of plant and crushed it in a fist, rubbed it against her body. "Let me get your back," said Dee, who pressed the pumice scrub-stone to Erin's shoulder. Erin gave a yelp. "Has to be done," said Dee. "The dirt's caked on. One thing about warriors is that they're fastidious. Remember that. Many a warrior is judged by odor. The most fearless deed might go unheralded if the fighter stank. There's a cleanliness about the sweat and musk of battle. The stench of an unbathed body, however . . ."

"You didn't smell so good yourself about five minutes ago," Erin grumbled defensively.

"I've a habit of pouring whiskey on myself," said Dee matter-of-factly. "As I said, many a warrior is judged by her smell. It's a handy disguise, odor." Dee left off scrubbing Erin's back, but pulled on the string around her neck, asking, "What's this trinket?"

"I don't know," said Erin. "A crystal pendant. Sometimes it glows at night."

"Another thing about warriors," Dee snapped. "They don't meddle with sorcery."

Erin swam away, toward the bank. She climbed out and stood drying in the sun. Her two swords lay by her feet. Dee's whale-like corpulence continued to swim about with shocking grace. At length Erin replied, "That being so, perhaps you ought not meddle with me."

"You say *you're* sorcery?" The fat woman laughed, crawled out of the water to fetch her swords and rope. She led the way toward the cottage. The wide warrior and the narrow one entered. The inside was uncluttered, simple, clean. Dee went to a closet, found a robe for herself. It was a grey material, with a slightly different shade of grey barely forming the shapes of hawks swooping down from the shoulders to the legs. She found another robe which was a light blue, with slender threads embroidered into it in the shape of clouds. "This will fit you," she said to Erin. Erin was surprised.

"You plan ahead," said Erin.

"I always do that," said Dee. "There's no girdle

for you, however; it would be audacious of me to
provide that. You'll have to clean that fisher's girdle of yours. The peasants will love you if you fight
with that on! They'll call you 'hero of the people,'
the fencing fisher. Other warriors will call you
scum. That's one reason for you to learn fastidi-
ousness. You must know in your heart they're
wrong, or they'll weaken you with names."

Shadows of doubt were etched in Erin's expression.

"Put the garments on," said Dee, annoyed again.
"Your tits'll catch cold. Hungry?"

"Perpetually. I'm used to it."

"Fetch wood out back. You're about to learn
what a lovely cook is Dee the Rope."

That boast proved a joke or a lie. Before long,
Erin sat at a short table in a shorter chair, samp-
ling a gruel not much better than the stuff she
scrounged in the streets.

"Warriors are austere," said Dee.

"You live well enough," said Erin, letting gruel
drip off her spoon into the bowl as she added, "except for this."

"So I can't cook. Soon I won't have to. This cottage isn't mine to keep, just to borrow; but I'll
have a villa of my own in the warriors' quarter
next year, and enough capital to keep servants."

"Such austerity," said Erin, "and from a revolutionary."

"Revolution. Poo!" Dee smiled. "I'm a rouser. A
mercenary. I'm on the side that wins."

"Do you change sides often?" The tone of Erin's
voice was not the least friendly when asking this.
Dee stopped feasting for a moment only, said,

"I *never* change sides, once I've taken payment."

"Then how can you be sure you're on the side
that wins."

"My side is in the middle."

"That can't be so."

"It can. You see two sides: warriors, and peasants. But there's someone else. There's the merchants. Merchants control the flow of wealth. Not the little merchants—they're peasants, too, though they think themselves holier. But the wealth of the city, nay, the whole of this country, is in the merchants' hands. Dynasties of aristocrats and warriors have come, have gone; peasants have seen slavery, liberty, and slavery again. But the major merchant families have been the same throughout history. When nations are laid to waste, neither the people nor the armies win in that. But there's always a profit to be made by someone—that someone is who I serve."

"So," said Erin, "this venture we do tonight isn't out of friendship to Teebi. You're being paid."

"I'd've saved Teebi in any case, I think. I wouldn't have invited you. For *that* I was paid."

"By a man with sand-colored eyes."

Dee spat gruel, choking. She stared at Erin, but said no more on that topic. Instead, she said, "It's long before night. I have to sleep. You?" Erin shook her head. Dee said, "Well, then try not to get too lost in the gardens. You can explore if you like, but stay inside the gate." She got up and took Erin's unfinished bowl away. Soon Dee had thumped into a low, stout couch and was asleep almost instantly. Erin of Thar went outside to wash her girdle and old robe.

\*       \*       \*

Teebi swam upward through darkness and pain only to surface into darkness and pain. He was certain that some of his bones were broken. On inspecting himself, he found he was wrong. Not even a rib was cracked. A good torturer knows a well-pulled tendon or a hard-struck kidney is quite a bit more painful than a broken leg; moreover, the victim recovers more quickly and is able to withstand another cruel bout.

When Teebi heard footsteps, he thought to play unconscious, so that the torturers would not know he was recovered enough to hurt again. They'd test for that trick, surely, so Teebi tried to formulate a better plan. Aching though his muscles were, he climbed to a standing posture, and looked at the ceiling of his tiny, high-walled cell. Above, the stone was cracked, and had been reinforced with heavy crossbeams of timber. He might wedge himself between those beams if he could manage to reach them.

The footsteps were louder. Teebi jumped, grabbed a beam between palms, held himself for a fraction of a second, and fell back. *Can't be done*, he admitted. The footsteps stopped outside some other dungeon door, and Teebi's selfish heart beat more slowly with relief. Then the torturer-who-chose-another said nastily, "You be the Healer Valk? I be Hek, Scream-Maker, new to this ward."

Teebi's heart fluttered rapidly as he pressed himself into a corner and, with feet and hands against two walls, began to scale upward. *Surprising what impossibilities can be done when need demands*, thought Teebi, taking a passel of splinters all along his sides as he squeezed himself between two beams, wedged against the ceiling. From this posture, he cried out, "Hek, Scream-Maker can't make this one scream!"

A growling, heavy breath responded. "Who speaks so!"

Teebi was silent.

"Who dares deride Hek's skill!" bellowed Hek. Teebi heard Valk the Ear's cell being relocked. Hek, Scream-Maker began peering into other cells. Frightened, whimpering voices were saying it wasn't me, it wasn't me.

"It's only a mouse!" shouted Teebi. "Even mice

do not fear Hek, Yawn-Maker."

Teebi hadn't any true idea of this new torturer's abilities, but he recognized egotism when he heard it panting and slobbering. This Hek raged and champed like a wild beast, so insulted was that ego; and Teebi Dan Wellsmith sweated on hearing it. The torturer's face peered into Teebi's cell and saw only shadows. In such darkness, the torturer could not be certain if a cell were empty or not.

In a high, squeaky voice, Teebi said, "No one here but a mouse."

Hek roared and keys jangled. Bolts moved; the door swung open. The torturer was armed with a spear and had a bow-whip coiled in the other hand. Hek, Scream-Maker stepped into the cell. His whip licked out into a dark corner, found nothing, tested another corner, found nothing again.

Teebi dared not drop. The torturer's spear was planted haft to floor, point to ceiling. If Teebi dropped to attack, he'd be impaled. Slowly the torturer realized there was no one upon the floor, and he craned his bull-neck to look upward, a smile across his huge toad-face. Seeing Teebi's dilemma, the villain said,

"How will you get down, mouse."

Teebi returned the smile. "I guess I can't, now, can I, hey." He grinned at the point of the spear. "It was all a little joke, hey."

Hek, Scream-Maker thrust his spear's point straight up into the ceiling, passing through Teebi's shoulder. Teebi screamed for the scream-maker and dropped the length of the spear's shaft, straight into awaiting arms.

*     *     *

Teebi was flayed. Teebi was burned. Teebi's good eye was bashed and threatened, the bad one already monstrously swollen. He couldn't speak through swollen lips. He had long since stopped screaming, but Hek, Scream-Maker seemed to value almost as highly the sight of Teebi's mouth spraying blood with every grunting breath. Both his thumbs were broken. The wound through his shoulder was festered and oozing. The torturer had lost all concern for the subtleties of pain-with-out-bruises; this one would go to the bugs a piece of living hamburger.

Through puffy lips, Teebi said, "Wa - er."

"War is it?" bellowed Hek, laughing. "Aye. As good as any war!"

"Wah. Er."

"Ah! Water! Don't mind if I do! Give you a chance to rest!"

The torturer drank deep from a wooden ladle. Teebi's bent hands and broken fingers strained at their bonds, toward the dripping ladle. Hek threw the utensil aside. "My friend," he said, "I hope you're not tired of yawning," and a leather-bound fist big as two ordinary fists unhinged Teebi's jaw. The torturer dug a thumb into the place where the hinge belonged and Teebi winced. He wished for the simple mercy of unconsciousness, but the torturer was too good at his occupation to allow it.

Through the redness of pain, Teebi heard the words, "You'll suffer, man, but you won't die by my hand. A pity, that, for I'd enjoy seeing this to your last moment of life. But it's the stake for you, and a dismemberment more merciful than the slow stuff I have for you."

Teebi could see nothing anymore. He could only hear laughter.

\*     \*     \*

"It's near time," said Dee, pulling her girdle tight. She wore the robe which was her finest, hawks embroidered grey on grey. Her swords and their scabbards had been polished. The bristles of red hair were brushed flat atop her head. Erin wore the light blue robe Dee had given her, and the fisher's diamond-patterned girdle which looked almost as fine as the day Orline gave it to her, now that it was clean. Dee grabbed a slender rope from a chest of many. Erin was startled to see the rope was made of fine metal wires, woven as hemp would be. It was as supple as any common rope, but stronger, and on its end was a many-spiked ball of iron. Hanging it on the opposite side away from her swords, Dee said, "Do we look good? We should look good."

"Because we might die?" said Erin, not seeming to care if that were the case.

"Hells no! Because we'll be magnificent! We have to look the part."

"You look handsome enough," said Erin.

"And you. Good. Let's go."

It was the hour of dusk. The streets were abandoned for the night. All was strangely silent. As warriors did not quest for sacrifices in the rich merchants' quarter, Dee and Erin strode unmolested for several blocks of their journey. They came soon to the business district, where doors were bolted and lanterns doused. Here, a few warriors hunted the garbage bins and dark corners for vagrants. "Walk bold," said Dee. "They'll think we're doing what they're doing."

One of Shom Bru's two-swords whooped on finding a beggar cowering in a stairwell. "Got one!" he exclaimed gleefully. The beggar shot out of the stairwell like a rabbit. "Get him!" shouted the two-sword at Dee and Erin, but the women let the wretch escape into a black alley. Shom Bru's man looked perturbed and started to ask, "Why didn't you . . . " then realized the women were dressed too well for this kind of duty, and their girdles lacked the insignia of Terwold's army. By then it was too late. Dee the Rope cleaved his head open, cleaned the blade on the man's shirt before he had fallen over, and sheathed the *mai* when the corpse lay on the ground.

"Easy as that," said Erin, mildly surprised.

"Next one's yours," said Dee, striding off toward the low district where Shom Bru's warriors would be doing their best hunting. She hadn't gone twenty paces when suddenly she whirled, *mai* to hand, and used the flat of her sword to avert a dagger aimed at her back.

Erin drew her *mai* in kind, crouched, looked left and right at shadowed places. Dee the Rope whirled once more, to the sound of a dagger slicing through the air. Her sword knocked it away, but she could not turn fast enough to stop a third dagger from yet another direction. The short blade struck her high upon the shoulder, barely missing the big vein in her neck.

No one was visible. Erin said, "We're surrounded by assassins."

"*I'm* surrounded," Dee amended. "There aren't any knives coming your direction!" She reached over her shoulder and pulled the dagger out, a gush of blood darkening the grey of her fine robe. "Damn," she said. "I wanted to look my best." The wound clotted quickly. Dee's fat provided a protection of sorts, closing around such narrow wounds. "I'm all right," she said to Erin.

Erin put her back to Dee's so that no more knives could get the obese warrior from behind. Dee blocked another dagger. Erin felt helpless. She was not the target and could provide only a shield.

"Come out!" Erin shouted. "Fight me too!"

No more daggers were being thrown. From an alley on the left, a well-dressed child stepped into the dim light of dusk. To the right, a slender girl, equally well clad, stepped from between boxes of rubbish. A third youngster dropped from an awning, the underside of which had provided his hiding place.

All three bore additional throwing-knives.

"There's more of them than three," Dee whispered to Erin at her back. "I hear they attack in sevens, for luck. Probably only these three will show themselves."

"What do you want?" Erin called to the boy who had dropped from the awning.

He replied, "Our council says Dee the Rope will die for the murder of one of our guild's members."

"An error!" Dee lied. "I've never killed a child in my life, and would never think of harming one of the boat-guard guild!"

The slender girl said, "The boy was my cousin. He wasn't dead when you left him. He lived long enough to say you struck him down in order to steal a sword."

"Mistaken identity!" Dee insisted, holding her *mai* up in case it was necessary to ward off more daggers.

Erin said, "We've a mission of urgency tonight. Can your justice wait?"

"Justice!" grumbled Dee. "I confess to nothing!"

"Can you wait?" Erin repeated.

"We cannot," said the girl.

"Then you are my enemies, too," said Erin. "Your justice would cost many lives. Your guilt would exceed that of Dee the Rope."

Other children, hiding in the shadows, exchanged furtive whispers. The three who showed themselves listened for a moment. The boy beneath the awning asked, "How long to complete your mission?"

"Until the bug-folks march at least," said Erin. "By then, we will have succeeded or failed."

More whispering went through the shadowed places, echoing weirdly from the walls all around. At length the slender girl said, "We will wait until darkness is fully met."

The children withdrew into dark alleys. In a moment, it seemed they must be gone. Dee said,

"Some help you are! You as much as said I was guilty!"

Erin said, "You are. You killed the boy to get this." She held up the bared *mai*, then sheathed it.

"The circumstances!"

"The circumstances were that you were paid to do something quickly, and a child stood in your path. You're not my friend, nor Teebi's; but I'm not prepared to do this thing alone. So we will fight as comrades tonight. Afterward, you'll have to abandon your employer and flee Terwold, or risk the knives of every child upon the streets."

"It seems you do not trust me," Dee reflected. "I suppose there is no reason why you should."

Erin did not reply to that. She said only, "Please. Lead on."

\*      \*      \*

Fourteen prisoners, political and otherwise, had had their arms bound tight behind their backs, then strung together on a long, thick, hemp rope. Teebi Dan Wellsmith could barely walk, but the prisoners at front and back kept him from falling, pushed and dragged him onward through the gloomy, torchlit halls and to the grey streets of Terwold. Two-swords met the turnkeys and torturers at the prison gates and took charge of the silent prisoners. One of Teebi's swollen eyes opened a speck and he recognized the back alleyways he and thirteen others were being led through. This was the same rarely-used route that he had been told to use if he wished to find his way unseen to the frightful prison. He knew this route would eventually come out in a square of cracked cobbles. Not far from that point there would be a gate leading out of the city.

Teebi tried to see where Valk the Ear was in the line. A soldier kicked Teebi back into place when he broke the single file. His one eye he could see from a bit was cut and bloodied, the other swollen monstrously so that he could not open it at all. He was not able to see enough to figure out if Valk was in front of him or behind him.

There was no pain, miraculously; Teebi's blood rushed so quickly, his breathing came so fast, the adrenaline striving to burst out of his veins . . . the only thing he felt was dizzy. There wasn't much strength in him, despite the adrenaline. In his best form, he would have been hard put to burst the bindings of his wrists; in his present state, it was entirely impossible.

He felt so foolish to allow himself to be led like this, led without a struggle. Yet the two-swords urging the procession onward would not hesitate to cut a tendon to cripple a complainer, leaving him to be dragged on by others. So Teebi shambled on, almost blind, hunched over, barely able to feel that every bone and muscle was twisted or torn, every finger's width of flesh bruised black or brown or yellow. His robe was stained with dark blood from the wound clear through his festering shoulder and from the gushes that periodically issued from his nose and mouth.

He seemed to be pulled along for hours, though it had not been very long. Once he fell and was jerked back to his feet either by a two-sword or the prisoner behind him.

He knew where he was being taken. He knew he was going to die. *Surely there is something I can do*, he thought. Even if he died doing it, some sort of action would be better. Or perhaps his thinking was wrong. Would Valk the Ear struggle? The Healer would not take the lowest villain's life to save his own. Perhaps there was valor in not struggling. This idea tried to settle comfortably, but wouldn't quite. Kill or be killed was a nasty sentiment, certainly; but what about killing to save others? If there were some way, couldn't Teebi Dan Wellsmith burst into a killing frenzy to save other innocent people? Would Valk the Ear forgive him under such a circumstance?

Teebi groaned. It sounded like a groan of pain, but the pain was in his mind, not in his myriad injuries.

Someone pushed him from behind and sent him rolling. He rolled and rolled, for this particular street was on a hillside, and somehow he was no longer bound to the other thirteen prisoners. He lay there, waiting to be snatched from the cobbles and tied back in line. No one grabbed him. Instead, he heard scuffling, the clash of steel. On craning his neck, he saw faintly that Erin of Thar was fighting with one of the two-swords in charge of the prisoners. She had cut the rope so that prisoners were scattering like beads off a broken necklace. *I should help*, thought Teebi, but his body wouldn't move. He craned his neck further, trying to see Valk the Ear. He saw the white-clad Healer being led away by three warriors, down the street which would lead to the gate leaving the city. *No*, screamed Teebi's mind. He couldn't speak. He couldn't shout for Erin to hurry, save the Healer, forget the others!

Then the hulking presence of Dee the Rope was over him. She was looking him in the face. She said, "You're a sorry sight, man. We came to save your ass, but there's nothing much to save. If you want to be put from your misery, there's enough left between us that I'm happy to oblige." Dee raised her *mai* and, shaking her head sadly, prepared to kill Teebi, who for all appearances was beyond any other kind of help. As her sword descended, Erin of Thar made a tremendous leap and struck Dee's *mai* aside.

"What the Hells are you trying to do!" Erin screamed angrily. The prisoners had fled. The two-swords lay writhing on the cobbles, dying. Erin knelt at Teebi's side and lifted his head, looking at his beaten, swollen face. She said, "Praise Durga's tits, you're living."

He tried to talk, but only spat blood.

"He won't live long," said Dee. "Best to kill him outright."

"The Healer," said Erin. "Did he get away? I only saw him for a moment. We've got to find him for Teebi."

Dee didn't say anything.

"Did you see him?" asked Erin. Dee nodded. "Well, which direction?"

Dee pointed down the street which led eventually to the gate. "Soldiers took him," she said.

Erin tried to lift Teebi, but the man was too big. "Help me," said Erin pitifully, but Dee only watched.

Teebi's bent hand raised and tangled itself in Erin's hair. He pulled her head down, and she didn't fight him. When her ear was close to his face, he whispered hoarsely, "Don't . . . trust . . . Dee."

"What's he saying?" asked Dee the Rope, moving closer, her *mai* still drawn: Teebi rasped close to Erin's ear,

"She . . . showed . . . way in. Said . . . she was once . . . inside. I heard . . . torturers say . . . she was best . . . she was one of them before. She was . . . never . . . prisoner."

Erin pulled Teebi's fingers out of her hair. She let his head down easily, then stood, faced Dee, said, "Teebi tells me you helped him find his way into the prison. You told me you didn't know anything about it until afterward."

"He's injured," said Dee. "He's delirious."

"You tried to kill him a minute ago so that he couldn't talk. Why did you lead me on this fiasco-mission if you wanted him dead? Why not let him go to the stake?"

"I was . . ."

"I know. You were paid. Paid to lead me around by the nose. Why?"

"I don't ask questions," said Dee, backing away. "I think I'm a better swordswoman than you, Erin, so I don't fear your anger. But I can't fight with you. My employer wanted you dragged up from the depths to which you had let yourself fall. I didn't like risking Teebi's life for it, but as I told you, once I've accepted payment, I can't shift sides. Not even a little."

"You . . ." Erin strode forward, shoulders square, *mai* pointing in the direction of Dee's throat. Dee, in response, sheathed her own *mai*, saying,

"I'm not to kill you."

She removed the steel rope from her hip and began to trace a wide circle about herself. The iron mace whirred around and around, passing within a hand's width of Erin's face. With Erin at bay, Dee bartered,

"You need Valk the Ear to save Teebi's life. You need me to help."

Erin would not be fooled. "The only warriors killed just now, I killed. You made a good show, but allowed Valk the Ear to be taken away to the stake. You deny it? You're a professional rouser. If Valk the Ear were martyred, would that rouse people to action? If he lives to spread his notions of pacifism, would that go against your master's intentions? Merchants alone gain from war."

As the mace-ended steel rope passed by again, Erin raised her *mai* into its path. The rope wrapped around the blade and Erin pulled as though attempting to draw a whale from the ocean. She said, "Now I am a fisher of villains."

Dee could not be budged. She was too much heavier for Erin to win any game of tug-of-war.

Dusk was done. The moonless dark had begun, with Valk the Ear by now staked, and the insects marching. Erin felt her anger welling, but was not certain she could defeat Dee.

Then at the top of her vision Erin saw a child crouching on the roof of a leaning porch. Dee's keen senses felt the presence at the same moment. She dropped the steal rope and whirled, *mai* sliding from its scabbard. She successfully deflected the child's razor-sharp dagger, but now Erin was at her back. Dee moved sideways, turned, struck Erin's sword aside. Another dagger was flung at her from darkness and struck the base of her neck. Her nape's fat kept her from bleeding profusely. Erin kept her too busy to deflect smaller weapons. Yet another dagger struck her, this one near the thigh, through the eye of an embroidered hawk.

"You'll die," said Erin.

Dee leapt away from Erin's slash. She bowed to snatch the end of her steel rope from the cobbles, instantly tangling Erin's legs in it. She boasted,

"Dee the Rope can only die rich and old!" Her *mai* swung up, deflecting a dagger. She pulled a previous dagger out of her thigh and threw it toward the roof of a porch. It took the boy there in the stomach. Erin had untangled herself from the rope, only to see Dee whip the iron mace across the street and strike someone in the alley. It was the slender girl who staggered out into starlight. She fell with forehead crushed. A half-dozen daggers came from every direction at once, two of which she batted aside, four of which pierced her in various places, including major arteries. She couldn't last much longer.

Erin approached more carefully. She knew that Dee was fighting for her life, not for her employer. The next time that iron mace shot out, it might be Erin's forehead crushed.

"I relent!" screamed Dee, deflecting still another dagger from its course. "I relent!" she screamed again, this being a warrior's plea for mercy. She wrapped one end of her steel rope around her own neck and began to whirl the iron mace madly. She screamed one last time, "I relent!" and gave the mace a terrific toss upward. Erin heard the sound of the bones in Dee's neck separating.

Children stepped out from every corner, drawing closer to the place where Dee collapsed. They began to collect their daggers, and took Dee's two swords as well. Two pairs of children carried off the ones Dee had killed. The two-swords previously killed by Erin were ignored. A boy tried to come closer to Erin, but she withdrew as from a hideous demon. Several paces away, he said,

"Teebi Dan Wellsmith was once a member of our guild, when he was a child of the piers like us. Perhaps he undertook missions like our own at one time or another. Be that as it may, we are still charged with protecting his boat, which responsibility we view seriously. We are prepared to take him back to his boat. Someone has already gone for a cart. He is dying, it is obvious. You, if you so desire, and are so capable, can save Valk the Ear so that he might heal Wellsmith. Otherwise, we will care for him gently in his last hours."

Erin tried to sound composed. "I will bring Valk to the piers."

"No. It won't be safe in the city. One of us will take Wellsmith and his boat out of the city by the channel gate, before trouble erupts. The channel runs away from the paths of the bug-folks, so there should be minimal danger. If Valk the Ear comes to save our ward, we are willing to help the Healer escape his enemies in Terwold."

A cart was being wheeled along the cobbles. Erin could not see it in the dark, but heard its wooden wheels clattering on the street. Erin said, "What of Dee's corpse?"

"The *rint* can have it on the dawn. We will take her swords and her girdle, so that no one will know she was a warrior. That is our final revenge."

Erin overcame her dread of these child-avengers and returned to Teebi's side. She helped load him onto the cart the children brought. She said to him, "Don't die, Teebi. You'll live to see me be a hero yet. Can you promise me?"

Teebi bubbled red froth and managed a hideous smile, which Erin took to be his promise.

*     *     *

A sense of personal power and importance coursed through Erin's veins as she rushed along a street which opened into a courtyard of cracked pavement. There she stopped to regain her bearings in the darkness. Seeing the way, she went headlong, trembling. She did not shake from fear, but from expectation. Just as Dee the Rope had longed for wealth, Erin longed for a hero's recognition; everyone had their petty greeds, of one kind or another. The fact that Erin had been incapable of useful heroism had driven her to the pits of the low districts and emotional collapse. Something had snatched her from that despair . . . something like a rope, but stouter: she owed her recovery to Dee the Rope, whom Erin had repaid in a righteous pique—repaid with death. Erin stumbled, but only a little. *It was just*, she told herself, *and Dee took her own life.* Justifying herself thus, Erin was able to hold her course, and came to a halt only when the gateway was visible.

Great bronze and iron doors were being sealed, the last of the warriors having returned to the safety of Terwold. For a moment, Erin saw beyond the gate to where a row of struggling blighters were bound to stakes. Then the view was blocked by the huge doors.

Erin charged. She screamed maniaçally, causing the single-sword guards to back away, and the two-swords to pause and take measure. She'd killed three in a trice before they realized it was only one swordswoman, not a whole horde of demons. Her *mai*'s edge took the throat of a man moving a bolt across the double-doors. When he fell, Erin pushed her weight against the doors, and one began to pivot open. She stood in the gateway battling four at once. Outnumbered, she was forced back, over a flat bridge which crossed the pits before the gate. At least they could not get behind her. One of her opponents leapt back from her sword's thrust, only to slip into the pits, his scream cut short when he struck the spiked ground with a sickening *gunch.*

The others withdrew into the city once more, attempting to pull the open half of the gate closed. Erin leapt forward again, showing them the folly of their ploy, for the game of open-and-close could go on without end, and they were forced to fight her at any cost. She was mad to push them thus; mad to think she could battle all at once. But often madness wins over rationality, as witnessed the two-sword who fell upon the bridge, his gut sliced by Erin's *mai.*

She took the *mai* one-handed so that she could draw the *i* with her left. Her teeth shone in the dark, not evidence of fear, but enjoyment. She shouted in a guttural dialect, taken from the pariah class she had lived among: "Come for more, my fellows!" They came. She killed two at once, one of them slipping from the bridge.

Behind her she heard the wet clicking of insect mandibles and the crack and clatter of their exo-skeletons. The march was coming! The warriors at the gate were dragging their dead back into the city, those which had not fallen from the bridge. They tried once more to seal the gate against Erin, and against the insect-folk. She let them. She turned and fled up the hillside, seeing the jerky postures of the insects silhouetted against star-light. She had to save at least one of the prisoners: Valk the Ear.

The furthest staked prisoner was already being dismembered. Erin approached from the opposite end of the row of sacrifices, cutting ropes as she ran toward the grotesque insects.

Most of the intended victims were too weak from torture and ill care to flee. They merely col-lapsed at the base of the stakes, awaiting dismem-berment.

"Run you bloody bastards!" she screamed, and a few stumbled away toward Terwold. Archers were on the wall. Who fled toward the imagined protection of the city found feathers in their feet and knees. The sacrifices collapsed and insects came in threes to collect their due.

Erin felt her heroism already dinted, already proven useless. The insects swarmed around, but did not approach Erin, whose diamond pendant raised a dim aura about her body. She charged one bug, swept its head off its shoulders with one stroke, but it continued carving apart its victim with its sickles and meat-knives. Cursing wildly, Erin hurried to the white-clad man whose head hung down, whose hair covered his face. "You at least will run!" she demanded, cutting him loose. He fell as had the others, head upon his knees.

Erin grabbed his hair and jerked his face up to command him angrily, but the face made her gasp instead,

"Válkyová!"

He muttered something she could not understand. His eyes were white with fear.

"You're speaking Czech!" she shouted above the clack and din of insects and their victims. She slapped Válkyová to try to get some sense out of him, but he only said,

"Not Czech. English. Have you forgotten?" He pulled himself into a ball, refusing to budge or to say more in the desert dialect of Durga's Lathe.

The sight of Válkyová brought Erin's memories flooding back, the memories of Earth she had tucked away. But of English she remembered only a few words, and had no grammatical context for them. It had all been erased. She recalled the voyage through limbo, the invasions of her mind . . . something or someone had impressed upon her the key languages of Durga's Lathe and surrounding countries, and lent her to understand the variant dialects. Simultaneously—by accident or design—her own native tongue had been eradicated. Hadn't the same thing happened to Válkyová in the transferal between worlds? Why did he speak the desert tongue with his European accent intact?

Insects gathered around to peer menacingly at the white-clad man bathed in the light of Erin's aura. Válkyová shrank further into himself. He refused to stand, refused to look at anything (including Erin), refused to acknowledge the final screams of the last dismembered victims. Arms and legs and divided torsos were being hauled away by trios of anthropoid insect-creatures. Erin had seen it before; Válkyová clearly had only heard about it, and never imagined the fullness of the horror. He seemed visibly smaller, withdrawing psychically from the unthinkable carnage.

"Snap out of it!" she shouted, pulling him up one-handed and pressing him against the pole. She took the diamond pendant between her fingers and held it outward, causing the insects to draw further away. "We're safe from them!" she yelled at Válkyová, as though he were deaf, as indeed he seemed to be. She explained, "They won't come near this needle-sized sword." She put her shoulder to his stomach and let him fold over her back, then she stood. Válkyová was of slight build and Erin was more than strong enough to carry him, but it was a nuisance all the same. With the shining pendant held before, she moved down the hillside, the insects parting from the eerie light of the tiny, glassy weapon. Válkyová clung to her like an infant ape, shaking, afraid. She said, "Don't look at them. Think of something else." He blathered in Czech or English—Erin could not tell which, knowing only that it was no tongue of Endsworld—his terror not easing one iota.

Arrows were unleashed from the crenels of Terwold's walls, but Erin and Válkyová were beyond range. She moved sidelong, far from the walls, in the general direction of River Yole and its numerous little tributaries, canals, and channels. She continued to speak to Válkyová, trying to calm his unrelinquished fear:

"There's a boat waiting for us. It's away from the insects' paths, and Shom Bru's men won't pursue us until the insect-march is done." She wasn't really sure of that assumption, but it sounded like a good bet. She said, "You're saved, Val. I saved your bloody skin."

Through all, her burden whimpered.

\*     \*     \*

A child poled the boat through the shallows near the bank of the River Yole. Stars were bright overhead, glinting between overhanging branches. Erin sat in the bottom of the boat near Teebi, watching and helping Válkyová Idaska put to good use the skills he had learned as a medical student and used as an emergency medic. A clay pot of burning charcoal warmed an iron pan of water, in which string, needles, and sponges were boiling. Against the coals themselves, Idaska had placed a brand. After cleaning Teebi's wounds with fanatical fervor, Válkyová proceeded to cauterize or stitch the worst of Teebi's rents, while Erin held the fevered man still. Once, Teebi half-regained consciousness and tried to slap away the hand which caused him pain, but saw the face of Válkyová above him, and went limp and submissive. "Poor man," Val whispered. "You took all this for me . . ."

"Will he be all right?" Erin asked, fretful.

"We'll have to cool him off," Válkyová said, not answering Erin's query. Erin found rags which she wetted off the side of the boat, and used them to soothe and cool Teebi's flesh. Válkyová said, "If he shakes with chill, we'll have to cover him with something dry; otherwise, his wounds and his hot skin can use some cold air. If the fever doesn't kill him tonight, and we can keep infection from those wounds, he'll heal in two weeks or less."

"That quickly?"

"It's a conservative estimate, Erin. If I had antibiotics, I'd have him on his feet in three days."

"But that shoulder . . ."

"A clean wound all the way through. You'll be surprised."

For the first time since they reached the boat, Erin breathed relief. She took Válkyová's hand for the quickest moment, looked him in the eyes, and said, "Thanks, Val. Thanks." He looked away, embarrassed. He still felt ashamed of his panic when the bugs appeared; he was in no frame of mind to believe he merited thanks. He said,

"I nearly got both of us killed."

"It was interesting," said Erin, half kiddingly. "You babbled all kinds of nonsense while I was carrying you along the river. I kept trying to get you to use the desert dialect you speak, so that I could understand you. You wouldn't."

Válkyová grinned despite himself. "If I remembered what I was saying, I'd tell you. Probably calling for my grandma if I was speaking Czech. Someone else if it was English. Very strange you can't tell the difference."

"It's strange to me you can still speak Earth tongues! You came to Endsworld the same way I did; it should have affected you the same."

Valkyová shook his head, puzzled, unable to offer a theory. Erin continued,

"I was taught to understand the languages of Durga's Lathe. Someone or something entered my mind to do it, and the first person I met—a blind priest—I could talk to him fine. Whatever did that for me, or to me, managed to interfere with my ability to speak English. Not that it'd be much use here anyway."

"I was less lucky," said Válkyová. "I was dropped in a desert, not a stitch of clothing, and nearly cooked to death before someone found me. I couldn't understand them at all, nor they me. Later I learned they thought me an angel who'd slipped from one of the twenty heavens. To them, my Czech and English were divine tongues. I figured out their speech fast enough, by listening constantly, and became known as Valk the Ear as a result. I used my medical training to help the desert tribes, thinking thereby to earn my keep, and they began to call me Healer."

"You did more than that," said Erin, antipathy at the edge of her tone. "You played Jesus Christ with them."

Val looked away into the darkness, then at the boy poling the boat along the river. "I think Ghandi is a better comparison myself—but I didn't start out like an egomaniac with a messiah complex, truly. I had no idea healing was a holy occupation to these people. They cast the role on me. All the while, the violence I observed was getting more and more upsetting to me. My grandmother used to tell of such brutality, but I never understood . . . until I'd consumed myself attempting to patch up boys who'd gone fighting with people of other tribes, sweated with primitive medicines and inadequate tools, only to see them, as soon as their scars heal, run out to get themselves completely killed. I finally broke. I started telling them what I thought of it, and I wasn't pleasant about it. I was certain they'd cast me out for being disagreeable and challenging their way of life . . . but they liked to hear me rant. They'd honestly never thought of things like peaceful cohabitation with ones brothers and sisters, all that rot. Peace seemed an alien concept to them. Pacifism stranger still. I laid a little Moses on them. A little Barbara Demming. They were interested and I began to believe I could get through to them, so attentive were they, so curious to learn these things."

"But you didn't change a thing," said Erin, comprehending, remembering her own failures of a different sort.

"It only gives them another thing to fight each other about. The more I begged and demanded and cajoled and threatened, the worse things got, the more violent. The ones who followed me most devotedly—all dead. Shom Bru's warriors found our camp and I saw . . . I saw men and women devoted to a cause . . . shit, all I made was a passel of martyrs, and that's sick, too, you know? It's the same as those swords of yours! It invites violence, praises death." Válkyová had more to say, but could only cover his face, and weep for the folly of his ways and humankind's. Erin felt an unexpected pity for the man, but no greater than that which he felt for himself. She said,

"I think you don't belong here, Val. You weren't given the language because this thing you brought me, this jewel, was primed for me alone. Somehow I dragged you through the portal the jewel carved. I apologize for it."

"No," said Válkyová Idaska, looking up, his eyes suddenly melancholy. "It was I who wouldn't let go of you. I couldn't let you come here without me."

"And now you regret it, eh?"

"Until now, yes," he said. "But only because it was without you." He looked at Erin with big, earnest eyes, which made Erin cuss quietly. He said, "You're brave, Erin."

"Shit."

"It's true. You are."

"Listen, you're a pitiful wretch who doesn't fit in this world. You can't change it by preaching, and it can't change you. I'm not even sure I belong here, but I seem to be getting the hang of it a little. Anyway, I've seen the man with sand-colored eyes, the one who gave you this little necklace I wear. It was him, or his Endsworld twin at least. I think he has the power to send you back. He as much as threatened to do it to me."

"It would be good to go back," he said, looking far away. "I strove hard for my American citizenship. This world is too cruel for me."

The boat came to a slow halt, abrading the silty river bottom. "Shhh," hushed the boy with the pole. He pointed out into the center of Yole. A boat was anchored there, no light showing from it.

"What?" asked Erin, to which the boy repeated, "Shhh."

He crept over the boat bottom on all fours and came where Erin and Válkyová sat near sleeping Teebi. The boy whispered in the lowest possible monotone,

"There lies a ship without a brand on deck, without a sound on top or within. I'll tell you what they're doing: they're listening. The whole crew is likely sitting with their ears pressed to the timbers. They may have heard us coming, for I saw it not in time."

Erin glowered at the silent, black ship, then whispered to the boy, "How could it be before us? It couldn't have navigated the river's deep center by night, and it couldn't have gotten ahead of us without our knowing it . . ."

"It's a river-guard," the boy explained. "It's been here all along. But not silent like that. Runners must have come to it in a beeline, whereas we poled slowly 'round winding Yole. They know about us, all right. In fact, look:" The boy pointed to the further bank. There, a palanquin sat near the water's edge. "Not just runners, but palanquin bearers. That means they brought a three-sword."

"They want me that badly?" asked Válkyová, his voice too loud, so that the boy said once more, "Shhh."

"Or me," whispered Erin. "We're both of us notorious by now. I've been warned a few times not to face a three-sword, though. Still, it's dark. Perhaps I can resort to the uncouthness of assassins and not confront some master's sword face-on."

Válkyová winced, hearing this. He said, softer this time, "We can run, that's what. If boats guard along our route, we'll have to go overland. To the desert, I say. I've supporters there still."

"I know where I have to go," said Erin. "It must be to Yole's birthplace: the Heathen Hills, and Black Mountain behind them."

A brand was lit on the guard-ship, and a curved mirror held behind it, making a searchlight.

"As I feared," said the boy. "They've heard us."

The light swept the nighted waters, but it would be difficult to see the little boat tucked between overhanging limbs, where the boy had smartly put it. The light passed within a hand's breadth of the hull.

"We can't stay here until dawn," complained Válkyová. "They'll see us then for sure. Overland is our best bet."

"Teebi can't be moved," said Erin. "You go to the desert if you want. You can't tag along with me anyway." To the boy she said, "I'm going to draw them away by going back down the river a ways and making a racket. You get Teebi and Val to safety; yourself as well. I'll be all right."

"You won't!" said Válkyová, and the searchlight swept back their direction. Erin made a forward open-handed stroke at Válkyová's diaphragm. He collapsed with the quickest "oof."

"He'll be an abysmal pest," Erin warned the boy. "First group of desert tribespeople you see, dump him on them. He'll only be unconscious for a few minutes. By then, you'll have to be well out of here."

"There's a maze of tributaries a little further down-river," said the boy, and Erin nodded. She climbed up into an overhanging branch and went quickly to the bank. Running along the path, only the darkness kept her from being in plain sight. Several hundred paces away from Teebi's boat, Erin began throwing largish rocks into the Yole. The searchlight was immediately aimed at the spot, revealing naught but circles of ripples.

She scurried another hundred paces and threw

more rocks. She heard a small boat being lowered by means of creaking pulleys and ropes. A second torch was lit on the prow of the tiny sloop. A mirror was held behind that one, too. Erin led the sloop on a goose-chase away from the guard-ship, away from Teebi's boat, giving the clever boy thereon ample opportunity for escape. She couldn't see Teebi's boat going, but neither would anybody else.

A suspension bridge drew Erin's attention. She climbed a particularly high bank to reach it, then began to run across at top speed. The bridge swayed as she went. Both searchlights found her at the midway point, and an arrow was unleashed from the sloop. Erin fell flat to avoid it, then stood and ran the rest of the way to the opposite bank. There, she slid down to the riverside, looking silly as she went bumping on her rump, but hardly caring about that. She ran back toward the place where the guard-ship was anchored, and both searchlights followed. An arrow struck a tree bank. She could barely see him in the darkness, behind the palanquin, thinking it would provide cover, but she had guessed wrong. The palanquin bearers had been hiding inside it. They leapt out at her with single swords drawn. Erin's short *i* cut left and cut right, killing her big but unskilled opponents. Erin panted.

The sloop had come aground a hundred paces behind her, and a three-sword stepped onto the bank. She could barely see him in the darkness with spotlights in her eyes, yet she could tell with what self-confidence he strode. She had a sudden vision of herself stooping beside the palanquin, and thought she must look as though she were cowering with fright. Perhaps she was doing just that. Peeved by the thought and the image, she stood upright in the light, troubling herself to look as bold and proud as the three-sword.

"Merilia!" crowed the three-sword, drawing the long, exquisite *oude* from across his shoulder. "I killed you once, I will kill you once again!"

It was Shom Bru himself! Erin stepped backward, *i* to hand. She drew the *mai* as well, and bit her lip. Now she could see him better as he approached, all dressed in silken red, a regal color on Endsworld. She had never seen him before, and yet recognized him as the man she had seen in dreams, old dreams while she was still of Earth. She recognized him also as a grander, more remarkable version of a mere kendo opponent lying dead at her feet. Erin crowed back,

"No. It was I killed you. Have you never dreamed it the other way?"

Shom Bru held back, for indeed, as Erin knew, he had dreamed of Jerry Mason the same way Erin Wyler had dreamed of Merilia. She had dreamed herself mighty, and he had dreamed himself weak. Her words struck close to his deepest insecurity— that he was that other fellow after all, and not a mighty warlord and king. Erin surmised these things, but what else could be the truth? What else did this warlord think when he had such visions, in which he was a pale shadow of his Endsworld self, only a chubby young man with strange obsessions that kept him outcast? And if the dreams of Jerry Mason had lately not recurred, wasn't that only because Shom Bru dreamed the death of his other self—and been puzzled by it, and relieved by it, and afraid, all at once? Understanding herself, Erin began to understand her nemesis. She shouted,

"It was foolish of you to face this emergency personally. Another three-sword could have been sent, while you sat safely in your tower. Was it not you sent retainers in your stead, to a certain ocean shore at a certain hour of a certain day and month, questing, perhaps, for the stolen corpse of Merilia, where star-gazers said she would be found with life restored? Your retainers reported footprints leading to the sea, saying that if Merilia lived anew, it had been only long enough to throw herself into the sea to drown!''

''How do you know these things?'' Shom Bru growled, for indeed the retainers had been sent upon a ship, but no one else had known.

''I know it because no one fears me more than Shom Bru. I know it because so many prophets have read it in our stars, yours and mine, and augured it in the holes of their cheeses, in their cards, in the leaves of teas, and along the far-off roads of *penm*-induced trances. Only Shom Bru could command a ship to search that lonely shore; only he would have so invested an interest. I fooled your men that day, for I had not walked into the sea, but away from it backward. You could not, and cannot rest until you have seen my body burned, stirred the ashes yourself, to be sure I never rise again from ocean or from hill. Fear resides inside you, fear of the prophecy and dream that I can cut you to the spine. The dream was true! It was *I* who killed *you*. It shall be done again!''

Shom Bru's way had always been to face his fears, and he was accustomed to seeing those fears dissipate before his might. That Erin did not dissipate was confounding, but her boldness did not increase his fears one whit. Rather, each threat and true-enough speculation on her part infuriated him. He rushed toward the palanquin without another hesitation. Erin caught the downward slash of his *oude* in the crook of crossed *mai* and *i*. Shom Bru twisted deftly, powerfully, and Erin went flying over the top of the palanquin and into the cold waters of the Yole.

She did not come up. Shom Bru went to the water's edge, peering down. He motioned with his hand, and archers on ship and sloop loosed arrows, striking the whole surface with an intense barrage. Shom Bru let his longest sheath slip from his shoulder to his hand, then replaced the *oude* therein. He cursed undramatically. But his fears were lessened, had dissipated after all. For he knew now that this could not have been Merilia. That she had stopped his attack was impressive, but hardly genius. She was not the master of swords that her look-alike had been, and everything she said and everything she appeared to be was, after all, only a trick. She was no threat to Shom Bru, no threat to his government. Eventually, she would die.

VI·DISCIPLE

# VI. DISCIPLE

The last coals of Erin's fire were dying down.
She lay uneasily, wrapped in her robe. Even sleeping, she sensed the dark and stony faces of Black
Mountain, visages carved by aeons of wind and
rain. A breeze played over the round, hollow
mouth of one such strange visage, causing the
beastly face to whistle a sardonic note.

It had taken three days to reach the multi-
peaked Black Mountain. The moon had become
the Sky God's Boat, silvering the country in its
wake. The black and eerie faces of the cliffs, peaks
and escarpments were given highlights by that
young moon; and as the night progressed, the
moonshadows changed, so that each visage's
expression went from hateful ugliness to grinning
malevolence and then again to vacant stupidity.

Such monsters watched the woman sleep.

No tree or bush survived in the stony crags, for
Black Mountain seemed blasted by extraordinary
heat, enough to leave it glazed and glassy, with
barely enough soil to support an occasional brown
or grey lichen. At least that was the case with the
western approach Erin had used. Perhaps the
morning side of the mountain would prove less
severe.

The sleeper shivered in her robe, although it
kept her warm.

The moon passed along the sky, vanishing behind one peak, reappearing, then vanishing behind another. Of the seven summits of Black Mountain, it passed four of them, before descending completely from view. The stars shone with shocking brightness at this altitude, so that darkness was not so pervasive; yet what visions the stars kept unveiled were none to lend security to a camping mountaineer.

Throughout her uneasy slumber, Erin kept an unusual awareness of all this, as though she stood outside herself watching over her own body. If she dreamed this awareness only, then she was helpless after all; but it seemed that, should danger approach, she would sense it, even see it, and quickly wake herself.

A shadow came loose from the darkness when the last ember of Erin's campfire winked out. Silver starshine glinted *through* this apparition, which stood over Erin in a threatening posture, the dark shadow of a sword held in its hand. Instantly Erin was upon her feet, for it was true, as she suspected, that she would awaken herself at the first signal of danger. But there was no one about, least of all the anthropoid shadow that had hunkered near her. Had she imagined, or dreamed, the uninvited guest?

She remained crouched, shortsword to hand.

"Come out!" she commanded, gesturing with her *i*. Before her voice had finished echoing off stone monuments, the apparition stepped partly into view. It was a patch of darkness in the star-shadows between two narrow points of rock. For a split second, eyes glinted redly, and Erin launched herself murderously at those eyes.

There was nothing there. There was no sound of the monster fleeing.

"Stand and fight me!" Erin commanded. "Mine is a charmed sword! It fights even ghosts!"

This was a lie, and the phantom likely knew it.
She heard it make a soft, horrible sound—laughter, no doubt—and she charged toward that
sound. *I can't really fight a ghost*, thought Erin,
but sought the encounter nonetheless. It occurred
to her that she was not fully in possession of herself—that, like a sleepwalker, she pursued some
course of subconscious logic which, on waking,
would make no sense at all. It was a problem she'd
had as a youth; and she remembered the childhood
experience of awakening underneath the kitchen
table, where she had piled slices of bread in a pattern meaningful to her sleeping state but senseless
on wakeful examination. Her mother had spoken
of seeing Erin partake of other midnight sorties,
from which Erin rarely did properly awake;
rather, she would usually return to her bed, never
to recall those pointless adventures. She was sent
to psychologists about the problem, but her
parents were told not to worry about it overmuch,
that the child should be left to wake herself. *I
must wake myself*, a grown Erin remembered, but
she pursued the phantom instead.

Her *i* remained drawn, the longer *mai* sheathed
near to hand, in case it were needed too. There
were so many natural monuments that a foe might
leap at any time from atop or from behind any of
them. Erin was alert.

Not once was there a clear, honest view of the
wraith. Yet, not once did it lose her altogether.
She was being led! Perhaps it even held some control of her, investing her with this desire to
pursue. Even suspecting this, she could not give
up the chase. Why this was so, she was uncertain;
but it always came back to the same feeling: a
dream. In a dream, the mind can think one thing
while the self does something else.

Since regaining her memories of Earth, she was
more than ever inclined to doubt the reality of

Endsworld *or* Earth. This being so, reality being
nothing, there was no need of fear, no need to
fight the ghost's compulsion. As in a dream, she
followed over a dark, steep, lifeless terrain, quick
as a leopard after easy game. But the game was
not easy and, indeed, it seemed to delight in being
hunted. A low, batwing sort of sound resounded
from the throat of the phantom.

There was a flat mesa above, visible where the
starry canopy ended. The chase would end there,
for the labyrinth of boulders, monuments, and
gulleys would give way to a plain on which the
specter could neither wend nor hide. Erin
welcomed whatever she would meet! Stupid and
senseless as it might be, she welcomed it. The
chase roused her blood. Her lust was for a battle!
She could hear her own heartbeat in her temples,
and the steadiness of it gave her a sense of order
and correctness, so that she did not doubt her
occupation. The thin air of the mountainous
heights lent to her exhilaration. Though it might
be that this bloodlust and feeling of power was
thrust upon her by the ghost or else her own
somnambulistic state, she could not stop; the feeling was that of an excellent vintage wine which
was too grand to throw away, drunkenness not-
withstanding.

The ground was hard as the concrete of San
Francisco streets, and as steeply graded. The comparison was like a knife thrust into her consciousness. The elder dream of Earth impinged upon this
current place: dreams within dreams and nightmares within nightmares. The monumental stones
to her left and right had turned into skyscrapers;
the hard paths through gulleys were streets and
avenues.

Erin ran crazed up the San Francisco-covered
hillsides. There was no car in sight. Neither
vagrant nor police officer populated the nighted

city. There was not a single light in any of the massive buildings. Earth was dead! *I've lost control of the dream*, Erin thought wildly. The vaguely evil, almost happy sound of batwings laughed at her from the mesa above.

"Wraith!" she cried. "Wait for me and we will fight!"

She climbed the last few meters and came to flat ground. The first rays of dawn glowered between the peaks of Black Mountain, striving to achieve the seven summits surrounding the flat mesa. The phantom ran over the terrain but Erin could not make out its shape, for something like a shadowy cape fluttered behind the fiend. As she watched it fleeing, the phantom faded completely from existence—for all phantoms are despairing of light.

Erin looked back the route she came, shocked by the amount of treacherous ground she had covered swiftly and without careful step. The sharp, brilliant stars were fading with the growth of dawn, but the mountain's shadow on the land below seemed darker. Far off over Durga's Lathe, the shadow of Lone Black Mountain came to an end, and was slowly shortening.

The sun peered over the fingery peaks as Erin shook her head as might a stunned lion. She felt as though she had just awakened. Between two peaks, in the direction the wraith had been running when sunlight devoured it, Erin spied the first greenery since setting foot on Black Mountain. From her vantage-point, the place ahead appeared as a microcosmic paradise sitting in the midst of some scorched, eternal hell.

That the mysterious Teacher lived there, Erin had no doubt.

\* \* \*

Amidst peaks-guarded forest was a garden and in the garden were all the aromatic herbs that one could imagine. There were wide, pebbly paths which wended through this place, and sturdy little bridges over creeks, and a natural shelter beneath a waterfall through which three paths converged and came out the other side as one. Throughout the medicine gardens there were statues of wonderful, wise-looking beasts who were men and women with four legs and cloven hooves, and each had a braided tail. They weren't exactly centaurs, for their bulk was less than that of horses, though slightly more than deer, and the horizontal portion of the back was less than that attributed to Earth's extinct or else fictitious counterparts. The whole of each stone representation was only slightly larger than ordinary humans, not counting that which reached out behind; but they were more imposing than many a gargantuan model could have been, because they seemed more real.

Erin dawdled here and there before certain of the statues, studying them one by one. Some were made of marble, others out of granite, one of glassy obsidian, and others of hard or soft stones she lacked the expertise to name. The features of most were weathered, but this varied, and all retained the apparently inherent handsomeness of the race, beautiful in form, of visage, and proud of posture.

Each statue's hands carried some object. Certain of these Erin could not name, while others were familiar: tablet-and-quill connoting the author, compass and globe indicating the navigator, and so on. None of these statues were placed together, as though each were a solitary being, or as though the artistic renderings were intended to be appreciated without reference to the others.

She observed that some of the statues were less worn than others and, at first, assumed this was due to better protection for some, set as they were amidst ancient, twisting, though sometimes dwarfish pines. But she gasped aloud seeing a certain one, for it seemed newly made. No lichen or bit of moss marred the smooth surface of its tawny stone, and there was not the least wear of time upon it. This particular statue held a halberd in her hand, and a belt of knives had been carved around her waist. A warrior perhaps. Or a guard to something holy. This latter seemed more apropos, for the creature's gorgeous face looked upward as to the twenty heavens, an expression suggesting the absolute moment of enlightenment.

It was difficult to tear her gaze from this remarkable work of art, but she did so, and strode on along the paths, overwhelmed by grand odors, reminded of a different garden—a flowery one, not herbal—wherein Dee the Rope had been a squatter. Old pangs of guilt returned, remembering the fat warrior, to whose suicide Erin had contributed. She tried to rationalize her guilt away, but instead found herself taking on additional guilts, ones which should not be hers. She fancied herself the root and cause of Teebi's being beaten near to death, of Válkyová's miserable homesickness for his adopted United States. It seemed that every crime or misdeed or misfortune or sorrow in the whole of the world could in some way be traced back to Erin, if one gave it enough thought. Certainly she could not evade responsibility for Rud and Orline, her foster parents torn to pieces by bugs, in the great tragedy triggered by Erin's meddling and ignorance.

Caught between her own self-blame and self-pity, and the soothing, almost hypnotic odors of the garden, Erin did not hear the tappa-tapping at first. It was more noticeable away from the waterfall. She stopped finally, turned her head, scanning with her ears. She took a path which led up a rocky stairway. The rocks seemed natural rather than purposely arranged, but that might have been a trick performed by some artful designer; certainly the steps were handy. At the top of these stairs, there was a clear view of a cavern's maw atop yet another flight, this one built of mortar and cut stones grown over with bright moss.

The cavern had not been visible from the bottom of the slope. Possibly it could not be seen from anywhere else but where Erin stood presently. Another angle would find it hidden by firs. On looking back from the landing between stairways, she could see the whole of the medicine gardens, in which the beautiful stone creatures were arranged most pleasingly. This, clearly, was the superb and well-chosen vantage point of whosoever lived within the cave.

Before she had set foot on the first stair of the second and longer set of steps, Erin heard the tapping again, and it was not from the cavern after all. She moved along the horizontal path instead, into another area of the gardens. The tapping varied in intensity and measure as she listened. There were pauses now and then, and an occasional scrape or chink. She moved toward a thicket from whence the sound originated. She was leery, though not frightened, and took her *mai* from its sheath in case some danger waited there.

Silent though she moved, she must have been heard, for the tapping stopped before she could see who made the noise. She found the place and saw that a sculptor had abandoned tools. A great block of yellow stone was beginning to take on the vague outline of another of the four-legged race. Erin bent to the ground where a chisel lay, and found it hot from use. She looked all about the area, but saw nothing, heard nothing beyond the sound of a tiny, tinkling stream.

Carefully, she moved toward a dense area of brush, prodding with her sword as a blind man might do with a stick. When she did this, the thicket erupted. A being reared up on its hind pair of legs, kicking with its front. Erin leapt backward from the giant, who turned out not to be so dreadfully tall when it came back to all fours. It jumped from its hiding place with the grace of a gazelle, and a sword was borne in the hands of its human torso. Erin's *mai* was struck with such strength that it went flinging from her hand, sticking deep into the trunk of a tree.

In an eye-blink she was flat upon her back, a four-legged man above her, his unusually curved *oude* to her throat. "Cursed mortal!" he complained. "You dare to prick my arse! Cannot a fellow retire to his pissing-place without the likes of you interrupting?" The creature rubbed his rear thigh where indeed Erin's *mai* had touched him, its sharp point leaving a rent. As Erin looked at the small wound, it closed itself miraculously. The four-legged man's temper seemed to heal as quickly. He sheathed the *oude* across his back while Erin rolled over onto all fours to humble herself completely.

The creature ignored her apologies and turned his rump to her, starting along the path. Erin got to her feet, brushed herself, and scurried to the tree in which her sword was stuck. Beyond the tree was a noxious smelling trench. Realizing that the sculptor had not hidden from her after all, had probably not heard her coming, she might have laughed at the episode. But she was too confused and shocked for laughter, and annoyed that she could not get her sword out of the tree.

The four-legged man heard her grunting and, looking perturbed, he sauntered back to pull her sword from the trunk. Handing it to her, he asked belligerently, "What is it you seek, pilgrim? Herbs? I've plenty! What have you to trade?"

"I was told by Father Kes," said Erin, "to come to you on this mountain."

"That was some while ago," said the creature coldly, admitting in this way that he knew who she was. He turned away again and moved his girth toward the stairs to his cavern. Erin trailed behind, saying,

"I was delayed!" Then, more honestly: "I feared you meant me harm."

He stopped with each hoof on a different step and looked back over his shoulder. "I meant you severe tests!" he said sharply. "You failed them."

"I've yet to fail the last one," she reminded. "You bound Father Kes to fight me, and I've scant months to prepare for that day. Tardy I may be, yet I have come to the Teacher of Black Mountain as bid. Will he leave me to Kes's hammer, my head bashed in and nostrils stuffed with cotton, proof of no one's skill and everybody's folly?"

The four-legged man stopped at the top of the stairs, looking back to where Erin stood halfway down. She was small before his presence. He echoed with vague petulance,

"*Every*body's folly?"

"Yours too, yes," she said, and was adamant in this. She went up the last steps and stood before the imposing creature, telling him her thinking. "I came from a world called Earth, knowing neither how nor why, and instead of explanation I received challenge—a challenge sent by you. If I fail your tests, it will not be because you were too wise for me or anyone. It will be because you thought to test an infant against the fully grown."

The weathered, handsome face of the beast leaned forward until his eyes were even with Erin's. She beheld sorrow in those eyes as he studied her features, and she studied him. He said,

"A pilgrim passing twixt the peaks of my mountain told me where and when another-world Merilia could be seen. I was never told this Merilia was an infant. Had I known, it is possible I would have been less hasty in binding Kes to the duel."

"Was this pilgrim a man with sand colored eyes?" She knew she had guessed right. "He has many guises. To a woman named Dee the Rope, he was a merchant. To me, he was a *penm*-vendor among pariahs. Who he really is, I hope one day to know. He told me that such as you would not even notice an insignificant fellow like himself existed. Yet he manipulated you as easily as he has done me. He has brought us together for some great scheme that is, perhaps, his own, if not interwoven with the larger schemes arranged by Fates and Destinies. A score of prophets thought they saw the fall of the Bru Dynasty at the hands of strong Merilia, and her death was both shocking and unwelcome to some. The magician with sandy eyes doubtless hopes I am the one actually foreseen."

"Such matters intrigue me minimally," said the four-legged man. "Long and long ago I made a habit of meddling in the affairs of common men, but nothing made them better. I could easily sleep for the length of a dynasty! They mean nothing to me anymore—neither humans nor their affairs. I am very old, but never old enough to die; my pleasures are those which pester even mortals in their old age: comforts, memories, security. Please, enter my cavern. You will find it more relaxing than the stair, and less austere than many have supposed."

She went with him into the cave, the first chamber of which was ordinary, but they did not stay there. In the next chamber there was a habitable place not so different from many another home, though the furnishings were oversized and made of stone. The stonecutter and quarryman was evidently the Teacher himself, who presently moved his girth backward into a very large and simply constructed chair. He folded first his back legs and then his front into a meditative posture. He looked like the carving of a god sitting thus, the fire of oil-lamps bathing the whole of his body in highlights and shadows.

Erin stood in the middle of this room and turned full circle, her face revealing wonder. The walls were lined with shelves bolted into stone, and these shelves were piled with scrolls and tablets and great leather-bound books. Beside the chair in which the Teacher sat was a stone table, on which several books were stacked near to hand, along with inks and quills and blank papyrus sheets and scrolls.

"You are an author?" asked Erin.

"Merely an illuminator," he said off-hand. "The old books crumble in a fortnight, or so it seems to me. Because I value them, I copy them from time to time, from age to age, and give the older copies to passing pilgrims so that they can be confounded by them."

"Many pilgrims come?"

"I never counted."

The place did not smell of musty books, for all across the ceiling herbs were hung to dry. The air was full of sage, thyme, heather, savory, hen's bane, broom, dill, mint, glorious teas and medicinals . . . There were side-rooms into which she could see. Ones walls were also shelved, and lined with apothecary jars in the cool, unlit interior. In the main cavern itself, there were four lofts, each with thick stone stairs leading up between stalactites. In these lofts the Teacher kept many possessions, mostly ordinary things.

"The elderly are collectors," he explained. "Someday I shall have to throw that old stuff out, or else find another mountain."

There was an iron door at the far end of the chamber, the only room with any door at all. Over it hung weapons of various sorts, including a sickle of the insect-folk, and odder weapons still, all of which piqued Erin's interest in things martial.

"Find comfort there," said the four-legged man. Erin bowed quickly and removed her two swords from her belt, set them beside one of the big stone chairs, and climbed up onto the edge. The creature said, "I take a lot of space to live my life, but really I value nothing more than the herbs and my library. My treasures have no intrinsic value, unless it is the books. I fancy it is priceless, but human folk don't think so, for books are not made of gold. Mostly they are military treatises written aeons ago; although other topics are represented, too. The languages are nearly all forgotten; I've nothing new. I should know them all by heart by now, but a settled man needs possessions, for possessions are like anchors against useless wanderlust . . . I've been settled here for centuries, I suppose; I've lost track. Ah, but forgive me if I grow tedious, as old men are wont to be; and do not encourage melancholia from these decrepit bones! Tell me instead your name, for I only know you as Merilia, and it is too painful to call you by the name of my late, most gifted pupil."

"Kes called me Erin of Endsworld, but I think he teased. I am known as Erin of Thar."

"Humble names are best," said the four-legged man. "My own name is Kiron."

Erin was startled by the name, and Kiron, noticing this, asked,

"As I have known you before, so have you known me?"

"It's not that," said Erin. "But on the world called Earth there is the story of a Centaur who taught the heros of a classic age the martial arts.

The centaur's name was Cheiron, and his wards included Achilles, Jason, Atalanta, Asclepius, Heracles . . ."

"The names are unfamiliar," said Kiron, looking edgy. "What exactly is meant by 'centaur?' "

"It is half man and half horse."

"And what is meant by 'horse?' "

Erin was uncertain how to explain. There was no comparable beast which she had seen in Durga's Lathe; the commonest means of travel was by boat, foot, and palanquin (for the wealthy), and even the common design of clothing—long robes—were peculiarly unsuitable to riding any sort of animal. Carefully, she suggested, "It is a noble animal friendly to humans, capable of holding large burdens on its back."

"Then I venture that this Cheiron of Earth is no kin of Kiron of the Black Mountain!" Kiron clambered off his big chair and began to pace around his large quarters. He'd been belligerent earlier, but now he seemed almost nervous. He said, "Once my race was used as beasts of burden, because we have long backs on which loads might be tied. When we revolted against the ones who ruled Endsworld in that antique era, all of us were killed for our struggle, all except myself, who the killers made immortal by means of weird sciences and magicks. I was the last one, after all, which they would preserve like any artiface! Perhaps it was meant as a kindly gesture, although I think those destroyers knew no kindness. In any case, it has only been a curse to me. I soon could not bear to see the changes in the world, living through more epochs than human scholars know existed. That is why I am a hermit now, bothering only rarely with the world below Black Mountain, sculpting the likenesses of the lost heros and great minds of a time none but I recall. They are poor company, never speaking; and so at times, in my loneliness, I speak with creatures like yourself, and train them to be heroes . . . much, I suppose, as your famed Cheiron once did." His pacing brought him to Erin's chair, over which he towered. "But I am not a 'centaur' or a 'horse.' I am my entire race! And if you consider beasts of burden to be 'noble,' then, Erin of Thar, I say that I am not noble, but that I am the greatest of living gods!"

She shrank from his vehemence, but collected her courage and sat up squarely.

"Who," asked Erin, "could keep a people as large and strong as yours in thrall? Surely the human race would be trampled beneath the greatness of such gods."

"You are sarcastic?" asked Kiron, and almost smiled to hear his transient egomania fed back at him so well. He settled down a bit, cantering toward the stone table, resting a hand thereon. He said, "It was not humankind who enslaved us. In that age, humans either did not yet exist, or were still scavenging in the trees. I do not know if humans are native of Endsworld or not, for none of them were important enough for anyone to notice. I remember when I personally noticed them—when in the early centuries of my immortality I wandered, always finding their settlements and cities. I had lived on far continents, away from their development, and they had not saved much of their history, and no other race recorded it— only mine could have done so, I venture, but there were none of us left to do so. The histories in these books around us make no mention of humanity, being as they are the histories of my dead race. It is possible the first humans came to Endsworld, like yourself, from one or more of the twenty hells or heavens. Or they may have lived unnoticed in the trees, like apes, until something encouraged them to come down and to grow. As for what race, if not humans, enthralled us . . . that is part of the riddle of Endsworld which you will resolve in good time. For now, your major quest must be the sword, or Father Kes will kill you in the match. If humankind held no importance to the Endsworld of antiquity, then your race will amend the situation in the future of this planet! It may be that you, Erin of Thar, will be among the heroes to shape the future, if you learn your lessons well. I will groom you for the destiny that might have been Merilia's. If the goal is set too high, then you will never be anything at all. It depends upon whether or not you can master the swords you own.''

Saying these things, Kiron bent to an oil lamp's wick and blew away the flame. There was another, smaller lamp elsewhere, but it only made the shadows in the room more severe. Erin felt a chill go up her spine. The room which had a moment before been comfortable was now threateningly strange. The herbs hanging over her head gave off a pungency no longer soothing, but oppressive; she was reminded of *penm*: a sick sweetness that closed upon the mind.

Before her stood the red-eyed shadow that had led her over the darkling mesa to the forest.

"What is this?" demanded Erin, slipping from her tall stone chair and reclaiming her two weapons. When she faced the shadow-man again, she saw that he had multiplied, becoming three. In a blink, he had become five. She looked at Kiron, who watched impassively, then to the shadow-men once more—who now numbered seven. No more than that appeared. Each of them bore long shadow-sabers, which they held out at their sides.

"They will be your opponents," said Kiron, his voice deep and resonant. "You cannot hurt them; they are shadows, as they seem. They are the spirits of the seven peaks of Mount Black. An eighth spirit is a shadow-dragon who lives beyond the iron door, and down. She is Black Mountain's roots. I cannot command her. But these shadows I have used for ages to help me teach the sword. They do not communicate well, so I do not know what they think of their commission; but they perform it well. Ah! See! They prepare to attack!"

"I cannot take them all at once!" Erin exclaimed, backing away from the seven crouching shadows. They began to surround her, their shadow-sabers raised upward in a pattern Erin recognized: the blades were arranged as were the peaks of Black Mountain! Erin drew her *mai* and held it two-handed. She asked the stern Teacher, "Is any trick allowed?"

"Any trick," said Kiron. "This time."

Erin moved toward the small oil lamp and put the tip of her *mai* to it, threatening to tip it over. She said to Kiron, "Your library then. I will burn it. The light will scare these shadows away. That, or I'll fight just one."

Kiron grumbled, sounding himself like a mountain. "You will learn to respect these ancient tomes, Erin of Thar; but I did say any trick was allowed."

By some unspoken command, six of the shadow-men vanished, and Erin engaged the one remaining in combat. The shadow-saber struck hers well, and deflected each attack as would any steel sword. But there was no clangor, no more sound than there would have been in touching an ordinary shadow. It gave her a strange sensation, but she refused to be unnerved. She concentrated, hoping to impress the Teacher, certain that she couldn't.

The shadow-man's saber made a clever sweep across the top of Erin's shoulders. She felt a numbing cold streak across her throat and fell backward, instantly drained. The last shadow-man vanished, but did so as a victor. Erin felt her throat, her head, surprised it had not gone rolling away across the cavern floor. She had failed. She felt ridiculous and unskilled.

"Not bad," said Kiron. "Not good either. You will have to learn to fight all seven. The cold you felt as the shadow-saber passed through you was akin to the heat *they* will feel when your sword passes through them. I will do with you what I can. I will devise a tough agenda. Tomorrow, you will learn about my herbs, meditate until it bores you, and fight the shadows until they strike you down. I will plan the schedule tonight, so the rest of this day is your last one free. There! That corner. Make it yours. There are cupboards for what little you own. The stone pallet will be your bed. Blankets are in a chest in that loft there. They are thin blankets. Prove yourself hardy and use but one."

Erin was still feeling the cold band around her throat when night had fallen. The night was a cold one, so she slept in her robe, hoping Kiron would not notice that one blanket was too few.

*       *       *

The days passed swiftly with aching mind and muscle. Those first days Erin thought herself the most foolish of fools, incapable of memorizing the names and uses of herbs magical, medicinal, or good to eat. Slowly she ceased her effort to memorize and began to understand them and know their names and value as she might know a friend. She looked into Kiron's books, too, but found the scrawls therein meaningless. When she begged instruction in these, Kiron said, "Next year, if you live, and choose to stay with me, I will teach you. You must study other things for now."

Each day she met the Shadows in a dark grotto where a black lake was hemmed in on one side by overhanging cliffs, and by gigantic gnarly trees on the other. Little sunlight filtered into this place, and the shadow-men would come to her at any time, and fight her on that small lake's shore. Sometimes Kiron would be there to watch and give advice. Other times, she was left to learn by trial and error.

It was a contrast Kiron insisted was important, to balance her studies between the exertion of martial exercise and the quietude of gardening or meditation. She helped harvest herbs in their prime and hung them to dry. Those dried she would take down from their hangers to shred or crush and store them in stone bottles with wooden caps.

Thus her chores were varied: sometimes domestic, sometimes personal and meditative, sometimes done with swords. This last seemed most important to Erin, but Kiron warned her not to place too much emphasis on one part of her tutoring above all others. "You must emphasize the calm with the active," he would say, "or get too big on one side and fall over." She laughed, for he had meant to be funny, but when she thought it over privately, she began to understand.

After the first week, she began to meet two shadows instead of one, and fight them simultaneously. At the end of a month, she was fighting four of them at once. Her *mai* or *i* would touch them, and they would collapse and writhe as though set afire, and she pitied them their soundless anguish and wondered why they always returned another day for more. When they touched her with their shadowy weapons, she would collapse likewise, as though overcome with rheumatism and blue chills. It was painful to be touched by those sabers, regardless of the lack of wound. She paid dearly for her errors, therefore, and after each mistake must study other things less physical, until she recovered from the coldness of defeat. Yet she returned to the grotto each new day, just as the shadow-men did, and perhaps—as she had wondered about them—they were curious why she should always return for more.

Kiron was likewise busy, sometimes in his gardens, or tutoring her in duels, or working on his statue which he seemed to like doing the most, or dickering herbs for drygoods and other foodstuffs (and sometimes absurd trinkets) with visiting pilgrims who treated him like the oddest of gods and the most remarkable. He would never let Erin talk to these priests and monks herself, for he said any news of the outside world would only interfere with her concentration on matters at hand. But she often watched who came, for the view was excellent at the foot of the steps from the cavern. She never saw the one with sandy eyes.

At night, Kiron often climbed onto his stone bed very late, for he would sit at his table for long hours copying old books and making them fresh. This was a slow task for each character was a work of art. This work was Kiron's meditation.

Her own meditations were abysmal, for usually she could not clear her mind but thought herself into depression. Sometimes she was depressed because she seemed to advance slowly. More often, her various guilts came pecking at her like horrifying little devils. Now and then she found herself at the waterfall, wishing the roar to drown her thoughts, and sometimes her thoughts were of throwing herself from the top to drown everything else about her as well. This she never did.

Once, on a day when her footwork had been awful, and four shadowy opponents "cut" her with their swords, she lay in the grotto freezing and alone (for the victorious shadows went away, chortling in their batwing fashion). After a while she crawled into the sunlight outside the grotto, trying to get warm, listening to the chink-a-chink of Kiron who was nearby with his chisel and mallet, but beyond sight. She fell into unconsciousness for a bare moment, but in that moment suffered horrid nightmares of Earth. In these dreams the whole of that world was populated by shadow-people and to be touched by them was to be frozen to the heart, and there was no happiness there, and only two choices: to be a cold shadow herself, or to be forever lonely. It was really but one choice.

She awoke shivering fiercely and staggered to her feet, trying to find Kiron though she was still dazed from cold slumber. When she stumbled into the clearing where he was cutting stone, he was startled, and his chisel slipped. A finger of his left hand was severed by his blunder—or Erin thought it had happened, could have sworn she saw him snatch the finger as it went falling, cursing all the while. But her daze continued, and when she finally shook herself fully awake, and felt a bit warmer, Kiron's finger was attached where it belonged.

He set aside his tools and cantered to where Erin had collapsed to her knees, her expression puzzled, her eyes clearing as her befuddled brain cast off the effects of the unplanned nap.

"You were defeated badly today," said Kiron, recognizing the effects of the shadows' cold knives.

"Kiron," she said, then, "Teacher." She sat up on her knees, and Kiron got down on his four, and they conversed there in the clearing where his work-in-progress stood. Erin said, "I am periodically annoyed by the feeling that I am dreaming, that none of this is real. Sometimes this feeling is so strong that it becomes difficult for me to continue in anything I do, for what use, if all is illusion."

Kiron reached a hand toward her shoulder, the large hand of a sculptor whose works are massive. His face was concerned, which was unusual for him to reveal; he was usually impassive, or worse, a bit irritated. Today he was much kinder, perhaps perceiving Erin's loneliness, a feeling for which he held much empathy. He said, "If you think you must find the proof of reality, Erin, then yours is a fool's quest indeed. You will have to go away from Black Mountain emptier than you came, or else gain a firmer sense of reality by ceasing to question it."

"But . . . if I accept the authenticity of this world, I am left to wonder if lost Earth was but a dream, and what my life really was before."

"Is it so hard to bear that Earth may not exist? If that world you lost reclaims you, it will be because you could not let go of that other reality and hold this one. Would you like to return to Earth?"

There was no hesitation in her reply. "I would not."

"Then accept that it was the dream. That way, you can only visit it in dreams and never in flesh, as once you only came to Endsworld in your dreams."

"It is hard for me to think as you counsel," she admitted. "If I cease to question the reality of Endsworld, then I can no longer excuse the deaths of people I have caused to die. I brought doom to all in village Thar, and have killed others since, with various justifications and sometimes with no justifications at all. If nothing can be doubted, then I cannot live with the certainty of my guilt."

"You would rather die?" asked Kiron. "Good! A warrior is always ready for death. A warrior does not merely face death, but seeks it. The minute you desire life, you are worthless in the fight."

Erin pondered this. Her eyes focused on a stone chipping at her knees. Teebi Dan Wellsmith had worried overmuch about what he perceived as Erin's suicidal streak. Yet Kiron suggested that such a tendency might be a boon. If she was always ready to throw her life away, she would remain unafraid of battle.

"I feel better now," said Erin, waiting for Kiron to rise to his feet before she rose to hers. On standing, she said, "I am grateful that you share your wisdom."

Kiron was in a good mood indeed, for he laughed at Erin's gratitude, and Kiron's laughter was rare. He said, "I am as ignorant as you, Erin. I have not yet grown weary enough of knowledge to seek understanding instead. There is a statue in the gardens, near where the dragon's bane is planted, twixt thick small pines. I've seen you visit her on times. *She* was one who unburdened herself of all knowing. She, not I, was wise."

"Someday," said Erin, "I should like to learn the history of your race."

Kiron took up hammer and chisel and moved toward his recent project. He said, "It is not what you need immediately to survive; but I am flattered by your interest. If you are with me next year, I will teach you the ancient tongue of my people, that you might understand the texts I keep. Only, remember: it is knowledge, and so a barrier against wisdom greater than mine."

\*   \*   \*

That Erin performed more and more of the gardening freed Kiron to work longer hours on the yellow-stone statue, and this made Erin feel less a burden and more useful. "It is coming along," he told her one afternoon. "I would ask you not to look at it until it is finished." He was embarrassed to ask this, but Erin thought she understood the artist's mind, and promised not to go into the stand of trees which hid his current work. It became one of only two places Kiron had set beyond her limits. The other was the passage beyond the cavern's iron door.

The door infatuated her, the mystery it encompassed, the personification of Black Mountain who Kiron said lived below. But Kiron warned her not to go through the door, not saying it meant danger, but that it meant a breach of his trust. That was enough to keep curiosity at bay, to not pry into Kiron's secrets.

In time, he fenced with her himself, and it was one of the many marks of his great skill that, even when she was not quick and balanced, he never once cut her. He would attack with a variety of weapons, some so strange she could not at first cope against them. Often the sharpest of blades or daggers came within a hair's-breadth of her skin. Subconsciously, she devised a way to defeat Kiron, which relied on the conscious knowledge that he would never actually injure her. But Kiron was ahead of even her subconscious. Her ploy ended in a swift strike to her shoulder with the backside of his one-edged sword. The bruise would last for days. Only beyond hours of meditation did she understand what she had done. Thereafter, she strove to better her skills and did not seek the shortcuts of cleverness or trickery.

In the full of one day's noon, Erin repaired to the coolness of the dark grotto while Kiron chipped away at his slow creation. That day she called upon herself five of the shadow-men at once, and fought them well. She was proud of herself that day, and so was anxious to fence with Kiron himself, to prove to him that she was improving not by small increments, but by bounds. She hurried from the grotto. It was by then long after noon.

Kiron was annoyed to be called out from the

stand of trees where he'd been sculpting in solitude. Yet he agreed quickly to the match, doubtlessly sensing her pride. He defeated her with a single stroke. Her *mai* was flung from her hand so that it stuck into a tree, just as on the first day of their meeting. It went too deep for her to get it loose. In anger and frustration, she fell upon her knees before the tree which would not unleash her sword, and she complained unhappily and with bruised dignity,

"I am anxious to be skillful! I cannot stand that my progress is slow!"

Kiron stepped near, hovered above her mightily; but by now his presence had become more comforting than imposing. He said, "Impatience damages the worth of your work, Erin. You want to learn quickly? I will tell you how. Cease to consider time. It will all be done quickly then."

"That is easier for an immortal to believe. You have eternity upon which to achieve and ponder everything you consider worthwhile. You have lived long already and have resolved many of the mysteries, at least to your personal satisfaction. I on the other hand have barely begun to resolve those mysteries. I have not understood the world, or myself, or my swords, or the meaning of our lives."

"You would do well not to imagine profundity," he said. "Anything that seems of momentous occasion should be dwelt upon as though it were of slight note. Conversely, trivialities must be attended to with the greatest of care. Because death is momentous, give it no thought; because victory is important, give it no thought; because the method of achievement and discovery is less momentous than the effect, dwell always upon the method. You will strengthen yourself in this way."

\*    \*    \*

Some lessons were difficult, but others seemed impossible. Patience was the virtue Erin lacked the most. One night she lay wide-eyed upon her stone pallet in the cavern, her thoughts glum. Kiron slept on a pallet of a similarly polished slab of stone, thrice the size of hers. He snored loudly beneath his one thin blanket. Usually his snoring was a comfort, but tonight it annoyed her supremely. She stood, put on her sandals, robe and girdle, and slid *i* and *mai* into her girdle. She went from inner to outer chamber, and then out into the night. The stars were misted and dim. The air was moist and cold. She felt her way to the stairs and descended the first flight, and then the other, and went the route she knew with eyes closed, to the grotto where she was used to fighting the shadow-men.

The entrance to the grotto was a narrow breach in an otherwise unbroken wall of trees. She stood before these pillars, listening to the sound of frogs chirping in the cold waters of the pond within. In a moment, she whispered, "Shadow-men, come out. Come into the night you rule. One, four, five, seven. I will fight you all tonight!"

Two eyes like red amber appeared beyond the rent between the trees, and then another pair. The shadow-men stepped out. Two more shadow-men appeared to her left, for none of them truly lived in the grotto and might appear anywhere they chose, so long as it was dark. To her right, another pair of shadow-men were standing. The seventh was behind her. Erin drew *mai* in right hand, *i* in left, and held them to her sides. She turned around and around quite slowly, watching the seven pairs of coal-bright eyes that floated.

"I can see you well enough," she said softly. "You will each feel my fiery sword before I feel yours of ice!"

The battle was engaged. Her *mai* swept left, her

*i* swept right; she stood with arms crossed and leapt out of their sabers' way. She blocked. She attacked with sweeping strokes. She thrust and stabbed. She was as swift as light; they, as swift as darkness. They dizzied her, making her turn quickly one way then the other. Her sword passed through one and he fell back, the glimmer of his eyes dying. She would have to touch six more!

Blocking left and right, she broke from among the six, ran wildly down a hillside into the gardens, the shadows in pursuit. They laughed their fluttery laughs, and Erin knew they loved the chase. She stopped abruptly, her back against one of Kiron's statues. They could not surround her now, and could only approach a couple at a time. She battled them thus for some while, but it was a strictly defensive stand; she could not put her swords into any of them. One of the shadow-men had climbed atop the shoulders of the statue, prepared to leap upon Erin, but she burst into a sprint toward the forests surrounding the medicine gardens.

Among the trees, she could plan assaults as well as defenses; but this was true of the shadow-men as well. They surprised each other time and again, playing hide-and-leap-out for a long space of time. The only sounds were those of her breath and heart, for the shadow-men's swords were silent in striking hers, and her various ploys kept them too fretful to make their bat-wing laughter.

She began to suspect the extent of her folly when her lungs ceased to expand enough to draw the amount of air her body required. She had to rest, but the shadow-men came on without relent. Then, she broke the guard of another and, turning full circle to block a rear attacker, she came back to face the first opponent and took him across the belly as her sword finished the hundred-eighty degree sweep. Now there were five.

As her energy waned further, it was everything she could do to hold her good defense. When her second wind came to the aid, it allowed her merely to carry on the defense, not to attack. Soon after, she was weak indeed, gasping for air as she battled. An icy stroke slid down her back. Another, through the chest, found her heart. A third shadow-saber slipped from top of pate to chin; a steel blade would have cleaved her skull, but the shadowy one merely left her feeling dull and stupid.

She collapsed and began to crawl away from the vengeance of the five shadow-men. Two more strikes were made at her back. She moaned, shocked, never suspecting the shadows of such cruelty. They had won, but would not stop. She wondered if they meant to kill her. She fell from hands and knees to her side, and rolled down a sharp incline, lay at the bottom, freezing, shaking. The ground was bare. She'd slid onto the scraped path leading from Kiron's quarry. It was along this trail he brought sculptor's blocks of stone, rolling them across logs-as-wheels. She felt one of those logs and clung to it in terror, sniveling with the pain.

The shadow-sabers were thrust into her vitals and her eyes. *Yes*, she thought, *they mean to kill me*. They would not let up. She tried to crawl further, for the quarry-trail would take her through the forest and back to Kiron's gardens. But she could move no longer. She let go of the log, rolled on her back, watched the five sabers strike at her prone form time and time again. Her lips were blue but moved to form the words, "Please . . . I . . . relent."

The shadow-men stopped. They turned in a flourish of shadowy capes and walked away in different directions, toward the respective peaks of Black Mountain whose souls the shadows were.

Perhaps they had meant no malice after all. Even Kiron did not understand them. Erin had, after all, asked for their ultimate attack, thinking that it would force her to treble her rate of improvement. "Fool," she whispered hoarsely, chastising herself.

In a while she was able to crawl along the trail, pitiful, defeated. She doubted she could make it back to the cavern and her bed and warmth. Suddenly, there was light before her, and she looked up, saw Kiron standing there with a small oil lamp in his hand. He grumbled something she did not understand, in his race's old tongue she supposed. Then he grabbed her one-handed by her cloth belt and lifted her up, carrying her through the gardens and up the stairs like a big, limp parcel.

In the cavern, he threw her in the corner on her hard pallet, and for the first time she felt like it was a dog's corner, an out-of-the-way and inconsequential space which the dog's owner had no better use for. She felt on the verge of tears, and so cursed instead, and rolled weakly to her knees, pushed herself up with her hands, and demanded to know,

"Will I never perfect my skill?"

It was a kind of lament, like a sad dog's keening. Kiron was heating water over a larger oil-lamp, while blending herbs to make a curative tea for Erin. When it was made, he brought it to her in a battered copper cup (the copper being part of the cure) and while she drank the warm, pleasant stuff, he said to her in his most measured tone,

"Your quest is for perfection? Give up your quest and you will have achieved it. Strive to be a little more skillful each day. Never say, 'It is done,' but, 'It is beginning.' Never say, 'I do well,' but, 'I will do better.' Seek to perfect nothing. Rather, seek to improve. Assume nothing achieves its apex."

She looked up at him, eyes big, still pitiful; but glimmers of hope, understanding, and patience were budding there. She asked, "But . . . if I do not let myself know when I am good, how will I know that I can overcome my foes?"

"A warrior has no foes," said Kiron. "Always remember that. Say, 'I have no enemies,' regardless of what may appear. Enemies are invented! Then they are maintained at great expense of will. They exist in the memory of the past and the thought of the future. A true swordsmaster lives only for *now* and therefore has no foe. Don't seek skills to defeat another! Learn to defeat yourself."

\*       \*       \*

There came a day when Erin realized that she loved her gruff taskmaster, and considered his lofted cavern to be her home as well as his. The medicinal gardens and the forests between the peaks were hardly a vision of paradise; but the place had certainly become her own ideal retreat. Occasionally she wondered about Durga's Lathe, if in that country revolution still brewed, had come and gone, or if things went on unchanged. Did Válkyová Idaska still play Christ and Shom Bru the Devil? Perhaps they'd both died of some common sickness, or assassination. Did Teebi still sell fish, or had his fierce wounds found infection after all, and taken his life away? From all of this Erin had, like Kiron, withdrawn emotionally. Even intellectually, she only in rare moments considered matters of the plains below.

Patience she learned, but pride did not lessen. She yet wished to be a hero, though for what cause she could not imagine. This desire felt suddenly within grasp when, finally, she succeeded in defeating the seven shadow-men at once. It had been a difficult victory, but the victory was hers. When

Wendy Adrian Shultz

the last shadow was vanquished, light seemed to shine inside her mind, and she staggered breathless and grinning from the grotto, swelling with excitement. She could not find Kiron fast enough, and so stopped before the statue he had made of the female with spear and knives, whose expression faced heavensward. And Erin thought she understood what that enlightened warrior was thinking. Erin fell onto her knees before the statue, and said, "Surely we are alike! My swords will be avengers! My strength will carry the weak! I will struggle against injustice throughout Endsworld!"

Kiron had overheard. He was nearby, his fists clenched around bundles of herbs. He approached Erin, and he looked unhappy with her naive, boastful words. Erin was embarrassed to have been caught speaking so boldly of herself and to a statue.

"Pride, if valuable at all," said Kiron, "is valuable within. If it must be shown to others—whether to gods in prayer or to the meek in terrifying deeds—then it was false pride all along, seeking support from outside the self. Those who are insecure require proof of their greatness. True greatness neither sees itself, nor asks."

Now Erin was more than embarrassed, but also ashamed, and it made her feel defensive. She asked, "Is it only pride that makes me ache to see justice prevailing here and there?"

"Of justice you will find none, not among the twenty heavens or twenty hells, and not upon Endsworld. To judge is evil. To mete justice, more appalling still. Act from compassion and you will do better than to devise any code or facade of justice."

"What of . . . what of . . . chivalry?" Erin stammered, sounding ludicrous even to herself. "What use is my sword if I do not use it to right evil?"

"Despite your growing skill, Erin, there is weakness in you. If I sent you into the world today, you would kill when you became angry. You would slay from indignation. You would be self-righteous. You would advocate the faith of pride and justice, those all-consuming falsehoods."

Kiron's words reminded her of the death of Dee the Rope, and Erin became more defensive still. "I would never use my swords at all if I followed your advice!" She was confounded and angry as she continued, "I cannot strike when angered or proud or righteous. There is no dignity and no justice. There are no reasons left to fight! If all who pursued the sword thought as you, there would be no use of swords!"

"That is true," Kiron agreed. "Embrace that truth. Otherwise, you can only perpetuate the things you wish will end."

Erin had been on her knees before the statue all this while, not really looking at Kiron as they spoke. Now she stood, faced him, thinking. Her mood calmed. She asked, "Then how can I know when properly to battle?"

"The warrior who lives each moment as it falls," said Kiron, "does not need justification. End each day with a clear mind, and you will wake to start anew with the same clear mind. If you are disciplined within, you need not reason with yourself before beginning."

"You tell me not to consider the cruelty of the world or my part in it," said Erin. "I do not see how to unburden myself of guilt, of past errors—how to clear my mind. And when I see unfairness, it makes my fist grow tight! Perhaps it is only myself I wish to punish, but there is no way to avoid thoughts of things I would set right, given so much strength."

Today, Kiron practiced the patience he often preached. He revealed no irritation as he studied her expression, searching, perhaps, for sincerity—and, perhaps, finding it. At length he said, "Strike in anger, Erin, and you strike for the sake of ego and are weakened. You will lose. The ego wants to live, to be correct, to prove matters. It is righteous and self-righteous. The ego is unwilling to die and will never protect you. It is never best to strike in anger." He handed Erin one of his two handfuls of aromatic herbs, a gesture which calmed her further. She asked,

"Should I then be contemplative?"

"No, you should not strike from contemplation either. I have taught you there is only evil in judgement and judges. Whether good and evil are separate and opposing, or subjective interpretations of identical situations, is unworthy of debate. When people reflect deeply on this or any matter, it makes them slow. A crisis proceeds with encouragement at such sloth. After the emergency is over, there is no longer value in action—unless in vengeance, which is also for the ego. Compassion is a greater source of activity than intellectual investment. Compassion is antithesis to the ego. Compassion has no anger, no intellect, no fault. When genuine, it is swift. Activity born of compassion cannot fail."

"Action born of compassion," Erin said, looking inward.

Kiron nodded. He said, "You should make it your precept."

\*    \*    \*

It had taken all her life to arrive at this little bit of peace, this modicum of freedom from herself. She doubted she had really let go of her ego, for she still envisioned her swords involved in heroic sweeps; but her guilt at least began to pass, and with it, her need of vengeance, and her anger. She felt a higher degree of acceptance for the fact that her foster parents and village Thar were gone. She had acted, then, from compassion; she had no cause for guilt. As for Teebi, Dee, Valkyova . . . they sought their own fates, she did not lead them. They, too, provided no proper cause for guiltiness. Whatever might seem to be her failures she could forgive if her motivations were pure; conversely, her successes would each be meaningless if pursued without purity of reason. She had learned that a good ending never justified evil means, and tragic outcomes could not revoke well intended means.

At the same time of Erin's coming to this acceptance of life and death as they exist, Kiron began to behave more erratically. It was as though she had become a part of him and he a part of her: the sorrows she had lost, he had gained. She wondered why.

Her home became less warm with her Teacher unwilling or unable to communicate, to share. He rarely fenced with her anymore, and when he did, he neither praised nor belittled, and his comments were superficial. The shadow-men still came when she beckoned, so her fighting skills improved; but she missed Kiron and the more rewarding lessons his tutelage embodied. She even missed his recurrent annoyance with her. The situation worsened so that eventually Kiron abandoned his teachings entirely and, despite his continued presence, Erin was alone.

He also abandoned his illuminations of manuscripts. He bedded early, woke late. She asked if he was ill, and he almost laughed at that, for he could not recall a day of sickness.

On a cold day in winter, with snow outside the cavern, Erin returned from fencing the shadows in the grotto and found Kiron huddled near a brazier oiling his *oude* absent-mindedly, a single tear in one eye. She squatted down by the coals and whispered, "A warrior does not consider the past. A warrior does not contemplate."

"I am no warrior," he said, his voice gentler and sadder than she had previously heard it. "A warrior is ever prepared for death. I have forgotten what it is like to be prepared for that! I can never die." He ran his wrist along the edge of his *oude* in a suicidal gesture that made Erin gasp. The weapon was inconceivably sharp and Kiron's hand fell into the burning brazier. Blood did not spill from Kiron's stump. There was no smell of burning flesh in the brazier. Impossibly, horrifyingly, the hand began to crawl out of the coals, to scale the slope of the brazier. Kiron put his fresh stump to the wrist of the severed hand, and it reattached at once. Kiron said, "Neither fire nor ice can slay me. I expect to be the last witness of Endsworld, when Time has worn this planet out. You may think it is far away, that future, that ultimate loneliness; yet the aeons race so quickly for me now! Without a sense of my own mortality, eternity is but a day. You cannot understand the feeling! And thank whatever gods you may that that is so.

"I have long known that I was no warrior, no hero, not even a proper aesthetic, weighted as I am with the possessions pilgrims bring me. But I have always thought myself at least the *trainer* of warriors, of heros . . . yes, even I have my delusions. I failed Merilia, and I fear I've failed you."

"You're wrong," said Erin, trying to soothe. "Yours is no delusion. I have never been so strong."

"Yet others have been stronger," said Kiron. "I raised Merilia from childhood. How could I hope, in months, to give to you the skills I gave to her in years? You may be the match of Father Kes by now, I am not certain. But you are not the match of me, as Merilia nearly was. Great as she was, some trick of Shom Bru's felled her. It confounds me still. You will die the same way, I fear, unless the riddle can be solved."

Kiron stood from the brazier, went to a cupboard and took from there a huge jug. It was wine given to him by one of the priests who traded for herbs. Kiron opened it with his teeth, spat the cork, and drank deep of the fluid within. Erin asked, "Do you do this often?" When he did not understand the question, she was more explicit. "Drink, I mean."

"Often enough," he said, and drank deeply once again. "Would you like to test it?"

"If it is part of my training," she said.

"Then don't." He drank again.

"You've changed this last month," said Erin, to which Kiron laughed. He moved nervously about the confines of the cavern's main chamber, looking as though he needed to escape.

"I never change," he said. "Your illusions are only shattered."

He snatched up a sledge hammer from among his many tools and virtually bolted out of the room with it, and with his jug. Erin was encouraged to follow him into the snow-covered gardens of a cold day and to the place of his work-in-progress. She had not seen it for a while, the area having been off limits. The statue was still not finished, but it was assuredly well along. She recognized the face as Kiron's own. It was to be his first self-portrait.

Raising the sledge like a sword above his head, he said, "What vanity to think my own likeness belonged among the great minds and heros of my vanished race!" He smashed the face into fragments. He struck again and the head toppled off, rolling across the snow between him and Erin. The whole statue quaked, snow slipping from its back and shoulders. He struck over and over until the torso cracked, but he stopped of a sudden, already remorseful. Erin watched without comment, with sadness in her eyes. Kiron dropped the sledge and took up the bottle again. He sat down so abruptly it looked as though he had collapsed upon the snowy ground, and he drank more deeply than before.

He fixed an expression on her which was accusing, as though she had driven him to this. But she had learned her lessons well enough that he could not force her to feel guilty. Self-blame was ultimately an egotistical thing. To think oneself the hub of the whole world's anguish was irrational. Those who feel such extraordinary guilt, who believe they can take the sins and sorrows upon themselves, perhaps to die for others, do not feel these things with compassion. They feel these things to be true because of their self-centeredness. A sense of guilt was in many ways a buffer against greater pain; empathy for another was much more terrible.

"Erin," said Kiron, then, "Merilia . . ." Confused, he reached toward her face, toward the scar at her hairline, but she sat too far away. He said, "I can teach you nothing more."

"That is not so," said Erin. "You promised to teach me your books. You promised to . . ."

"Those things are insignificant now. The only thing I can tell you is that Kiron is weak, and Kiron lies."

"That's not . . ."

"I will tell you! Priests came recently and gave me news which I have kept from you. The one called Valk the Ear—a friend of yours, you've said— has raised an army in the desert. It is an army without weapons which intends to martyr itself against Shom Bru's warriors, their white-clad general striding at the front."

Erin could not hide her shock. She had thought

her own ego great, but Valkyova's was unimaginable! Kiron did not let her interrupt, but added,

"What they intend to accomplish by mass martyrdom may or may not be noble in concept, but I tell you this: it will come to nothing. For three generations the Bru Dynasty has had at its command a weapon it has never called into force. Most of the people have forgotten that once the insect-race moved by day as well as night, and moved without regard for the moon. Their marches are limited by treaty, not by nature. If Valk the Ear's suicidal gambit triggers a rising, as indeed it must, Shom Bru will call upon the heads of his enemies a horde of murderous automatons. There is only you to stop it, Erin. You wear the sword-shaped pendant which is the bane of the insect race."

"If I can!" said Erin, hoping her readiness would ease the burden Kiron obviously felt. Once she had desired to destroy the insects out of vengeance, but her motivation was different now. She would do it for love of Kiron, who seemed to wish it.

The wine had loosened Kiron's tongue, and he made his next confession. "I have told you revenge is for the ego and a warrior must have none; but I've also told you I am no warrior. For aeons I have hungered for revenge! I have trained heros time and again, never telling them what it was I hoped they would perform in the fullness of their careers. The race that once enslaved my kind, that killed us for desiring freedom, that cursed me with this endless life . . . it was a mighty race indeed, a gregarious race whose billions of minds were linked as one tremendous sentience. Today that race consists of a perverse queen who takes human lovers, and her tiny empire of mindless workers and drones. Yes, it is the insect folk I mean, once the masters of Endsworld. Their numbers fell below the billions needed to sustain the overmind, so that their intellect collapsed."

"Then your race did not die for nothing," ventured Erin, still hoping to make him feel better.

"It was not my kind, but yours. I lied to you about now knowing the origin of humankind. They were brought here by the sciences of that overmind, drawn from the twenty heavens and hells to live in sties, the strong raised to be slaves, the weak culled as fodder. Their new slaves were less strong than my race had been, and even the gargantuan intellect which encircled the globe underestimated the will of puny humans.

"There came a time when the slaves were made to perform every unlovely but necessary labor of an increasingly complex and advanced technological society, geared to the service of the insects. The humans gained control even over the workings of the power-crystals which charged the many objects of that wondrous technology. Humans worked magicks and sciences of their own upon the crystals to make them inimical to the multi-celled eyes of the insects. The engines which produced the crystals under tremendous pressure were destroyed; the existing crystals snatched the very same hour in a world-wide conspiracy of incredibly fine execution. Without the crystals, the insects' technology ground to a halt. Even the humans had failed to foresee the results. The whole of an artificial environment on which both insect and human life depended was gone. The collapse of a cruel civilization drove insect and human alike to the brinks of extinction. Plague, droughts, starvation . . . immortal Kiron was witness to it all.

"The humans would eventually rebuild the world much as you see it. The insects, having lost the density of population required to sustain the overmind, vanished into the background of the environment for centuries upon centuries. They and their weird sciences were nearly forgotten. The highest orders of priests and priestesses, who had held the stolen power-crystals as holy relics and talismans, one by one lost the devotion of their descendants. The value of the talismans was forgotten; the crystals themselves were lost, hidden, or destroyed. When the insects resurfaced, they were not remembered as the masters of old, but seen as a new and much simpler menace.

"The long-lived queens had passed along certain knowledge from antiquity to now. They have adhered to an ancient plan, striving to raise the population of their workers and drones to a level sufficient to recreate the overmind. At this very moment, beneath the junk-yard of their shattered technologies, their population expands toward the limits of their confines. Soon, the colony must divide. Daily, a new generation *winged like their queen* is being nurtured to maturity. They will scatter across Endsworld to create new colonies. Then the days of humankind will be measured not in millenia, perhaps not even in centuries, but in dark and fearful years."

Erin fumbled at the pendant around her neck and asked, "This can stop them?"

"The sorcerer you mentioned, the man with sand colored eyes . . . it is my guess that he is among the last, if not *the* last, of the ancient lineage of priests descended from the ones who masterplanned the ancient revolt. Clearly he has made the crystal your possession, has keyed it to your aura, made it operable only in your hands. As it is the power source of many forgotten technologies and hidden machines, you bear at your throat the potential downfall of the oldest Endsworld race. You may well be the savior of your people, and the avenger of mine. I am ashamed to want it so badly. My desire reveals my weakness. But it is still my desire."

"Whatever I can do," said Erin, "I will do. But now my friend, drink no more. It is making you ill."

"I am never ill," he said, his old belligerence resurfacing at the suggestion of putting the jug away. He drank again, then cursed, for the jug had run out. He got to his feet awkwardly and staggered through the snow toward the stairs which would take him back to the cave. Erin followed helplessly, heard him say, "If I drink enough, I will know, however transiently, oblivion akin to death!"

In the cavern, from the cupboard, he retrieved a bottle only slightly smaller than the jug had been. In a terrible moment of inspiration, Erin flung herself at Kiron, trying to take the bottle away to break it on the stones outside. He raised it above her reach and with his other arm swatted her expansively so that she was flung into the air. She landed on her feet far from him, but launched herself more fiercely in his direction. This time she made her body into a feet-first missile which struck Kiron below the chest and sent him staggering back and plunging to his knees.

"I relent!" boomed Kiron, who was suddenly laughing, not with any sort of humor, but from hysteria. Erin backed away, fearing him near madness or on the verge of a drunken rage. He hugged the bottle near his chest and said, "I feel the guilt I told you to cast away. I must send you down from the Black Mountain not the ultimate warrior you would need to be to defeat the combined infamy of the insects and of Shom Bru who unwittingly protects them under his grandfather's secret treaty . . . I must send you down an ordinary if determined fighter, to your doom. *Unless!* There is one last confession I must make, which will reveal to

you your one most desperate chance of learning
not only all that I had taught Merilia, but also
answer the riddle of Shom Bru's occult style. It is
time for you to see what really waits beyond the
iron door! Go, Erin! The door is no longer forbidden! Now, leave me to drink myself into merciful oblivion."

Erin turned from Kiron toward the forbidden
door. It was open. In it stood the shadow-men,
three of them, their eyes glowing redly. They
beckoned her. They moved from her path to let her
enter. She looked back once to see Kiron flat upon
his side, his head and torso thrown back, guzzling
from the bottle. The iron door was closing behind
her.

*          *          *

A softly moving, humid draft went up the
tunnel, then down, then up the tunnel, then down,
in long, slow breaths which gave Erin the sensation of passing through a dragon's lung. There was
darkness; but by the echo of her own breath she
knew the roof was low, and she could feel the
walls close at either hand. Ahead, there was a light
which at first seemed far, far off, but it was not. It
was the tunnel's end which opened into a gigantic,
rounded chamber. The walls and ceiling joined as
a kind of rough dome, natural bracings looking
like ribs which met at the backbone overhead. The
soft, eerie breeze continued around her, one direction and another, somewhat soothing, somewhat
unsettling.

The source of light was a glowing, crystalline
box taller than Erin and a little wider and deeper.
It stood in the center of the chamber upon a round
pedestal which might have been the stump of a
severed stalagmite. She could not see into the box
because of the dazzling brilliance, but as she came

nearer to it, as she entered into the light and it surrounded her without shadows, she could make out the outline of a human figure standing erect within.

She moved closer still, then stopped, frightened by what came into view. It was the image of herself! It was her Endsworld twin, Merilia, clad in funeral-white robe, eyes closed, looking like a doll in a case—a warrior doll, of course, although her swords were stolen. Erin knew at once that the two swords she bore had once belonged to Merilia; she wondered why she had not guessed it before, since they'd been gifts from Kiron from the start.

Merilia was beautiful in her androgynous way, more beautiful than Erin, which was odd to say, their features being the same, their glistening black hair the same shoulder length. There was a greater serenity in Merilia's expression which Erin had never approached, perhaps could not approach in life. Merilia's handsome beauty was marred, horrifyingly so, for where Erin bore only a scar, Merilia bore a rent. Above that seemingly-sleeping visage of serenity, a sword had cleaved through bone, exposing part of the brain.

Erin's natural instinct was to turn and flee, for frightening paradoxes might unfold should she face her own self. But the light held her in its grip, and the corpse drew her closer, death seeking life, life seeking death. She took another step forward and would have halted for certain *because Merilia's eyes had opened*, but she was caught in the spell and could not resist.

Their eyes held one another and Erin felt herself losing herself, knew for the smallest fraction of a moment what it was truly like to have one's ego nullified. Then she was gone into the dreary limbo between worlds and dimensions . . . and then she no longer existed as Erin but was, instead, the child Merilia studying fencing and warfare and a

multitude of matters with Kiron. She grew to
womanhood under his tutelage and finally went
off to see the world, to become involved in private
battles and the wars of others, learning by chance
the connection between the Bru Dynasty and the
insects' terrorism, swearing herself the Dynasty's
foe and coming, eventually, to the famous encounter with Cal Bru, slaying him, becoming
thereby the most popular folk hero of Durga's
Lathe, but also the most hunted.

In all these remembrances, the mind of Erin of
Thar never once surfaced, never once came to
these events as a detached observer, but lived
them wholeheartedly as her own.

There was heartbreaking failure in the wake of
her successes, for instead of encouraging the
necessary revolution, the peasants only gained a
greater faith in saviors, more certain than ever
that their input was not needed. Hero worship was
an evil thing, she saw, for those worshippers grew
in apathy, believing that an avenging angel or
white knight would win them freedom without
their having to take the risks.

She rode with the puny force of rebels, relived
their slaughter, went through the same motions of
her last insistent stand. Erin-cum-Merilia found
herself ultimately in confrontation with Shom
Bru, heir of Cal who she had killed, last of the tyrants waiting before her sword! She quickly discovered the young, cruel ruler was not the equal of
his father, and she knew she could kill him easily.
He gripped his *oude* no better than the three-
swords she had plowed through to reach him; although she must credit him a lack of fear.

His sword flung from his hands and arced
through the air and, seeing it, Merilia held back,
ever chivalrous, waiting for him to draw one of his
shorter blades, so that he could die with sword to
hand as befits even a tyrant of a warrior. But the

sword had not gone flinging from his grip at all. It
was some occult trick. His sword had become invisible and she did not realize the illusion until the
white fire of his steel cleaved her skull. Life
flowed out and away, out and away . . .

Erin staggered through the blinding whiteness
of death, slowly recapturing herself, regaining her
bearings, seeing that the whiteness was not death
but the glass coffin's shining. The experience had
been as overwhelming as living her own life twice
in different ways, and it was strange to feel that
second life underpinning her own. She now knew
Shom Bru's occult swordplay. She knew all that
Kiron had taught Merilia, too, and understood for
the first time how painful it must have been for
Kiron to see, each day, Erin's blundering, while
remembering the twin's extraordinary ability.

Merilia's eyes were closed again. Her expression
was still one of bliss eternal. The light blazed from
the upright coffin, though it was not as bright as
when the spell had gripped Erin. Although she
could not yet tear her eyes away, it was from no
outward compulsion, but only a sense of awe at
her twin's incredible prowess and tragic demise.

That awe was tripled knowing by the feel of
every muscle that Merilia's abilities were now
Erin's. It was heady stuff. Only the memory of
Merilia's death—death felt as though it were her
own—kept Erin sober, kept her from headlong
flight from Black Mountain to Terwold, challenging all Shom Bru's army to prove herself invincible. There was nothing invincible about her, and
she must bear it in mind. Superior skill could add
up to nothing if over-confidence bred carelessness; and as Merilia proved, the very Fates and
Stars could favor her, and still the slightest error
could end it.

The light of Merilia's coffin was softening. Looking about, Erin saw that there were a score of en-

trances to this chamber, all identical to the one
she had come by. Which one had she taken? As she
stood wondering, the light went lower still, until it
was nearly dark. Seven shadow-men were
standing one beside the other, their shadow-
sabers drawn. They did not offer battle, but
salute. When they bowed together, Erin returned
the bow. When she raised from the bow, she saw
they were pointing to the tunnel at the furthest
end of the chamber, which couldn't possibly be
the one she had entered through, unless she were
utterly turned about. She did not fear the shadow-
men's advice, though, and so she took that route,
descending through the dragon's intestines and
finally through its sphincter to the plains below.
There had been no farewell with Kiron, who
would have found his transient oblivion by then in
any case. She would see him again, she was certain; he had promised to teach her his books, after
all. Yet she felt sorrow in leaving, that which every
fledgling must feel on slipping from nest to branch
and thence into flight.

She found the road which led across the plain.
There were no villages, so Erin, perforce, fasted.
The road led only to Black Mountain and few but
pilgrims went that way. Winter was shorter on the
plains and, though snow still covered Black Mountain making its peaks no longer black, it was
almost spring down here. Still, she had left without provisions, and her first night was miserable.
In the morning she broke camp and started off
anew, seeing before noon a pilgrim in the distance,
moving with long strides and putting his staff far
before him.

Most of the monks and priests were martially inclined, but by his outline far ahead, this one
carried neither *i* nor *mai*, though if her eyes were
not mistaken, he carried an *oude* across his
shoulders. It was rare that anyone carried such a

sword without also owning the others; but sometimes religious sects varied from the norm of secular warriors.

The mystery was resolved when he was closer. Erin saw that the head of the priest's staff was a hammer, and he was blind. When they met, there happened to be a little shrine at the side of the road, this one built to honor the Shades of Black Mountain, having seven stone monuments erected around it, and the carved wooden representation of a dragon resting within.

"My first year on Endsworld is over," said Erin. Father Kes grinned toothlessly, bowed, then tapped the stone wall of the little shrine and said, "Shall we make prayers to Black Mountain before we duel?"

"The Shades and the Dragon have blessed me already," she said. "You may pray if you wish."

"I have prayed to dark Durga a little earlier today, and to my hammer as well."

"Need this battle be? Would you accept my word that I can defeat you, and let me take the third sword which is mine?"

"I think not," said Kes. "I am bound by oaths to this duel."

"It makes me sad," said Erin. "You are no foe of mine."

"A warrior has no enemies," Kes intoned, yet smiling. "A true warrior has only opponents. I will not disappoint you, I should say."

"I know. As I shan't disappoint you, though I did before. Have you any request or message I should deliver, when you're slain?"

"None. Bury my corpse behind the shrine. It will be enough."

"So you know I will win?"

"In fact, I do not. Kiron taught me for as many years as he did Merilia. It could be that we are evenly matched."

"Kiron told me Merilia was his finest student. I dare say, without boast, that I am now as good as she."

"The Teacher does not know what I have learned in my austerity as a priest!"

"Do you mean to say I need not feel badly about this match?"

"I can hold my own. You may be in greater peril than you imagine."

"Then," she said, "if it is I who falls, I request you give Kiron my apologies, and a vast jug of wine."

Kes the Hammer agreed. Then the battle was enjoined. Erin did not hold back, yet did not achieve the quick victory she expected. Kes was quick as ever. His hammer had the reach of an *oude*, which her *mai* could not equal. If she bore the *oude* already, she would have him. But she would have to defeat Kes *before* acquiring the weapon she needed to do it easily.

As the hammer whisked by, barely missing her temple, Erin realized it was thoughts of the *oude* which made her weaker. Why consider the merit of weapons not in hand? She cleared her mind and fought with *mai* alone, not drawing *i*. Kes was then on the defense entirely, hardly threatening her at all with his hammer's head. When she cut him, they both had not expected it; it had happened swiftly, naturally—and the cut was deep. His hammer was flung from his grasp into the brush between the shrine-monuments. He went immediately to his knees and began to pull cotton wads from a pocket in his girdle. He was sworn never to spill blood, and that included his own as well as that of others. He stuffed cotton in the stomach wound and pressed compacts to the outside, trying to keep the blood from seeping out.

"I am sorry," said Erin, flicking blood from her *mai*'s tip with a single gesture then sheathing it.

"It is all right. I shan't spill any blood at all. If I die, it will stop in my veins; if I live, I will hold it in stubbornly."

"I will help you up Black Mountain!" she said, going to his side. "Kiron's medicinals will cure you!"

"You've more important things to do. Have you not heard that a pacifistic movement rises in the desert? Hundreds plan a March of Death to the walls of Terwold. I have important information for you, which my big ears overheard from the lips of one of Shom Bru's frightened servants, the Maker of the Beds. It seems the tyrant has long been the lover of the insect-queen, as were Cal Bru and Joor Bru before him, and it is debatable which rules the other in the perverse arrangement. Elsewhere, I learned that Shom Bru has already sent trusted aides to the queen's stronghold to plot, with her, the attack of Valk the Ear's peaceful army. The plan is to have the insect folk attack them in the desert before they reach the hills and forests around Terwold; they will not expect it, for most have come to believe the insects will not appear save on moonless nights. If the pacifists can be exterminated without anyone ever learning their fate, it will avoid the embarrassment of slaying them outside the walls of the Capital, and circumvent the reaction of witnessing peasants. If you can stop the aides, Valk the Ear's plan will not be aborted by Shom Bru's insect allies, and the pacifists will make it to their chosen doom instead. Of course, it would be better still to avert tragedy altogether, but that will be more difficult."

Erin said, "I know of a route which by-passes Terwold and leads more directly to the insects' stronghold. But it will be difficult to arrive before Shom Bru's aides if they have left Terwold already."

"You can only try. They will be three-swords, although Shom Bru used to send two-swords as emissaries, until less than a year ago a group of them were murdered (*your* handiwork, according to the fishmonger Teebi Dan Wellsmith). You will need the *oude* from my back. Take it! You have earned it."

She took the *oude* which was the match of her *mai* and *i*, completing the set. It felt proper slung across her shoulder, but it did not much console her feelings about Kes on his knees upon the road, desperately holding back his blood. He said, "Where is my hammer? It is my eyes! I need it!" She fetched it for him, put it in his hand. He used it to stand and without further word or adieu began to walk toward Black Mountain. Erin called after him, "Do not die, Father Kes! I've debts of gratitude to repay!"

He staggered on, not looking back, not replying, staff reaching before, hand clenched to belly. Erin of Thar went the other way.

VII·WARRIOR

# VII. WARRIOR

"I am a man of peace," said Teebi Dan Well-smith to the motley group of peasants, pariahs and renegades who fancied themselves rebels. They had gathered in the temple in the low district, whose priest was a sympathizer. There were less than a hundred of them, hardly an army. But there were other groups like this one, some in the villages, some elsewhere in Terwold, scattered and with poor communications, which didn't make them exactly a united force, but it did make them pretty much invulnerable to major treachery. They had one thing in common, these groups: each was prepared to rise in arms if the coming pacifists were met with the regime's typical violence. The whole of the city and the countryside was a packed, dry tinderbox waiting for the spark to come to them from the desert.

Teebi went on, "But there are only so many cheeks a man can turn. I'm with you on the morrow, with a good fine hook for slaying." He raised the barbed bale-hook meaningly and, having said his part, sat down in the pews. Others swore allegiances as well, confessing their pet grievances, telling of the injustices they had witnessed, showing their own scars of torture, lamenting their murdered families and friends, praising Valk the Ear for his magnanimous plan

. . . Teebi listened to the complaints and oaths and righteous vigor of the destitute who had nothing left to lose. He knew he could not and would not withdraw from his role in the rising, for his oath was given and there was no turning back. He harbored doubts nonetheless. Valk the Ear, for whom half the city was willing to rise in arms, clearly would not approve of such support. The paradox was that someone *had* to fight to preserve the Healer's philosophy or it would die with him; but, fighting, the pacifistic philosophy died anyway. Teebi's mind struggled with this over and over: if the pacifists were destroyed, the Bru Dynasty would gloat unchallenged; if the people were at last outraged enough to revolt, Valk the Ear's teaching would be trampled by warrior and rioter alike.

There was no resolving these dilemmas, not that Teebi's simple approach to things could manage, so finally the only thing that made sense to him was this: save Valk the Ear at any cost. If the burden of murder and violence were carried upon the shoulders of the likes of Teebi Dan Wellsmith, who anyway was unworthy of salvation (thought he), at least the preacher himself would live to spread his gorgeous notions, even to chastise the ghosts of his self-sacrificed protectors.

Sitting in the darkness of the pews in an old and holy place, surrounded by the vile smelling volunteers and ragamuffins, Teebi Dan Wellsmith began silently to weep, as he had done too often in these last months. His cheeks glistened with moisture, but no one around him noticed. He thought: *Let it cost my soul; I do not care.* If he were too weak to champion an idea, at least he would be strong enough to champion its progenitor. He knew only this:

Valk the Ear must live.

\*       \*       \*

The relics of a forgotten age reared their ugly, variegated shapes above the trees, against an orange and darkening sky, looking like something no less bizarre than a nightmare-twisted carnival. The last few miles of her trek were easy, for she had found the well-tramped and bloody path of the insects themselves. It led straight toward the crazy junkyard of technologies best left idle.

It was dark when she reached the place, newly so, and her eyes had not quite adjusted. A full moon would be rising soon, but it was below the rim of the world just now. She moved carefully through the shards of glass and steel, trying to remember the layout of a place she had seen but once before. By the sound of moist clicking, she found her way to the tunnel leading underground.

Erin of Thar tucked the sword-shaped pendant into the fold of her robe, let it dangle against her flesh, above her heart. It was not presently glowing, but she knew it would do so in the presence of the insects. There was no need for her to be a beacon in their midst, so she hid the object until such time as she was spotted and needed the power-crystal to avert their tearing her part from part.

She descended into the black tunnel.

The path wound downward to a point that leveled off. She felt her way along, felt the entries to chambers which she did not explore. A peculiar sound stopped her once. From one of the dark chambers there came not the usual clicking of insects, but a sound less comprehensible: wet linen pressed against rocks at a riverside, squishing, oozing, dripping. The hair at the nape of her neck prickled, for Erin knew that nothing so innocent as laundry reposed in that room. Curiosity outweighed common sense and, since the room seemed to contain no sound of the insects themselves, she bared the crystal, which now glowed a small amount, enough to reveal the contents of the room.

White, elongated shapes twice the size of melons, half egg and half maggot, writhed within the confines of octagonal nests against the walls. Their squirming produced the sound. The ugliness of the blind monstrosities caused Erin to hide the light of her pendant, and hurry along the bending tunnel. It ended in a lighted place: a squared passage apparently built of steel at ceiling, floor, and two walls.

The ceiling of this long hallway held tubes set lengthwise, glowing greenly. The light was not much, and not attractive, but it sufficed. Erin went along the corridor, leery of the side-passages which were all on her left. From each she heard the gurgling clicks of industrious insects and the oozing, squirmy sound of the white, blind children. The sour smell of meat wafted out from certain of the side tunnels.

She stepped suddenly into one of the side passages, for a trio of insects was emerging from a passage further along the hall. They hadn't seen her. She pressed herself to the wall and heard their feet clattering upon the steel floor in exact unison, slowing down as they approached the passage she was hiding in; and she knew she must act swiftly, for her refuge was their destination.

She stepped out with *oude* drawn and with a swift stroke beheaded all three. Their bodies did not fall. She evaded their grasping claws and snatched up the three heads and rolled them down the winding tunnel she had leapt from. The insects' minds could control the bodies even severed, but as those heads tumbled beyond view, they could no longer see their own standing bodies and could not direct them properly. They thrashed and grasped, but Erin had already moved far along the corridor.

The telepathic link between trios was also, apparently, weakly linked to the other insects. The moist clicking rose to an excited pitch, and Erin knew they were all aware of what she had done to the first three. The side passages were sounding with the clatter of the insects' scurrying arms and legs. They were coming in a rush up into the steel hallway, intent on stopping the intruder.

Erin ran the length of the hall, came to its end, turned to see the horde of demonic creatures flooding out of the various tunnels. Trios of them, armed with daggers and sickles in their various arms and claws, stalked in her direction. The sickly green light glistened over their black shells, a perfect dream of horror.

Erin held the *oude* straight forward, wondering how many she could cut to pieces and how much good it would do if she couldn't manage to destroy their walnut-sized brains in the process, since even decapitated, they would fight. She pressed her back to the wall at the corridor's end, prepared for the worst. The wall gave way behind her. She stumbled backward into another room. The wall resealed itself, barring the insect horde from entry.

Before her stood three warriors, three-swords like herself, older men and dignified, and frightened of their most recent commission, she could tell. The room was lit in green. The floor was tiled with diamond shapes alternating blue and deeper green. At the further end of the room was an ebon throne, upon which sat the breastless, hairless insect queen, majestically feminine, her multi-celled eyes watching the humans with curious detachment. It was not possible to find human emotion registered in that almost robotic or sculpted face.

There were other things in the queen's room, things Erin had not expected: a control panel of some sort was set against a wall, over which was a viewing screen in which Erin saw herself. So she had been observed the whole time! She pulled the sling of her *oude*'s sheath from her shoulder, put her sword therein, and slung it across her back again. She could draw any of three swords in a fraction of an eye's blink, so she was not fretful on that account; yet, the sheathing of it was a peaceful gesture, and Erin needed to buy time.

One of the three-swords stepped toward Erin, growling, "What offense do you plan? Who sends you?"

The insect queen made a hissing sound which caused the abusive three-sword to be instantly cowed and silent. The insect raised a long-fingered hand in a languorous sweep, and she spoke. Her voice issued not from the throne, but from a sound system hidden in the panelled walls. Her voice was sweet, sardonic, ultimately feminine, but also somewhat mechanical as she said,

"It has been long since we met, Earth woman. The emissary of Shom Bru is rude, but asks the proper question. Do you plan some offense?"

"I do," said Erin.

The three-swords moved as one, as a trio of insects might do. It made Erin grin, thinking their infamy was comparable to that of the insects they feared but required. The hiss of the insect queen made them stand back again.

"It will be difficult to succeed alone," the walls' feminine voice said, and Erin thought there was humor in the tone. The insect queen continued, "The emissaries have asked that I send my people to destroy a certain group of desert-humans who are coming toward Shom Bru's city this night. I have told them my storehouse of human flesh is full from the month's sacrifice and can hold no more, although I am not adverse to bargaining about the matter of assistance. I have asked that my lover Shom Bru commit himself to spending one month in every ten with me in my tunnels, in exchange for my continued observance of the old treaty, and for various services rendered in the present matter and others."

The three emissaries swelled with indignation, but minded their tongues and tempers. They were torn between watching out for Erin at one end of the room, and keeping eyes upon the terrifying queen at the other.

"It strikes me as a decent bargain," said Erin. "But you forget that I have a weapon which will make all bartering moot."

To Erin's right, a panel opened at some command she neither saw nor heard. The panel opening was an arm in width and half that tall. Inside the wall was a crystal not unlike her own, but cracked—a flawed diamond. It was held at the tip of a tubular structure, the ends of which were pronged. Webs of energy reached out from the crystal in all directions. The queen said,

"You refer to the battery you wear at your neck like a bit of human jewelry. As you can see, I have one also, and it is keyed to my bodily systems as yours is keyed to you. Mine is used to sustain this underground complex, but the flaw in its structure makes it unreliable. I would like to replace it with your own, although I cannot touch yours as long as you live. For this reason I must alter my bartering position with these emissaries. If they can kill you, I will send my people into the desert to destroy my lover's enemies, and take your crystal as my only payment."

The three men were clearly delighted with this change of events, having thought the queen's previous demands unreasonable. The one who had earlier spoken gruffly to Erin spoke more kindly to the insect queen. "If that is your condition," he said, "we happily oblige."

"It is my condition," said the sweet, sardonic

voice from the walls.

Erin drew her *i*, her shortest blade against three opponents, but realized she was boasting, so drew the *mai* as well. The emissaries drew their *mai* blades only. The *oude* would be too awkward for them in the confines of the room, since all three attacking with long sweeps could result in their cutting each other instead of her. The middle-sized blades, then, were most practical.

Erin blocked with her smallsword, blocked her second attacker with the *mai*, ducked between their blades to be missed by the third attacker. She made a rush for the throne, but a power-shield stopped her, dazed her. The insect queen did not move. Her large eyes closed and opened slowly, and she seemed to be, if anything, bored. Erin leapt into the air to avoid a cut to her legs, and as she came down, slashed her nearest opponent across the side of his neck. He collapsed, red spurting from his jugular onto the blue and green diamond tiles. The remaining two men arranged themselves on either side of Erin. She sheathed her *mai* and *i* in a quick motion and drew the *oude* from across her shoulder.

The insect queen hissed.

"You cannot defeat her," said the queen.

They attacked together. Erin fell to one knee and slid backward, *oude* reaching left then right then back to a centered position, so swift the two men did not realize they'd been cut. The one on her left fell first. Then the one on her right.

The insect queen stood from her throne, descended the steps, moved along the far side of the energy field in the direction of the control panel against a side wall. There, she pressed a single button, and the green light brightened in the room, seeming to come from no special point unless from the whole of the floor itself. The three corpses Erin had created faded as the green light went back to its previous, dimmer level. Erin felt the power-crystal warm above her heart, and she knew it was busy keeping her from the same vaporization as the corpses.

"I admire you," said the insect queen. "Perhaps I can bargain with you."

"As you bargained with Jorr Bru many years ago? Do your tastes extend to human females as well?"

"I never considered it," said the queen. "It is a proposition with some merit. I have always liked new ideas of this sort."

"I won't bargain with you. I've come to destroy your people."

"Not a noble construct," she said through the sound system, her sardonic voice seeming to surround Erin as a tangible thing. "Extinction," said the queen, "is irrevocable. My own race has never been responsible for the extinction of a single species."

"Not even the four-legged race?" asked Erin pointedly.

"Not even them; not so long as Kiron of the Black Mountain lives, which will be forever. I know you think my race is cruel, because we eat human flesh, but I find human nature more incomprehensible. Since humans came to dominate Endsworld—and it was partly my kind's fault, I readily admit—many things have disappeared forever: species of fish, huge lizards which were hunted to the last specimen, birds decimated so that humans could decorate their hats with feathers, numerous larger creatures rendered moldy trophies . . . It is the nature of my kind to hunt, and to feast upon, only that which can easily replenish itself. It is a better order of things, if you consider it objectively. Soon, my people will have achieved the population necessary to join all minds as one, to regain our past intellect and glory, to restore a sensible order to Endsworld. With the help of the battery you have brought into this stronghold, I intend to better protect my kind for that coming day of restoration."

While she talked, her fingers played over the control panel, as upon the keys of a musical instrument. Erin knew something was in the works. She felt that it was now the queen who was biding time, and the moment was upon Erin to act. She edged toward the console by which the queen stood, even though the near-invisible shield shimmered between them. She raised her *oude* one-handed, holding it as though intending to thrash at the barrier, while the other hand made a deft, unnoticed toss in a different direction. Her *i* shot toward the open panel which contained the flawed power-crystal.

The *i* struck its target squarely. Erin felt the warmth of the hot, red flash of light at her back; had she been facing that light, it might have blinded her. She turned to see her handiwork, and was disheartened to see her *i* had lost its fine point —the tip was melted blunt. The crystal had fallen loose from the pronged rod which held it, and lay in two pieces on the floor of its nook. The lines of power which webbed it flickered, changed. The green light of the floor went bright and dim, bright and dim. The insect queen made a curse Erin thought only to hear from humans, then slipped backward through a secret panel.

Then: darkness. The power of the shattered crystal had bled away. Erin bared the talisman, let the white light of it hang outside her robe. The energy field had fallen. She was surprised to find it crumpled like cellophane at her feet. Fetching her blunted *i* from the floor where it had clattered, Erin used it to pry at the panel through which the insect queen had vanished.

It opened. She felt a gust of metallic air as she

stepped into the joining room. The light of her talisman revealed to her rows upon rows of winged insect people standing in crystal boxes similar to the one dead Merilia had been encased within (Erin had not guessed before now that Kiron had preserved the corpse by ancient insect technology). But these were not corpses. They were newly matured adults, awaiting release so that they might fly into the clouds and go out across the lands to found new colonies. As Erin passed among them, they cringed inside their glass prisons, averting their eyes from her crystal's light.

There were hundreds of them stacked one atop the other, one beside another, one behind another . . . She could see through the glass cases to the ones behind, and the ones behind those. Hundreds? Nay, thousands! Erin struck at the glass of one of the cases, but it would not break. Could she hope to kill them, even if the cases could be opened? It would be a time-consuming effort at its best.

The insect queen hissed in darkness. Erin turned. The queen could no longer speak, having lost the aid of her machinery. She rasped, "Er-ta-wo-man-*die-eeee!*"

The glass boxes sprang open all at once. The winged insects began to climb out of their containers. They weren't flyers yet, for their wings were too moist. It might take mere moments for them to dry. Their wings rustled as they were exercised. Erin was quickly surrounded.

She thought herself safe, for the insects could not approach the light of the crystal. But she had not counted on the clever queen instructing her people. Mandibles and claws reached for her as the creatures approached *with eyes closed!*

She fought her way back into the throne room, littering her path with fragments of claws and wings and severed heads. The door at the further wall of the throne room was open. Through it came trios of wingless workers and drones, blocking her escape with sickles and daggers and mandibles and claws. She did not think, did not plan; a warrior moved by training and instinct, not intellect. She charged into the swarm, reaving with her *oude*. They could only approach her with eyes closed, which handicapped them in the actual fight. She felt the scrape of their claws upon her body. Their sharp weapons rent her clothing. But she was too swift to be dealt a serious wound. She went through them like a ferocious whirlwind, carving a path, fleeing through the square steel corridor, then up the winding tunnel, injuring the insects at every step and turn. She came out into the chilly night, a bright moon overhead, clouds few. Oh, what she would have given for the myth to be the truth! The insects did *not* fear the moon, and swarmed up after her.

They were clumsy and stupid trying to catch her with huge eyes shut. She evaded them, but more and more of them flooded up onto the ground, filling up the junkyard with their presence. There was finally no place for her to duck, so she began to climb upward through the skeletal framework of some grotesque machine. If she were treed, there was no helping it, no other choice.

The young fliers were preening and testing their wings. Some of them were bold and took to the sky awkwardly, trying to get close to Erin inside the structure. Their wingspans were too great for them to fly amidst the girders. Wingless ones were climbing up from the ground. Erin was amazed most of all by her lack of panic. She had no plan and nowhere to go, but her mind remained clear and calm, and she proceeded by that warrior's intuition which was the most forceful weapon anyone could have.

She found herself sitting in a familiar seat, one

which did not really fit her bottom. Calmly testing the levers and buttons, a two-pronged lever popped outward at her eyes. It looked exactly like the rod which had held the queen's flawed crystal.

Erin burst the hemp thread which held the sword-shaped pendant and set the talisman between the prongs, then pushed the rod back into its spring-lock. What she was activating, she did not yet know, but it certainly *looked* like some huge instrument of destruction, and might prove a useful weapon.

Part of the machine reached outward like the arm of a monstrous crane, at the end of which dangled a number of loose cables and wires. As the machine activated, the ganglia drew upward as might serpents, then wove themselves into a basket shape. In the middle of this construction a cold light glittered. Erin pulled the thick lever toward herself, and a glistening ray of inconceivable coldness struck the young fliers, stopping them in mid-air, turning them rigid. They plunged to the ground, shattering as even steel would do at such a low temperature.

At the same time, the machine itself began to rise on telescoping legs, six of them in all, shaking the climbers loose and crushing them in its gears and hinges and hydraulic lifts. It was less crane-like thus animated. It was a gargantuan mosquito braced on its six legs, swivelling its dreadful snout in search of blood. The ice-ray spread along the ground, freezing the insects in their places. Those who tumbled, broke.

Scores and then hundreds withdrew into their underground lair to escape the killing cold, but the murderous machine would not be evaded. Erin experimented with the few odd controls, learned the mosquito-juggernaut's operation as best she could, and was surprised with each new discovery regarding its abilities. The machine reared back, almost shaking her from the knobby seat, and stood on four of its six legs, using the front legs to scoop into the ground.

As it dug into the underground habitat, part by part the colony was exposed. The steel corridor and other metal-reinforced passages and chambers buckled and burst in the juggernaut's digging feet. The rooms and tunnels which were carved in mere ground collapsed upon themselves. The maggot-like eggs were exposed and began to make high-pitched whining noises, wiggling their more pointed ends frantically as their octagon housing was crushed and tossed about. Workers and drones scurried over the ruined nest crazily gathering the eggs in their claws, only to be stayed by another frigid bath of rays, blasted into twisted statuary.

The front pair of legs continued digging into the ground, exposing the storehouse of human flesh. Arms and legs and heads and quartered torsos rose out of the earth in a grey mass.

Another deep scoop ripped out the roof of the throne room. Erin looked down from her high seat and saw the diamond patterned floor, the ebon throne, the ruined console and viewing screen. She did not see the queen. In the next moment, the room was buried again, covered in dirt and meat and the numerous corpses of frozen insects.

The glassy cases from which the fliers were unleashed were uncovered. The scooping forelegs of the juggernaut plowed through these, raising a din of knells and tinkles as the cases were crushed upon themselves, and the insects fleeing between the rows were crushed as well.

There was surprisingly little vindictive feeling in Erin's activity. She did think momentarily of Rud and Orline, of the sacrifices she had seen outside the walls of Terwold, of the generations of terror these monsters had delivered to the peasantry. She thought, too, of Kiron's pleasure and inevitable grief, seeing his obsession obtained, knowing not how to spend the rest of his eternity. But Erin felt neither vengeful nor righteous. She was not certain that what she did was necessary or proper. Yet, somehow, none of these considerations were important to Erin personally, and her true motivations were obscure even to her. The deed was witnessed by no fellow human who could later sing her praises, so it could not be that she was seeking notice as a hero, the thing she once believed she most wanted. "The ego requires feed," Kiron had taught her. "A warrior must nourish other things." Erin scarcely realized it, but it was no longer important to be noticed for her performance. It was enough to know, in herself, that she had acted in accordance with her training and values.

At the bottom line of it all, there was only this: a warrior must *act* and act unselfishly. The death she wrought here was quick and merciful. By her deed, thousands of human lives were saved, and an age of terror ended.

She felt sorrow for the insects nonetheless. The words of the queen were true: extinction is irrevocable. But it was not for Erin to champion those who fed upon the human race. The insect queen had pursued lusts perverse for her species. Had she spent her time at better occupation, she might have bred or become the champion of *her* people, as Erin was for humankind. The fates even of the insect race had been, and remained, not in Erin's hands, but their own.

In the distance, above the trees that surrounded the technological heap, and against the light of a swollen moon, Erin beheld a group of fliers being led away by their queen. The panic which Erin had not experienced beckoned at the back door of her mind, for the queen and an entourage were escaping. Erin punched the controls of the mosquito-juggernaut and sent the whole structure bounding foreward, first on four legs, then on six. It stepped between the trees below, getting stuck among dwarfed verdure, uprooting trees when pulling loose. The insects flew toward the horizon in a straight line and Erin could not hope to overtake them in this hobbled contraption. She could only hope the range of the icy ray could reach them.

The basket-shaped snout of the mosquito swung upward and the glittering ray shot out over the countryside. Those insects at the rear of the retreating swarm were frozen in their flight and fell from the sky. Another frigid bolt took more of them, and more. The wings of the surviving few beat frantically, though they were too far away for Erin to hear the whirring, and her vehicle's stressed creaking and humming drowned out everything else. The remaining fliers made a wide circle behind their queen, protecting her from icy bolts. Erin picked off two more of them; they had spread themselves out so she could not get a lot of them at once.

The snout of her vehicle reached forth as far as it could. The rear legs raised to take a new step through the forest. The front legs snagged upon the pines. And the whole of the machine became unbalanced.

Erin clung madly to her seat and was jostled around in the cab as the juggernaut toppled, slowly, slowly. The last ray of coldness went wild, firing uselessly into the heavens. The mosquito began to crumple upon itself, girders and miscellaneous parts warping and bending under the pressure of their own unbalanced weight. It might have been a stronger machine in the millenium it was built; now, it could not hold itself, nor catch itself, nor remain whole in its collapse. Erin pulled the pronged rod out of its place, reclaimed the miniature sword-talisman held at the rod's tip, and tried to climb free of the falling machine. A buckling girder struck her alongside the ribs and she grunted, unable to breathe. At last the thing had ceased to fall and Erin lay at an odd incline, looking outward at a wreckage of metal and splintered trees. She was surprised to be alive.

\*     \*     \*

Throughout that day there had come striding over desert sands men and women old and young, clad in the coarse yellow linens of desert tribes, their leader clad in funeral white. He was pale compared to them; or usually he was pale. The long march, already in its third day, had left him baked a brilliant hue. He was of stout spirit, but unused to his adopted country, even after this full year. He was pathetic by contrast to the tawny people who followed him. They admired his stamina, did not revile his puisance.

Darkness fell swiftly, but was not absolute. Starshine and then the rising full moon urged them over the shadowy plain. As they went, they sang songs, their voices pleasant blendings of old men's basses, children's sweet choruses, and the modulated contraltos of desert-toughened women. These songs were godless yet holy. They were songs of a libertine empire.

Later, mothers and fathers carried children, who were all asleep. The old ones were beginning to tire, but were eager to carry on. They came, that third night, to the desert's edge, and knew their goal was near. Beyond the forested hills before them stood the capital of Durga's Lathe. Valk the Ear, weakest among them though their leader, suggested that camp be made here at the desert's edge and that they break camp before first light so that they could complete the last leg of their

journey in the coolness and pulchritude of dawn.
To this, all agreed.

Despite the suicidal nature of their mission, these people were of good cheer as they laid out their night's bedding, and they slept peacefully and deeply. When wings fluttered high overhead, only Valk the Ear was awake to hear the sound of another race's shattered hopes. He watched the flying creatures cross the starry heavens, saw the minimal swarm pass before the moon. He thought it was a dream, for the insects never went abroad save upon the new moon (for which reason this march had been planned as far from the new moon as possible), and only their queen was known to fly. *Everything* had come to seem a dream to Valk the Ear, or more acutely, a nightmare, so the vision did not shock him.

He was not afraid that tomorrow would find him at the ledge of death. He would lead his devoted congregation to that cliff and off it, certain he would awaken from this awful place before he struck the ground. No matter if the rest awakened or not, so long as *he* could return to Earth. His motivations were never voiced. These people thought him holier than this, self-sacrificing, loving, committed to a future world of peace. If these had meant anything to him before, he did not remember it. He had ceased to be these things the desert people saw in him, and he had become something simpler. He had become mad. This, no one guessed, or at least no one suggested. It has been said the insane never realize their condition, but Válkyová *knew*, and hid it. He would pursue this nightmare to its end, and awaken from it if he could. If he could not awaken, he would at least not die alone.

The handful of flying creatures vanished over the horizon. Valk the Ear slept at last, never recalling the vision.

*     *     *

Teebi left Terwold by the canal to River Yole a while before dawn, soon pulling his boat out of the river and hiding it beneath branches and brush. There were an alarming number of guards upon the walls, so he crept carefully, sometimes on all fours, evading the attention of sentinels along the battlements. He came to a stand of trees on a hillside, from which he had a good view of the gate to the city. There were six other men and two women in the gulley he found, armed with an assortment of sharp implements ranging from farm tools to heirlooms and trophies, including one good sword among the eight people he could see. He had never seen any of these men and women before, but knew they were from groups akin to his of the night before. The stand of trees doubtlessly held six score more; and other stands along the hillside would be equally packed with the hidden rebels who had slipped into the hills during the night. Inside the city, there would be even more women and men, lurking behind every door and in every shadow, awaiting the response of the warriors to the pacifists.

The dawn seemed a long one. The guards on the city walls grew in number; Teebi was appalled to see it. Usually the bulk of the guards were one-swords, but an unusual percentage of two-swords were among them; and three-swords were there as generals to oversee whatever matters unfolded. The pacifists were not in sight, but no one doubted they would come.

Someone on the wall of the city pointed. Others joined to look. They had spotted some motion in a stand of trees—not where Teebi hid at least. The city gate opened barely wide enough to let one through at a time, but the bridge was not lowered over the pits; rather, a plank was set across, and a

half-dozen two-swords went out to check the area.
Teebi watched through briars and bushes, seeing
only a little. An encounter in those trees seemed
inevitable. Afterward, the three-sword generals
would wonder why a group of armed peasants had
been hiding there. Then they would have the rest
of the area searched.

Someone darted from the trees—perhaps the
very hapless fellow who had been fool enough to
let himself be seen before. He had a rabbit in his
hands, held by its ears. *What luck to find it*,
thought Teebi. The warriors stopped the man,
questioned him. Teebi couldn't hear any of it; but
hunting near the city was the prerogative of
warriors only, and this peasant was, therefore, a
poacher. He effaced himself before the six two-
swords, flat upon his belly, but they forced him to
sit upright on his knees and bow his head at an
easy angle for decapitation. Teebi admired the one
rebel's sacrifice, as would the hundreds of others
who secretly watched this typically cruel spectacle.

When they'd killed him, they gave a hasty glance
about, then returned to the city. They took the rabbit with them. The gate was left open its crack.
The plank was left down. Not long afterward, two
corpse-collecting *rint* in somber robes came out to
fetch the corpse and its head.

There were no other untoward happenings
before the desert people appeared on the last hill
before Terwold.

The yellow-clad group of about three hundred
stopped on the hilltop, did not approach the walls
where archers stood and watched. These people
had come to the place where stakes were set into
the ground, where sacrifices were made on each
new moon. Here, they followed the preacher's lead
and got down upon their knees, as though they had
arrived at some holy place, and folded their hands

before their faces. Whole families began to chant
monotonously, and the desert dialect was not so
different from the common speech of Terwold
that it was hard to understand the words: *May
tyrants fall and the world discover peace; may tyrants fall and the world discover peace; may tyrants fall and . . .*

The warriors did nothing but watch. The chanting went on and on as the sun raised ever higher.
At last they changed to a new if equally monoto-
nous phrase: *May the ghosts lay down, may the
dead find peace; may the ghosts lay down, may the
dead find peace,* faster and faster until Teebi was
amazed to hear it said so quickly.

Spring winds parted the grasses, whispered
through the scattered stands of trees. Teebi was
unnerved by the electric stillness, shattered only
by the drone of three hundred people chanting.
The warriors had still made no move. The
thousand hidden in the foliage and the trees were
bound to grow careless from the tedium of
waiting.

*May-the-ghosts-lay-down-may-the-dead-find-
peace . . .*

Someone behind Teebi, supposedly hiding and
keeping silent, began to take up the chant in
religious fervor. Someone else leapt on him, creating a scuffle. There was a sharp sound of a blunt
object against a skull and the lone chanter in the
trees went silent. With luck, the warriors would
not be able to tell that one voice among the hundreds had not been on the hilltop.

Two-swords began to leave the city in single file,
over the narrow plank, the gate still barely open.
They lined themselves before the wall, but made
no approach. They stood attentively.

The day never grew quite warm, not even when
the sun had reached its zenith. But Teebi sweated.
He looked at the few companions within sight, and

they looked edgy also.

The quick chant stopped abruptly and a new phrase was devised, starting at a slow, slow pace: *Praise to the wonderful law, peace is the regulation; praise to the wonderful law, peace is the regulation.*

Only about fifty two-swords had left the city. Six times as many prayed upon the hill; but the besieging "army" was indeed, as promised, unarmed. Fifty could kill three hundred easily. Yet there was a back-up of a thousand warriors—archers, one-, two-, and three-swords. Of course the regime would suspect peasant reprisals, and were prepared to respond.

A three-sword on the wall shouted some command.

The two-swords before the city began to march toward the hill.

The chanting ceased. Valk the Ear and his people lowered their faces, exposed their necks for the oncoming warriors. They were so silent, they might already be headless corpses waiting for the *rint.*

When the warriors reached the side of the tree-dotted hillside, a group of peasants rose from tall grass and from behind trees to throw a number of knives. Three two-swords were killed instantly, blades in their throats and faces. Then rebels were rising everywhere, overwhelming the two-swords with sheer numbers. There were more than Teebi had expected!

The city gates were flung full open. The bridge began to lower. Inside the gate, Teebi saw that scuffles had begun there already. The first sounds of rioting were beginning, would soon rise to a din.

Warriors charged out of Terwold (one- and two-swords only) to join the fray on the hillside. Teebi had as yet engaged no one in battle, but his hook

was to hand, and he was running the right direction. A two-sword was in his path, closer, closer
. . . a *mai* swung at Teebi's head, but he leapt into a roll, tumbled down the slope, catching the two-sword by the leg and ripping out muscle with his hook. The warrior shouted useless blasphemies, was felled and could not walk. Teebi left him for another to kill, and tried the trick again: he jumped, rolled, evaded a warrior's *mai*, ripped the fellow's leg. Teebi thought: *It keeps me from having to kill.* The third time, his trick failed. The warrior leapt into the air as Teebi rolled beneath. As the warrior turned to dash his sword at Teebi, Teebi caught the *mai* on the barb of his hook and twisted with his great untrained strength, breaking the sword halfway down its length. While the warrior looked sadly at the hilt of the broken sword, Teebi was able to get to his feet. The warrior, cursing at the indignity of having his *mai* ruined, drew his *i* and leapt upon Teebi, knocking him to the ground again. Teebi grabbed the warrior's knife hand and simultaneously plunged the hook into his attacker's stomach, pulling out intestines.

It was not a new sensation for Teebi. In his day he had been a rogue among rogues, a murdering, marauding pirate. He had often felt the blood running down his bale-hook, gushing on his hand. It had meant little to him in the past, but now it seemed a tragedy unbearable. Valk the Ear had cleansed Teebi of all sinfulness, had twice healed him of bodily and spiritual damage; and here he was blackening his soul anew. He pushed the warrior's corpse away, stood with shoulders squared, a look in his eyes which said: *My soul is lost already.* He began to swing his hook with killing purpose, using the barb to catch, bend, and break warriors' swords; using the curve of it to gut them. Teebi was no warrior by training, but there were

styles of fighting even peasants could learn, and
certainly pirates could practice in good encounters. He murdered well.

Others among the rebels were skilled in the martial use of tools, so it was a bloody fight for both
sides. Unless or until the three-swords joined the
battle, the rebels had an equal chance of winning
this first engagement.

Teebi smelled smoke. He looked toward the city
and saw flames lick up from behind the walls. The
din of rioting within the capital was now a fevered
pitch. The three-swords on the battlements had to
observe and direct battles at front and back. Soon,
some of them would be forced to enter the fight
themselves, to decide key positions. Teebi had
seen their methods often enough; the bulk of any
fight would be left to one-swords and two-swords,
while the greater warriors operated as tacticians,
involving themselves more fully only at critical
points or against particularly worthwhile foes. In
a war between counties or nations, the three-swords would engage only enemy three-swords on
the field. In a peasant uprising, proud generals
considered it beneath their dignity to fight
inferior rabble. If forced to do so, they would use
their *i* as a kind of insult. Teebi was not anxious
for them to come down from the wall, for there
were few if any rebels to stand against them. At
the same time, their haughty natures annoyed
him, as did their calmness as the city burned; and
he would like to see them sweat and smell.

The fight went on. Teebi felled another two-sword and, in a moment of inspiration, committed
the sacrilege of stealing the killed man's *mai*. He
swung it madly at another warrior, a fellow who
had seen and been outraged by Teebi's crime. That
warrior fell, too, and Teebi stole a second *mai*. He
put his hook behind himself and slipped his arms
out of the robe's sleeves, let the garment hang

loose from his girdle. He held the pair of *mai* upward, growled like a fitful beast, and carved the men of Shom Bru's army with shocking ease.

How he fought so well with swords was difficult for most to understand, for he had minimal training in their use, being not of warrior blood. Teebi was a man ready to die, or convinced that he was already dead, so sorrowful was he to go against the ideals learned and believed. He growled and warred and was such an imposing, hairy thing devoid of fear, that the stoutest two-sword was weakened by his appearance, surety, and clumsy style. Not wanting to be killed by such an apparition, the two-swords became weakened, and fell before the pair of *mai* like grass before the scythe.

All this while, the desert tribes people had remained on the hilltop. All but Valk the Ear were still upon their knees. The preacher had stood and raised his arms to the twenty heavens, and started a keen with every word drawn out like a wolf's cry: "Woe upon Endsworld! The Heavens weep! Woe upon Endsworld! The Heavens weep!" His people took up this terrible lament.

From other hills came villagers, and Teebi knew that revolution was real. The motley groups of rebels circled that one hill on which three hundred non-fighters chanted. The violent protected the meek while professional soldiers strove against this fervent opposition.

By now it would have dawned upon the three-swords that their army could not breach the fanatical defense of the hill unaided. The ultra-skill of the generals themselves would be required, or else they would never snuff the flame of all this: Valk the Ear. Numerous three-swords came down from the battlements. Some went deeper into the rioting city. A group of seven came through the gate and strode toward the hill. Teebi was used to seeing them fight singly or in pairs.

That they came in a group of seven meant, to Teebi, they hoped to prey upon the superstitions of peasants, who considered seven a tutelar number.

No peasant could stand before a three-sword without facing doom. Teebi fancied himself an exception. In his heightened state of murderous capacity, he thought he *might* kill a three-sword, if only one. The bulk of the rebels would have no such chance. There were a few renegade warriors among the rebels, but not one of them a three-sword. Yet the rebels had foreseen this event and were prepared for the three-swords. The plan was excellent and simple: they would run from the greater warriors given any chance, and attack the one-swords and two-swords as eagerly as they avoided those with three.

What this plan was not good for was stopping the three-swords from moving through the quarrel and up the hill to the sacrificial place, intent on executing Valk the Ear and the desert people who chanted against the din of rioting and battle.

The gate (and other gates not in view, no doubt) could not take the crowd of citizens seeking to flee the burning capital. As they came across the bridge, many were forced into the gaping pit below. Others poured out onto the countryside, trying to evade the numerous small battles, desiring to escape city, warriors, and rebels with as much upon their backs as they could carry. Many gave up their possessions in the panic, so the hillside was soon littered with various valuables. Some of them were killed by one- and two-swords out of sheer vindictiveness. Others made a late decision to join the revolt, there seeming small chance of getting beyond the battlefield anyway.

Teebi killed those warriors in his path, trying to make headway up the hillside, thinking only himself capable of stopping the three-swords heading

for the yellow-clad people and their white-clad
leader. For a moment, Teebi fancied himself divinely appointed to keep Valk the Ear alive. But he
could not get up the hillside, so hemmed in was he
by ally and foe. The way parted easily for the
three-swords, but Teebi had to fight every step.
His goal was made hopeless, and his heart began
to sink.

The next moment, he knew who the divinely
appointed protector would really be. Erin of Thar
appeared from the far side of the hill, strode
among the pacifists, looking at them as though she
did not respect them one whit. She was always a
contrary sort and Teebi could forgive her ill
glances at his own hero Valk the Ear; only, she
must see to his defense, to the protection of them
all.

That she had spent these many months with the
Teacher of Black Mountain could not be doubted
now; for Erin of Thar had returned a three-sword,
one who still wore a fisher's girdle. Many rebels
and warriors had their attention drawn to her, tall
among the knelt pacifists. If they could see her
girdle, they would know she came as a champion
of the trammeled classes. Some who saw her
might even think they knew her by another name
than Erin. Everyone, without exception, would be
expecting some wonderful action from her. Even
the three-swords approaching the pacifists held
back to judge their position, and hers.

Teebi fought absent-mindedly but well. He
strove to watch Erin rather than his own field.

She had drawn the *oude* from across her back.

*      *      *

Erin stood among the yellow-clad people, the
hilltop high enough to see inside the walls of the
capital, where here and there were buildings set

aflame. The desert folk were chanting, and
Válkyová Idaska was leading them in this useless
occupation. She gave him a severe look, and he
grew silent, and his followers did likewise. He fell
upon his knees, his arms held up to Erin, and he
pleaded, "Leave us to our sacrifice! With our
blood the sins of the world will be cleansed!"

"May you drown in Durga's milk, you damned
whoreson from the nineteenth Hell!" Erin drew
her *oude*, but was not threatening Válkyová. There
were seven three-swords coming up the hillside,
each with *i* to hand (for they considered longer
steel too good for slicing peasants). Most of the
rebels drew aside, apparently (and wisely) instructed not to engage generals on the field.

She glanced about at the people in yellow: old
women, old men, children among the rest. She
shook her shaggy head in dismay. They were
silent. They watched her. She said, "I will save
your bloody lives, but you will know first who you
worship. It was I brought Valk the Ear to Endsworld by mistake. Ask him to deny it! If he is sent
by some gentle god, then that gentle god is *me*, and
my gentleness will be expressed in lengths of
tempered steel. Válkyová! Tell them if what I say
is true!"

Their beloved Healer fell from knees to face,
pounded the ground with his fists and, wailing to
be forgiven, confessed: "I came not to die for love
of peace, but for hatred of this planet!" He raised
himself on his hands, looked around with soil
upon his face, madness in his eyes, and shouted, "I
am nothing holy! I am just a man!"

The families who had come so far with him
could not give up their own illusions as quickly as
this. They saw not his craven weakness, but his
humbleness, his refusal to accept the godhood
which was his, his desire to know every pain and
lack of reward which was ever the lot of mortals.

They accepted Erin's godhood quite as well, and found it not the least difficult to believe that gods should make one another cower, that one should make another weep as Valk the Ear was weeping. Now their eyes were upon him, and if anything, their worship of him was increased. First one, and then another, began to chant, "Praise be the wonderful law, the regulation of peace. Praise be the wonderful law, the regulation of peace." Válkyová Idaska relaxed his arms, fell on his face anew, and whimpered like a caged and injured dog.

Erin strode down the hill to meet the seven generals.

\* \* \*

Of the seven, one stepped forward, confronted Erin. All his swords were sheathed, but a hand rested on the hilt of his *mai*, a gesture which was a common greeting, but one which showed readiness as well. Erin had her *oude* at hand, but its edge and point were held away.

"You have joined these rebels, three-sword?" he asked. He was lank and swarthy, greying at the temples, a veteran of many wars.

"I am party to no group or crime," said Erin of Thar, and the seven generals were obviously relieved. "But," she added pointedly, "I will not allow the slaughter of foolish lambs. I am the bodyguard of the few hundred you see behind me, with minimal interest in the thousands who revolt. I suggest you settle the outcome among those who are willing to fight, and leave my idiot wards to their meaningless chanting."

"You play games with words!" complained the veteran. His weathered hand gripped the *mai*'s hilt better. Erin turned the edge of her steel toward him in reply.

"You would rather fight without discussion?

Then tell me your name that I know who I kill!"

"Jai Strongarm of Tine," he replied, and drew his *mai*. Erin stepped forward, opened herself to attack, then struck aside his blow so powerfully that the *mai* flung from his hand. It was the maneuver Kiron had used on Erin enough to make her learn it. Jai Strongarm was startled and nearly ran to retrieve the weapon, but stopped, chagrined, his dignity dented. He asked, "And who are *you*?"

"Only Shom Bru knows who I am, for he dreamed of me before I existed. Give him this message for me: the Woman of Black Mountain has returned to claim his soul!"

With recognition blossoming, seven *oude* whisked across seven shoulders, and the generals surrounded Erin. Jai Strongarm of Tine said, "Shom Son of Cal Son of Jorr believed you drowned in the River Yole, but warned his generals that it might have been a trick, and you might one day return. He told us that he crossed swords with you those many months ago, and discovered you no better than an average two-sword. We know you are not Merilia despite your appearance and the scar. We will not take your insulting message to Shom Bru, but will end your fool's charade right here. After you are riven, we will slay the ones you purport to protect."

Erin looked from left to right, her situation precarious. Seven three-swords hemmed her in; seven *oude* were poised and ready to strike vertically. She said, "Very well. I will fight."

Her blunt *i* came quickly from its sheath and in a single motion was cast toward the heart of the foremost three-sword. He turned his *oude* downward to deflect the *i*. Erin drew her *mai* in her left hand, kept the *oude* in her right, and fought with long and longer swords, blocking to each side, front to back, and all around. She avoided the

seven with quick maneuvers, cut one near the
groin. He continued to battle, though favoring one
leg.

Blocking two *oude* at once, crossed upon her
*mai*, her longer saber carved across the bellies of
both her opponents before they could withdraw to
strike again. She did not look for them to fall, but
turned to block elsewhere. The one whose leg
she'd injured was unbalanced. As he stumbled, her
*mai* tore off his head, and her *oude* smote another
direction to cleave through the shoulder of
another three-sword. Opponent's arm and *oude*
fell to the ground; but three-swords could be stub-
born. He drew his *mai* with his remaining arm,
and Erin ducked aside to avoid his onslaught. The
momentum of his missing blow carried him past
her and, at his back, she cut downward with her
longer saber, removing his remaining arm. While
she fought the remaining three, the man with
neither arm stood helpless, blood running out, and
died standing up.

The fifth fell before her sabers. The two remaining withdrew a ways, shocked by the decimation
of their number. Jai Strongarm of Tine, the
veteran of so many wars, was for once in his
career visibly shaken. He stepped forward, but not
close enough for confrontation, and said, "We will
take your message to Shom Bru."

As they retreated, cheers rose up from one side
of the hill. A group of rebels had pulled free of the
battle to watch Erin's swordsmastery. She took up
her blunt *i* from the ground and ignored the
childish praise of spectators. They returned to
arms, dejected, while Erin of Thar sat down on the
hillside to watch the battle, to guard the pacifists,
to await the inevitable return of a greater number
of three-swords, perhaps with Shom Bru directing
them personally.

\*      \*      \*

Rioters surrounded the imperial mansion. From the tower wherein Shom Bru waited uselessly for his unholy ally, he watched the streets and roofs, where small battles raged in great numbers, and where structures had been torched. The defense of the mansion itself was solid, and there were secret routes to escape, even the worst of circumstance; but the tyrant still feared the day, feared the collapse of everything he had inherited and fought to maintain.

He strode to the standing screen, pushed it angrily to one side, glowered at the soft-whips, penetrating devices, instruments of artificial torture, fur gloves, and velvet ropes, all arranged upon a shelf of black and gold lacquer. What use his horrific games of sadistic and pretended love? What reason his years of honoring a bargain made by a grandfather who, perhaps, enjoyed the sporting more? What avail the personal sacrifice of self-esteem? His slavish service to a gravel-throated monster had led only to betrayal in the Dynasty's first moment of need! Shom Bru turned to the grotesque tapestry his great-aunts and grandmothers had created for this room, and tore it from its mountings. He cursed with the frustration of finding it too tough to tear.

This day could never have been, had the insect queen hearkened to his call. The peasants would have remained at bay, tamed by their own fears. But the Dynasty's trump had vanished. The insect folk proved mere scarecrows in the most important test. The walls of the city would have held against any outside invasion, but revolution from within was always the bane of best defense. His council of generals would refuse to believe it, but the only end would be the indefatigable three-swords standing midst a prefecture reaved of peasants, sunken into tremulous waste and destruction. Decadence had weakened the council's judgement, as it had weakened his own grip on the nation. The government in Terwold would fall. But Wevan was a big country, and Shom Bru thought the rising might be contained here. He was not yet convinced no good could be made of things. There were still tricks to pursue.

A calculating look came into his eyes and Shom Bru became calm once more. He went to the rack on which his swords were mounted horizontally. The scabbards of these swords were of brilliant hue, matching the satiny crimson of his robe. He took first the *i* and placed it through his girdle, then the *mai*. The *oude* he carried by its scabbard. He went from the tower room into a torchlit hallway, descended stairs, came to a windowless chamber wherein the finest of his generals stood over a table which held the layout of Terwold and surrounding environs. From smaller doors in the back of the room, young boys came and went through secret passages, bringing the council news of positions and events, taking commands back to the field-generals. The members of the council, each clad in blue as silky as Shom Bru's crimson, leaned nearer the map, shoving game-pieces around the three-dimensional layout. "Burning," one of them said. "It spreads *here*." He pointed with his finger and someone set a carved ruby there to indicate a blaze.

When they saw their commander had returned, they stood erect with hands to hilts of *mai*. Their *oude* were held on the racks against one wall but, in the war-room, it was tradition to retain two swords at all times, as though the war were with them and not outside the imperial mansion and the city walls.

Shom Bru waved aside their formalities, demanded, "It grows worse?"

"We suggest sealing off the city," said the senior council member, a grizzled man whose lines of age wove among the scars of old battles. "Our archers are useless now, but if we withdraw our warriors, a relatively small group with bows can defend the wall. Then we can concentrate our efforts on quelling the violence in the streets of Terwold."

"Entrenchment is defeat," said Shom Bru. "Take Valk the Ear alive. That one hostage will bring silence to the city so sudden it will astound you." He approached the map, reached for the several blue and one crimson miniatures which stood inside the model of the imperial mansion, and moved those pieces beyond the wall. He set them by the pieces representing pacifists and, with a thumb, knocked the yellow miniatures over.

The council was aghast at this suggestion: *they personally*, and Shom Bru with them, cast into the fray outside Terwold? It was the inner city they must defend; each general believed this. Their own quarter of the city, the warriors' district, must at the least be protected from peasant torches, or else their personal wealth and holdings would not be intact when the emergency had passed.

"Sire," said the scarred senior, stalwart for all his years. "Why fight rabble ourselves? For sport? Even field-generals are above that! We must design our tactics upon this board, and send our advice to the marshals in the field. Otherwise we will lose primary positions, no matter how successful our encounters, for there will be no one at the map to judge each move before, during, and after."

Another said, "Joining the battle ourselves would only make it that much greater."

"Ah, my proud men," said Shom Bru, shaking his head at them as though disappointed. "Can it be you've grown soft in these few quiet years? You prefer your comfortable mansions to be unburned, your swords to be unbloodied? My

men, we must face the truth that this city will fall!
It burns! The best that we can do is drive the
rebels into their own fires, torch personally whatever remains of Terwold, cast this land into irrevocable poverty, and take an Eastern city for our
new capital!''

There. It was said. It was how Terwold origi-
nally became the capital, after all; the trick had
worked for Jorr Bru, and the example made of the
city *he* abandoned was enough to show the country that violence begot violence which served only
to enrich the warrior elite. If it had worked for the
saint Himself, it would work for his grandson.

A young messenger entered through a back way,
burnt and soiled, panting, wild-eyed. He had come
in time to hear Shom Bru's clever-seeming plan,
and piped without permission, "Sire! Dignitaries
from the Eastern prefectures have come begging
reinforcements. They did not know our plight was
the same as theirs: *the eastern cities riot!*''

Shom Bru looked less shocked then chagrined.
His generals grumbled alarm. It was the whole
country, then. They knew now.

Jai Strongarm came behind the young messenger, sheathed *oude* in his hand. It was unusual
for a field general to come personally, so he
immediately won attention. The senior council-
man asked Strongarm to speak.

"This message: 'The Woman of Black Mountain
has returned to claim the . . .'. You'll excuse me,
sire, gentlemen, 'to claim the tyrant's soul.' My
men and I thought her a fraud and fought her. Five
generals were slain with ease.''

Shom Bru's fist grew tight. His uneasy reserve
was breaking. His eyes narrowed, fear and anger
mixed. He stormed, "You come to me without her
head? Fool! Coward!''

A three-sword, a general, a veteran, a likely
candidate for the Council itself . . . Jai Strongarm

was unused to hearing himself called fool or coward. His lips grew thin, his jaw tighter than Shom Bru's fist. When he found his tongue, he said, "Sire, I will return to die by her sword if you require it. I and one other withdrew so that you would have this information. But sire, I felt the strength of her fighting style. I promise you this: There are not two men in this room to stand against her. There is only you, who has done it once before."

Shom Bru turned upon the gaming table and swept his arm across it. Soldiers, peasants, buildings, jewel-fires, walls ... everything erased, tumbling upon the floor. It would be next to impossible to reconstruct exactly those little scenes of carnage, for they were the product of long hours of information coming and going. The council gave a collective groan. Shom Bru shouted at Strongarm, "Idiot! It is not a ghost who haunts us! My spies named the woman months ago. Her name is Erin of Thar, the only survivor of a fishing town massacred by the insects. What magic makes her look like Merilia, I know, is confounding. But she is not the warrior whom you fear."

"What magic is in her appearance," said Jai Strongarm calmly, "has seeped into her swords. *Three* swords."

Shom Bru looked at the scattered miniatures, then to the council, and at the young, frightened messengers standing ready to leap into the underground passages if they could. He addressed the generals:

"Gentlemen! You are so anxious to play upon a map and not a field! I can tell you how to end this rising *at once*, and you will see it done. Take Valk the Ear alive. Slay this Erin of Thar. If you cannot capture an unarmed man and kill a common fisher, you are not generals, you are not three-swords, you are not men."

Reluctant though they had been to abandon
solid planning, loath as they were to see their
material holdings swept away as swiftly as Shom
Bru cleared the table . . . they were yet obedient
men, and certainly unafraid of peasant rabble.
Each bowed with hand to hilts of *mai* and, hurrying to the racks to take up *oude*, these finest three-
swords in the whole of Wevan *nee* Durga's Lathe
were gone into the tunnels.

Jai Strongarm had held back until only he and
Shom Bru were left to leave. He took the liberty of
touching the dictator's shoulder, holding him
from the tunnel an extra minute. He said, "Sire.
You may wish not to use it. But it does no harm to
prepare. A palanquin awaits you at the Shrine of
the Eighth Avatar."

Shom Bru considered this a moment. He was
eager to see the battlefield himself, true to his
nature of confronting fear head-on. Too, he was
curious about the swordswoman who, apparently,
had improved her style since their previous meeting. He would not flee in easy defeat, but it was
indeed wise to prepare alternatives. He said, "You
are Strongarm of Tine? Go, then. Await me at the
shrine you mention. You will be one of my palanquin bearers, for we will trust no peasant this day.
Despite this action I impose upon the council, Terwold is bound to fall, and as there are no safer
cities, I will find safe exile. On your way, gather as
many three-swords as you can find. None others.
Take this!" Shom Bru removed a signet ring, gave
it to Strongarm. "This ring will authorize you to
indenture whom you please. Those whom you
choose will return to this country someday, con-
querors again. Now we must go different ways. I
may be a while in coming."

They ducked into separate tunnels.

\*       \*       \*

Teebi's forehead had been clipped. It was a superficial cut, but bled well. He kept shaking the crimson from his vision. One of the stolen *mai* had broken two-thirds of the way down the blade, for he had used it improperly for a block. He kept it anyway, jamming the broken end of it up into the vitals of a surprise-faced two-sword. The good *mai* went the other direction, cutting across another warrior's eyes. The blinded warrior staggered backward, striving to cleanse the blood from his eyes, apparently unaware of the nature of his wound. Teebi struggled free of the corpses at his feet, some of which seemed to clutch at the hem of his robe.

Now and then he had a clear view of Erin sitting high on the hillside, properly guarding the people of Valk the Ear. She had not seen him below in the carnage. He tried twice to wave a greeting with his two filched *mai*, but every waving sword looked the same no doubt, and she seemed fairly disinterested in what was going on besides.

He fought his way to a knoll on which he thought to wave again. His melancholy was for the moment cast off. He forgot his dread of killing, and killed without remorse, for his goal was to be seen by Erin. It was a silly goal, but important to him. He'd missed her these many months, feared her dead, was excited to see her, more excited still to have seen the way she defeated the three-swords. As he made it to the top of the knoll, a track of corpses left behind, he was shouting the whole while, "Erin! Hallooo! Erin!" and finally she heard and stood up abruptly. He waved again with the *mai*, and she, somewhat reluctantly, not looking very glad, saluted with her smallsword.

It was probably that she was worried about him that she scowled, but Teebi was insecure enough to think she *might* be displeased to see him. He looked about himself at the gore he was making, once again ashamed of what he did. From the knoll, he could better see the sanguinary horror of various small battles. It dawned on him that for long moments he had been killing without remorse, without sorrow, without any feeling in the least, but only the foolish desire to be seen by Erin of Thar. How quickly a man is desensitized to slaughter! His sensitivities returned in a surge of self-loathing. He could not fathom in that moment what had driven him to this place, what had convinced him that murder could possibly be a dutiful occupation. He had not been doing the responsible thing; he had fooled himself thinking so. It was wrong to kill. Yet, even thinking this, Teebi's two filched swords—one whole and one broken—dashed around and around, slaying on every side.

Through the city gates (his view was superb) three-swords marched in force, led by older men, generals of the highest echelons. Incredibly, Shom Bru was among them himself. He was not at the front of their wedge-shaped formation, but strode between the two flanks, perfectly protected. Even so, his presence cast a horrifying sense of sure defeat upon the rebel fighters; it was superstition only, or Teebi hoped it was.

He knew where that force was heading: to fight Erin of Thar. Or should her name be Erin of the Black Mountain? Teebi caught himself desiring to watch the swords of Kiron's disciple, to see if legends were true, if Erin had been made invincible by Endsworld's One Immortal. He wouldn't be able to watch for he had to fight in his own field. He shouldn't *want* to witness such carnage like a kid at a carnival. He should want it to end.

As his swords whirled fiercely, his mind reeled confused. Shameful to admit, he *did* enjoy the physical power he possessed. He was a killer born, clearly, minimally trained but good and clever. That's why he was below the hill fighting rather than atop it chanting! The realization shook his very soul. He had never been a man of peace at all.

Teebi knew that his heart was filled with love of the world and humanity, and yet he loved these killing chores, despite himself. If even good men could not be stopped from violence, how could there ever be the kind of world envisioned by Valk the Ear?

There *was* a way. There *had* to be. But good men had to make better decisions than Teebi Dan Wellsmith had ever made. They had to confess that there was darkness inside each of them as vicious as that inside their enemies. No one must ever fancy another human being so much more evil than themselves that killing was justified.

A man bigger than Teebi Dan Wellsmith was coming toward the knoll, a man Teebi recognized, whose spear he recognized as well. It was Hek, Scream-Maker who had put scars on Teebi's flesh in Shom Bru's prisons.

Hek, Scream-Maker champed his teeth like a wild beast and drew fierce designs with his spear, clearing the way to the knoll, intent on taking the life of Teebi Dan Wellsmith. Teebi searched for a need to avenge his treatment at the torturer's hand, but could not find it. Seeing the torturer seemed to ease the turbulence and guilt of Teebi's thinking, and he knew at last what needed to be done. There was no such thing as a "proper" time for peace. If good men always waited for a better moment, there would never be anything but death and death and death all around. Teebi roared with this enlightenment, but it sounded like a monster's shout to the fighters who surrounded him, and they withdrew a few paces, watching for his next move.

On the hillside further off, Erin of Thar had plowed into the formation of super-warriors, holding her own against a score. Teebi's interest in it had lessened. He saw the faces of the warriors around his own self, saw their fear, their desire for life, saw that each one of them was a desperate human being pursuing a crazy road the end of which they could not see. What shock there was in their faces when their ferocious opponent did not renew his attack, but threw his swords down and growled,

"I relent!"

The one- and two-swords surrounding him stood firm, perhaps not believing a man of less than warrior blood meant relenting as more than a clever peasant's ploy. The torturer broke through the circle to face Teebi Dan Wellsmith and growl back at him,

"A criminal cannot relent!"

Teebi's jaw was firm. Hek, Scream-Maker commanded,

"Pick up the swords and fight!"

Teebi had never shown much temper, but he had a streak of stubbornness equally perturbing to everyone who'd ever known him. He would not pick up the swords, no matter how badly threatened. He repeated with child-like adamance, "I relent."

Without further argument, Hek, Scream-Maker raised his spear and cast it at such close quarters Teebi could not hope to duck aside. In the next moment, the whole ring of warriors ascended the few paces up the knoll and stabbed in front, in back, to each side. Pierced a dozen times, Teebi plunged to his knees, grunting like an animal, straining to say again, his voice smaller and quieter, a defeated but defiant boy: "I—do—I—re—lent . . ."

The warriors backed away. Only the torturer stood over him, taking the spear by the haft and yanking it out of Teebi's breast. Blood gushed from that wound and others. Hek, Scream-Maker

turned to fight elsewhere, and Teebi was left on
the knoll, on his knees, feeling not so much his
wounds as the hot tears streaming from his
clenched eyes. Distantly, he heard a friend calling
his name, screaming at him frantically, but he
couldn't quite remember who she was. He
couldn't open his eyes to see. There was something
very dark closing in around him which he didn't
think was common night. He fell upon his side,
thinking to himself again and again the phrase
that any decent warrior would have respected
from another warrior, *i-relent-i-relent-i-relent*, but
which warriors thought meaningless from the
mouth of a mere fishmonger.

His breaths came in short, jagged bursts and
everywhere he placed his hands upon himself, he
felt the blood and rents, but he still could not open
his eyes to look at the damage to himself. He
thought: *It takes so long to die.*

\*       \*       \*

They came in two long lines joined at the front,
like bright blue geese going along the clouds in
neat formation, a single red goose protected in the
wedge. They slew whoever could not move from
their path quick enough, for none could interrupt
their aiming the arrow of themselves up the hillside. Their target was obvious, but Erin stood in
their way, her *oude* to hand.

She would not use one of the smaller swords for
her plan was to use a minimal number of blocking
maneuvers and to use her agility and quickness to
avoid being cut, sprinting among them with her
longest blade strictly on the offense. She began
her headlong rush to meet them halfway, striking
like a mad small beast, eager to deliver them to
Durga for judgement. The man at the front of the
V was older than she'd expected to see on the

battlefield; but she was capable of judging strength by the way a sword was turned, and she knew that age was no handicap for this man. He blocked her *oude* with shocking ease, but a three-sword to the older man's left went down instead, for Erin caused her deflected sword to move across that next man's throat.

That quickly she had broken through their formation and saw Shom Bru in front of her. He did not draw any sword. He looked at her intensely, as though trying to penetrate a disguise, unwilling to accept who she was or who she might be. The three-swords, mighty generals all, moved into a more complex set of maneuvers which Kiron had described to her but which were dizzying to see. They cut her off from her approach to Shom Bru and surrounded her with a perfect circle, their swords pointing her way. She'd become the "farmer in the dell"; no direction to go without facing a wall of ready warriors.

She stood motionless, her *oude* held loose in one hand, looking as though she were off guard, but these men were not fooled by that. She looked more at the ground because it actually increased her field of vision. The circle moved counter-clockwise, intending by the motion to hem her in more completely. From Kiron's lessons, she knew what to expect. Three of the warriors came loose from the perimeters: one left, one right, one behind. Only three could safely attack in tandem with anything so long as an *oude*. Erin moved to one side swiftly, so that all three could not converge simultaneously as they planned. The one to her left was a mere arm's length closer than the other two, but it was enough for her to kill him first then face the other two.

Their *oude* waved before her like two hypnotic wands. Her own was held between the two, unwavering. They attacked and she withdrew, sensing that a new third had come inward from the edge of the circle at her back. She dashed sideways to avoid the rear attack, and kept going towards the circle of men, intending to cut through them and try for Shom Bru again. The three pursued her as the circle moved in such a way as to keep its distance equal from her at all quarters, to hold her in the center.

She reeled, ducked a blow, thrust the point of her *oude* up under the first attacker's diaphragm, ripped sideways through his ribs as she rolled to avoid another's slice, and cut the third man's leg off at the knee as she tumbled.

There was only one opponent at the moment, but two more came loose from the circle to make it a trio again. She went rolling through thorny grass and came back to her feet before the threesword who was oldest among them, the one Erin knew would be the best among them. She blocked his immediate blow—the first block she was forced to do—but she made good use of her *oude*'s sudden deflection from its original course, startling one of the other two with a slice across his arm, deep enough to sever tendons and cause his *oude* to slip from his hands. The old general had not lost time with his second attack, which Erin avoided by rolling onto her back, somersaulting backward, and came to her feet holding in addition to her own *oude*, the one which had fallen to the ground. When the old general pressed the attack, she blocked with one long saber and struck him with the other. He staggered back with intestines threatening to squeeze out the slice in his gut.

He attacked again.

Erin had to evade another warrior at the same time, wounding him not severely. A new man was coming inward from the edge of the circle, for the one whose arm she ruined had fallen, apparently in shock from loss of blood. She was most worried about what the older warrior would do, for she expected his sword's quickness to pursue her again. But when she caught him in her vision, she saw that his guts had oozed out and unravelled at his feet. He stood there with his expression calm, revealing no pain; but he could not step forward with his legs roped in his intestines. He dropped the *oude* in front of himself, unsheathed his small *i*, and slit his own throat, as Dee the Rope had once chosen to die at her own hand instead of another. At that moment, a musically authoritative voice called,

"Withdraw!"

Shom Bru's men let him through. He had still not drawn a weapon. He no longer stared at Erin so wonderingly, so may have accepted who she must be, though his first feelings might have been more correct. He asked, and his voice was surprisingly gentle when he did, "Do I fight Erin or Merilia? Is there a difference between the two?"

Erin felt the memories and training of Merilia like a ghost at the back of her brain, and could only reply, "I do not know if there is a difference between the two. But my name is Erin of Thar, the Last Disciple of Endsworld's One Immortal."

Shom Bru nodded as though it made sense enough. "I will fight you," he said.

As Shom Bru was reaching over his shoulder for the hilt of the *oude*, Erin heard from somewhere behind her a growling shout loud enough to rise above the din of battle further down the hillside. It was the cry of Teebi Dan Wellsmith and it caused Erin to turn her back on her opponent, in time to see the spear cast into Teebi's chest and a dozen more warriors closing on him with swords. She whirled back to face Shom Bru in time to deflect his incredible blow, a blow which sent her staggering. She was caught up in the hail of his onslaught,

but her only thought was of Teebi, and she could
not do more than defend herself. She made one
good counter-stroke which clipped a bit of
crimson cloth from his sleeve, but in the process
left herself open to a slice toward her stomach
which was so strong it took the handle off her *i*
which, at the front of her girdle, saved her from
being gutted. Tears were blinding her. She nearly
stumbled on the corpse of the old general. *Teebi*,
her mind cried out. *Teebi*.

"I relent!" shouted Erin, and Shom Bru stepped
back, obviously surprised. Erin was surprised to
hear herself say it, too. But she confirmed it. "It's
true. There is something else I'd rather do than
fight you. Please forgive my being rude, but I must
help a fallen friend." Saying this, Erin turned and
fled down the hillside toward a certain knoll.

Shom Bru stood above the corpse of the general
whose throat and stomach were cut. This man had
been on the council of Cal Bru, was an elder states-
man and warrior without peer, and was in fact the
tutor of Shom Bru. The tyrant could not find actual sorrow for the loss of the old man, for Shom
Bru was not loving in any sense; but he could find
a degree of wonder that this man had been defeated. If Erin of Thar could kill the grizzled states-
man, then she should have made a better showing
against Shom Bru himself.

"She has revealed her weakness to me," said
Shom Bru, loud enough for the warriors gathered
around him to hear. "She is concerned with
friendship before duty. We must remember that."
Then he motioned his men to follow him up the
hill, where Valk the Ear and his people no longer
chanted, but prayed in silence.

\*    \*    \*

Only when Teebi fell did she realize what had brought her back to Terwold. The delivery of ruin upon Shom Bru's insect allies was her most important task; that completed, she might have gone anywhere. Certainly she was of minimal value in the peasants' rising. Even Merilia had learned, in her last desperate days, that it was useless and perhaps immoral to play hero to the meek, for it only made them meeker, kept them from the knowledge that they could serve themselves. Nor had she come to Terwold to protect Válkyová from his own madness; suicide was a personal quest and, if he and his devotees wished to pursue it, for her to interfere with their resolve was mere audacity. It was Teebi who drew her back to Terwold, and it was for Teebi's love of Valk the Ear that Erin had defended the pacifists' hill. Now, Erin's motivation lay dying, or already dead, upon the knoll.

She ran over the quietening battlefield, hopping between twisted and twitching corpses, scurrying through a gulley toward the place where Teebi lay. There was only one encounter along the way. A spearman, big as a wall, stood in her path. It was his spear struck Teebi first, as Erin had witnessed from afar. She evaded his thrust and ran on past him, not stopping until she had reached Teebi's side. She left behind a headless man, still stabbing in the air with his spear, his body unaware that its shoulders now were bare.

She knelt at Teebi's side, lifted his head onto her knees, leveled a long series of curses at him, not one of which she wished would come to pass. In a moment he stirred, opened his watery eyes, eyes which looked in two directions but recognized her anyway. He smiled. He said, "Hey."

She had hoped to find most of his wounds superficial, had thought her knowledge of medicinal herbs would heal him if she could get him to a place to nurse him. But even Kiron would have shook his head to see such rents. "You're stabbed a hundred times!" she exclaimed accusatively, appalled by each new wound she found.

Teebi made a choking sound, then said two words: "About . . . twelve." She hugged his head tightly, wiped dried blood from a cut on his forehead. Despite the blinding moisture in her eyes, there were no tears falling. Teebi posed a half-formed question: "Valk . . . the Ear?"

Erin glanced at the top of the far hill. The pacifists lay already scattered on the ground, their heads loose from their bodies. Válkyová Idaska was bound, was being led beyond the rise, away from the scene of battle in the company of Shom Bru and Terwold's retreating three-swords. Troops of ragged, weary peasants followed after, vanishing over the rise, but could not hope to get the Healer back. Erin was honest: "He's hostage now. They won't hurt him. Shom Bru is bound to seek refuge in another country, now that the people have risen across the land. Valk the Ear is his safe passage out of Durga's Lathe."

Teebi was upset. He tried to sit up, but could not. He looked at Erin, pleading, knowing he was about to die. In a weak whisper, he asked, "My last wish, hey?"

"All right," she said, knowing what he wanted. "I'll get him, yes. I'll save the life of Valk the Ear. But it's for you, Teebi. It's for no one else."

Then Teebi's life was spent. Erin held a smiling, peaceful corpse. She rocked the head in her lap and thought the only holy thing any side of Black Mountain was gone from Endsworld, and the last of the battle receded from consciousness or concern. The pain was hard to bear. Kiron had taught her much but, being immortal, could not prepare her for a loss such as this. In a while, she began to pull herself together. The battles were petering

out, or else most of it had gone in hopeless pursuit
of Shom Bru.

Erin tried to lift Teebi but, despite her strength,
could do little more than drag him. She refused to
abandon his corpse for an unlabelled pot of ashes
or, worse, the *rint*.

*He'll have a bloody damn shrine*, vowed Erin.
*Vagabonds will rest beside his monument. Pil-
grims will come to pray.*

She looked about for someone to help her carry
Teebi away and saw a cowled man standing near,
watching her. Only his sand-colored eyes showed
from the hood. She said to him, "Help me, you
misbegotten manipulator of human lives!" He
said nothing. He took Teebi's legs. Erin had his
shoulders. Together, they went from the battlefield at dusk, leaving Terwold to its fate, the
people to theirs.

*          *          *

Between the day of the full moon (the eve of the
revolution) and the second-quarter moon after the
fall of Terwold, the complexities of a regime's falling peaked and dwindled. Three-sword naval com-
manders of a port city called Ucho staged a coup
against Shom Bru's appointed governor, and
would have taken control of Durga's Lathe's
coastal provinces but for this: after fighting into
the palace and out again, they returned to the
docks with the governor's head, only to find their
warships burning. Peasants had set the flames
upon the cleverly oiled water. Meanwhile in an
Eastern city, a destitute old woman was found to be
distantly related to the earlier aristocrats of
Durga's Lathe. A group of high-ranking officers
pledged service to her, raised armies in an instant,
and met the suffering remnants of Shom Bru's
forces in the fiercest engagements yet. The old

woman died of stress and senility, but it was believed she had a cousin in some monastery, and he was being sought as another rally-flag. Shom Bru proved his valor as often and as stoutly as he had before proven his cruelty; but the numbers of men devoted to his cause grew fewer and his inevitable day of exile drew nearer and nearer.

Of Valk the Ear nothing was heard or seen throughout this time, although it was rumored he was held captive in some sea coast burgh while Shom Bru made his last attempts to regain control of the country. Erin of the Black Mountain was also not in evidence during these and other crises, although always it was expected she would appear to change one tide or another (she never did). The tales spread of how she routed the generals of Terwold, so she was on everybody's tongue. And a novice of the Hammer Cult, privy to conversations within his order and loose of tongue afterward, gossiped the story of Erin being sent to fight the insect queen alone. His version was ridiculously inaccurate, and even the truth would have been hard to believe; but when the next new moon came and went without a single incident of terror (aside from those of human perfidy), the monk achieved some degree of credibility (and ousting from his order) while people speculated Erin had died in that brave encounter (for none knew the deed was done *before* she fought at Terwold).

Beknownst to none but a man with sandy eyes, Erin had spent some of this time in Thar. In the year since the massacre, many of the shacks had tumbled down, the tiny docks were mere poles sticking up from mud, and anything of value had been pillaged by human vultures.

What she had done was rest in the pitiful tumble-down which had been the house of Rud and Orline. Also, she moped a bit, but finally set to work. She took what good wood she could salvage

from the broken houses and burnished the best
with a flat stone and stained each plank with an
oily herb she knew about. In a few days she had
created a good amount of aged and gorgeous
lumber. With this she built a stout building in a
place where it could be seen from either the river,
or the highway running parallel, and above the
doorless entry she carved the name of Teebi Dan
Wellsmith, following it with the symbol signifying
"saint."

After the battle of Terwold, Erin and the man
with sandy eyes had built a pyre for Teebi, during
which ceremony the strange man proved himself a
priest by performing a bold litany of praise and
sorrow. He took the ashes afterward and placed
them in a leather pouch, promising Erin that he
would have a special pot made and bring it down
the River Yole on a raft to the place Erin required.
So it was that after the few weeks, a raft came
down the Yole to Thar, and on the raft were several flowering plants with roots wrapped in
burlap, the man with sandy eyes, and a huge
ceramic work with intricate carvings and runes
and a lidded dent on top to hold the ashes.

The priest had brought pulleys which, attached
to trees and with ropes strung through them, allowed Erin and the priest to tug the heavy ceramic
monument up the river's bank and get it inside the
shrine-house. The priest then performed a rite as
excellent as the one he'd done during the crema-
tion weeks before. Afterward, Erin was able to
speak to the sandy-eyed priest without the least
anger, for she well appreciated his impressive services for Teebi. She asked, "Why do you care
about him, too?" The sandy-eyed priest was busy
around the shrine, creating a garden by clearing
away some sorts of bushes and saving others, adding the plants he had brought, packing stones onto
a curving walkway twixt road and river. He said,

"The paths of your Stars and of Teebi Dan Well-smith crossed and crossed upon my charts. He was as important to this adventure as yourself."

"You're an astrologer," said Erin, still trying to resolve the enigma of the man.

"Or to that effect. The Stars did *not* foresee this man dying. He was to be a greater influence on your life than this, but something altered the normal course of his destiny. Such things happen. But the interference must be something strong."

"Válkyová," said Erin. The priest looked up from his gardening labors and said,

"When the sword-needle was pressed into your hand, no one could have known your strength was great enough to draw another across the threshold. The soul of Valk the Ear is not one ever meant to walk the face of Endsworld. He is an unknown factor whose Stars cannot be read in these heavens, and he is proving more a nuisance than can be contended."

"He wants to return to Earth," said Erin. "Is there some way you can send him?"

"It is for you to do, and I will show you how. It is unfair that I ask you, for you have already done the thing for which you were intended. You have decimated the insect race. That was to be Merilia's destiny, which you fulfilled in her stead. As last of my ancient religion and direct descendant of the forgotten heros who freed humanity from dominion, it was for me to set the stage for you to perform the annihilation. By rights, you should be free to live your life as you please, with my presence no longer in your Stars. But so long as there is the other one from Earth, nothing is certain, nothing is safe."

"You want me to kill him," Erin knew. "But I promised Teebi I would save the Healer's life."

The priest ceased fussing about the shrine and set his tools by the doorway of the structure Erin had built. She sat beside him on the step, thinking Teebi watched from inside. The nameless priest reached into his robe and came out with a transparent tube which looked to be made of ice, but did not melt. It reflected dappled sunlight in rainbow patterns, and Erin recognized the material as the same used in making Merilia's crypt; and her own diamond-like needle was but a harder, denser form of the same substance. He held it to Erin and she took it.

"You can see there is a depression in one end," he instructed. "The crystal you wear at your neck fits within. It is an artifact, of course, created by the blessedly extinct Overmind aeons ago. It seems to have been part of something larger, something used to bring human and other species to Endsworld from the Twenty Heavens and Twenty Hells, of which Earth is one. I have worked with it for some while, and think I have rearranged its structure in such a way that it can send Valk the Ear back to Earth. If it fails, and you will not consider the second option of killing him, then all Endsworld may regret it."

"And Shom Bru?"

"It has never been the pursuit of my line's religion to change the hearts of humankind, but only to free those hearts from dominion by another species. Shom Bru was not the target of my machinations. He ceased to have importance when his allegiance with the insect race was shattered. You will need to know where he has gone, certainly, for Valk the Ear is still his captive. A camp has been made in a cove near where the Yole spills into the sea. Yes, you know the place, for it is where you were brought at the beginning of all this. Shom Bru has gone there in secret, with less than a dozen men, to await the ship of an ally willing to carry him into exile. Let him go if it pleases you; only, do not let him take Valk the Ear. The fallen

tyrant knows that he has captured someone who
might become a tool of power. Shom Bru must be
severed of that tool by any means."

Erin handled the glassy, tubular object, looking
at the end with the depression, then at the end
which was smoother. She asked, "It is *aimed*?"

"No, no. The flat end must *touch* him. It may not
work. It's very old and very fragile in its own way.
If it fails, I cannot impress upon you too strongly
to recant your promise to Teebi Dan Wellsmith.
Should you find it necessary to slay Valk the Ear,
you can return to this shrine and pray for Wellsmith's forgiveness. Only, believe me, your fellow
Earthling must not be left to live on Endsworld."

"I will search my conscience," Erin promised,
"and act accordingly."

\*      \*      \*

Válkyová Idaska sat cross-legged in the tight
confines of a wicker cage, eating a meager repast.
His cage was not close enough to the campfires,
and the sea's wind chilled him. After three weeks
being buffeted from one dark confine to another,
the cage was almost a pleasant change. He had
long since lost his terror, for it was clear Shom
Bru wanted him alive for future plans.

It was dark. The sky was clear, stars brilliant.
Shom Bru sat on an unrolled mat near one of the
campfires, which were also beacons; and he was
discussing matters with four men. Válkyová could
not hear the conversations. A sentry stood on a
jetty with a torch, looking out to sea. They had
been waiting two days for the ship to take them to
a small island principality. It was a nervous wait
for everyone. Válkyová could not see where the
other half-dozen men had gone—further up the
margin, perhaps, to watch the sea beyond the
cove.

The ocean's waters glistened with luminescent plankton, green and gold and red. The partial moon passed before the Arch of the Sky, which on Earth was a less curved Milky Way. After some while, he began to hear a distant sound, a sound like women quarrelling—winds screaming in an eerie way. He knew what it was from stories. But having lived mostly in the desert of Durga's Lathe, he had never seen the sea's wind-sirens.

The sentry at the jetty's end waved his torch back and forth. Shom Bru and the four men beside him stood from their mats and discussions to gaze toward the Arch. Through it came a shining ship, seemingly from the Heavens, wind-sirens filling up the sails. The sirens were invisible, but the sound of them grew louder as the ship approached the cove.

Something moved behind Válkyová's cage. He tensed, looked around, and saw Erin upon her belly in the sand, her longest sword across her back, her *mai* and its sheath in her right hand. She placed finger to lips, urging silence. Crawling to the back of the wicker cage, she climbed over a driftwood plank and sat up casually, grinning. She whispered, "I've brought a gift for you." From her girdle, where her missing *i* belonged, she took a cylindrical object and said of it, "It's your passage home." She took the diamond-bright needle from the string on her neck and inserted it into one end of the cylinder. It began to glow, which startled them both, for it would give away Erin's presence in the camp. They heard the sound of soldiers running along the beach. Alarmed, Erin put the cylinder on the ground and covered it with a little sand, hiding the glow. Behind her, a half-dozen three-swords stood with bows. Arrows were nocked and aimed. She remained sitting, but turned halfway around to face them.

The screaming sirens in the ship's sails quietened, rested. The ship slowed down in order to be brought into the cove carefully by oars and human hands.

Shom Bru approached the cage, not surprised to see Erin. She dared not move; even supposing she could duck the arrows, if she did so, the caged man would be feathered in her stead. "We expected you," said Shom Bru, looking satisfied at her position. He was a weary man, having aged much these last weeks. But his clever mind forever plotted. He said, "I knew you could not abandon Valk the Ear, for friendship is your weakness."

"What makes you think he is my friend?"

"If I doubted it," he said, "your presence proves it now." He motioned to his archers and said, "Kill her."

The arrows were unleashed.

Erin pulled the driftwood plank up to serve as shield and the arrows struck deep. She was on her feet in the next instant and, before the archers could drop their bows to draw swords, three of them lay dead. Three more drew *oude*, but backed away with their weapons held defensively. They knew from previous matters that they could not match her.

Shom Bru spoke in melodic tones. "We will duel without relent, if you are unafraid."

Erin dropped her guard a bit, stood straight, bowed her assent and replied, "Without relent." Shom Bru said, "We will begin."

They met each other near the sea's edge. He drew *mai* and *i* against her *mai*. For some while they only stood each other off, followed one another back and forth along the margin, sizing, judging. From Válkyová's view they seemed to glow, for the sea's bright plankton gave them auras.

Finally they clashed. It was Shom Bru's offensive, but Erin hardly moved. Shom Bru fell back, surprised. He was too good a swordsman not to realize what he faced this time; so he sheathed his *i*, stuck his *mai* into the sand, drew the *oude*, and charged Erin before she could get her longest sword. She blocked and he attacked again, giving her no time to draw the sword which matched his own. She dodged into shallow waters, the hem of her robe becoming heavy like a sponge. Shom Bru followed her, still on the offense, but now Erin had drawn her *oude* and held a sword in each hand. His double-handed blow was stronger than her two single-handed defenses, and Erin was forced into deeper water.

Although she appeared wholly on the defense, Válkyová observed Shom Bru, and saw that the warrior did not look the least confident. Perhaps Erin was only holding back for the perfect time.

The illusion of their glowing seemed strongest for Shom Bru. This puzzled Válkyová, who began to study every part of his captor. He saw, as an ornament on the hilt of Shom Bru's *oude*, a faintly shining gem akin to the one Erin had placed into the butt of the cylinder. It was smaller than Erin's needle, a mere chip; but it cast its slight shining over Shom Bru. It made Válkyová wonder if it had some protecting value, and if Erin were in more danger than she realized.

Erin burst forward from the waves with her first attack and made an upward swing *with the back of her sword*, striking the *oude* so fiercely that it was flung from Shom Bru's grasp. Válkyová watched the long saber twirl through the air and strike the sea without a splash. Válkyová looked at the waves into which the *oude* had fallen and wondered: *Without a splash?*

Erin blocked against an invisible sword and continued the fight, oblivious to the illusion. She said to Shom Bru, "Your occult swordplay cannot work on me. I have seen it once before."

Did the tyrant grow pale? Valkyová could not be sure in the darkness. Certainly it was Shom Bru on the defense now. His sword slowly rematerialized, and Valkyová was surprised to see the tip had been broken off when Erin previously struck with the dull back of her own *oude*.

Shom Bru backed away, then turned to flee in the direction of the wicker cage. Valkyová forgot he couldn't stand and bumped his head trying. Erin pursued Shom Bru, but a sword with broken tip had been thrust into the cage and pressed against Válkyová's throat. He couldn't move or swallow. To everyone's surprise, and most especially Válkyová's, Erin did not slow her pace, did not seem to care if Válkyová's neck were pierced. Shom Bru reached with his other hand for his *i*, but Erin was too swift. Her *oude* cleaved from an upward angle through the wicker cage and out the other side, striking the underside of Shom Bru's elbow, and continuing in its upward arc to strike aside her opponent's *i*.

Shom Bru backed away, his arm missing from the elbow. His broken *oude* lay on the floor of the cage, hand still clinging to the hilt. Válkyová's heart thumped rapidly and his throat was slightly cut, but he realized Erin had sliced the wicker so that he could force it apart and climb through. Shom Bru's remaining men surrounded him to protect him, but he reminded them angrily, "This is a duel without relent!" The sentry had returned from the jetty; it was Jai Strongarm of Tine. He said, "Sire, let me fight her in your name! Let me die instead of you!" But Shom Bru shook his head, took a new *oude* from Jai, and made his stand one-handed.

"It's over," said Erin.

"It is never over while both of us are living! We are the worst of foes!"

Erin said calmly, "A warrior has no enemies."

"I can still defeat you!" shouted Shom Bru. He was outraged. The music in his voice was gone. Erin replied,

"That is not what is important. Can you defeat yourself?"

Shom Bru glowered. Hate was in his eyes. His men looked embarrassed for him, but they were faithful, and would welcome his order to attack her, though all die by her sword.

A dinghy from the foreign ship was being drawn ashore. Erin said to Jai, "Take your master to the ship. Look after his injury."

Válkyová Idaska approached Erin from behind, and she stood there to shield him as the warriors went past. To her surprise, she felt something touch her back, and it tingled. The one-handed warrior and his last retainers became a blur before her eyes. Válkyová's voice was a whisper, an almost sensual thing, saying to her, "I'm sorry, Erin, but my work here is not complete. Ends-world does not need another killer." Then everything was darkness. She was caught in the chaos between dimensions and worlds. *As quick as that*, thought Erin, too startled even to react with anger. She was tumbled through limbo and sent plowing into the sandy beach of a place not Ends-world but Earth. She knew without turning that the cliffs overlooking the sea would no longer be wild forests but waterfront homes for the rich. At least she was clothed! The cylinder had worked matters differently than the needle-sword had done. She had her swords as well, whatever good they'd be in so wickedly civilized a place as Earth.

She raised herself to her knees facing the sea, watching the tide in darkness, her spirit swelling with disbelief and sorrow. Dawn moved toward the horizon. Erin sat motionless. Somewhere far away, a dog was barking. She thought she heard the wind-sirens of Endsworld, but it was only an ambulance speeding to some heart attack or car accident. She feared to look behind herself, to see the houses lined up along the cliff. She fell instead into a meditative trance.

When the sun warmed her back, she still sat thus. People started coming to the beach with radios and blankets and umbrellas, with dogs on leashes and with children. They looked at Erin and thought her some looney eccentric, clad as she was, and with swords which might be real. A group had come to the beach to practice Tai Chi Chuan in unison, and several people thought Erin must be with them. She scarcely knew so many watched, so deep she was in meditations, striving to recapture the world so quickly lost. But Endsworld faded as dreams do, and tears slipped through closed lids to track the woman's cheeks.

· EPILOGUE ·

# NINETEENTH HELL

Wendy Adrian Shultz

# EPILOGUE:
## NINETEETH HELL

*Confidential Police Report:*

On March second of last year, a Caucasian male, Válkyová Idaska, gained entry to rooms and records of a mental health facility by misrepresenting himself as a physician. Findings show that he had been accumulating photographs and data regarding a patient in the facility, Erin Wyler. Idaska, a naturalized citizen, had apparently developed a fixation on Wyler after responding to a call in his capacity as emergency medic. At that time he calmed Wyler's hysteria and tended her injuries. It is presently believed that Idaska kidnapped Wyler on March second, when both of them disappeared under unclear circumstances. Wyler reappeared one year later, seeming to suffer from amnesia, and was placed under psychiatric observation. Válkyová Idaska remains at large. Warrants have been issued.

An earlier investigation of a possible manslaughter led to Wyler's initial institutionalization. She had killed one Jerry Mason during a martial arts exhibition between their respective schools, with a large number of witnesses mostly in agreement that it did not look like an accident. As psychiatric consultants declared Wyler incompetent to stand trial, she was placed in the institution from which she was later kidnapped by Idaska.

Shortly after the disappearance of Wyler and Idaska, new evidence regarding the alleged manslaughter was brought to police attention. The alleged victim, Mason, had kept an elaborate diary in which he recorded bizarre fantasies of being an evil king whose worst enemy was a woman. His penned descriptions of this life-long "enemy" match the description of Wyler. No other connection between the deceased and Wyler has been established. The present theory is that Mason, a deranged young man with few friends and only one interest outside of books, was so shocked to find his martial arts opponent the coincidental match of his fantasized enemy, that he initiated unprecedented violence during a public competition. He attempted to kill Wyler in exactly the fashion alleged by her immediately after the fact. Although unusual and puzzling ends remain, Wyler has been cleared on all charges.

\*    \*    \*

*Confidential Psychiatric Report:*

The patient was discovered on March third of this year, sitting on a beach, dressed in a costume the origin of which has not yet been established, and carrying two unusual swords also of unknown origin. She was unable to understand spoken words but was able to speak at length in a totally fabricated language of her own device. Dr. Sorenson, who wished to study the articulation in his linguistics lab, recorded many of the patient's frenzied monologues. His report is appended and itself helps to understand the complexity of the patient's schizophrenia.

By August fifteenth, the patient was using English, having recalled it in stages. She continues to speak with a consistent accent and to be uncommunicative as to her whereabouts for the past year. Amnesia is suspected. Police reported no incidents of violence during the period she was missing, irrespective of the weapons she was carrying and which she claims were merely gifts, although from whom she cannot or will not say.

Although the patient can by no means be considered well, and indeed the nature of her illness is deep-rooted and profound, it is at the same time the opinion of her attending psychiatrist that she is not dangerous to herself or others. This opinion is put forth in spite of her previous psychiatric record. Police evidence strongly suggests that she had acted in self defense in the violent incident recounted on her previous record and was not psychotic at the time, but suffering from hysteria for having to defend herself *against* a psychotic individual. Her present schizophrenia may have been induced by the incident of accidental manslaughter, her subsequent kidnapping, and the unknown events of the past year. The patient will not discuss, and in fact may be unwilling to remember, the missing year, which we assume therefore to have been traumatic.

In light of the non-violent nature of her present illness, it was recommended that she be afforded out-patient status. This was made effective May twenty-seventh. She presently lives in her own apartment with some assistance from her parents. She is attending weekly psychiatric appointments although to date she remains strikingly non-communicative.

\*       \*       \*

Erin stepped off the transit into the heart of the city, looked upward along the lines of a tremendous bank tower, and hugged her long, thin parcel. What she planned might well reopen the troubles with legal and medical investigators, but to let things pass might create problems equally annoying. Glad as she was to find herself cleared of murder charges and freed of the loony bin, it was disconcerting to learn what piece of evidence convinced everyone that Jerry Mason, and not Erin Wyler, was the psychotic in the deadly encounter. His diary revealed what the authorities called "fantastic delusions" that Erin had killed his father (who had actually died of cancer) and that eventually he would have the opportunity to kill her in armed combat. It was pretty convincing stuff, and Erin was absolved of any misdoing. The problem, of course, was that Erin had a diary very much like it which might raise eyebrows if compared to that which the police received. And her parents had given her diary to a certain meddler who convinced them it was for their daughter's benefit.

Apparently the legal matters had been pursued in her absence not because Erin's parents wished it, but because a wealthy businessman with the noisome name of Theodore Wilson Hendrison III, heralding from a family older than the thirteen colonies, exerted influence in the case. Erin could not imagine what his interest was in her; but he had apparently obtained Jerry Mason's diary as well as her own, and turned the former over to police detectives without mentioning the latter. Erin hoped to recover hers.

She pressed the elevator button. The door startled her by opening immediately. Inside, she pressed the number "26." Her stomach sank.

In the front office, she was denied access to Hendrison's chambers. She glowered at the secretary —a young and fey fellow—who rather shrank beneath her gaze and made no attempt to stop her physically. She entered the plush chamber unannounced and stood on the edge of heavy carpeting looking far across a room to a huge desk. Behind the desk sat the man with sandy eyes, or a somewhat plumper look-alike.

Hendrison was smiling. It was an inviting smile. He pressed a button on his desk, said, "Phil, I'll be taking no calls, thank you." A faint all-right-mister -hendrison reached her ears before the *click*. She heard a faint whirring as well. It was not the air conditioner.

"Well, Erin, I suppose I've been expecting you."

She walked to his desk and sat her long bundle on it. She reached behind the desk and pulled open a drawer. A tape recorder was turning. She pulled a wire loose and it stopped. She then proceeded to unwrap the bundle on his desk. It was her *mai*, sans sheath. She said,

"I came to thank you for your various influences on certain bothersome legal matters, and to request the return of my diary."

His sand-colored eyes peered along the curve of the weapon, its hilt toward Erin, the point nearest him. He did not stop smiling.

"As you may suspect," said Hendrison calmly, "I am uncommonly attached to my Endsworld counterpart, and our lives parallel closely, even though he is a priest and I am, I suppose, a tycoon. Money has replaced gods and heros in our world, so perhaps I am a priest after all, and a magician as well, for money can work as many miracles as the artifacts of Endsworld. At the same time I fancy myself a sort of socialist and philanthropist. I've learned to live with certain hypocrisies and deceits to see my fortunes grow . . . but I use this wealth for revolutionary purposes. You'd be surprised what sorts of organizations I support. You might approve. You would also be surprised how events of Endsworld affect events of Earth, and vice versa. My counterpart and I are careful of each of our machinations. The fates of two worlds hang in the balance."

"*Your* fate, I venture, is presently influenced largely by me," said Erin casually. "I seek only the diary. It's personal and it's mine."

"Let me explain something to you, if I may be so audacious. First of all, a sword will serve you nothing but trouble on Earth, and it would please me if you'd wrap this one up and take it away. Second of all, it is you and not the Czech who is useful on Endsworld. I am your link with that other world, your only one; and I hazard you would be upset afterward if you were to, shall I say, 'sever' that link. My counterpart would like to retrieve you, but the crystals are rare, and the one you had is now in the hands of the Czech. That is most unfortunate, for without it, it will be most difficult to find or create an entry into Endsworld. I also hope you will forego this obsession with your diary. It is, shall we agree, 'security.' If things can be arranged, you will hear from me under a more auspicious occasion than today. Assuming, that is, that you *do* wish to go back someday."

Erin hovered across the desk, glaring at him a while. In a moment, she began to rewrap the sword and, taking the bundle from the desk, turned to leave. As her hand touched the door handle, she looked back across the sea of carpet and said with stinging sarcasm, "I'm sure you have my best interests at heart."

He was still smiling when the door closed behind her.

*     *     *

The roads were made for cars, not humans afoot. At times there was no shoulder but a ditch. Cars honked if she walked in the road. Passing wheels stirred a ghastly dust.

She wore a backpack with a sleeping bag on top of that; for, despite the fact that there were hundreds of dwellings along the way, no one here helped travelers across the land, and all ones needs must be carried.

Dust, cars, exhaust and muddy gutters wore upon her mood. She sought an alternative route, but private properties were fenced, dogs were a nuisance, and people as well as dogs barked from their houses. "Get out!" they shouted, or "Can't you read the signs?" Eventually she found a railroad track which provided the closest thing to a reasonable route. Trains forced her off to the side only occasionally.

In less than a day she came to the foothills which, from the city, had looked like smudgy humps. The air was purer here, but not so pure as Erin could have hoped. There was a river beneath the trestle and Erin climbed down to it. She followed along the banks until she discovered a reasonably wild place to make camp. She propped her backpack and roll against a friendly seeming tree, and she sat, striving to recapture some of the old sense of glory in the world; tried to forget the newspapers with their daily synopses of violence and villainy which eternally lacked the bold valor of events on Endsworld; tried to forget the smell of machines and factories and trash; tried to be alone.

In the beautiful rapids, an aluminum can glistened. There was a swirl of water between two boulders, where a mound of suds was trapped and whirled around. The birds grew momentarily silent as a private plane buzzed the forest.

After a repast of dried fruit, an avocado sandwich, and Kool Aid from a thermos, Erin unrolled her sleeping bag. It was not yet dark for the sun went down late at this time of year. But she was weary from the stress of her long walk (which was not a physical stress) and so she climbed into the bag. Even in the forest there were so many reminders of civilization; it seemed her only escape was sleep. Through the evening and night, she abandoned herself to dreams, but forgot them on waking.

Birds were making a ferocious noise in anticipation of dawn. It was not yet light. Erin heard a *thump* near her sleeping bag, which was a flying squirrel missing its mark in the branches and gliding heavily to the ground. She faced it and they stared at each other, it more surprised than she. It panted, dark-eyed, showing her its yellow teeth and pink tongue. Then it sprinted away, darting up some tree. A frog or fish splashed in a pond beside the river. Erin rose and rolled her sleeping bag.

She found roots and herbs which she boiled in river water with aid of fire and pot. She added green leaves which tasted like spinach. When the concoction cooled a bit, she drank it from the pot, taking the roots out with her fingers to eat those. She had brought food from the city, but the wild stuff around her seemed better. There had once been a tremendous, ages-old evergreen nearby, which was now a flat stump wide enough for a square-dance; foresters had poached the giant, long enough ago that the stump was starting to rot. A bush grew from one part of it, laden with small, red, somewhat bitter berries which served Erin as dessert.

Not once had she felt release. She wondered if there was a place anywhere in the whole of the world which would not have been injured by human hands. She took up her backpack and bag and started further up the river. Before noon, she had said hello to a variety of hikers, mostly loud boys and giggling girls who seemed bright, and healthy, and safe in the world. She kept going and kept going until the terrain was rough and there were no more fun-loving youths along the way. She found a tumble-down log cabin and explored around it absent-mindedly. The only thing interesting was the evidence of long-ago picnickers: an old, returnable Coke bottle of a design long discontinued. She went further up the river, which by now became a gorge.

Toward evening she came upon a cliff overlooking a falls. She made her camp there. Below, she saw a lone fisherman casting with a rod and reel. He was somehow unobtrusive so far away, the falls disguising any noise he might have made. He stood in the shallows with hip-boots and was wearing a hat. She watched him for a while, from her high place, thinking negative things about sports fishermen, remembering village Thar where fishing was no game but the difference between survival and death. But there was a grace about the man's casting which Erin admired, even while appalled, and finally, watching him, she felt calm. Something about the lone man's activity seemed right, or at least the closest thing to right anything could be in such a horrifying world. She moved away from the cliff and prepared a fire site for later that night. She had decided to stay here a day or so.

Night found the sky overcast and the countryside chill. Erin huddled near her campfire, liking the feeling. A second campfire gleamed down below; if the fisherman had not noticed her before, now he would, by the light of her fire.

She stood abruptly, for someone was climbing up the steep path from the river below. "Hello!" the man cried out. "Hey! Hello!" She saw him coming up the slippery path, through the darkness like a ghost. He was wearing a crumpled hat with hooks-and-flies all over it. The big man came awkwardly to the top and stood in Erin's firelight, grinning like an idiot, his eyes looking two ways at once, and Erin breathed the name,

"Teebi . . ."

"Eh? Hey? Name's Daniel Wells. Danny. You? I didn't know anyone but me and the Army Corps of Engineers knew about this place. You know they want to put a hydroelectric plant right down there in the gorge? Shee-it!" A big, hairy hand reached out to shake Erin's. "What did you say your name was?"

She was gaping at him as he pumped her hand. It took a moment for his question to register, and she answered at last, "Erin Wyler."

"Mizz or Miss?" he asked, and it seemed to be a joke.

"Just Erin."

"Great! Well, there'll be winds up here tonight. I don't mean to tell you how to pitch your camp or anything, but you may have noticed the sky's a bit bleak. Gonna be a right fine storm by morning, I swear-to-god. And I don't mean anything wrong by it either, you understand, but my camp down there is pretty well protected from the weather, cuz of this hillside and cliff you see; and I was thinking we should share the spot if I don't seem like too rotten a company."

"I . . . " Erin was still amazed by the man's appearance. She said, "Actually, I came out here to be alone."

"Oh. Well. Sure. I did that myself. I'm sorry. Here, though, I brung up some dried meat." He handed her a wrapper of jerky. "Dried it myself. It's moose. Friend of mine killed it in Canada. I'm just a fisherman myself, can't abide guns personally, but don't mind a free shank now and then to dry up. Hope you like it. Sorry to be a pest. I'll be going back down now. If it gets cold up here, don't you worry about me saying 'told you so' or like that; just come on down and in the morning I'll show you what a wilderness cook I can be."

He seemed terribly embarrassed, but Erin had not meant to rebuff his kindness. When he was gone back down the steep path, she sat a while gazing at her fire, adding no more wood to it. Before long, she went to the top edge of the falls to fill her pot with water and returned to the fire pit to douse it and bury it in mud. Steam rose up around her, anticipating the lowering mists. She took up her backpack and sleeping bag and started down the hill, chewing on a piece of salty meat.

Not everything on Earth would be so bad, she reckoned.